EMPEROR'S EYES

EMPEROR'S EYES

BY GEORGE VASIL

iUniverse, Inc.
Bloomington

Emperor's Eyes

iUniverse books may be ordered through booksellers or by contacting:

iUniverse
1663 Liberty Drive
Bloomington, IN 47403
www.iuniverse.com
1-800-Authors (1-800-288-4677)

ISBN: 978-1-4620-1237-4 (sc)
ISBN: 978-1-4620-1238-1 (hc)
ISBN: 978-1-4620-1239-8 (ebk)

Library of Congress Control Number: 2012919640

Printed in the United States of America

iUniverse rev. date: 11/14/2012

NOTES

Archimandrite: rank in the Eastern Orthodox Church, just below that of bishop; or an abbot.

Caesar: a top rank of nobility. Caesars were family members or trusted friends of emperors.

Cataphract: a heavy cavalryman or a group of heavy cavalrymen.

Dalmatic: an overrobe worn by the rich, or the commoner on special days. It had long, tight sleeves and fell to the knees. It was heavily decorated and frequently worn with a belt.

Dromon: a fast galley

Euxine: the Black Sea

The **folis, miliaresion,** and **noumisma (*pl.* noumismata)** are coins: copper, silver, and gold, respectively.

Ister: the Danube River

Koumbarro: best man at a wedding and usually thereafter, a godfather to one of the children.

Mese: the arcaded main street of Constantinople. It was lined with shops and booths.

Metropolitan: Eastern Orthodox equivalent of **archbishop.** I use the terms interchangeably.

Papou: Greek for Grandfather. **Yiayia:** Greek for Grandmother.

Propontis: the Sea of Marmara

Scutati: a heavy infantryman or a group of heavy infantrymen.

Stola: a woman's equivalent of the dalmatic. It was heavily jeweled and decorated.

Strategos: essentially a high-ranking general.

Superhumeral: decorative collar worn over a stola or dalmatic; very decorative, jeweled.

Tribune: a mid-level officer, such as a modern major.

Tunica: a basic article of clothing; a shirt-like garment worn by all classes. It was tighter in the arms and wider around the torso. Held in place by a belt, it would fall to the knees or ankles. The wealthy often used it as an undergarment. It was usually wool or linen but could be cotton.

Turmarch: a high-ranking senior officer, like a modern colonel or brigadier general.

FAMILIES

Dukas

Romanus IV Diogenes==2==Evdokia==1==Constantine X Dukas   John Dukas

                 Michael VII   Andronikos   Constantine

                                           Irene==Alexios Comnemnos

Nikopoulos   Phillipos

     Demetrios==Aspasia   Martha==Basilios Alexander Leo Theodore=Anastasia

Maria   Eftihia   Athanasiou **Eleni**===**Justin** Paul John

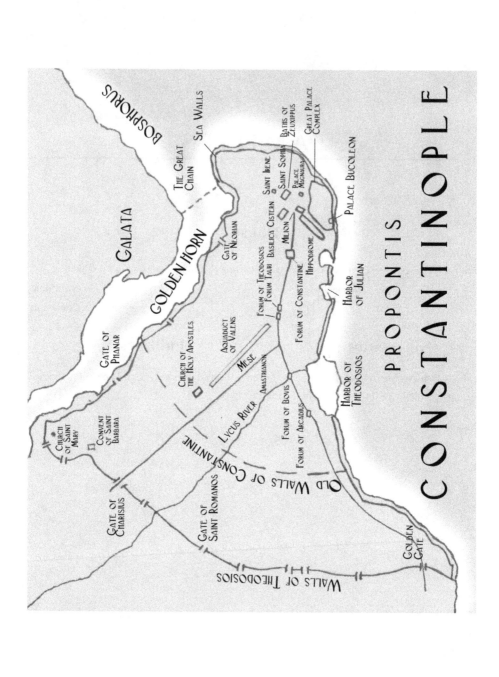

CONSTANTINOPLE

PROPONTIS

BOSPHORUS

GALATA

GOLDEN HORN

SEA WALLS

THE GREAT CHAIN

GATE OF NEORIAN

SAINT IRENE

SAINT SOPHIA

PALACE MAGNAURA

BATHS OF ZEUXIPPUS

GREAT PALACE COMPLEX

PALACE BUCOLEON

BASILICA CISTERN

MILION

FORUM TAURI

FORUM OF THEODOSIOS

FORUM OF CONSTANTINE

HIPPODROME

HARBOR OF JULIAN

GATE OF PHANAR

CHURCH OF THE HOLY APOSTLES

AQUADUCT OF VALENS

MESE

AMASTRIANON

HARBOR OF THEODOSIOS

LYCUS RIVER

FORUM OF BOVIS

CHURCH OF SAINT MARY

CONVENT OF SAINT BARBARA

OLD WALLS OF CONSTANTINE

FORUM OF ARCADIUS

GATE OF CHARISIUS

GATE OF SAINT ROMANOS

WALLS OF THEODOSIOS

GOLDEN GATE

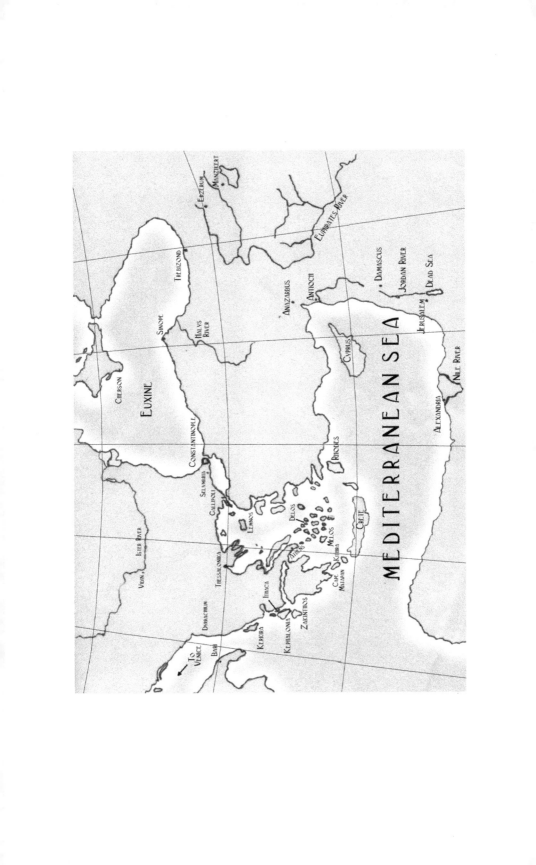

Part I

INTRIGUE

CHAPTER 1

"Lunacy, Tasso. They call it lunacy."

"What was that, sire?" the confused Tasso asked, shivering as he rubbed his chilled hands together.

Tasso had briefly fallen asleep while he and his lord waited outside the door of a rain-soaked stone building in the early darkness of a cold winter morning. Long black cowls obscured their cold faces. Frigid water vapor streamed from their nostrils as each wrapped his arms tightly around himself, fighting the icy weather's best efforts to freeze them.

"Lunacy," the lord repeated to his servant, his gaze fixed on the heavens. "A preoccupation with the moon." He enunciated each syllable with precision.

Tasso watched his lord continue his trance-like gaze at the bright silver orb that owned the night. A few thready clouds streamed past this mistress of the dark sky in a feeble effort to obscure her.

"Sire?" the puzzled servant asked. His master's thoughts had raced over his head. Perhaps the energy-sapping cold kept him from following the meandering course of his master's logic.

"Actually, more than a preoccupation," the lord said, more to himself than to Tasso, his devotion to the full moon above unwavering. "Some say it is an intermittent insanity which varies in intensity with the phases of the moon."

Tasso again failed to gain the same appreciation his lord held for the heavenly object.

"But I see the moon — the ancient goddess Artemis — as a symbol of life."

"Life, sire?"

"*Life*, Tasso," he said as he shifted his gaze to his confused minion. "You see, a man is made out of nothing; then he grows, reaches his full size, realizes his full potential, only to shrink, to decay with age and return to his origins, to nothing."

Tasso had given up trying to follow.

"The new moon is invisible," the lord said as he looked heavenward. "It later waxes from crescent to gibbous; then it reaches its complete potential as it becomes full." He paused as he savored these words. Then he broke his own silence and announced with the sobriety of an ancient Hebrew prophet, "And tonight, Tasso, the moon is full and our potential is realized."

"Yes, sire," Tasso responded obsequiously. He still had no idea what his lord meant. He pulled his cowl tighter, sensing the wind from the harbor picking up abruptly.

Suddenly a loud rattle startled the lord and his servant. A massive oak door opened behind them. They turned to see an officer of the imperial army coming toward them. The officer greeted them both and saluted the lord.

"Will your man be accompanying you, my lord?" asked the soldier.

"No," the lord answered indifferently.

The officer led both men through the portal. He directed Tasso to an anteroom twenty feet to the right, grabbed a torch from the wall, and led the lord down two flights of lightless stone stairs to the structure's deepest dungeon. A soldier stood in front of a bolted door. When the lord and the officer reached the door, the soldier snapped to attention and saluted his superiors. The officer returned his salute and reached for a key on his belt. The soldier automatically stepped aside as the officer unlocked and opened the door. Inside the cell, another man stood waiting for the lord.

"Welcome, sire," the man in the cell said.

"Homer," the lord nodded coolly as he stepped into he darkened room.

The door behind them creaked loudly as the guard outside closed it with an abrupt *thud*.

"It's good to see you, *Caesar*." Homer Skleros added with a subtle smile. "Were you compromised in any way, sire?"

"Not in the least, Homer," the lord replied confidently. "As far as any one knows, Caesar John Dukas is still confined to his estates in Bithynia by order of Emperor Romanos Diogenes." He smiled contemptuously.

"Very well, sire," Homer's smile grew. "Follow me."

Skleros guided his lord across the cold, damp cell that the two torches on the wall illuminated poorly. Water trickled down the walls and dripped from scattered green spots in the ceiling. The persistent precipitation heightened the cell's dank stench. The men stopped at a white marble slab in the middle of the room. A lifeless body lay upon the cold stone.

"When did he finally die, Homer?" Dukas asked as he inspected the bloody corpse.

"About an hour ago, Caesar," Skleros replied.

The two men, now alone with the corpse, stepped forward to the edge of the slab. The caesar shivered and pulled his cowl tighter around his chest as he surveyed the contorted, pale, naked body. He shuddered as he heard and felt rats scurrying over his feet, kicking blindly at them in disgust.

Finding the lighting inadequate for a detailed inspection of the corpse, Dukas grabbed a torch from its mounting on the wall and silently recoiled in horror as the torchlight revealed the collection of mangled flesh before him. He resisted displaying any weakness before Skleros; such behavior was unbecoming of a caesar.

The dead man's dried blood coated the cold marble. The caesar braced himself before continuing his investigation. He surveyed the poor soul's face. The torturers had slit open the nose and torn it away. All that remained was a dried clot. This time Dukas could not hide a grimace. The torturers had gouged out one of victim's eyes. The other remained, frozen wide open, as if to testify to the horror this wretched creature had endured. Hair pulled from the scalp and beard lay scattered beside the head in bunches. The torturers had broken each and every finger of the corpse's battered hands, some so badly that in places bone protruded through the bruised and broken skin. The caesar turned away from the corpse to ask Skleros a question but also to relieve him of this gruesome sight.

"Did he provide us with any information?" Dukas asked.

"Nothing useful, Caesar," replied Skleros blandly.

Dukas recovered and returned to the mutilated body. This time he held the torchlight closer to it and beheld a battered scrotum, swollen four-fold and possessing a brilliant purple color. Someone had given the testicles a good throttling. The caesar was powerless to control his revulsion at this point. His suddenly dry mouth made swallowing difficult. He quickly moved on to the dead man's legs and feet. The torturers had bashed and bruised them mercilessly after they had extracted each of the toenails. The torturers had wrenched and twisted the knees with such force, shearing ligament and tendons from their attachments, that below these swollen joints, the lower legs lay limply at right angles to the upward-projecting kneecaps. Yet this striking derangement of the dead man's anatomy strangely fascinated the caesar as he grew more accustomed to the grisly mess before him.

"Do you know who he was?" Dukas asked, his attention still riveted to the dead man's legs.

"He was known as Paul Arslanian, sire. Supposedly he was the son of an Armenian merchant who lives here in Constantinople. He worked as a servant for your son, Prince Andronikos. Aristotle Markos caught him yesterday eavesdropping on a conversation between His All Holiness the patriarch and your other son, Prince Constantine, in the patriarch's library," Skleros continued. "They were discussing some *sensitive* issues."

"Such as . . ." The caesar still fixed his attention on the dead man.

"Our plans to dispose of Diogenes."

Dukas turned brusquely and faced Skleros. His eyes narrowed as he scowled. "That is indeed sensitive."

"Yes, Caesar," Skleros agreed.

The caesar turned away from the bloody slab, wringing his hands. The corpse that had so enthralled him only minutes ago was now insignificant. "Homer, I've dedicated every available hour to removing that bastard Diogenes from the throne ever since that usurper married my sister-in-law three years ago," he fumed. "Nothing is going to get in the way of this!"

"Yes, sire," Skleros began. He too turned away from the corpse. "But Caesar, your plan is unfolding perfectly. I'm certain Diogenes knows nothing of what you have in store for him."

"What makes you so *certain*, Homer?" the caesar snapped back. "My brother Constantine appointed me to the office of caesar to help him rule this empire and to make certain the Dukas family retained control after his death. I recall his dying words to this day. 'John, keep the throne however you can. Don't let it slip through our fingers.'" Caesar John Dukas discretely wiped the mist from his eyes. "And then his wife breaks her promise to him and marries a man who just a few years before plotted to overthrow him! Can you believe that? Marrying the man who tried to overthrow your husband when he was emperor?" He turned and spat on the floor. "She's a damned whore!"

"Empress Evdokia—"

"Evdokia has made a mockery of my brother and of the entire Dukas family!" the caesar bellowed. "I don't want history's sole recollection of the reign of Emperor Constantine Dukas to be that he was outmaneuvered by his wife!"

"Yes, Caesar."

"It's bad enough that my brother left Michael to inherit the throne. The boy's more fit to be a schoolteacher than an emperor. Psellos has taught him too well to be a philosopher and not a ruler."

"Perhaps Emperor Michael will grow into the position. He is still young—"

"Unlikely, Homer," the caesar growled. "Michael is already twenty. His feebleness gave Evdokia the excuse she wanted to marry again, 'to provide the empire with the strong leadership it needs.' Damn her! Now that the usurper Diogenes is co-emperor, he's running everything. My nephew has no power. Michael may as well be a cypress tree in the imperial gardens!" He snorted in disgust. "My brother must be turning in his grave!"

"Yes, Caesar, but once your plan succeeds, your brother's honor will be avenged and you will again hold the reins of power. The empire will remain in the grasp of the Dukas family for generations to come!"

Dukas smiled with satisfaction as he thought of his revenge. "Michael will become sole emperor and the Dukas family will maintain the stewardship of the empire it has been granted by God Himself."

"Yes, Caesar."

"Of course I'll *assist* Michael in everything," Dukas added.

"Yes, of course, Caesar. Michael will sorely need your assistance."

Dukas, drained of his vitriol, returned to the corpse. Continuing his analysis, he asked, "Who supervised the torture?"

"Sklavanites, sire," Skleros replied as he followed Dukas around the corpse.

"He does, eh, *exceptional* work." The contorted figure before him that had once been a human being again enthralled John Dukas.

"Yes, Caesar." The cold Skleros was still unmoved by the horror of the corpse.

Dukas turned and walked toward the door, then suddenly turned back to Skleros. "Who is in charge of dealing with Diogenes' allies?"

"Archbishop Mavrites, sire."

"Ah, the venerable *metropolitan*," the caesar chuckled. "The Raven. Good choice."

"He is the best we have, sire."

"Indeed . . . Has the patriarch committed to joining us?"

"Not quite, but I've Psellos' assurances that His Holiness will soon be an ally."

"Good." The caesar turned to the corpse and surveyed it one more time. "It's hard to believe that he didn't break. Diogenes found a dedicated spy. Poor bastard. I'm impressed."

"Indeed, Caesar."

"Homer," Dukas said with a grin, "I used to bristle at the intricacy of our efforts. 'Let's just poison him and be done with it!' I thought. 'Hire an assassin and send an arrow through his heart!' Indeed, many emperors have met such fates." He sighed. "But these modern times require more finesse. Things aren't quite as simple as they appear, Homer."

Skleros looked inquisitively at the caesar.

"If we dispose of Diogenes so carelessly," Dukas continued, "his supporters in the army and the Senate, not to mention some of the wealthiest families in the empire, will rally round the empress and she will probably choose another husband."

"And we are right back where we started."

"Worse, if we're implicated," Dukas added. "And a civil war is out of the question. I don't want to destroy the empire just to get rid of Romanos Diogenes." Dukas placed his hand on Skleros' shoulder, as a teacher would before he reveals a forgotten truth to a favorite pupil. "But, Homer, if we drive a wedge between Diogenes and his supporters, isolate him, and deprive him of his power, the throne will easily come our way. Do you see now why it must be so?"

Dukas stepped toward the door and Skleros followed.

"Yes, Caesar," Skleros answered. "Will you be staying in Constantinople for long, sire?"

"No," Dukas replied as they reached the threshold. "It's probably just before dawn now. I'll leave in about an hour or so."

Skleros called to the guard who opened the door. Dukas and Skleros walked out of the room and climbed the stairs as the guard locked the cell door behind them.

CHAPTER 2

As the young man awoke from a pleasant sleep, the sun rose over the placid *Propontis*. The low eastern clouds deflected the sun's rays like a prism, coloring the tranquil waters with bands of pink and periwinkle. The glistening sun dominated the horizon. The wind was still. His bedroom was perched on the third floor from the ground level, the fourth, uppermost floor, of this home to three families and their servants. From there, he lost himself in the panoramic vista and thought about the events of the previous day. He could still smell the incense he lit last night as he said his prayers before retiring.

He was a soldier, in particular, a *cataphract*, or heavy cavalryman. Yesterday, at a lavish ceremony, his commander honored him and five other officers from his cohort for their bravery in battle. Today, he and his five comrades would join ten other brave soldiers for an audience before the imperial court. He was eager, yet anxious, to attend. To be invited to appear before the emperor and empress was a signal honor. "Certainly every soldier dreams of days like today," he thought. A simple man at heart, he felt self-consious about pomp and ceremony. He was no stranger to these kinds of celebrations, though he disliked being "shown like a prize bull." Yet he hid his disdain for such circumstance well.

A satisfied smile projected from his handsome face. The young horseman had married just three days earlier, so having his young bride and his parents with him at yesterday's ceremony had doubled his pleasure. He thought of the look he saw on his bride's face as he was called to the front of the arena. Her warm smile made him feel as though he were the only soldier being honored. But today, only the soldiers would attend the ceremony before the imperial court at the Palace Bucoleon. The young man found this disquieting but, as a soldier, he was expected to accept orders without question. He had heard about the grandeur of that great palace and was eager to see it for himself. Unfortunately, his wife and family would have to settle for just his description.

As he reached for a cup of cool water on the small table ahead of him, the young man saw three sailing ships becalmed in the Propontis. The lack of wind had paralyzed them short of their goal, the Golden Horn, where the still water of the docks would later welcome them. He thought with amazement about the mariners who traveled the length and breadth of the Mediterranean to bring their treasures here to Constantinople, the largest and richest city of Europe and probably the entire world. The thought of sailing fascinated him, too, though he had never been on a boat of any significant size.

Indeed, this beautiful first morning of March was the most spectacular the year 1071 had yet seen. Sparse cloud cover and mild temperatures were not unusual for late winter. The color splashed across the morning sky grew as the day progressed. The young man felt it fitting that such an important day for him should begin so beautifully. Perhaps he could overcome his disdain for the fanfare that would accompany today's ceremony and simply enjoy himself.

The young man moved his gaze to his right where the Golden Horn met its mother, the Propontis, at an angle of about forty-five degrees. He then reversed course along the Golden Horn and looked to the northwest, following this slender arm of water toward its origin. Its docks teemed with anchored ships, their crews only beginning to stir. To the northeast, beyond the Golden Horn, he saw the Bosphorus, the narrow strait just north of the city, which separated the rugged western shoulder of Asia from its counterpart projecting eastward from Europe as it linked the Propontis to the *Euxine*. He turned back to the southeast and followed the Propontis as far to the south as he could. It appeared endless.

His eyes skimmed across the crenellated parapets of the twenty-foot high sea walls that stood between the city and the sea.

He remembered hearing his father and grandfather tell stories of how these walls had protected the city from countless pirate raids and naval assaults. For a moment, he imagined fast imperial galleys, called *dromons*, attacking a pirate fleet while imperial soldiers manned the walls and catapulted fire, rocks, and giant arrows at the marauders.

He again looked beyond the walls and saw a galley of the imperial navy move through the Bosphorus. Ah, the glorious past of his home city! Capital of the empire known to him as the Roman, or Christian Empire. Although he was ethnically Greek, he and his compatriots saw themselves as Roman. Were not the people of this empire the only remnant of the great Roman Empire of days gone by? Didn't the lineage of the Roman emperors continue here at Constantinople? Had not the western part of that great empire succumbed to barbarian invasions to be occupied now by backward Germans who could barely read?

However, he knew that foreigners didn't share his feelings and those of his countrymen. The aliens sometimes referred to the great empire as the Byzantine Empire, after the name of the ancient city, founded some 1500 years earlier. Eight centuries later, Emperor Constantine the Great moved the Roman Empire's capital there, renaming the city after himself.

More often, though, outsiders called the empire the Greek Empire. However, this was quite inaccurate. This city and its empire were composed of a rich mixture of ethnic groups. At the top was a thin veneer of Greeks and, below them, a mélange of others: Slavs, Armenians, Vlachs, Syrians, and Cappadocians to name but a few. But it was the Greeks who formed the aristocracy. Most aristocrats were Greeks but not all Greeks were aristocrats. Constantinople was an eleventh-century Greek reflection of first-century Rome.

As two seagulls flew past his window, the young soldier stretched and reached into a basin on the console just below the window. He splashed cold water on his dark, olive-skinned face. He gently stroked his closely-trimmed black beard, continuing to relish the beauty of the morning.

This tall, muscular man had graceful, almost woman-like hands. His eyes were large and of the darkest brown. A small scar from his childhood bisected his left eyebrow—the only impediment to his handsome face.

He turned his gaze away from the window to the bed where his wife lay sleeping. With her long auburn hair, hazel eyes, and light olive skin, she was a woman of striking beauty. She was slightly shorter than the average Greek woman of her time. Her hands were soft and supple and did not betray the secret strength they harbored. Her legs were gracefully sculpted, leading slowly to statuesque hips. Her breasts and shoulders were a perfect complement to the rest of her body. Her round head was her crowning glory, accentuated by a thin, tapering nose that flared perfectly at its end . . . thin crimson lips, pearl-white teeth, and gently sloping cheeks. A thin sheet that had draped over her earlier in that warm morning had fallen to the floor, exposing her naked form.

On the fourth finger of her right hand, she wore a delicate gold ring. Although her physical beauty struck him, as it always had, his overriding thoughts in the moment were absorbed in his deep love for her. Although their marriage was only three days old, they had known each other since childhood. For twenty years, her family had lived only a short way from his. They attended the same church, Saint Irene, the Church of Holy Peace, and he had seen her almost daily from her birth. He was present at her baptism. Their fathers, retired career soldiers, had served together frequently. The government rewarded their years of loyal service with large tracts of fertile land in Thessaly. Farmers worked these tracts and the owners allowed them to live on the land and save some of the profits for themselves. The lion's share of the income went to the owners and afforded them a comfortable living.

Her brother Athanasiou had been his age. They were constant playmates until Athanasiou died of pneumonia at age fifteen. From the age of four, she would secretly watch him with her brother playing games in the street. Later she would furtively escape from home and follow them on their capers around the city. She was clever enough to avoid being detected for nearly a year.

One August day, the two boys spied her following them near the Cathedral of Saint Sophia, whose name means "Holy Wisdom." They confronted her and warned that her parents would be most unhappy with her for leaving the house so clandestinely. They lectured that once they brought her home, she would be in deep trouble.

But this clever child refused to be so easily intimidated. She discovered that her brother was wearing one of their father's daggers on his belt and reminded him that such an infraction would demand serious punishment. To purchase her silence, he would have to let her accompany them. From then until her entry into young womanhood, she became their constant companion. The three of them enjoyed many adventures together. He would often see her at school, for girls were given the same opportunities in education as boys. Today, he was now twenty-two; she was eighteen.

As beautiful as she was, however, she attracted this young man for other reasons. In eighteen years, he had discovered an intelligence that transcended mere cleverness, a flair for kindness and warmth that he found in no other, and an inner strength that he deemed greater than his own. He felt fortunate that his parents and hers had agreed to arrange their wedding. Women weren't usually wed at such a late age. Most young women married by sixteen or even earlier. Perhaps it was because she was the youngest of three sisters that her parents decided to keep her at home longer than usual.

As the young man though lovingly about his bride, he heard her stirring and watched her wake up. Once her eyes were open, she looked straight at him, unaware of her nakedness, and smiled. When she realized her exposure, she quickly scooped the fallen sheet from the floor and covered herself. She looked back at him with a sparkle in her eye, the previous night's sensual interlude still fresh in her memory.

"You are up early, Justin," she said. "The dawn is a rare sight for you when you are at home." She smiled as she saw that her dart had hit its mark.

"This is an attribute you have determined after a mere three nights of sleeping with me?" he asked.

"I've known you my entire life. Your mother is right when she says it would take a team of horses to get you out of bed before the third hour of the morning."

"What else has my mother told you?" He grinned as he moved toward her with a mischievous look in his eye.

"I'm not about to divulge any more secrets," she replied, playfully retreating under the bed cover.

Justin rushed to the foot of the bed. "Eleni, you're not being a good wife," he teased.

Upon hearing this, she sprang from beneath the covers, caught him totally off-guard, and pinned him to the floor with her body. "So, Captain Phillipos," she said, "will you surrender quietly or will I need to get rough?"

Justin looked into her eyes and felt his heart flutter. "You win. I give up," he chuckled.

"You're too easy," she said.

"I know."

Justin winked and smiled back at her. He moved his right hand to her forehead and tenderly brushed her hair back. She smiled and kissed him. He slid both arms around her and held her tightly. Their lips met passionately. His hands moved upward to her head where he combed his fingers through her lustrous hair. She caressed his muscular shoulders and neck. Their mouths separated and he peered deeply into her gorgeous eyes.

"Eleni, you are more beautiful now, at this moment, than I can remember." A look of complete fascination filled his face.

"Thank you, Justin," she responded, her eyes welling up. "You are the kindest, most sensitive man . . . ."

Justin then pulled her toward him and kissed her moist lips softly. His passion grew but his wife gently disengaged her lips from his.

"I know you'd like to spend the entire morning here," Eleni reminded him, "but you do have somewhere to be this morning."

He was startled realizing he had already forgotten the morning's imperial audience. "The army calls once again," he groaned. "Perhaps the emperor won't miss me today."

"I doubt that," his wife said. She stood up and held her hand out to him. "Come on, get up. This is important." She grabbed a long-sleeved white cotton *tunica* and pulled the undergarment over her head and body.

Justin arose and walked to a closet in the corner of the bedroom where he stowed his soldiering gear. On the way, he grabbed his undyed cotton tunica. He held up the undergarment, quickly checked its long sleeves, slid it over his head, and let it fall to his mid-thigh. He put on his blue tunic and then belted it with a broad leather waistband. Eleni helped him with a waist-length corselet, which was made of small plates of iron fastened to leather backing. From this protective vest hung metal strips over leather backing, forming a short protective skirt. He deftly pulled on and laced up his boots, then applied iron guards cushioned with cotton to his upper arms and greaves of similar construction to his shins. Around his waist, he placed his sword, suspended from a baldric, and slung a protective mantle over his left shoulder and fastened it on his right.

"Is the honeymoon over already?" Eleni kidded.

"Not if I have anything to say about it," Justin smiled, casting a sensual look her way. Suddenly, he looked apprehensive. "Uh, Eleni . . ." he stammered.

Eleni looked sharply back at Justin. She knew that his pending announcement would mean some type of imposition for her. She had been in this position before.

"Peter told me that we're supposed to meet with our commander after the ceremony today. It may take a while."

"You just now remembered this?" she groaned. "Justin, we were going to spend this morning with my parents. Don't you remember?"

Justin knew he had no excuse. He looked sheepishly at her, his eyes silently begging her forgiveness.

"After the ceremony, you were supposed to meet us here!"

"I'm sorry," Justin pleaded. He was as angry with himself as his wife was. "But Peter said it was very important."

"How could you forget to tell me something so simple?" Eleni added, thrusting her hands on to her hips.

Justin was in desperate straits. His situation begged for a different approach. He wasn't going anywhere with his current tack, yet a frontal assault would be suicide. *Perhaps a flanking maneuver . . .*

He acquired a philosophical air as he stepped toward Eleni. Justin raised his right hand as if he were a priest about to begin a benediction. "How can a man remember his own name, let alone an important engagement, when he is in the company of such beauty?" he asked, pointing his open hands at his bride. "Most men needn't worry about bearing such a burden . . ."

Eleni rolled her eyes. She was used to Justin's antics. She was still angry with him and her face showed it, but she was entertained by his lame efforts to defuse the matter. Justin's pathetic, self-mocking diatribe grew more contrived and humorous. As Eleni listened, she could feel the steady, silent current of Justin's amusing defense eroding her ire while he continued. "Alexander was not burdened by such heavy diversion, nor was Julius Caesar."

Justin had no excuse and he knew that anger burned in the pit of her stomach. But there was no good reason to chide him further. It would only frustrate her more. If he could amuse her, perhaps that would salve the wound. "And many of the great men of science," he continued. "Maybe the greatest—"

"What do you know of science?" Eleni interjected, sternly extorting contrition from him.

"Well, only what my Uncle Theodore tells me, but I've been particularly attentive to his lectures lately . . ."

Then the corners of Eleni's lips curled upward. Justin saw this and smiled. Her smile grew and he responded with a much broader grin of his own.

"Justin, I have every right to be very angry with you right now."

"I agree."

Eleni looked sternly for a few more seconds, then suddenly embraced him and asked, "Why can't I stay angry at you?"

Justin tried to soothe her. "I love you, Eleni, and I do not mean to hurt you." He held her close to him. "I will be back as soon as I can, I promise."

Eleni looked into his eyes and kissed him. His soothing words had done their work. Justin grabbed a conical helmet from the table and placed it on his head. He adjusted the tuft of blue horsehair coming from its apex and looked back at Eleni. "I promise," he reminded her. He kissed her one more time and left the room.

Eleni's patience abandoned her soon after Justin left their home. Instead, frustration again welled up. In a fit of passion, she silently rescinded her forgiveness. *How could he be so inconsiderate?* This Eleni had known about Justin forever. His lackadaisical attitude had been amusing to her in the past, but it had become an obstacle she was tired of overcoming. This likeable foible, she decided, was now a nuisance. Justin's absent-mindedness was nothing new to her. Yet, for some reason, this morning this annoying flaw in her new husband especially frustrated her. Why couldn't he overcome it? "Justin!" Eleni groaned under her breath.

As Eleni looked at his eyes just minutes before as his feeble defense stumbled onward, she remembered how kind and gentle he had always been. He would scrape the bottom of his purse to give his last coin to an orphan playing in the street. He was always the first to help an elderly widow carry her shopping. And when the son of the fishmonger had been lost at sea, he came to that family's aid when others avoided them. He was always there for others but not always for her.

Eleni walked to her closet where she found the green and gold *stola* her mother had given her just before her wedding. This over robe was the most lavish garment she owned. Eleni felt it was not right that her father had spent such a great deal of money for it. She threatened to refuse the gift but both parents were adamant that Eleni would have it.

She held it over her arm and ran her fingers over the beautiful silk brocade. The round collar was heavy with pearl and topaz and the outer hem, gold-filled, would run to the floor when worn. The flowing, bell-shaped sleeves were long and comfortable. Eleni realized that the gift was to be treasured as were those who gave it to her. Again she thought of Justin. She paused, put back the silk stola, and grabbed a plain, light, linen one and put that one on instead.

"Justin, why do you do this to me?"

CHAPTER 3

The farmer led his donkey down the crowded *Mese*, past the dozens of open booths that lined the main boulevard of Constantinople. It was packed that afternoon with hundreds of people, men, women, and children. A tall woman, perhaps the farmer's wife, wrapped from head to toe in a dirty brown shawl, rode silently on the donkey's back. They walked past vendors from all over the world: Chinese selling silks, Russians selling furs, and merchants from North Africa, Venice, and Persia selling gold, spices, perfumes, and cotton fabrics. She heard the customers haggle with the women who ran the booths. (Women ran nearly all of them.) They passed silk merchant, after metal smith, after jeweler, after artisan before reaching a grocer. Unlike the other merchants, grocers kept an enclosed shop rather than a simple booth.

The farmer handed the donkey's reins to one of the grocer's sons outside the shop, helped the woman off the donkey, and led her inside. There, the grocer was busy inspecting a recent delivery of garlic while his wife spoke with the customers. At the back of the shop, squid and onion grilled on a brazier, their delicious smell pervaded the busy atmosphere. When the wife caught a glimpse of the visitors, she motioned with her eyes to the farmer who led the tall woman through a doorway. As the farmer closed the door behind them, a young woman greeted them and led the tall woman to another room.

The young woman pointed to a chair in front of a wide silk crimson screen. The tall woman nodded and the young woman left the room. The tall woman sat and removed the shawl, revealing that she was no farmer's wife at all. She wore a beautiful blue woolen over robe, a stola, with beautiful gold brocade on its long sleeves. A delicate pale blue scarf covered her hair.

"Did you have a comfortable journey?" a male voice from behind the screen asked.

The tall woman was briefly surprised but responded that she had.

"I'm sorry for the masquerade," he said. "But security, you know."

"I understand."

"You are one of the empress' servants?"

"Yes."

"Are you free to move about as you wish?"

"Yes, quite free."

"Do you have her confidence?"

"Her *complete* confidence, I assure you."

"Perfect! This will work well!" the voice said and then went silent for several minutes.

The woman tactfully cleared her throat as she thought the man had forgotten about her.

"Oh, please forgive me," he said. "There. Look down by your feet."

The woman looked to find a blue velvet pouch. She carefully picked it up. It must weigh ten pounds, she thought as drew the strings apart.

"I hope you will find this an adequate first payment."

The woman gasped as she looked inside. There were over three-dozen large silver *miliaresion* coins in the pouch. "Yes, sir!" she replied. "This will be more than adequate!"

"Good. We will contact you through one of our agents in the Palace Bucoleon. I trust you will keep us well informed."

"Absolutely, sir."

The young women reappeared in the room and helped the tall woman with her shawl. She guided her back to the farmer who indifferently led her back down the Mese.

Vendors, selling everything from fish to silver jewelry to linens, farmers carrying young lambs to market, traders bringing goods to and from the city's many wharves to shops and artisans in the city, and other Constantinopolitans exercising their daily routines, all clogged the streets. The loud din was not unusual to one who called this city his home. The congestion slowed Justin's walk from his home near the Gate of Neorian more than he had anticipated, but he knew his delayed departure was the real cause of his tardiness. He arrived late at the sprawling grounds of the Great Palace Complex. The complex included dozens of imperial buildings, which included the Palace Bucoleon, other palaces, churches, and administrative buildings.

As the guard at the gate showed him into the garden, Justin saw some of the young officers assembling on the far side of the imperial gardens. They busily readied themselves to enter the imperial presence in the Palace Bucoleon. A few of the officers knew him and waved to the young captain. Other than a handfull of gardeners and as many guards in view, these officers were alone.

He walked over to join them, noticing the intricate detail of the expansive, well-manicured gardens. The gardeners kept each tree of a certain type at a height equal to the others of that same variety. And the distribution of the trees demonstrated flawless geometric symmetry. The same was true of the bushes and the few crocuses that had poked through the soil on this late winter's day.

Justin arrived in the company of the young officers. As was characteristic of his pleasant, outgoing nature, he made the acquaintance of those he didn't know. Of course he also greeted those with whom he had been honored the day before. All were of about the same age so conversation came easily. The soldiers regaled each other with more-or-less exaggerated stories of their personal bravery in battle. As the soldier's stories became more unbelievable, Justin looked for his friend Peter Argyropoulos. Where could he be? Peter wouldn't miss this event. The emperor was honoring him today as well.

The conversations among the young officers came to an abrupt halt as their commanding officers strode toward them from the Palace Bucoleon. Word spread quickly from the commanders that they would be entering the emperor's presence very soon. It was there, among the commanders, that Justin spotted Peter.

Peter and Justin had served together in frontier detachments on the *Ister* for the past six months. During that time, they had forged a strong friendship. Justin had four more months of service than Peter and, as a result, was his superior but Justin never exploited this position. They got along well, so well that Justin asked Peter to be his *koumbarro*, the best man at his wedding. Such an honor was usually only bestowed upon one's godfather. Since Justin's godfather had died several years earlier, he chose Peter.

Peter was half a head shorter than Justin and had a muscular build. His sandy red hair was beginning to recede along the forehead and at the temples. He had a physical agility, which, when coupled with his strength, made him a skilled combatant. His usually calm, quiet demeanor combined with his superior tactical cunning complemented his physical attribute and made him a skilled officer. By nature, Peter was wary of most people, unlike Justin. He had few friends but those he did have treasured their relationship with him. He was more likely to finesse his way out of a situation than to act impulsively. Although he was more than capable physically, his wits had saved him more often than his brawn.

Justin acknowledged Peter as he walked over to him. Peter was dressed in a military uniform similar to Justin's except Peter's corselet was armored by small pieces of horn laced together rather than metal strips. Justin remembered his friend saying the lighter weight of the horn allowed for more quickness and agility.

As Peter approached, Justin saw the sour look in his friend's eye and knew that something was not right. "Good morning, Koumbarro," Justin said.

Indeed, the usually cool-headed Peter was quite upset. "Justin, where the hell have you been?" he snapped.

Justin opened his mouth to speak but Peter angrily stopped him.

"Did you meet a beggar on the way here?" Peter asked. "Did you have to escort him to the imperial bread kitchen for the day's food and drink?"

"What are you—"

"Did you forget that we were supposed to meet with Tribune Apostolas before this morning's ceremony?"

Justin, alarmed by his own forgetfulness, could feel his face flushing. "Oh, no! I'm so sorry, Peter! I thought we were meeting after the ceremony! I'm—"

"You should have heard the story I concocted to save your skin! I told him that you had been asked to inspect Senator Kastros' personal bodyguard by the senator himself. Hmmph! What a lame, pathetic tale that was!"

"Thank y —"

"Apostolas acted like he believed my explanation but I knew he didn't believe me." Peter ignored Justin's efforts to reconcile. He had Justin up against the wall and wouldn't back down. "Why do I stick my neck out for you? It's a good thing he likes you, Justin!"

Justin waited to make certain Peter had finished his tongue-lashing before trying to speak. "I'm truly sorry, Peter," he apologized, hoping to calm his friend. "I was certain that we planned to meet after the ceremony."

"Justin, we talked about this just yesterday!" Peter jabbed back in exasperation. "We had agreed to be here an hour early to meet with Apostolas. What happened?"

Justin failed to manufacture a suitable reply.

"Newlyweds!" Peter said curtly, shaking his head, although now a smile was breaking through his stone-hard face.

Then, to Justin's growing embarrassment, he saw Tribune Apostolas approaching. He could feel his throat tightening as his commander approached.

"Well, Captain Phillipos, how is the good Senator Kastros today?" The tone of the tribune's voice confirmed that he had not believed Peter's story.

"He's, uh, fine, sir," Justin answered.

"That's good." Apostolas looked Justin squarely in the eye. Justin felt fortunate that the usually unbendable Apostolas was letting him get away with such an egregious offense. The look on Justin's face promised that this would never happen again. This wordless interrogation and confession appeared to satisfy the tribune. Once appeased, Apostolas addressed both of them. "Gentlemen, I believe the emperor and empress are requesting our presence at this moment," he said, maintaining his chilliness. "Please fall in with the others." Apostolas walked over to the other commanders while Peter and Justin assembled with the junior officers.

On the way, Peter whispered to his friend, "You're lucky you got through that in one piece!"

The short, stocky fifteen-year old strutted slowly into the public bath, looking around as he proceeded. He carried himself as well as a man of twice his age, probably because the young man was an aristocrat and commander in the imperial army. When he reached the changing room, a red-haired man signaled him to follow.

The redhead led the adolescent to an isolated room, well away from the crowd.

"Welcome, cousin," the short man heard as he walked through the door.

He looked into the room to see a man a generation older than him seated by himself in a six-foot-square pool enjoying a steaming hot bath. Five armed men stood outside of the bath.

"Care for a bath?" the bather inquired.

"Why have you sent for me?" the younger man asked.

"Must you be so rude?" the older man growled back. "I'm not certain how that ambitious mother of yours raised you, but I was taught to be respectful when speaking to an older kinsman."

"I'm sorry, cousin," the young man said.

"That's more like it, Alexios," the older man smirked. He turned and instructed the servant to bring more hot water. Again he addressed his guest. "As you know, cousin, these are turbulent times. A treacherous usurper is on the throne and we of the Dukas family must unite to meet any, uh, *challenges* he may send our way."

"Challenges?" Alexios asked.

"Oh, yes!" The older man grabbed a cup of water and drank. "The usurper keeps Emperor Michael from his rightful place."

"Constantine, you bring me to a public bathhouse to tell me this?" Alexios asked.

"Exactly, cousin. This is a public place. Probably one of the few places not patrolled by Diogenes' spies."

The younger man glared back and asked, "So what do you want from me?"

Constantine Dukas grabbed a white cotton towel and rose from the water. "The Dukas request the aid of the Comnenos family in securing Michael's rightful place. Do we have it?"

Alexios Comnenos balked. True, he had wed into the powerful Dukas family. His mother, Anna Delassena, known for her extreme ambition and political savvy, had arranged his marriage to Irene Dukas, daughter of Andronikos Dukas and granddaughter of Caesar John Dukas. However, he was more concerned about his own highly political family than the Dukas.

"Do we have it?" Constantine Dukas asked. This time he demanded a reply.

"Of course . . . cousin," Comnenos answered.

"Good! Good!" Dukas said as he extended his hand.

Comnenos took the offering and smiled reassuringly at his kinsman. "Two great families and one great cause," Alexios added, still pumping Constantine Dukas' hand.

"This moment was long overdue," Dukas added. "The caesar will be most pleased."

"Cousin, might I leave now? I was in the midst of some family business when your man accosted me."

"Certainly, cousin," Constantine said, slapping Comnenos on the shoulder. "Good day to you. And God's blessings on your family."

"Good day and God's blessings to you and all of the Dukas too," Comnenos replied as he sped out of the room.

The red-haired man walked over to Constantine Dukas after Comnenos had left. "Do you believe him, sire?"

"Do you?"

The redhead didn't answer but the look on his face begged for his lord's opinion. Constantine Dukas thought for a second and answered, "Can anyone truly trust the Comneni?"

The commanders, followed by the young officers, proceeded past four of the Varangian Guard and into a large antechamber. These rugged Viking soldiers were the personal bodyguards of the emperor. Originally, the Varangian Guard was a gift from the Prince of Kievan Russia earlier in the century. Subsequent recruits hailed also from Germany, Saxon England, and Norman Italy, as well as Scandinavia.

Once in the antechamber, Justin marveled at the grandeur around him. White marble columns braced a high vaulted gold ceiling. Beautiful mosaics, glittering with gold, sparkled from the walls. Gorgeous silk tapestries of red, blue, and green, each with its own intricate design, hung gracefully from the golden ceiling. He smelled sweet frankincense in the air.

From the antechamber, the young soldiers slowly walked forward into the enormous golden audience room. In the distance in front, they saw a large marble platform where the imperial family sat on their golden thrones. Ahead, Justin could see Emperor Michael Dukas. The throne to Michael's right was lower than his. On it sat his mother, Evdokia, the empress and wife of Romanos Diogenes. On the throne to Michael's extreme left, which was equal in elevation to his own, sat Romanos Diogenes. Between the two co-emperors was a fourth golden throne, higher than the rest and occupied only by a bejeweled, golden book of the Holy Gospels. Everyone regarded this as the throne of the Lord, Jesus Christ, Son of God, and the True Ruler of the Roman Empire and the world. Any emperor served as Christ's Vicegerent, the Executor of the Will of God.

Justin's eyes widened as they took in the wonders of the audience room unfolding before them. Flora and fauna of all sorts and amazing, seemingly magical, man-made devices embellished the gigantic chamber. Small silver boats floated on pools of mercury. Ornate mosaics of precious and semi-precious stones covered the walls and the thirty-foot high ceiling. Potted exotic trees from the far ends of the world towered over the court. Elaborate water fountains projected a veil of water toward the ceiling. Domesticated cheetahs, lions, and tigers waited in the galleries that flanked the audience room. They were leashed to porphyry columns by tethers of red silk inlaid with silver and gold. Colored lights reflecting from a multitude of mirrors made such a beautiful array that Justin felt as if they were at Heaven's Gate.

Two hundred years earlier, the Emperor Theophilos awed his supplicants at the Sacred Palace with roaring mechanical gold lions and chirping brightly painted, jewel-encrusted wooden birds that performed at his command. And if that weren't enough, he'd raise his throne high in the air and look down on those below.

Some of the younger officers stood still, too overwhelmed to continue moving forward on the white marble floor. The chamberlain came up from behind them and urged them onward. The walk to the imperial family was but a mere one hundred feet; to many, it may as well have been several miles.

As he took in the splendor around him, Justin remembered a verse from *Ecclesiastes* that a priest friend often quoted: "*Vanity. All is vanity.*" Several dignitaries of the court, both secular and clerical, among them John Xiphilinios, the patriarch of Constantinople, stood at the base of the platform facing the commanders and their junior officers. Almost everyone in Constantinople had seen the patriarch at one church procession or another. This brilliant man established the School of Law at the University of Constantinople at the behest of Emperor Constantine Dukas. He appeared to be a quiet, reflective man whose gentleness could soothe any sinner. The patriarch, first of all churchmen of the empire, wore flowing jewel-studded vestments of golden cotton and silk. A jeweled, golden-domed crown rested on his head. When he raised his golden staff as each soldier approached, Justin saw how this silver-bearded ecclesiastic was seen by many of the common folk to be the earthly image of God Himself.

The bearded metropolitans, bishops, priests, and deacons wore similarly lavish clothing, but not to the degree of their overlord. The monks, bearded as well, kept their garments simple: black with occasional accents of gold. There were other courtiers as well: philosophers, wearing gray, and physicians wearing blue.

To the right of the patriarch stood Michael Psellos, who, although he was technically still a monk, wore a white silk and linen *dalmatic*, patterned with multiple interlocking gold and silver circles. Its flowing sleeves widened at their ends. They were buried in gold and silver bands sewn into the fabric. This same pattern appeared at the hems and seams of the over robe. Its collar was embellished with black onyx studs. Psellos, another intellectual giant, had created the School of Philosophy at the university for Emperor Constantine. He held his head high and Justin glanced at him. *He's quite full of himself.*

At the patriarch's left was Andronikos Dukas, who wore a blood-red silk dalmatic interwoven with a golden material. This aristocrat sneered as he watched these common soldiers file into the room. Justin saw the man scowl. *He doesn't want to be here.* Because of the multitude of golden rings on Andronikos Dukas' hands, it appeared that the gold of the dalmatic's fabric overflowed on to his hands.

To Andronikos Dukas' left was his younger brother, Constantine. His bright gold dalmatic was studded with diamonds. He didn't scowl like his brother but his gaze betrayed an uneasy wariness. He closely examined each officer as he entered the room.

Opposite the patriarch stood *Strategos* Joseph Tarchaniotes, known to be the emperor's most capable general. Tarchaniotes held his chiseled chin high as the soldiers marched their way into the imperial presence. His stern countenance demanded obedience. The strategos wore a blue silk tunic with an accompanying leather skirt, similar to what any soldier would wear. He also wore a golden breastplate embossed with the figure of a charging lion. Near the bottom of his bare legs, one could see his modest laced leather boots, nearly identical to what the lowliest soldier in the imperial army might wear.

Beyond the courtiers, the imperial family sat tall on their thrones. Romanos Diogenes, in his mid-thirties, six feet tall, muscular, and dashingly handsome, was easy to identify. Contrasting his rugged physical appearance, his elegant silk robe was red and purple with the purple sleeves visible at his wrists and covered with gold medallions, pearls, sapphires, and rubies. His head was capped with the magnificent imperial diadem. A beautiful small enamel icon of the Risen Christ augmented this perfect union of gold and precious gems. Only the Vicegerent of the Almighty was worthy of wearing this heavenly creation.

Empress Evdokia Macrembolitissa was a physically stunning woman, her dark brown eyes soft and warm. What was visible of her hair revealed a black color with subtle streaks of gray. She appeared quiet, contented, satisfied with yielding control of these proceedings to her husband. She wore a beautiful robe similar to that of her husband, though its jewels were smaller and more subtle. Her diadem, while quite exquisite, was less opulent than his.

Emperor Michael appeared immature, both physically and emotionally. Although he was about twenty years old, his mannerisms and posture were those of a boy of twelve. He refused to sit still and he slumped in his throne. Michael was shorter than most men, and some women, of his age. His puerile mannerisms only amplified his pitiful efforts to appear majestic. The young Dukas' emerald silk robe was embroidered with one-inch golden

Greek crosses. His diadem was similar to that of his stepfather but he had chosen a small icon of Archangel Michael crushing the serpent's head as its ultimate adornment.

Justin watched nervously as he and the rest of the soldiers reached the foot of the platform. As each man did so, he prostrated himself before the imperial family. After the last had done so, Romanos Diogenes spoke.

"Arise," Romanos commanded in a deep voice, his booming voice reverberating off the marble palace walls. "Our world is once again in great crisis," Romanos began as the soldiers stood at attention. "The last of our lands in Italy have been taken by the barbarous Normans; the Ishmaelite Arabs have held the Holy Land for three hundred years and have recently taken Antioch. And now a new threat has surfaced in Asia. The uncivilized Seljuk Turks have penetrated our eastern frontier, striking deep into Armenia and Anatolia. And while they have neither taken any land, nor claimed any, their raids have destroyed many crops and killed many Christians. Last year, our army pursued them throughout the Anatolia with limited success. Our commanders Bryennios and Alyattes are in the field at this time, awaiting our orders and the expiration of the current truce with these Turks. The truce will end shortly and we must be ready to attack as soon as possible, catching them off-guard so we can eliminate them as a threat to the empire."

Romanos continued, holding up his hands and spreading them apart as he spoke. "The Roman Empire, but five hundred years ago, stretched from the Spain to Syria, from the coast of North Africa to the Alps and the Ister. These were days of glory, under the mighty Emperor Justinian."

He set his arms down. "But his conquests were lost. Many brave emperors waged daring campaigns to recover these lands. Even at the beginning of this century, the second Emperor Basil, the Bulgar Slayer, made the empire the dominant power in the Mediterranean. When he died, the empire stood poised to recover her former glory. However subsequent emperors have allowed the strength of the Roman Empire to fade since those golden days."

The gigantic room became as quiet as a tomb. Everyone recognized this last comment as an affront to the Dukas family and their allies. Andronikos Dukas seethed at Romanos' words, and Michael Psellos and the patriarch were obviously disturbed. Emperor Michael stood and attempted to speak but his mother curtly motioned to him to sit down.

"This neglect of our defenses has had disastrous consequences. Our enemies now see us as weak and ripe for attack," Romanos continued. "It has been three years since our assumption of the throne. In that time, our paramount goal has been the reconstruction and rehabilitation of our military and naval forces to assure the safety of the empire of Constantine the Great and all of Orthodox Christendom. This will be a long process and we will need fine officers of your caliber to facilitate that transformation."

Romanos paused, perhaps anticipating a response from the court. He didn't seem surprised when it failed to arrive.

"In one week," he continued, "you are to join us in Asia where you shall witness the Turk being brought to heel. The foundation of the empire will be strengthened. Then the reclaiming of the Holy Land and Italy thereafter can be planned!"

Not one in this cavernous room applauded. Justin was perplexed. What was going on?

Yet Romanos did not appear to be disturbed by his court's lack of enthusiasm. He seemed to expect it. He motioned to his chamberlain who brought each commander, one at a time, directly before him. Each warrior prostrated himself as he arrived before Romanos. The emperor would then call out each soldier's name, have the man rise, and present him with a gold medal and his personal congratulations.

Once he had finished with the senior officers, Romanos moved on to the younger men. Justin and Peter were the last of their group to be called. Both of them waited eagerly as the chamberlain approached. He stopped in front of Peter and led him up onto the platform. Peter walked solemnly to the throne of Romanos Diogenes and dutifully flattened himself before him.

"Peter Theophilos Argyropoulos," Romanos' voice boomed.

Peter rose and Romanos presented his right hand, which Peter firmly grasped and shook. Romanos looked Peter sharply in the eye and held his hand for several seconds. Peter released his grip several times but Romanos maintained his. He wasn't going to let

Peter go until *he* was ready. Then Romanos released his tight grip and presented the soldier with the medal.

"We thank you for your service, Captain," Romanos said softly.

Peter bowed and joined the other soldiers back at the foot of the platform.

Justin watched Peter and the emperor with anticipation. Romanos had taken longer with Peter than with the others. Why? The look on Peter's face was familiar to Justin. He had seen it many times. Peter's eyes were slightly narrowed and Justin could see his jaw muscles tensing. He was obviously uncomfortable in front of the crowd. Justin tried to imagine the thoughts going through his friend's head when he suddenly felt the chamberlain tap his shoulder. Justin glanced over his shoulder at the older man and then followed him to Romanos Diogenes, where he prostrated himself.

"Justin Basilios Phillipos," Romanos announced.

Justin rose and shook the emperor's hand. As he maintained his grip on the young captain's hand, Romanos studied Justin deliberately. Justin felt Romanos' eyes pierce through him. He was beginning to feel conspicuous and uncomfortable. The seconds dragged on like hours as he received the same scrutiny as Peter. Then the emperor released Justin's hand, presented him with the medal, and offered his congratulations.

"We thank you for your service, Captain," Romanos said softly.

Justin thanked him and made his way back to his comrades.

The ceremony ended with a long prayer, led by the patriarch and enjoined by all of the clerics in the room. Thereafter, the chamberlain motioned to Tribune Apostolas and the commanders filed out of the throne room, followed by the junior officers.

Justin left the audience room with mixed feelings. He had just had a great honor bestowed upon him and for that he felt proud. But the strange relationship between Romanos Diogenes and his court bothered him. He had been called before the ruler of the empire, set apart, and identified as part of the emperor's plan to change the empire. Yet the powerful court seemed indifferent, if not angry. Perhaps the change Romanos wanted was unwelcome. What would this mean for him? Justin wondered if Peter would know.

CHAPTER 4

Eleni descended the two flights of stairs that separated her parents' home from hers. Eleni's parents, Demetrios and Aspasia Nikopoulos lived on the first floor above the ground floor of the four-story dwelling. The ground floor was used for storage. On the next level up lived Eleni's sister Eftihia, who was six years older than Eleni and had two young sons. Her husband Manolis worked as a bureaucrat in the imperial treasury. Maria, Eleni's senior by eight years, lived with her husband, Lukas, in Athens. He was a sophist, a privately paid teacher, who taught architectural antiquities.

Mateos, a Nubian man, met Eleni at the door. He had been a servant of the Nikopoulos family for twenty-six years. She politely refused his escort and walked up the stairs and into the central great room. She could smell the mint tea her parents had with their breakfast.

Beautiful glazed tiles adorned the white plaster walls. Eleni looked at them and grinned, remembering the look on her mother's face when her father had brought the tiles home. He had read a great deal about North Africa. Although he had never been there, that locale fascinated him. One day he came home with these half-dozen-or-so tiles. Her mother was so upset with him that she refused to allow the servants to help him lay them. She even threatened to destroy them. So he mounted them himself. Her grumbling continued for several months; more than once she threatened to remove them but he knew that she wouldn't so he said nothing.

Some of the painted tiles showed acacias, others cheetahs, giraffes, or elephants. A third group of tiles featured paintings of beautiful desert flowers. Eleni had always loved these tiles and, she thought, her mother had finally softened to love them as well.

Aspasia Nikopoulos was surprised by her daughter's visit but greeted her enthusiastically with a generous hug and three kisses, one on the right cheek, one on the left, and the last again on the right.

"We weren't expecting to see you until after the ceremony," Aspasia said to her daughter.

The older woman was forty-eight years old and an inch or two shorter than her daughter. She outweighed her by a good twenty pounds. Aspasia wore a long-sleeved, ankle-length tan stola with a dark brown sash and brown leather sandals, which laced up to the middle calf. Her long hair was prematurely gray but full-bodied; she had braided it into a single strand to be clasped by a beautiful silver band, which was engraved with two owls. The garrulous Aspasia met any endeavor with endless enthusiasm. She lacked subtlety but was unswervingly honest and sincere.

"Let me tell your father that you are here," Aspasia said as she turned toward the end of the hall to fetch him.

Eleni's father, Demetrios Athanasiou Nikopoulos, was in his library reading from Epictetus. When he heard Eleni speaking to her mother, the fifty-four-year-old man disengaged himself from his reading and came to greet her. This short, wiry, olive-skinned man had the same color of auburn hair as his daughter. He had always been close to Eleni, although his heart still longed for his son who had been taken from him by death early in his manhood. Perhaps it was because the father shared with his youngest daughter a keen ability to find an answer to any problem, no matter how difficult. Even Aspasia would complain to Demetrios that he was closer to Eleni than he was to her, his wife.

"Eleni!" Demetrios greeted her, kissing her three times as her mother had. "How can I help you, my dear?"

"Well, Father," Eleni stammered, "I've came to see Mother."

Aspasia and Demetrios looked at one another, surprised.

"Your mother," Demetrios said, thinking he had not heard her the first time.

Eleni nodded.

"Me?" Aspasia gasped.

"Yes, Mother," Eleni answered, understanding her mother's surprise. "I need some help with my hair," she added as she twirled a strand with her fingers.

"Hmmm," Demetrios began. "Hair . . . Certainly . . . Well . . . That's good." Then he added clumsly, "I think I hear Epictetus calling." He smiled at his daughter, turned and walked down the hall toward his library. Just before he reached that room, he abruptly turned toward Eleni and added, "I'll be in the library if you need me, Eleni."

"Thank you, Father," she replied, then turned to her mother.

Aspasia stood in front of her daughter, her disbelief unabated.

"Mother?" Eleni asked. "Are you all right?"

Aspasia startled as if she had been awakened from a daydream. "Oh, oh, I'm fine, dear. I'm fine."

"Good." Eleni gently touched her hair to remind her mother of the reason for her visit.

"Come with me, dear," Aspasia said as she led her daughter down the hallway.

In the dressing room, Eleni sat on a backless chair facing the mirror of a pine vanity painted white with gold accents. Aspasia took her spot on a stool directly behind her daughter. For the first few minutes, each waited for the other to begin. As Aspasia gathered and inspected the brushes and combs, Eleni looked down at the surface of the vanity. To her left she saw a silver crucifix. The image of the suffering Savior gave her pause; she scanned the letters over His head: INBI, the Greek initials for Jesus of Nazareth, King of the Jews. She crossed herself discretely three times with her right hand, touching her forehead, then her mid-abdomen, then her right shoulder, and then her left. The weight on her shoulders was momentarily lifted, but as she felt the burden easing, the same force that lightened the load reminded her why she had come to her mother.

Eleni tried to resist her need to speak to her mother. *Mother and I are so different!* But she knew the problem she was facing could only be addressed with the help of that woman. Yet she still resisted. Inviting any distraction, Eleni looked to her left where her mother had laid a silver hairbrush and comb. The hairbrush was engraved with a scene from Greek mythology, one Eleni knew well: a relieved Daphne changing into a laurel tree as she is pursued by an over-amorous Apollo. Her mind returned to a simpler time when she had first heard the myth.

But the present problem, as if under its own power, blotted out the innocent past and demanded her attention. As she handed the comb and hairbrush to her mother, she wet her lips and readied herself for this conversation she had been dreading for the last hour. "Confession," Eleni remembered her father say, "is the emptying of the mind so that the heart can be filled."

"Thank you, Mother," Eleni said, as her mother ran the comb through her hair. She became quiet, her courage failing her.

Aspasia put the comb down. She saw that her daughter's need to see her mother and not her father was as foreign to Eleni as it was to her. She had to penetrate her daughter's unusual quietude. "Eleni," she began. "What's wrong?"

"Wrong?" Eleni asked, turning around and trying to brighten her countenance. She was retreating even further.

"Eleni, you're a hundred miles away. Three days married and you're as quiet as a mouse. That's so unlike you," Aspasia said. She thought for a second and chuckled, "When I married your father, I was bubbly for months but you don't seem happy at all."

"I'm sorry, Mother." Eleni looked at her mother and realized that she couldn't keep up the deception any longer. "It's Justin."

"You'd think you'd know some one after eighteen years," Aspasia joked.

"Mother," Eleni hesitated, still not wanting to broach the subject. "Justin will be late this morning."

"Oh, is something wrong?" the mother asked, pulling her stool closer to her daughter.

"Well," Eleni began, "he told me that he had to meet with Peter after this morning's ceremony —"

"But I thought you two were going to spend some time with your father and me!" Aspasia protested.

"Mother! Please, let me finish!"

Aspasia was taken aback by her daughter's sudden outburst.

"I'm sorry, Mother."

"Go ahead, my child," Aspasia said as she lovingly put her daughter's hand in hers.

"When Justin left, I was so frustrated with him—"

"It won't be the first time, dear," Aspasia said, remembering her experiences with her husband.

"He had known about this meeting with Peter for some time. He says he just forgot to tell me about it."

"That's not hard to understand."

"But how could he forget something so important?"

"Maybe he was more preoccupied than usual. That boy's always got something on his mind. He's a dreamer. Sometimes I think he's in another world—"

"Mother!" Eleni pulled her hand out of her mother's gentle grasp and placed it on her own lap.

"I'm sorry," Aspasia begged. "Please continue."

"What's bothering me is that I've known Justin all of my life. I've always liked him as he is and I've never thought that anything that he did would ever bother me. But what happened today has truly annoyed me."

Aspasia grinned and asked, "Is that so?"

"Yes, it is!"

"What is it about marriage that suddenly transforms us?" Aspasia began, smiling like a sage with a new pupil. "We are selfless at the altar, only to grow more selfish as we walk away from it."

At first, Aspasia's response went in through one of Eleni's ears and out the other. But as Eleni thought about it, she was thrown off-balance by her mother's thoughtful analysis. Words of wisdom flowed only from her father's lips, certainly not those of her mother. Eleni looked at her mother as if to ask, "What do you know about this?"

"Yes, my dear," Aspasia said, patiently. "I am very familiar with this problem." Eleni remained incredulous. "This happened to your father and me, to my mother and father . . . ."

"But why, Mother?" Eleni asked. She was intrigued by her mother's insightfulness. She had never thought of her mother as a wise person.

"We come to think of marriage as ownership. We come to the wedding table wanting to take but it is really our duty to give."

"What do you mean?"

"The wife is to love and obey her husband," Aspasia continued. "How can she do either if she loves her husband only for what he could be and not for what he is?"

Eleni sat quietly as she considered her mother's words.

"The duty of the man is to love and honor his wife, to love her as Christ loves the Church. Doesn't our Lord love us as we are and not just for what we could be?" Aspasia waited patiently, admiring her youngest child's auburn hair.

"Mother, you surprise me," Eleni said, still trying to appreciate what her mother had said. "What you have said seems wise . . . ."

"No, my dear," Aspasia interrupted, "these aren't *my* words of wisdom. My mother told me this soon after I married your father. And for all I know, her mother told her this after her wedding, too."

"So, you're saying that I need to accept Justin as he is."

"As you have for all of your life, before you were married."

Eleni shook her head in frustration.

"Do you love him, my dear?" Aspasia asked.

"Of course I do, Mother, but his forgetfulness will only cause more problems."

"Eleni, by your own admission, you've known him forever. Many women know their husbands for less that a year before they are married. You weren't promised in marriage to a man you hardly knew. Your father and I saw how much you and Justin loved each other growing up. We knew that you could be happy together so when Justin asked your father . . . ."

"But, Mother, what does this have to do with Justin's forgetfulness?"

"You had eighteen years to get to know you husband. Don't start splitting hairs now!"

Eleni looked away from her mother. "You don't understand," Eleni said, looking at the floor.

"Do you love him, Eleni?" Aspasia asked gently.

"Of course I do," Eleni answered.

"Then . . . ."

Eleni sighed and hugged her mother saying, "Mother, it's not that easy!"

"I didn't say it was," Aspasia said.

Eleni stood up to leave but her mother motioned her to sit. There was more on Eleni's mind that Justin's forgetfulness and she realized that her mother had figured that out.

"What is it, Eleni? There's something else, isn't there?" The stern look on Aspasia's face demanded an explanation from Eleni. The young woman found it difficult to speak to, or even look at, her mother now.

"I feel ashamed, Mother," Eleni said as she looked away from her mother.

Aspasia scooted her stool closer to Eleni. "About what, Eleni?" she asked tenderly. This woman, the youngest of her daughters, had never before shown such timidity.

"After Justin left," Eleni began, choosing her words carefully, "I convinced myself that he was not being honest with me. He and Peter were up to something, I was certain."

"Eleni!" Aspasia snapped, her patience suddenly gone. "Justin doesn't lie! How could you think such a thing?"

"Mother, I know that Justin wouldn't lie."

"So what's wrong?"

Eleni was extremely embarrassed. She wanted to get up and go home right then but she stayed seated. She knew she couldn't delay any longer. Eleni looked straight at her mother and confessed, "I had Iakovos follow him."

"What?" Aspasia shrieked. "You had someone follow your husband? God help us all!"

"It wasn't just anyone; it was Iakovos."

Aspasia sprang to her feet and threw her hands into the air. "Oh, so you're using one of our servants to do your dirty work!"

"Mother, I know what I did was wrong—" Eleni stood as she tried to explain.

"Then why did you do it?" Aspasia thundered, jabbing a finger at her daughter. "This is not loving and obeying your husband!" Aspasia crossed herself with rapid, deliberate gestures. Eleni could hear her muttering an invocation to the Almighty under her raspy breathing.

"I admit I was impulsive." Eleni's face showed that she knew her guilt. She looked into her mother's eyes, desperate for her forgiveness. "I'm sorry, Mother."

"Apologize to your husband, not me!"

"I will—"

"Damned right you will!"

Tears formed in the corners of Eleni's eyes. She stood and moved toward the door. She said, "I'm leaving now, Mother."

But Aspasia was closer to the door and arrived there before Eleni. She saw her mother's face had softened considerably.

"You will tell him?" Aspasia asked.

"Yes, I will, Mother," Eleni answered.

Aspasia sighed in relief and hugged her daughter. Tears trickled from Eleni's eyes as she welcomed her mother's forgiveness.

"Eleni, what bothers me most is that this behavior is so unlike you," Aspasia said. "You're not a suspicious person. This is the act of a petty, weak woman. You've allowed a demon into your heart that will only destroy you." Her voice softened as she held her daughter in her arms and asked, "Why did you do such a thing?"

"I don't know and I don't think I ever will," Eleni sobbed. "I guess that's why I'm so bothered by it."

Aspasia squeezed her daughter tightly. "My dear, dear Eleni. You are a strong, honest, bright woman. Don't do anything else so unworthy of yourself . . . or Justin."

"I won't, Mother," Eleni promised, still crying. Relishing the warmth of her mother's warm grasp and her forgiveness, Eleni continued to hug her mother.

"And go easy on Justin. He's a good man."

"Yes, Mother," Eleni answered, still feeling that her mother was asking the impossible.

"Shall I call for the chaplain so you can confess?" Aspasia asked, maintaining her gentle tone.

"Perhaps later," Eleni answered.

"You will tell Justin, won't you?"

"I will tell him, Mother."

CHAPTER 5

"So what did you think?" Peter asked once Justin and he were alone in a corner of the imperial gardens. Robins exchanged chirps and flitted between the branches of the trees. "Kind of strange, don't you think?'

"Holding hands with the emperor while his court glares at us? What's so strange about that?" Justin asked sarcastically.

"Right," Peter shot back. "Makes me feel real comfortable, too." Peter thought for a few seconds. "The emperor has some serious problems with the company he keeps."

"What do you mean by that?"

"He's obviously not popular with them."

"Yeah."

"Then he insults them in public."

"So where are you going with this, Peter?"

"The extra time he spent with us. He's publicly showing his favor to us. He's bringing us into his fold."

"You can't say that," Justin countered. "He never said anything like that."

"That's right but what he did gave the *appearance* of an alliance, a special relationship."

"No—"

"Justin, if they decide to off him, we'll be next."

"What? That's ridiculous!"

"I'm serious!"

"Peter, that's just a little too far-fetched for me to believe."

"Open your eyes, Justin!"

"Can we change the subject?"

"Justin!"

"Please!" Justin paused for a second and continued calmly, "Please, Peter. Let's talk about something else."

"All right," Peter conceded after a moment's hesitation.

"Thank you."

"So, Justin," Peter began playfully, "since you don't have to meet with Tribune Apostolas and me after the ceremony, what are you going to do with all of that spare time? How about taking in a horse race at the Hippodrome?"

"Very funny, Peter. Listen, I truly am sorry about missing that meeting this morning. I could have sworn you said—"

"Justin," Peter interrupted. "I know you're sorry."

"And you lied to Apostolas to save my butt. You didn't have to do that."

"Apology accepted," Peter said, sensing that Justin's apology would drag on.

"I *am* sorry, Peter."

"You've said that a few times already."

"Well, then this is my final apology," Justin added as he held out his hand to Peter.

Peter took Justin's hand, smiled, and shook it vigorously. "Apology accepted."

As they turned to leave the Great Palace Complex, they nearly collided with a short, bearded man wearing a black cassock. "Good morning, my children," the priest said. He held out a small black bag. "Perhaps you would like to make a donation to the widows' and orphans' fund? Remember that our Lord encourages us not to forget those in need."

Justin and Peter looked at each other hesitantly, then reached for their money, and looked into the black bag. At the bottom of the empty bag was a note. They looked at the priest's face.

"Don't hesitate to be generous, my children. The Lord loves a cheerful giver," the priest said, motioning with the bag as if to encourage them to take the note.

Each of the young captains dropped a copper *folis* into the bag, Justin first. When he grabbed the note, the priest smiled.

"Your rewards are in Heaven, my sons," the priest said. He left them, chanting a familiar hymn.

The two young men looked at each other in complete bewilderment. Peter inpatiently snatched the note from Justin. "Let's have a look."

"Hey!" Justin complained.

Peter looked around to confirm their solitude, and read, "'You are to meet us at the Basilica Cistern immediately.' This is marked with the imperial seal!" He immediately looked around to see if they were being followed. "My idea doesn't sound so far-fetched now, does it, Justin?"

"Let me see that!" Justin demanded as he grabbed the note and inspected it.

"I don't like this," Peter groaned as he recalled the imperial audience that had just left. His worst fears were confirmed.

"It's genuine," Justin said, handing the note back to Peter. "That's the emperor's seal."

Peter read the note again. "I don't like this one bit, Justin."

"I hate it when you're right, Peter. It always means we're in trouble," Justin said, half-joking.

Peter didn't reply. He was deep in thought, anticipating the upcoming rendezvous.

"Peter, shouldn't we leave?"

Again Peter was silent.

"Peter, the note said 'immediately'."

"Uh, sure," Peter replied, as if awakening from a daydream.

As they set out, Peter and Justin speculated about the note's origin. They agreed this was too strange to be a joke but why had the emperor demanded a second audience and why in the Basilica Cistern of all places? From the walls outside the Palace Bucoleon, they headed north through the packed streets. They struggled to make their way past the many people and numerous beasts of burden along the way. The streets were littered with trash, animal waste, and fish blood and the stench promulgated a lucrative perfume trade. To keep the imperial olfactory senses protected from the odor of the street, the emperors ordained that all perfume shops must be within a stone's throw of the gate of the Great Palace Complex.

When Justin and Peter reached the Hippodrome, just to the west of the palace grounds, they ran into a large mob waiting to get in. This large stadium was shaped like of an elongated horseshoe, its east and west sides running parallel and its southern end curved in a semicircle. As Peter and he struggled through the multitude outside, Justin's thoughts drifted into the massive stadium. He remembered the long thin island that ran down the center of the stadium infield. It acted as a median for the horse races, chariot races, and other events. Numerous artful objects were implanted in this island. Three in particular were the most impressive. The first was a tall obelisk, brought to the Hippodrome from Egypt by Emperor Theodosius I in the fourth century. It rested on an eight-foot pedestal. Carved on each of the four sides of the pedestal's base were scenes of competitions in the Hippodrome.

Earlier in that same century, Emperor Constantine the Great had brought the second prize, the ancient bronze Serpentine Column, from Delphi. The column took the form of three serpents wrapped around a pole. Legend stated that after the Greek victory over the Persians at the battle of Platea, the bronze spears of the dead Persian soldiers were melted down to create this monument. Unfortunately, over the years, vandals had broken off two of the three heads but the ruined remnant still possessed a certain majesty.

In the preceding century, Emperor Constantine Porphyrogenitus added a second tall stone obelisk to this median and covered it in bronze. To leave one's mark in the most-visited edifice of the city ensured that emperor's immortality among his people.

Cretan acrobats had been performing in the Hippodrome all week. Few seats were to be found. The performance was about to begin and the throng outside the massive stadium was growing impatient. Despite the elevated social position people usually gave to soldiers, it was with difficulty that the two captains plowed their way through this mass of humanity. As they did, Justin thought of the performance of these same acrobats he had witnessed five years ago.

It was a warm, sunny day in early September. Justin, his youngest brother John, and their father Basilios had heard a great deal about these acrobats. The troop consisted of twenty-six young men whose acrobatics included tumbling of all kinds, diving from twelve-foot heights into pools of water, masterly sword handling, and horseback riding, among other feats.

Justin's favorite event involved three men and two horses. The two horses rode side by side; one man stood on the back of each horse's bare back and the third man stood on the inside shoulder of each of the other two men. The bottom two men held the ankles of the topmost acrobat with their inside hands and the reins to the horses with the others. The topmost man brandished a sword in each hand as the two horses trotted around the infield of the Hippodrome.

The horde of some forty thousand exploded in applause. From the imperial box in the middle of the eastern flank of the Hippodrome, the emperor at that time, Constantine Dukas, and his wife, Empress Evdokia, applauded courteously. Above them, frozen in a regal trot they'd held for seven hundred years, were four life-sized, gilt bronze horses. On their second tour around the infield, the acrobats thrilled the audience with more daring maneuvers. The topmost man sprang from the shoulders of his colleagues, swords in hand, backflipping ten feet to the ground behind the trotting equines. The spectators rose and roared with excitement. They repeated this four times, at different areas of the infield so the onlookers had the opportunity to see the performers in relative proximity. And to their delight the speed of the horses increased with each attempt. The amazed observers remained on their feet for the remainder of the spectacle.

For their final spectacle, the acrobatic trio jettisoned their swords and one horse and reassembled. The largest man stood on the horse's bare back. The next largest stood on his shoulders and the lightest stood atop the shoulders of the second man. The bottom-most acrobat urged the sturdy horse slowly onward until the group was directly in front of the imperial box. The Varangian Guard were visibly unnerved by the proximity of the entertainers but Constantine Dukas reassured the guard and the acrobats proceeded. The agile, topmost fellow leapt upward off the shoulders of his colleague and completed a triple flip before landing squarely upon the short wall two feet in front of the imperial couple. The multitude gasped and suddenly was anxiously quiet. That had impressed them but they held their applause. They wanted to gauge their response to that of their emperor.

As the acrobat dropped to one knee, his face fully bowed out of respect for his emperor, Constantine Dukas froze. The emperor felt violated by the presence of this common man so close to him but he realized that the thousands in the Hippodrome was very impressed by this troop. To indulge the masses and cheer this upstart would be to lessen his office, he believed. Yet the Hippodrome had a power of its own. Other emperors had learned too late that to snub the will of the crowd meant risking one's throne and one's life. Emperor or not, they would tear him limb from limb if they so chose. In the hippodrome, rulers and subjects sometimes stood on level ground. Perplexed, the emperor didn't know what to do.

The acrobat, his heart pounding rapidly and his breathing grew shallow and more frequent, felt beads of sweat on his forehead as he awaited a sign of approval from the emperor. Had he overstepped the bounds of appropriate behavior?

Empress Evdokia saw that the issue required quick resolution and her husband couldn't provide it. She slowly, majestically, rose to her feet and raised her arms upward. The masses roared loudly at the empress' signal, louder than Justin had ever heard them before. The empress smiled widely to the masses and then looked to her husband as if to say, "This is how it is done." The angry husband shot her a disapproving look and remained seated. But the prolonged ovation of the spectators obligated him to follow his wife's lead. Reluctantly, Constantine rose and waved to the crowd. The cheering intensified. The poor acrobat, still bowing in submission, suddenly fainted; relief from his tension had arrived too late.

From the Hippodrome, Justin and Peter hurried toward the Cathedral of Saint Sophia. It was here that Justin realized that they were being followed. He recognized the pursuer and chuckled to himself.

Peter was rescued from the depths of his concern by the sight of Emperor Justinian's great domed cathedral. Forgetting about the morning's furtive rendezvous with the diminutive priest, he briefly lost himself in this architectural marvel, the third church of that name, built on the same site of its two predecessors.

Peter recalled stories of the rioting between the rival Blue and Green political factions that began after the races at the Hippodrome five hundred years ago. As tension between the groups grew, Justinian jailed the rowdy ringleaders to silence the hostile groups and bring peace to the city. Three days later, as Justinian sat in the Hippodrome's imperial box, he was greeted with uproar rather than reverence. The Blues and Greens, now united against him, shouted, "Nika! Nika!" Usually this encouragement to "Win! Win!" was directed at the charioteers or horseman each side sponsored. But on that day, they were united against Justinian.

The emperor tried to soothe the mob by starting the races but the dissatisfied multitude erupted and spilled into the streets, burning all in its path, including Saint Sophia. Three months later, the rebuilding was begun by Justinian's architects, Isidore of Miletus and Anthemius of Tralles. Six years later, the cathedral outshone all edifices.

At Saint Sophia, Peter and Justin swung left to the entrance of the Basilica Cistern. The same Emperor Justinian built this huge cavern to store vast amounts of water for the city. Water was diverted from many areas in the southeast Balkan Peninsula to maintain the city in time of siege or drought.

Peter arrived just before Justin and flashed the priest's note in a guard's face. The sentry quickly read the note and summoned a second guard who escorted them into the cistern.

The few torches mounted on the walls of the Basilica Cistern gave little light to the dark cavern. The torch-bearing guard led the captains down a series of steps. Justin could smell the disagreeable stench of the cistern's motionless water as the three of them walked in near darkness for several minutes. Occasionally the light from their escort's torch allowed them to see one of several tall columns supporting this substantial cavern. The capitals atop the columns were tediously ornate; some designs were complicated latticework, others included small statuettes of Greek or Roman heroes. Others evinced a Christian theme featuring scenes from the Bible. The sound of their sandals hitting the stone flooring echoed throughout the huge cistern. As they walked on, they could clearly hear water dripping from the ceiling of the giant cave to the waiting pools below.

The guard stopped. He announced that he would return briefly and then disappeared. Soon after, a secret door in the stone foundation ahead ground open. The same guard appeared on the other side and escorted them into another room where three figures dressed in dark cowls awaited them. Although this smaller chamber was better lit than the huge open area of the Cistern, Justin could barely see those ahead, even as the guard led them to within four feet of their hosts.

"Leave us," the tallest of the three commanded the guard.

The guard exited, slowly closing the massive door with a mighty crash whose echo died slowly. The stone walls of the dank chamber were entirely featureless and the sound of dripping water gone. The room was silent until one of the three said something in a low voice to the others. Then someone, the tallest, spoke.

"Welcome, Captain Phillipos and Captain Argyropoulos."

Recognizing the voice of the Emperor Romanos, Justin and Peter immediately prostrated themselves.

"Please, gentlemen, refrain from the usual pleasantries. There is no need for that now. Your efforts are appreciated but we wish to make this meeting *informal*."

Standing up, the captains could discern the faces of their hosts, as one of the trio brought a torch from the wall forward. The two guests now recognized the second member of the party: Empress Evdokia. But the identity of the third, the torchbearer, remained a mystery.

The emperor and empress wore none of their imperial vestments but they had not shed their imperial presence. The empress motioned to the emperor who spoke to the young captains.

"You gentlemen are undoubtedly wondering why you have been summoned here," the emperor began. He didn't wait for their acknowledgment. "You two, above all of those honored at the palace this morning, have been chosen to serve your emperor and empress in a *special* capacity."

The young captains wondered what he meant but dared not speak. The unidentified man handed a book to Romanos Diogenes.

"Captain Justin Basilios Phillipos," the emperor read, "you have been serving us for the last six months along the River Ister. You have distinguished yourself in the heavy cavalry in actions against Pecheneg raiders and Bulgarian rebels. Previous to that you served in Syria, fighting the Arabs. While at this post, you were captured." Romanos looked up from the book and ordered, "Please tell us of this."

Justin nervously took a deep breath. "Your Majesty," Justin stammered, "yes, sire, I was captured."

"Go on," Romanos commanded.

"Yes, sire," Justin continued, slowly gaining composure as he spoke. "My patrol left the fort at night to raid the enemy's camp. Our raid was successful but I was captured."

"Captain," the Empress Evdokia began, her voice unexpectedly strong. "You are far too modest. Half of your patrol was captured as you rode away from the enemy camp after the raid. Upon your arrival at the fort, you realized this and remounted your horse and rode back to the Arab camp." It was obvious she had committed the whole story to memory. "Your commanding officer saw you leaving the fort, ran out to stop you, and ordered you to stay but you rode off; a daring act of disobedience."

Justin said nothing. *What could he say?*

The empress continued, telling the tale as if she had grown up with it. "You returned to the enemy camp under cover, neutralized a guard or two, found the tent where your men were held, freed them, and created a diversion which ensured their escape. Unfortunately, you were discovered as you fled the camp. You were captured and spent a year as the personal slave of the Arab officer who captured you but later you escaped by swimming out to a Roman ship anchored off shore."

Justin smiled, not knowing if he should speak or listen.

"That's quite impressive, Captain."

"Heroism seems to be a tradition in your family," Romanos said as he read from his book. "Your grandfather, Justin Basilios Phillipos, saved the life of the Emperor Basil by blocking a blow from a Bulgar cavalryman at the Battle of Balathista. He killed that Bulgar and a dozen others in less than an hour." He looked up from the book at Justin as if he were expecting confirmation.

Justin still said nothing.

"Your father, Basilios Justin Phillipos, served in action against the Arabs in Syria and also with the great George Maniakes at Monopoli, where he twice rescued his commanding officer from the Normans," Romanos read. "He completed his career as a military aid to our embassy in Venice," then he looked up from the book, "one of the few western powers that still respects us." He drew a deep breath and added, "You are a brave man from brave stock, Captain Phillipos. We have chosen wisely."

Then the emperor turned to Peter. "Peter Theophilos Argyropoulos," he said as he looked back at the book, "you have been serving us with Captain Phillipos on the Ister for the past six months. Prior to that, you served in our navy for two years, keeping the seas free of pirates and naval raiders. A squadron under your command defeated a larger Egyptian force that was raiding the southern coast of Crete." The emperor looked up from the book at Peter and then returned to it, quickly thumbing through several pages. "Your record is replete with similar acts of bravery." Romanos looked up from the book. "We have no record of your father," he said, inviting Peter to explain.

"Your Majesty," Peter began hesitantly, "when I was two months old, an Arab raiding party killed my parents. Nearly all of the inhabitants of our small island were massacred or taken away as slaves. My mother hid me before she was killed. Roman sailors discovered me there the next morning. The priest of our island had been badly hurt and left for dead but he survived the massacre. He identified me as he had baptized me only three weeks earlier. I was near death and taken to a convent on a nearby island where I was nursed back to health. There I stayed until I was four. Afterward, I was sent to a monastery where I stayed ten years. The monks trained me to be a priest but I knew I wanted to join the navy."

"And now you are in our army. Why is that?" Romanos asked.

"I had been in the navy for a long enough time and I was ready for a change."

"All of your childhood, you dreamed of being in the navy and suddenly you decide that you'd had enough?"

"Yes, sire," Peter replied.

The torchbearer stepped forward and whispered something to Romanos.

"Ah, yes," the emperor replied. "Gentlemen, this is Tribune Michael Attaleiates."

The tribune extended his hand to each of the captains.

"The tribune is one of our most trusted men. He is in Constantinople secretly; officially he is in Kiev negotiating a trade agreement." Romanos yielded to Attaleiates.

"Captain Argyropoulos," Attaleiates began, "it is of no use holding things back. His Majesty is aware of all of the details of your naval service. He is being polite in asking you your version of the events. Now, please tell us your reason for leaving the navy."

Peter balked.

"Captain?" Attaleiates demanded.

Peter was silent.

"Tell us, Captain!"

"I killed one of my sailors," Peter blurted out as he looked Attaleiates in the eye.

Justin was stunned. His friend had never told him this before.

"Please continue," said the tribune.

"I killed one of my sailors," Peter repeated. He was angry with Attaleiates for making him reveal this unpleasant event in front of his best friend.

"Captain," Attaleiates said, "you had a man executed because he disobeyed you."

Peter did not respond.

"You were his captain." When Peter maintained his silence, Attaleiates coldly added, "Execution of insubordinate men is standard practice in the navy *and* the army."

Justin didn't take his eyes off of Peter. Attaleiates was right. Justin knew that Peter was being too hard on himself. He silently tried to encourage his friend but Peter would look only at Attaleiates.

"Majesty," the tribune protested, "this is an obvious sign of weakness. Is Your Majesty certain that this man can fulfill his mission?"

"Captain," Romanos asked, "please answer the question."

Peter drew a deep breath, tried to cool his anger, and began his reply. "The first mate of our ship refused to execute a Norman pirate we had captured on patrol off the coast of Kefalonia." He bit his tongue before continuing, hoping to purge any emotion from his voice. "A year earlier, this same pirate was a sailor in o ur navy and had saved our first mate's life during action against the Saracens off the coast of Sicily."

"You took the correct action, Captain," the tribune said.

Peter was unmoved.

"Son," Romanos Diogenes said, "sometimes the correct action is the most difficult."

"Yes, Your Majesty," Peter replied, more out of duty than out of agreement, his eyes looking downward.

Frustrated by the digression of the proceedings, the empress spoke. "Gentlemen, the Roman Empire is in grave danger but you young men don't realize that the danger without is dwarfed by a greater danger within."

Justin immediately thought of the imperial court's reaction to the emperor's speech.

"The Seljuk Turks in the east and the Normans in the west are a mere nuisance. It is the Dukas family and its friends that are the true enemies of our realm.

Evdokia's words were strange, coming from one who had been a part of that clan. Justin saw Peter look up at her. The empress also spotted Peter's reaction. "Captain Argyropoulos, you are shocked that the widow of Constantine Dukas and the mother of the Emperor Michael could speak in such a seditious manner." She looked over to Justin who was no less shocked and added, "We were disillusioned by Constantine's abuse and neglect of the empire. We have always had a deep love for this land but Constantine and his family sought only to enrich themselves and their friends as they secured their grasp on the throat of the Roman Empire. He weakened the army so it would not be a threat to him and surrounded himself with flatterers whose only goal was extracting riches from the state, not serving it. He tried to fill the Senate with his kind and placed that leech Xiphilinios in the patriarchate. The empire is doomed with the likes of those vermin in control!"

"Your Majesty's son—" Justin began softly.

"Is a tool of his father's family!" Evdokia interrupted. "He is weak of mind and has no idea what is going on around him. We have no influence over him. His Uncle John holds more sway over him than we ever will. That demon would have Michael rule alone." She discretely wiped a tear from her eye. "As Constantine lay dying, he made us promise not to remarry after his death. Thus Michael would be assured the throne. With his supporters dominating the Senate and Xiphilinios as patriarch, we were bound by holy law to remain unmarried and therefore subject to the Dukas family."

"But you outfoxed them, my dear," Romanos said, losing a bit of his imperial finish as he stepped toward his wife. "As soon as you were widowed, you let it be known that you were interested in marrying Xiphilinios' brother. That hyena saw this as another opportunity for power so the old fool used every legal scheme he could to quickly invalidate your promise to Constantine."

"So Your Majesty was able to choose her next husband," Justin said. Then he realized his assessment was incomplete. "But why did Your Majesty choose His Majesty? Only a few years before, he had been condemned to death for attempting to overthrow your late husband."

Evdokia took no insult from Justin's bold question. "We knew that the empire needed the Governor of Serdica to save her," she replied. She looked fondly at Romanos.

"We have exiled John Dukas," Romanos said, "but his sons Andronikos and Constantine remain. Do you know of Michael Psellos, Captain Phillipos?'

"I've heard that he is a brilliant man, Your Majesty."

"He is that and very dangerous. His ink poisoned the life of the late Patriarch Cerularios, her Majesty's uncle. And now he waits for the chance to do the same to us."

"The jackals may appear to have the upper hand," Evdokia began. "But we will outmaneuver them. Fortunately, a slight majority in the Senate and many of the empire's powerful families share our concern. They see that the empire needs bold leadership but the loss of any of our support will tip the balance in favor of the Dukas."

"There are a number of senators who remain uncommitted," Romanos added. "If we gain their support, our position will be strengthened. If we lose it, my reign will end and Michael will rule by himself. The most expedient way to gain their trust is with a quick, convincing, military victory. We were unable to achieve that last year against the Turks. Their elusive mounted archers always managed to escape our grasp. Some of our political support left us as a result. However, now the Turks have a greater enemy in Egypt. The Turkish Sultan covets the lands of the Caliph of Cairo and, while his attention is there, we will attack and destroy his forces in Armenia.

"Next week, sixty thousand infantry and cavalry will cross the Bosphorus to Chalcedon. Two days before, you gentlemen will cross the Hellespont at Gallipoli with fifty heavy cavalry. We expect you at Nicea by the time our army is ready to move east. At Nicaea, you will join your new commander."

Justin and Peter eagerly waited for Romanos to reveal the identity of their new leader. Peter had heard many times of the bravery of Nikephoros Bryennios. He hoped that he'd be the one. Justin had heard that Alyattes, the Cappadocian, was an exceptional leader and wondered if he would be the one.

Romanos could see the anticipation in their eyes. He hated to let them down but this was part of their mission, the mission that was so important to his continued political survival. He cleared his throat and announced, "Gentlemen, your new commander will be Andronikos Dukas."

Justin and Peter recoiled. *Andronikos Dukas?*

"He's leading the levies of the nobility," Romanos explained. "They will be our second line in battle." When he saw the confused faces of the young captains, he tried to reassure them. "Which has you two more concerned, the fact that we are bringing him along or that we have placed you under his command? You think this is madness."

The young soldiers nodded discretely.

"Let us reassure you that we feel more comfortable with that viper within our grasp than in Constantinople, plotting our downfall with his family."

Romanos Diogenes smiled as he disclosed his second reason for retaining Andronikos Dukas. "He is also a hostage of sorts. His family will not put him in jeopardy by grabbing the throne while he is in our midst. And his command is the second line, the reserve.

We can keep him at a distance so he won't be able to upset our efforts on the battlefield."

"Your Majesty," Justin said, looking to Peter for support, "we fear that today's ceremony —"

"Will make you conspicuous in his camp," Romanos interjected. "Well, that's exactly why we are placing you there. He will assume you are my eyes in his camp. While his attention is focused on you, Dukas won't find our spies in his midst."

The sudden intrusion of a guard broke the conversation. The guard whispered something into the emperor's ear and stepped back.

"Excellent!" the captains could hear Romanos Diogenes whisper to the guard. "Bring him in."

The new arrival was a dark, stocky young man who appeared to be out of breath as he hurried into the chamber. One could tell he was an aristocrat by the way he freely exchanged greetings with the emperor, empress, and Attaleiates. A much younger man, he had the poise of someone twice his age. But who was he? Justin found himself fascinated by the new man.

Once the greetings were completed, Romanos Diogenes brought the new arrival forward to the two captains. "Captain Argyropoulos, Captain Phillipos," Romanos said. "This is Lord Alexios Comnenos."

CHAPTER 6

Comnenos. Peter knew the name well; every soldier and sailor in the emperor's service did. *Political brat from a political family.* Though he was boiling with contempt inside, Peter kept his feelings hidden. If it were apparent to the others, Peter could find himself in serious trouble. *Your ambitious mother will stop at nothing to have you on the throne, Comnenos. She even arranged your marriage to Irene Dukas to put you one step closer to her goal. Didn't anyone ever tell you people that greed is a deadly sin?* Indeed, Comnenos' mother, Anna Dalassena, sister-in-law of Emperor Isaac Comnenos, who proceded Constantine Dukas in that role, made it clear to all in her family that someday one of her sons would sit on the throne. *Funny finding you here, Comnenos. After all, it was your Uncle Isaac who abdicated and begged Constantine Dukas to take the throne. Had he chosen more wisely, we wouldn't be here now.*

Comnenos stepped forward and held out his hand. Justin eagerly grabbed it and bowed his head forward.

"Captain Phillipos," Comnenos said, "it is a pleasure to make your acquaintance."

"Thank you, sir," Justin replied.

Comnenos offered his hand to Peter who hesitated before he followed suit. "Captain Argyropoulos," Comnenos sensed Peter's suspicions, "it is my pleasure to meet you."

"Oh, the pleasure is all mine, sir," Peter said, glaring subtly as he took the young aristocrat's hand. He bowed his head and squeezed Comnenos' hand harder than usual.

Peter saw that Comnenos was good at cloaking his thoughts. "I look forward to working with you two in this most important endeavor."

"As anyone can see," Romanos Diogenes proclaimed, "we have assembled a formidable team!" While Romanos spoke, Attaleiates and Justin listened enthusiastically but Peter and Comnenos shot furtive glances at each other, as if they were generals sending scouts to the enemy's camp to procure vital intelligence. Romanos directed his words to Justin and Peter. "Tribune Attaleiates will accompany our staff on the campaign. Although Lord Comnenos would be a valuable asset in the field, we have ordered him to remain here in Constantinople to watch the Dukas."

Peter looked at Comnenos again. *You're staying here because your mother won't let you go. Yes, your older brother Manuel was killed last year fighting the Turks and I've heard you distinguished yourself well against them. The emperor even made you a strategos. But you'll stay home for this one. Mother doesn't want all of her prospective emperors killed off.*

"These men will continue your instruction in our behalf," said Evdokia, lifting her hand toward Attaleiates and Comnenos majestically. "Trust them with your lives."

Peter discretely snarled. *Never!*

"You will be contacted at the appropriate times," Romanos said. "We leave you now."

The four soldiers snapped to attention and bowed from the waist. They watched as the emperor and empress disappear into the darkness.

Once Romanos and Evdokia had left, Comnenos spoke. "These are treacherous times. I pray that our meeting today will be the first step, with God's help, in starting the Roman Empire back on its path to glory."

Peter glanced at Justin. He perceived Justin's admiration for the young aristocrat. However, his own disdain grew. He saw Comnenos' response to his hostility in the younger man's face and that filled him with a certain proud satisfaction.

Yet Comnenos recovered quickly. "The Roman Empire has been dangerously weakened and her future does indeed lie with her army. Were the efforts of my uncle Isaac in vain? The empire acquired a new vitality in his reign. This is what Romanos Diogenes hopes to duplicate and I believe in him."

Peter remained incredulous. *Comnenos must see Diogenes as a faster path to the throne. Crawl over whomever to sit on that golden chair!*

"My family and friends are unaware that I am in the city," the young aristocrat continued. "Few of them know my personal feelings toward the emperor or of my intimacy with him. Even my wife is unaware."

But I'll bet your mother does! Peter wanted to scream his thoughts but kept his composure.

Comnenos looked at Peter as if he had read his mind. "Captain," the collected Comnenos said, "I know that Captain Phillipos and you are unaccustomed to the intrigue one finds so plentiful at court. You are soldiers. What need do you have for these games of deception? This whole discussion is, to you honest and loyal soldiers, sordid and the work of the Devil. In many ways I agree with you. But to battle those who make these perfidies a way of securing their evil ends, well, an honest man must learn to play these games as well."

Michael Attaleiates felt compelled to offer his counsel, too. "Yes, gentlemen, politics are not for you," the tribune began, trying to reassure them. "What do you care if this man or that man is on the throne? You want safety for your families. You have shown yourselves to be courageous in battle. All the emperor wants now is your continued loyal service but in a different capacity."

Peter looked from the tribune to Comnenos. *Is it really that easy? Do you expect us to be elated about this deception we're being forced to join? You have praised us for being good soldiers. Let us be good soldiers, not your players in your perverse tragedy!*

"Now rest assured," the tribune looked at Justin, "that we will protect your family from any political entrapment. If the Dukas do attempt to overthrow the emperor, your family will undoubtedly be implicated as his friends because of your new association with him. Unfortunately those involved in political intrigue in any way may find themselves locked in the darkest dungeons of the empire, or exiled."

Justin's face went white. His earlier enthusiasm for the adventure evaporated.

"I know that you would not wish such a fate upon your family," Attaleiates continued. "So, the less they know, the better. Your wife and parents should be told only that you are going away on campaign. Their limited knowledge will protect them. As an added precaution, while you are away, your wife will stay as a guest of the empress among the ladies of her chamber in the Great Palace Complex, perhaps at the Palace Bucoleon or the Palace Magnaura." The tribune paused and looked at Justin and Peter. "Do you have any questions thus far?"

Justin and Peter looked at each other. *This man must be joking!* Of course they had questions, thousands of them, but how could they ask them? Why had they been chosen for this? Could they refuse the order and just walk away? Both knew the answer was certainly "no." Wasn't this undertaking too dangerous to involve mere soldiers? They were good at charging the enemy on horseback; they'd prefer to leave spying to spies. Why were they being placed in this dangerous situation for which they had no training or desire?

After Comnenos deemed his wait for a reply adequate, he said, "Gentlemen, while you are away, do not attempt to communicate with us. And do not attempt to communicate with the emperor in any fashion unless he initiates the action. He needs to distance himself from you as he leads the campaign. If any tragedy should befall the emperor, get word to me if you can or, better yet, come to Constantinople immediately and aid me in reforming the government for the emperor and keeping the Dukas from seizing control.

"There is a man here who can help you. Simon bar Levi, Simon the Jew." His voice soured a little on the last word. Oppression of Jews was common in the empire. "He lives between the Gate of the Phanar and the mosque near the Church of Saint Mary Pammakaristos."

"When do we meet him?" Justin asked.

"You already have," Comnenos answered with a broad smile. "He delivered the message that brought you here!"

"Do you mean the priest?" asked Peter.

"He is a master of disguises," Comnenos chuckled. "I don't even think he's really a Jew!"

Attaleiates joined him with a few guffaws and added, "He is a good man, a valuable asset. You can trust him."

"Remember," said Comnenos soberly as he and the tribune extended their hands to the captains, "we will provide safety for you and your family. I pray for the success of this campaign, the emperor and the empress, and your good fortune. When you return from your victory and the emperor is fully ensconced on his throne, you *will* be rewarded for your loyalty."

Attaleiates called for the guard and, before he arrived, Comnenos and the tribune disappeared into the darkness, unnoticed by Justin and Peter. The guard saluted them and escorted the captains to the entrance through which they had come earlier.

As they left the dark Basilica Cistern, they shielded their eyes against the late morning sun's radiance. Peter motioned to a stone bench nearby and the two men sat. "A few hours ago we were just two ordinary soldiers. Now were up to our necks in—"

"Exactly," Justin interrupted. "I'm still trying to figure out how we got into this. This morning I awoke a soldier but now I'm a spy! I don't want this!" He groaned as he looked across the grass to Cathedral of Saint Sophia. "But why do we need to be in this at all? And my family . . ." He threw his arms up. "Exiled or jailed or killed for this stupidity? Why? I can't believe this! Peter, we need to get out of this!" Justin added without really thinking.

"And how do we do that, Justin? We are soldiers in the emperor's service. We have our orders. Does the thought of execution appeal to you?"

"I'm sorry, Peter, but I prefer to follow orders that make *sense*," Justin snapped back. "Why does he have us in a special detatchment and not with the main army? That doesn't make any sense."

"No it doesn't but what can we do?" Peter asked. Justin looked away and sighed in disgust. "If we refuse to cooperate," Peter thought out loud, "the emperor will think we're with the Dukas. Since he has revealed his intentions to us, he'll consider us a liability and probably have us killed."

"We could approach Andronikos Dukas . . ." Justin ventured wrecklessly.

"Justin, complicity with the enemy is best avoided. And besides, if you were Dukas, would you trust us?"

"No," Justin answered. "Do you think the empress—"

"No!" Peter interrupted. "She'd have us killed for even thinking about not going along with them. She's the real strength behind the throne." He shook his head. "And Comnenos and Attaleiates . . . I don't trust them either."

"How about leaving the city?"

"Right!" Peter snorted. "That wouldn't be far enough away; we'd have to leave the empire! And where could we go? You'd have to take all of your family and Eleni's family with us. You don't think they're watching us and your family at this very moment?"

"Of course I do!" Justin fired back.

Peter recoiled.

"I'm sorry, Peter. I didn't mean to get angry with you."

"Given the circumstances, Justin, I don't blame you at all." Suddenly his face showed a dire seriousness. "Why does the empress need to keep Eleni at the palace?"

"They said to protect her."

"Wouldn't Eleni attract more attention in the empress' presence?"

"Maybe . . ."

"Justin, I think that the empress will be watching Eleni in the same way that the emperor will be keeping his eye on Andronikos Dukas."

"As a hostage," Justin concluded soberly.

"Yes but remember that the Dukas will know she is there as well."

"One mouse being watched by two cats."

"I'm sorry that she's been dragged into this," Peter said. "This is not the lot of a simple soldier we expected when we first began."

"No, not at all."

Peter paused thoughtfully before he concluded gravely, "Looks like we're stuck, Justin."

"Certainly does."

"Well, there's one thing we can hope for. If the emperor does get his victory over the Turks, we'll be home soon."

"And the quicker the better," Justin sighed.

"I've had more believable dreams." Peter leaned back on the stone bench and stretched his arms along the back of the bench. "It was so much easier chasing down Pecheneg raiders."

"Koumbarro, this might be one of those rare situations you can't get us out of," Justin added as he recalled their adventures together.

Peter appreciated his friend's efforts to lighten the pervading gloom. "This may be the one, Justin." He threw his arm on his friend's shoulder. "I wish there was something I could do. Eleni's and your families don't deserve this." He embraced Justin. "This isn't fair."

"Thank you, Peter," Justin answered. "Well, I'd better be headed home," he added as he stood.

"Sure," Peter replied as he stood.

Justin started toward home but then stopped. "Peter," he said, "why didn't you ever tell me about that sailor?"

Peter was caught off guard. He looked down. "I'd just as soon not talk about this now, Justin. That was the lowest point in my life."

"Peter, didn't you trust me enough to discuss it. Were you afraid of the way I might react?"

Peter looked up at his friend. "I appreciate your honesty and your concern. You are a great friend but I couldn't bring myself to talk to even you about it." Peter looked down again. "I've never even gone to confession about it."

"What's to confess? You committed no sin."

Peter was unmoved.

"Listen, Peter, we've been through a lot in the last six months. I know you well. Damn well. Don't ever hesitate to talk to me about anything. You can trust me."

Peter looked up again. He was deeply touched by his friend's directness. "Thank you. I'll remember that."

"You're welcome, my friend." Justin threw his arm over Peter's shoulder as the two walked onward. "Koumbarro, my family is having a dinner for Eleni and me in a few hours. Why don't you join us?"

Peter hesitated. "I don't—"

"Don't tell me you'd rather spend the evening at Missus Lambatos' boarding house!"

"Hey," Peter retorted, "it's a good place to live. She's a great cook."

"Yes but everyone else there is twice our age. You've got to be getting tired of listening to those old bachelors' stories, how Mister Butzes single-handedly sunk the caliph's fleet or how Mister Handakos nearly captured the king of the Bulgars."

"No," Peter said, "It was old Handakos who sunk the caliph's fleet and Mister Michaelithes who nearly captured the king of the Bulgars," Peter chuckled. "You've got to admit, they are colorful."

Justin smiled as he slapped his friend on the back. "Come. We're meeting at my Uncle Theodore's house. My other uncles will be there, too."

"Leo and Alexander?" asked Peter. "They're so entertaining, always arguing about one obscure thing or another. They've got a lot of fire in them."

"And they're a lot more interesting than old Butzes!"

"Undoubtedly."

Justin suddenly grew serious. "Peter, I have no idea what I'm going to say to my father."

"He's used to your going on campaign. He *was* a soldier, you know."

"Orders or not, I feel obligated to tell him more than that."

"Justin, that's not a good idea."

"I have to. I just have to."

"No. You don't. What about Eleni?"

"She's not going to live with the empress without an explanation." Justin paused. "There's no lying to her. Even if I don't tell her she'll know something's up. She can see right through me."

"She can see through anybody! Good luck thinking of what to say."

"Thanks. I'll definitely need it."

"About dinner," Peter interjected carefully.

"We'll meet you at the old Baths of Zeuxippos in a few hours? My folks live close to there."

"Thank you."

Justin groaned, "I'm *not* looking forward to telling her."

"I'll see you later, Justin."

Justin silently acknowledged his friend. He thoughtfully stroked his beard as Peter departed and then buried his head in his hands.

Peter started to walk home but then realized he had yet to address his uneasiness. He detoured to Saint Sophia. The cathedral gleamed in golden sunlight. *Perhaps a conversation with the Almighty is in order.*

Justin raised his head. *No use putting it off.* He stood and walked north up the hill. Ahead he saw two Chinese merchants perusing the silk displayed outside a local merchant's shop. He smiled as he remembered how two Orthodox monks visited China and smuggled silk worms out of that land by sewing their cocoons into their sleeves, thus bringing the silk industry to Constantinople. His concentration was broken by the odor of a passing fishmonger's cart. He sighed at the thought of his task and made his way toward the Gate of Neorian and home.

Saint Sophia had always been a favorite place for Peter to think, pray, and dream. This graceful domed giant was indeed an architectural wonder. As far as Peter and most of the subjects of the Roman Empire were concerned, the mathematician-architects had succeeded in creating the most spectacular temple in the world. Its rectangular base and countless elegant arches effortlessly supported its giant dome whose height was second only to that of the Pantheon in Rome. The massive structure appeared able to endure any cataclysm. In 558 A.D., an earthquake had severely damaged the cathedral. But by 563 A.D., the damage was completely repaired. Other natural disasters had affected it as well; but again the seat of the patriarchate of Constantinople remained undaunted.

Peter cradled his helmet in his left arm, and walked through massive ten-foot-high doors into the church. Inside the walls of the outer narthex were overlaid with numerous icons of the saints, composed of hundreds of precious and semi-precious stones. Ahead, in the inner narthex, at the emperor's entryway into the nave, two armed *scutati*, heavy infantrymen, in full dress uniform, marched slowly in place without stopping. The guards would change every few hours to allow the soldiers to rest. This imperial order had been in effect since the first Saint Sophia was constructed. Peter had seen the depressions in the marble floor created by five hundred years of laden soldiers marching in place. He wondered how much larger the concavities would be in another five hundred.

A black-cassocked monk greeted him. The dim narthex was illuminated by hundreds of candles lit by the faithful as they entered the nave. Each candle was placed on a large golden candle stand after it was ignited, adding to the shadows of flickering candlelight that danced on the walls. As he took a silver miliaresion from his purse to place it in offering, Peter noticed Emperor Constantine Dukas' image on the slver coin. Noting the irony of the moment, he shook his head and smirked. On the reverse he saw Christ the Judge, weighing souls with scales in his left hand, his right hand raised in admonishment. *Another irony? The lifetime of a man is but a minute portion of Eternity.* Peter dropped the coin into the ivory oblation chest, took a candle from a golden cask, and lit it from one of those on the stand. *Why have you placed me in the path of Evil, Lord Christ?* He sighed and placed the burning candle on the stand. Peter walked forward to an icon of the Virgin and Christ child standing on a small table. He started to cross himself but stopped. He stared angrily into eyes of the Holy Infant. *Why have you placed me in the path of Evil?* The absurdity of his new mission escalated his ire. *I keep your holidays and worship you faithfully and this is what you do to me?*

Peter turned away from the icon and glanced to his left at the icons hanging from the north wall. *Why has this happened?* Saints Thomas, Catherine, George, and the others just stared back. He turned again to his left and saw the doors through which he had just entered. Sweat began to form on his brow. "I can't do this!" he said to himself. "I've got to find a way out!"

Out of nowhere, a firm hand landed on Peter's right shoulder. "Aren't you going to go in?" asked the same monk who had greeted him a few minutes ago. The monk noted the sweat on the young soldier's brow. "Are you well, sir?"

"I'm fine," said Peter as he stumbled toward the exit.

"Sir, you don't appear well," the monk said with concern. "Why don't you step into the nave? I find it is a place of great healing, for the soul and the body."

Peter wanted to resist but couldn't. His muscular body was languid in the gentle grasp of the concerned anchorite. The monk slowly led Peter to the icon of the Virgin and Child.

"I believe this is where you left off," he said kindly.

"Thank you," said Peter awkwardly.

The monk acknowledged Peter's gratitude and went to the north wall of the narthex to admire and venerate the icons there.

Peter confronted the icon of the Virgin and Christ child again. *The eyes have changed.* As they beckoned him forward, Peter thought he heard a voice. He advanced uneasily. *What was happening?* When he reached the icon he leaned forward. Was this where the voice came from? He quickly kissed the image of the Holy Infant and that of His Mother, crossed himself three times, then briefly placed his right hand over his heart.

Peter advanced toward the nave. Above the imperial entrance to the nave was a mosaic icon of the mature Christ, as Judge of All. Emperor LeoVI lay prostrate before Him, begging forgiveness for violating a patriarchal proscription and marrying for a fourth time. The Virgin Mary, the Theotokos, the Mother of God looked on.

Peter heard the voice again, this time more clearly. *Welcome, Peter Argyropoulos.* Peter stared in disbelief at the icon and heard the voice speak a third time. *Welcome, Peter.* His first inclination was to drop to his knees but something directed him onward. Peter, feeling as though he were in a dream, took a deep breath and stepped into the nave through another entrance to his left.

Peter couldn't help but look upward in this formidable space. The massive dome owned his gaze like a loadstone. He recalled that this happened every time he entered this nave; there was no avoiding it. He walked into the center of the substantial room, now nearly void of people. A morning service had ended two hours earlier so the cathedral was nearly empty.

The stunning vault rose one hundred eighty feet from the pavement where the young soldier stood. The vault itself measured one hundred six feet across. Forty windows pierced the lower rim of the dome, allowing fingers of brilliant sunlight to shine through. *How could the architects have predicted that their handiwork would produce this divine image of shimmering golden silk threads from heaven holding the dome above the church?*

But the structure of the dome was only part of its magnificence. The ceiling, adorned by vertical blue lines on a golden background, led to a central circle at the dome's zenith. There, a sublime icon of Christ *Pantocrator*, Maker of All, gathered in these blue life-filled veins from the corners of Earth. It was as if he were looking up into Heaven itself. The overpowering majesty of the dome warmed his heart and began to dissolve his despair. He recalled the letters of Saint Paul: *If God is with you, who can be against you?* And as he lost himself in the dome above him, he felt that God was indeed with him. *I will never leave you nor forsake you.* His anger with God faded. The Almighty would protect him.

A sudden crash interrupted Peter's ecstasy. He gasped and instinctively spun around. One of the deacons of the church had accidentally dropped a gilded book of the Gospels on the marble floor while returning it to the sanctuary. Gently, the black-robed cleric lifted the treasured book, quickly kissed it, and crossed himself three times. When he saw Peter looking at him, he returned a friendly glance that the young captain interpreted as, "It's all right; no damage done; sorry to disturb you!" Peter, relieved by his discovery, returned the cleric's friendly smile.

Peter turned his glance again to the dome, his eyes stopping at the pendentives. Peter had read about the difficulties ancient architects had placing a circular dome on a square base. In this structure, the architects used spherical triangular members called pendentives to fit into each corner of the building and support the dome and the result was indeed spectacular. Each pendentive was covered with angel wings in mosaic on a gold leaf background. How appropriate: the pendentives themselves gave the dome its wings, its ability to hover above the ground.

Peter then made his way to the periphery of the nave and inspected its high marble walls. They were covered with stunning mosaics, gold leaf background, and various precious stones. He recalled that the builders of the church had selected marble panels of the same grain so that each huge marbled wall appeared to be one continuous piece of marble rather than several sections.

The nave was separated from the church's galleries flanking on the north and south sides, by arches supported by massive marble columns. These arches held the imperial chapels of the second story over the galleries. From here, an observer could take a breathtaking view of the nave. Another set of arches supported by marble columns held up the ceiling over this second story. From the tops of these arches projected the topmost walls, one on the north and one on the south. These parallel walls ran up to the rim of the dome on these two sides and were generously supplied with windows, allowing the gigantic structure to fill with light.

Peter recalled that during the construction of the sacred edifice, Emperor Justinian sent word to all of his territorial governors to send material, especially marble, to build Saint Sophia. The eight gray-green marble columns Peter had always liked most were brought from the ancient Temple of Artemis in Ephesus. He also enjoyed the eight porphyry columns, taken from the ancient Temple of the Sun in Rome.

Peter walked over to the south gallery and looked up at the graceful vaulted ceiling. The gold background highlighted the dozens of detailed mosaics, which clothed the vault. Some mosaics were of the prophets of the Old Testament, others the saints of the New. Some were splendorous designs, left open to the interpretation of the observer. In one, Peter thought he saw a pitched battle between the Archangel Michael and the Devil himself.

He returned to the nave. At the east end of the church, he saw the huge apse, which had three smaller apses projecting from it. It was at this eastern end that he saw the most glorious part of the church. The iconostasis, fifty feet in length, was made of solid silver. This icon screen separated the nave from the sanctuary where the altar was. Icons of angels and the saints of the church hung gracefully from the screen. In the middle of the screen were the Holy Doors through which only clergy could pass. There were two other doors through the screen, one several feet to the right and one of equal distance to the left, for non-clerical males to enter the sanctuary, when appropriate. Women were not allowed behind the iconostasis. *Strange. Women had played such an important role in the Early Church. Weren't the women the first to see the Lord's empty tomb?* As he peered past the Holy Doors he could see the high altar, which was covered with gold and precious stones from all over the world.

In the eastern apse, above the iconostasis and the altar, he looked at a stunning mosaic of the Virgin and Child. This larger-than-life portrait, an apotheosis of grace and compassion, nearly brought tears to the eyes of the thick-skinned warrior. *Mary has such a warm, comforting smile; she seems more a young mother in this icon than in others I've seen.* On the face of the infant Jesus, he noted a look of insurmountable joy. "The King of kings," Peter murmured under his breath, "the Lord of Hosts as a child; God on Earth, the Son of Man, the Son of God." The young soldier lost himself in contemplation gazing at the mosaic of the Savior. " . . . lo, I am with you until the end of the age," he swore he heard the Christ child saying, echoing the last verse of Matthew's Gospel.

Peter's spirit was renewed. This church had always had a strong effect on him. But never had the impression been *this* deep. He hadn't seen anything today that he hadn't seen before. However, today, his need was greater and God had indeed provided. *My cup runneth over.*

A bell from a nearby chapel rang and the giant cathedral slowly filled with clerics who began preparing the church for afternoon worship. Peter knew that if he didn't leave now he would be late for his meeting with Justin and Eleni. He, and nearly every Greek, knew that this cathedral held many of the great relics of the Church: the True Cross, found in Jerusalem by Saint Helen, the mother of the Emperor Constantine; Jesus' swaddling clothes; the table of the Last Supper; the burial shroud of the Lord; the Crown of Thorns worn during His passion; and countless others. Yet, Peter also knew that these were not displayed to the common folk for fear that each relic's holy power would so overwhelm the ordinary man when he saw it, that the holy power would certainly kill him.

Peter hurried out of church and into the sunshine. His visit to Church of Holy Wisdom had indeed bolstered his faith. He still couldn't begin to understand why Justin and he found themselves in this intrigue but he knew he could rely on God's protection. Peter knew he would have to keep reminding himself of this; he was a cynic by nature. God was with him, never to leave. Why had he doubted Him?

Peter turned back and beheld the cathedral one more time. *If one could enclose God within a building, this would certainly be the place to do so.* He thought of the Emperor Justinian, who, on entering his church for the first time, was heard to murmur, "Solomon, I have surpassed thee!"

Iakovos greeted Justin as he walked through the door of the Nikopoulos house. Justin stopped and turned toward the old servant. The tall, thin man of sixty-some years had been a servant of the Nikopoulos family for more than twenty. He was in the adjacent room when Eleni made her entrance into the world. Although he usually served Eleni's father, he was occasionally called upon to care for her.

This silver-haired, white-bearded fellow was as gentle as a lamb. The years had laid claim to his knees and hands but he never let that slow him down much. Since he had no family of his own and Demetrios' and Aspasia's parents had died within five years of their marriage, Iakovos easily fit into the role of a grandfather. And, of course, since he was a fixture at the Nikopoulos home, he was well known to Justin's family.

"Iakovos," Justin began, "were you running any errands today . . . say, down by the Hippodrome?"

The old man was caught off guard. He tried frantically to formulate a lie but it was obvious he had been discovered by the prey he had so clumsily tracked that morning.

"Don't worry about it," Justin said to put Iakovos at ease. "I'm a soldier. We're trained to know when we are being followed, even by the best."

"Uh, how did I do?" the servant asked.

"You were doing pretty well until you knocked over the apple cart. And next time you shouldn't fall into a horse trough. And toward the end there, you got kind of slow. I had to keep stopping so you could catch up. Captain Argyropoulos was getting pretty upset with me."

"So Captain Argyropoulos didn't see me?"

Justin was enjoying his little game with the devoted family servant. "He saw you before I did." Then he took on a more serious tone. "Iakovos, who told you to follow me?"

"I mustn't tell."

"Was it the Caliph of Baghdad?" Justin couldn't resist teasing him. "You know you shouldn't get involed in these foreign machinations. The emperor has offered a huge bounty for any spies—"

"It was your wife."

Justin was taken aback. "Missus Phillipos?"

"Yes, sir."

Justin didn't fully digest the revelation before saying, "Well that's okay. Spying on one's mistress' husband is not yet a crime so you're safe." He paused thoughtfully. "And Iakovos, thank you for telling me. Thank you very much." He put his hand on the old man's shoulder playfully. "And, so as not to endanger any potential future missions that Missus Phillipos may have for you, I won't mention a thing about this."

"Thank you, sir." The old man sighed in relief as he returned to his duties.

Justin made his way up the stairs. Why Eleni would have him followed? The first thoughts through his mind made him chuckle but those that followed were more disturbing. Did she not trust him? No, he and Eleni were almost like siblings. Worry was perhaps the more logical explanation for her behavior. But Eleni never worried, not to this degree. What could make her change?

Justin analyzed his own behavior. *It was so stupid of me to forget to tell her about my meeting with Peter!* How could he be so oblivious? And now his forgetfulness was being interpreted as neglect. How could he be so unfeeling toward her? His inattention had forced Eleni to send Iakovos. *This whole thing is my fault!* Didn't he love her? Had he changed? As he neared the landing jus6t before the top floor, he turned and headed down the stairs. *I'm not ready to face her now. I need more time to think.*

"Justin, is that you?" he heard Eleni call from inside their home.

"Too late," Justin muttered to himself. "Like it or not, I've got to make this right." Again he found himself hesitating.

"Justin?" Eleni called again, this time softly.

Better address this now. All the thinking in the world isn't going to help me. Justin turned around, climbed up to the landing, and went in their home. "Yes," he answered.

Eleni walked slowly out of the bedroom. Apprehension had replaced her usual certainty. "Justin," she began. She hesitated. "Justin," she began again, "I'm—"

Justin gently interrupted his wife. "Eleni, my darling, I can't stop thinking about this morning." He placed his helmet on the floor. "I've been angry with myself for forgetting to tell you about my meeting with Peter this morning."

Eleni listened attentively.

"It turns out I had forgotten that Peter had told me that our meeting was *before* the ceremony," he admitted, feeling the fool. "Boy, Peter was angry with me for that!"

"It seems that all of your close friends were angry with you this morning." Her tone was softer than that morning.

Justin nodded, sheepishly.

"But the ceremony shouldn't have lasted this long," Eleni noted. "Something happen later?"

Justin put his hand on his wife's shoulder and smiled. "As a matter of fact, yes," he answered.

Eleni looked at her husband curiously, as if she knew that this was going to be quite a story.

"After the ceremony, Peter and I were called for a second meeting before the emperor and empress," he said. "A secret meeting."

"Just the two of you?" she interrupted, incredulously.

"Yes. Just the two of us," Justin answered, unphased by her disbelief. "Peter and I are to accompany the emperor on a campaign in Anatolia."

Eleni was confused. "You two had a secret meeting with the emperor and empress just to be told that you'll accompany the emperor on a campaign? That's strange. You usually get your marching orders from your commanding officer. Why would the emperor *and* the empress meet with two mere captains to brief them on an otherwise routine campaign?"

"Believe me, Eleni, Peter and I are as confused as you are. We have no idea what's happening or why." He sighed and added, "And we leave in two weeks."

Eleni looked deeply into Justin's eyes. Although her fears and doubts of the morning hadn't vanished, they were now far away. Eleni saw in those eyes the handsome boy she knew as a child. Her childhood dreams of Justin meandered through her mind like a lazy stream on a summer's day. Eleni's heart reacquainted itself with those old feelings for Justin. It was time to put away her frustration and love this precious man.

"And that's just half of the problem," Justin continued. "They—"

Eleni slid her hand up to his face, gently placed her forefinger over his lips to silence him and kissed him.

Justin forgot what he was going to say. He tried to recover. "We are, uh, going to be, uh—"

Eleni's hands moved quickly and smoothly to unfasten his baldric. It and the sword it carried crashed to the ground. They both giggled. He ran his fingers through her hair and kissed her forehead. She undid his corselet, let it fall to the floor, its metal strips clanging as they hit the floor. She plunged her fingers beneath his tunic and tunica, and felt the hair on his chest. Justin moaned softly as Eleni moved her arms around his waist and held him tightly.

Justin slid his hands to the back of her head and down her neck to her shoulders. He leaned forward and kissed her, simply at first but then more passionately with each kiss that followed.

"I love you, Justin," Eleni said.

"I love you, Eleni," he replied.

Justin slid off Eleni's dalmatic and tunica in one motion and caressed her breasts with his hands. She disrobed him and rested her hands on the back of his muscular thighs, gently squeezing when the notion struck her. They slowly made their way to the wool rug on the floor below them. Her lips never tasted sweeter; his shoulders never felt stronger. Her fingers combed through his thick black mane. His powerful hands gently kneaded her soft, supple shoulders. She brought her hands down to his face, pulled away her lips, and looked deeply into his eyes.

Justin looked back at her, wanting to speak but realizing they were speaking volumes already. Eleni's bewitching green eyes held his gaze tightly, even as he leaned forward and kissed her lips. She closed her eyes. Their embrace grew tighter as their kissing intensified. She leaned backward, easily pulling him on top of her. Her hands found his hips and pulled them toward her. He slid his hands beneath her shapely thighs and gently lifted them with a slight squeeze.

"Justin," she whispered, taking him by surprise, "you're wonderful."

Before Justin could reply, Eleni facilitated their passion. Each groaned softly in ebullience. Any verbal reply would spoil this perfect moment. Their ecstasy was endless.

When the end of their frenzied commerce arrived, they were exhausted. Eleni looked lovingly at her mate. Her eyes beckoned him to follow. She stood up and held out her hand. Justin complied and walked with her, hand in hand, to the bedroom. She slid beneath the bedcovers and he followed. Her eyes gently spoke of her love for him; his replied. She leaned forward and tenderly kissed his lips. He hugged her and kissed her forehead. They smiled and closed their eyes.

Justin fell soon asleep but Eleni was too excited to sleep, reveling in her feelings for Justin. She rolled to the opposite side and looked at two small caskets on a small table next to the bed. She and Justin had received them as wedding gifts. Justin's parents, Basilios and Martha, had given them the ivory one. This one was as wide as the length of her hand and as long as the distance from wrist to just past her elbow. It had a flat, unhinged lid. The sides of the container featured carvings of Adam and Eve engaged in various domestic activities. On one side, Adam wore a belted knee-length tunic and laced leather boots. Eve wore a long-sleeved ankle-length garment and simple leather sandals. She operated the bellows of the forge her husband is manning. Other panels had similar scenarios depicted, man and woman helping each other through life. At the edges of each panel were deeply etched tessarae, inlaid with gold. It was customary for newlyweds to receive gifts like this to symbolize their new relationship together.

Eleni inspected the other casket. This was a gift of her parents and was made of whalebone. This rectangular box was slightly smaller than the one Justin's parents had given them and had a truncated pyramidal lid with gilt copper hinges and flanges and a gilt copper lock with a key to match. The carvings on its sides included depictions from the lives of Ruth and Boaz, Joachim and

Anna, Sarah and Abraham, and Isaac and Rebecca. The upper truncated portion showed scenes from the lives of Saints Basilios, Mary Magdalene, Cosmas, and Barbara. The topmost panel represented an Earthly paradise, serene and tranquil, populated by humans, animals, plants, and occasional angels.

This last casket reminded Eleni of a similar receptacle her parents had recently received as a gift from their children. The case was nine by seven by twelve inches and made of silver and was embossed with figures from Greek mythology and the history of the Roman Empire. Gilt was used liberally to accent the figures. It was composed of two truncated pyramids, a silver handle on each side to allow for easy transport.

Eleni knew that she had not allowed Justin to fully reveal his activities of the morning. Yet it didn't matter. And though his forgetfulness would undoubtedly stymie her again, she was determined to be patient with him. *Like Adam and Eve, they were to be partners in all endeavors throughout their lives. Would Heaven record their marriage with those of Ruth and Boaz, Joachim and Anna, and the others?* Eleni hoped so. She loved this man and now she remembered why. Their young marriage had been through a rough day but she was intent upon its ultimate success.

CHAPTER 7

"Excellent match!" Romanos Diogenes exclaimed to Joseph Tarchaniotes as they dismounted their polo ponies.

Tarchaniotes reached out to the emperor's outstretched hand and shook it. "Thank you, sire."

Romanos Diogenes increased the intensity of his grasp and pumped the strategos' arm harder. "You were excellent, Joseph!'

"Thank you, sire. You played well yourself," Tarchaniotes replied as they walked off the polo field and toward one of the many entrances to the Palace Magnaura.

"How are you doing with the army?" the emperor asked as they walked through a grand doorway, saluted the guards, and made their way to a small, ornately decorated room. Romanos Diogenes dismissed the two servants in the room and asked his favorite general, "Will it be any better than last year?" The emperor closed the door behind him and offered Tarchaniotes one of two golden goblets of red wine, which were resting on a small table made of ebony inlaid with gold.

"The troops are not yet fully ready, Majesty," Tarchaniotes replied as he picked up one of the goblets and took a sip. "Excellent wine, Majesty. The neglect the army suffered under Constantine Dukas has seriously disabled it. It can't function well as a unit. There is no comradery. Attacks are poorly coordinated. Defenses are poorly planned. It's no wonder we lost Bari in Italy."

"Well let's just make certain we don't lose anything else," Romanos said after he took in a substantial portion of wine in one gulp. "The military party has high expectations of us and we are counting on you to sharpen this dull and rusted sword. We need results and our hope is that the Turk will give them to us."

"Majesty," Joseph Tarchaniotes declared boldly, "you shall have your results. I promise you, sire."

"Mercenaries?" the emperor asked, changing the subject.

"We have found exceptional soldiers among the Uz. They are Turks themselves, Majesty, distant cousins to our Seljuk enemies."

"Very good, Joseph," Romanos Diogenes said with a broad smile.

"We still have a good number of Pechenegs, Normans, Armenians, and Serbs, as well," Tarchaniotes added, sensing the emperor's growing confidence in him. "Of course our Roman troops are still the backbone of our army, especially the Thracians, Isaurians, Cappadocians."

Romanos Diogenes patted the strategos on the shoulder. "We knew you are the right soldier for the task, Joseph. We know you will not let us down."

As the emperor led the strategos out of the room, he lifted his wine again and emptied the goblet in one final swallow. After their departure, one of the mosaics on the wall regained its original eyes. The man replacing them had substituted his own for the brief time that the emperor and the strategos were in the room.

"The archbishop will be very happy to receive this information," the man said under his breath. He reached into his purse and found a single copper folis. "Don't worry my solitary friend," he whispered to the coin. "You will soon have lots of company." He chuckled as he reached for the oil lamp he had place on the floor of the secret room. "Lots of *gold* company!" He sniggered quietly as he made his way down the passageway and into a tunnel, which would lead him, undetected, out of the palace.

Eleni and Justin left their home later than expected. They went downstairs to find that Eleni's parents were already on their way to Justin's Uncle Theodore's house.

"It sounds like you've gotten yourself in to a real mess this time," said Eleni, reflecting on what Justin had just told her about the rest of his morning. The two walked hurriedly south to the Baths of Zeuxippos. Disobeying the emperor's orders, he had divulged the entire situation to his wife but he felt that if the emperor were about to place him in such danger, he needed to tell somebody and who better than Eleni. Justin knew his secret would be kept safely with her.

"Some people are blessed by all of the misfortune they attract," Eleni teased.

Justin had to laugh at his wife's gentle barb. "You don't seem upset at the prospect of spending the next several weeks with the empress."

"Like you, I have no choice," she said. "A good soldier does what he is commanded . . ."

"And a good soldier's wife?" he asked.

Eleni became more serious. "Justin, you know me; I can endure anything. You've been off on campaigns before."

"Yes, but this time it's much more complicated. I feel that my life is in more danger now than ever before. And the fact that you and our families could be dragged into it . . . ."

Eleni spotted Peter across the street where he was giving directions to some visiting Persian traders.

"There's Peter." Eleni called to him. Peter acknowledged the young couple and headed toward them. "Let's enjoy ourselves and not let this ruin the dinner."

"I agree," he replied. "Thank you for being so understanding."

"Justin, you're a good man. Always remember how I feel about you. And always be open with me. Trust me; I can handle whatever you have to tell me."

"I'll remember that, Eleni."

Peter approached quickly. When he reached them, Justin and Eleni greeted him warmly. Peter and Eleni exchanged three kisses on the cheeks.

"Eleni, you look lovely as ever," Peter declared.

"Thank you, Peter," Eleni answered. She looked him over quickly and added, "You look very confident, like you're ready to take on the world."

Peter looked over to Justin. "Now why would you say that?"

"Justin has told me everything."

Peter glanced at Justin again and then at Eleni.

"You must trust in God," she added soberly. "He will protect you both."

"Yes," Peter replied. "I know He will."

Justin's father and mother, Basilios and Martha Phillipos, lived in a home that shared a courtyard with Uncle Theodore's home and the home of his other two uncles, Alexander and Leo, both widowers. All three residences shared the bathhouse in the middle of the courtyard. Daily bathing was the norm. Justin's parents' had recently moved here from their home near Eleni's parents, where they had lived for nearly twenty-seven years.

When Martha and Basilios married, her father and mother could not offer their tiny home, or part of it, as a portion of the dowry. She was the youngest of four girls and her parent's penury made the likelihood of her marriage poor. But the young Basilios Phillipos was willing to dispense with custom to attain this beautiful bride. His mother was shocked when he told her. His father at first resisted but soon realized that further discussion with his determined son was futile. He had saved enough money to allow Martha and Basilios to live with them in reasonable comfort for a short time. People talked disparagingly about the marriage arrangement but the thick-skinned Basilios, his wife, and their parents didn't pay any mind.

Eleni, Justin, and Peter walked up a flight of stairs to the front door. The ground floor was used as a stable and for storage. Theodore's wife, Anastasia, greeted them at the door. "Welcome! Welcome to the newlyweds! Welcome, Peter!" She hugged each of them tightly, kissed each three times, and escorted them into her home.

As they walked through the entry, their nostrils took in the familiar scents of onion and garlic cooking in olive oil, fresh-cut oregano, basil, and parsley, and roasting lamb. In a large room near the front entry, the women sat chatting. Among them were Justin's mother Martha, Eleni's mother Aspasia, Eleni's sister Eftihia, and Anna, Justin's younger brother Paul's wife of one year. Each rose to her feet and came forward to hug and kiss the new arrivals.

Martha Phillipos was a tall, thin woman with a sallow complexion. Her hair was as black as pitch; there was no sign of gray encroaching. In fact, the years had been kind to her; she looked fifteen years younger than her true age of forty-six years. Her husband often boasted of his wife's immunity to aging.

Martha quickly kissed her son and moved on to greet her newest daughter-in-law. "How are you, Eleni?" She lowered her voice and asked only like a husband's mother could, "Is Justin being good?" Eleni feigned an uncertain look in her eye and then they both laughed.

Aspasia saw this and hugged her newest son-in-law. She retorted in good humor, "Oh, don't you mind them! I know a good man when I see one." She threw her arms around his waist and hugged him tightly. She turned to Eleni. "You'd better take good care of him or I may steal him away from you!" Everyone within earshot laughed.

"Peter!" cried a voice from across the room.

Peter turned to find Justin's youngest brother John hailing him. "John!" He politely excused himself from the women and crossed the large room, its light blue walls decorated with wooden paintings of athletes, chamomile flowers, cypress and laurel trees, and figures from Greek mythology.

Peter and John stood before a small table. On it was a beautiful icon of the *Anastasis*, the Resurrection. Peter glanced at the beautiful image as he walked over to John, a friendly young man who looked just like his brother but was a few inches shorter. As Peter approached he threw his arm around the back of John's neck and pulled the younger man toward him. John jabbed Peter in the ribs with his fist and maneuvered an escape from the soldier's grasp.

"You'll have to try harder than that," John said, daring Peter to try it again.

"You're definitely getting better. You're ready to graduate to the next level of difficulty." Peter lunged at John but the younger fellow successfully dodged the attack. "Hey, when are you going to join us in the army?"

"Well, I thought I'd try the university."

The empire had always had its intellectuals but actual institutions of higher learning were transient. The sixth through the ninth centuries had seen a decline in higher education. In the tenth century, interest began to grow and, by the eleventh century,

Constantinople had a lively intellectual climate. By this time the University of Constantinople was still a fledgling but growing. The course of study was limited (law, rhetoric, grammar, literature, astronomy, mathematics, geometry, and some sciences) and it had no buildings to constitute a university *per se*; most classes were held in government buildings like the Capitol. The instructors, the sophists, earned their keep with a salary and gratuities from students or solely from student gratuities. And the university was at the mercy of the emperor. If he withdrew his patronage, the university would suffer a serious setback.

"The empire needs soldiers, not egg-headed intellectuals," Peter retorted, throwing up his hands. "Didn't Justin ever tell you that?" Peter loved baiting John on this subject. "Some of those fellows can't empty their bowels without thinking about it for twenty minutes. No, John, you need something more stimulating, more invigorating."

Used to Peter's teasing, John rather enjoyed it. "The university is stimulating: mathematics, medicine, art, rhetoric —"

"Rhetoric?" Peter wrinkled his face as if he had just swallowed a particularly foul-tasting bit of food. "Do you mean to tell me you need to be taught how to argue?"

"It will teach me how to formulate good arguments and present them in a logical fashion."

"I'd think a few choice insults at the appropriate time could crumble any argument easily."

"Perhaps in the army where two and three syllable words stress the intellectual capacity of the speaker, that argument may hold." John raised his nose in a patrician air. "But among those of us who are more educated, the presentation of the argument can be as persuasive as the argument itself."

"Isn't that what I said?"

"What of literature?" asked John. "What of Plato, Aristotle, Horace?"

"What do these pagans have to teach us?" Peter shot back. "If you want to study rhetoric, read the Old Testament Prophets and Ecclesiastes. If you desire music and poetry, study the Psalms and Job. To learn law, study Proverbs, Leviticus, and the Ten Commandments. And for history and genealogies, read Genesis,

Kings, and Chronicles. What is lacking in God's Word that you would supplement it with these pagan fables?"

John was caught off-guard by Peter's sudden seriousness. He quickly recovered and replied with equal solemnity, "The Holy Scriptures do not instruct us in the art of reasoning that is so important in defending the Faith from pagans, heretics, and infidels. Why not use the pagan's own weapons to destroy him? And besides, the ancients have much wisdom to offer."

Peter grimaced. He didn't want to admit that this young intellect's argument had merit.

John was encouraged by Peter's reaction and added, "I would submit that it is necessary the study the works of the pagan, not only to defeat him, but to exercise the mind and acquire eloquence!"

"I don't see why your father sacrifices so much of his money so that your mind can be filled with such useless information. Nearly all of your classmates come from very wealthy families. What do you have in common with these spoiled brats? How many students attend the university? Two hundred? Maybe three hundred? There are over one hundred thousand people in this city. Such a waste! I don't know why the emperor continues to support this nonsense."

"Peter, everyone who attends the university goes into government service. Those who study law become judges, notaries, and advocates. Those who study mathematics are invaluable to the imperial treasury. Taxes must be collected and tabulated properly. All intellectuals will serve the emperor in one way or another. Those who choose to educate at the primary or secondary level lay the groundwork for future scholars who will serve the emperor. Even the Church has made use of men of intellect. John Mavropous became metropolitan of Euchaita; Patriarch John Xiphilinios was the first president of the School of Law, and the great Michael Psellos founded the faculty of the School of Philosophy. He has served the emperor in a variety of posts, including that of First Imperial Secretary."

"John," Peter sighed, remembering what he had heard of Xiphilinios and Psellos that very morning, "you are so naïve in the ways of the world. These men don't acquire knowledge for the sake of knowledge. They grab for it because it gives them power."

"Isn't that what every man wants? Some control over his life?"

"Psellos and his lot want to control all of our lives!"

"Peter, that's ridiculous. Why are you so opposed to any intellectual enterprise?"

"I'm not! I just want you to know that some of these 'great' men you are trumpeting aren't as kindhearted and giving as you might think." He remembered the arrogant look on Psellos' face that morning.

"You sound just like my father!" John chuckled.

"I'll accept that compliment."

A servant came by and offered them wine that they both accepted.

"So, where will your soldiering duties take you and Justin next?" John asked.

"Rumor has it that we're headed to Anatolia to fight the Seljuk Turks."

"Weren't we just at peace with them?"

"Yes, but the situation has changed a little. The army spent a good deal of the last few years running them down and came up empty-handed."

"I hear the Turks are fierce horsemen and experts with the bow."

"That's what we hear," Peter replied. "What's most impressive is that their marksmanship is just as good whether they are riding on horseback or standing on the ground. But your brother and I have faced some tough enemies before . . . Pechenegs, Bulgars . . ."

"So you don't think the Seljuk Turks will be any different?" John inquired.

"No. No, I don't think this campaign will be any different than anything that we've faced before. We'll be home by summer. I'm certain the emperor will be presented with a triumph by the Senate." Peter knew that he was lying to John but he couldn't betray the mission and he certainly didn't want to worry Justin's family. In many ways he had adopted them as his own.

"Hey, I need to find Justin. He owes me a little money. Come with me."

"Okay."

John looked across the room but didn't see Justin. "He's probably in the back with the other men. Come on." John led Peter down the hall to a second large room. This room was about two-thirds the size of the large room off the entry. Its white plaster walls were covered with tapestries depicting scenes from lion and bear hunts. A mosaic of Apollo decorated the far wall. He held a lyre in one hand and a bow and two arrows in the other.

At a table in the corner, their host, Uncle Theodore, was busy mixing powders by the lamplight. Close by, Paul, Justin's junior by one year, was talking with Eleni's father Demetrios. Across the room, Justin gingerly attempted to discuss the morning's intrigues with his father. Justin's two oldest uncles, Leo and Alexander, were trying to resolve an argument. Alexander and Leo were notorious for their constant debating and trying to include Theodore in their discussions. Their debates usually ended in impasse and it was Theodore who would distill the *correct* answer to the deliberation of that day. But this time Theodore was too preoccupied with his project to show any interest.

Peter and John walked over to Demetrios and Paul who were talking over a new plan for increasing the yields from imperial iron mines. Paul, an engineer, oversaw a large operation in Macedonia.

"It sounds like it just might work," Demetrios admitted.

"Of course it will," Peter interjected as he and John joined them. Both of them knew Peter had not heard a single word.

"And what would a soldier know of mining?" Paul teased Peter as he shook his hand.

"Absolutely nothing!" Peter answered. He turned to Eleni's father as he continued to shake Paul's hand. "Hello, Mister Nikopoulos!"

Basilios Phillipos, now half a century in age, was a tall dark-skinned Greek who was strong both emotionally and physically. Usually reserved, he could be quite loquacious when the notion struck him. His full head of black hair was accentuated by the appearance of silvery strands at the temples. His penetrating dark brown eyes had often extracted the truth from a terrified, but nonetheless guilty, young Justin. Those same windows to his soul could stop any protest or argument dead in its tracks. Justin never quite overcame the control those eyes had on him. It was those eyes that played a major role in maintaining the gulf that existed between father and son. And now Justin was facing them again.

"What is it you are trying to say, son?" Basilios asked impatiently.

"This is very difficult, Father. I want to tell you so much about what happened to me today but I've been ordered by my superior not to," Justin replied. "This assignment could be very dangerous for me, and Peter and—" He wanted to say "and all of my family" but his father interrupted.

"Justin, remember that I was a soldier once. I know what orders mean and I know what their violation can promulgate." He sounded more like a tribune than a father.

"Father," Justin said, almost in desperation, "this—"

"Don't interrupt, son. You've told me all I need to know." He remained detached. "You are acting per your orders. If you've been ordered not to tell me, then don't." The frustration in his son's face eventually brought out some of his father's compassion. "Justin, you've been on campaigns before. Why are you so concerned about this one?"

Justin was encouraged by his father's change of heart. "This one is so much different," he began, "because we . . . ." He faltered, unable to put the words together. "We're going to . . . ."

"Son, I know that you want to tell me something you're not supposed to," Basilios said as he put his arm around Justin's shoulder, "but I don't think you want to jeopardize your position and that of your friend. So let's consider this matter closed."

"But Father! This is very different!"

"Closed, Justin!" Basilios was firm. "Be a good soldier."

Justin tried to muster the energy for another attempt but he couldn't overcome those eyes. Further attempts would be just as fruitless as the ones he had so ineptly executed. "Very well, sir."

"It's better this way, son." He slapped his son on the shoulder. "Say, where's my newest daughter-in-law?"

"Oh, she's with Mother."

"Well, I'm going to go give her a big hug," said the father. As he left the room he added, "Your Uncle Theodore wants to talk to you about something, Justin. Be sure to speak with him." This last statement was more of an order than a request.

"Yes, Father," Justin replied, defeated again by his father's iron constitution. He sighed as he realized his father could do nothing about his situation anyway. After his father's departure, Justin turned his attention to an energetic discussion involving his uncles Leo and Alexander.

Alexander was a physician. He was as tall as his older brother Basilios and possessed a full head of dark brown hair with a thick flowing beard that contained hints of gray. He was quite handsome, with perfectly shaped eyes and a nose and mouth that looked liked they'd been chiseled by Praxilites himself.

At the University of Constantinople, he had studied art, architecture, history, and literature. He had loved each of these subjects so much that he didn't dare concentrate on one, for fear of neglecting the others. A university education was expensive and few of the common folk had the money to send their children there. Alexander's father had a wealthy friend whose son had attended the university and had convinced the brave soldier that higher education could be a worthwhile investment. As a career soldier, his father had more money than most but was certainly not among the city's most affluent.

After leaving the university, Alexander served as a private teacher, instilling higher education into eager young minds, males and females. And this was not uncommon in the empire. But finding consistent work as a sophist was difficult so he studied medicine with some of his fellow academics. The group had to pool their textual resources and teach and learn as a group because there was no organized faculty of medicine at the University of Constantinople. Their chief sources were copies of ancient Greek texts from Galen, Soranus, Hippocrates, and others. Occasionally the writings of an Arab physician such as Rhazes or Avicenna would become available.

When he felt he had learned enough, he started his practice of medicine. He and others tried to form a faculty of medicine at the university. They gave free lectures but they were poorly attended. Soon, the faculty's interest in perpetuating the study of medicine dwindled. Alexander begrudgingly admitted there was more interest in philosophy and literature than in the healing arts so he decided to dedicate all of his time and skills to the practice of medicine.

He joined the army's medical corps and served as a field surgeon. The medical corps was a part of the army that had not lost its luster. Roman troops received the best medical care of any army; their wounded soldiers returned to duty faster than any others and suffered fewer deaths from battle wounds. An efficient ambulance and field hospital system assured this.

After three years of service, Alexander returned to practice among the people of Constantinople. He worked at the Hospital of the Pantokrator monastery on the medical ward. The hospital also had surgical and gynecological wards. The staff included a female physician, an herbalist, a professor of medicine from the University of Constantinople, and a kitchen staff that prepared patient meals, most of them vegetarian. Alexander pratcied general medicine but the city also had specialists, such as dentists, gynecologists, and ophthalmolgists. Alexander served for a time in the public health system. He inspected homes to make certain they had good plumbing to drain lavatories and waste water into the city drains that emptied into the sea. He later helped found a women's hospital, which was first staffed with eunuchs but soon female physicians replaced them.

Leo was a year younger than Alexander. About half a head shorter than Basilios and Alexander, he was nearly completely bald. His beard was of the same gray color as that small amount of hair on his head. He had a crooked nose, and his right eye was a quarter-inch higher than his left, and his face quite the opposite of his brother Alexander's.

Leo's father had destined him for the priesthood. Many felt, but wouldn't admit, that having a churchman in the family would increase God's favor upon them. Leo's father firmly denied this; he said he simply saw the church as a steady profession that could provide a reasonably good income. And indeed the church could provide a good living for a young man, especially a bright one.

A priest's duties were not limited to the spiritual well being of his flock. He was responsible for tending to the poor and running the local hospital for the sick, especially in small towns. The priest would also run the hospice for travelers and monks, and catalogue all births, baptisms, marriages, and deaths as well as providing spiritual oversight for the last three. Lay provincial bureaucrats had previously supervised these duties. In the last three to four centuries, the laity had lost interest in performing these functions and the church had assumed them because the clergy outshined their predecessors.

Leo initially had enthusiastism for a clerical career but soon lost interest. The monks at the seminary found this pupil intelligent but also argumentative and skeptical of church dogma. They and the *archimandrite* convinced his father that he belonged at the university. Leo's father had believed that another significant outlay of money, beyond what he was already paying for Alexander's education, was beyond his capabilities. But Alexander's success in academics persuaded his father that a university education could be valuable to his other sons, too. So Leo studied philosophy and law, after leaving the university, served as an advisor to the council of the patriarch of Constantinople. He now taught philosophy at the university.

Theodore, the youngest of the four and the brightest, was Leo's junior by about four years. His height averaged that of Alexander and Leo. He possessed a full head of dark brown hair splashed with accents of red, which were particularly noticeable in his beard. A thin four-inch scar on his left cheek drew attention. This had occurred during his service in the navy and at the hands of a friend, not a foe. A new recruit had hastily drawn his sword as their imperial galley approached a pirate ship and the new sword slashed through Theodore's cheek. The captain of the ship wanted to reprimand the novice sailor but Theodore defended the boy's mistake and punishment was fairly mild. The irony of the situation was that the pirates were surrendering. The naval vessel had been chasing them for the previous several days. The pirates found themselves trapped in a cove with the warship waiting for them at the cove's entrance and imperial soldiers waiting on shore.

While Theodore was still an adolescent, Alexander and Leo would bring him texts from the university. He'd read them voraciously and debated them with such skill that he proved an annoyance to Leo and Alexander. The two older brothers gradually sent him fewer texts as they grew busier but Theodore managed to obtain more sustenance for his intellect by exchanging letters with scholars at the university. These learned men had no idea they were sending this information to a mere boy.

While at the university, Theodore's studies included astronomy, rhetoric, mathematics, alchemy, and history. He had learned so much before entering the university that his instructors bored him. However, he aggressively discussed the issues. His superior fund of knowledge and his keen ability to destroy another's argument while soundly presenting his own made him many enemies among the faculty. After his first year, he was asked to leave and was only too happy to go.

His father was surprised and irritated that his son had been dismissed and had nothing to show for himself. Alexander and Leo recommended stern action but the father demonstrated considerable patience in dealing with this son. At the time, their brother Basilios was away campaigning against the Arabs. In his correspondences, he suggested "a more structured environment" might be of benefit for his youngest brother. So the father began to explore options and Theodore expressed an interest in seeing this world he had read so much about. When his father offered him a tour in the navy, Theodore gladly accepted.

The young man spent the next four years sailing the Mediterranean and the *Euxine*. His skill with foreign languages served him well. He was made a junior officer and acted as a translator. Peaceful interactions with the empire's perennial enemies (the Arabs, the Lombards, the Roman Papacy, the Normans) were common. His ship would dock at such ports-of-call as Alexandria, Jaffa, Naples, Cadiz, Syracuse, Ancona, and Ostia, the port for Rome. He also visited the cities of the empire and her allies; he traveled to Venice, Cherson, Trebizond, Bari, Thessalonika, Athens, and the ports of Cyprus. When able to go ashore, he would seek out the local intelligentsia to discuss astronomy, philosophy, art, religion, mathematics, and other subjects. Sometimes, if not given permission, he would sneak ashore. Over the years he established quite a network of intellectuals who could see beyond national and cultural boundaries and enjoyed exchanging knowledge for the sake of self-enrichment.

Now Theodore was rapt in the details of the potion he was creating. He repeatedly referred to a fragment of parchment he had on the table: mixing this powder with that one.

Directly adjacent to Theodore's table, the debate between Leo and Alexander heated up and demanded the attention of all. Justin watched from one side of the room; Paul, Demetrios, John, and Peter from another. Theodore remained at his table, appearing oblivious to all around him. Each discussant would make his point and then look to Theodore, as if trying to confirm what he had just said. However, Theodore remained aloof, to the frustration of Leo and Alexander and to the amusement of the onlookers.

"Well, it's obvious to me," argued Leo, "that Ptolemy had it all wrong. The sun is closer to the Earth than Mercury and Venus. It should occupy the second orbit around the Earth and Mercury the third, Venus the fourth. Otherwise his placement of the moon, Mars, Jupiter, Saturn and the stars is quite appropriate. Wouldn't you agree, Theodore?"

"And upon what evidence do you base this, Leo?" asked Alexander, obviously annoyed by the insinuation. "Ptolemy is well supported by nearly a thousand years of continued celestial observation. Isn't that right, Theodore?"

It was apparent that this exchange of opinions would go on for several minutes and, although each implored him to support his point of view in turn, Theodore still had yet to get involved. He continued to mix the powdered ingredients on his worktable, impervious to the storm around him.

In the heat of his argument, a frustrated Leo grabbed Theodore. "Theodore, you must help settle the matter. Alexander must be rescued from his descent down the path of arcane thought and be redirected to the intellectual Olympus of newer thought. He takes what he has learned and sits on it. He refuses to reexamine the evidence and arrive at a new paradigm."

Alexander rose and Leo released his grip on Theodore. Alexander retorted to Theodore, "Well, Leo obviously needs some type of medical help because he is suffering from severely delusional thinking. He is quick to adopt any new concept, no matter how absurd, and crown it with his diadem of truth."

While Leo and Alexander continued to dispute each other's intellectual abilities, Theodore returned to his work. But soon the volume of the discussion grew too loud for him to concentrate. Leo and Alexander began to pound on Theodore's table, each hoping the addition of physical punctuation to his argument might convince his unbelieving opponent.

Theodore saw that concentrating in this fracas was impossible and his brothers' blows to his table were coming dangerously close to upsetting all of his hard work. He loudly cleared his throat to gain their attention but failed to do so. Finally he stood up and clapped his hands four times. After the final clap, he had gained their attention, silencing his battling brothers.

Theodore sat down. He spoke slowly while he returned to mixing his powders. "Leo, you are wrong."

Leo was visibly upset and tried to respond but Alexander quickly interjected, "Another triumph for established scientific traditions!"

Theodore ignored Alexander and kept speaking slowly while continuing to mix his powders, "And Alexander, you are wrong."

"What?" bellowed Alexander.

Theodore looked up from his powders again. "Oh, I'm sorry: Ptolemy is wrong," he added as he returned to his mixture.

The older brothers were confused. They attempted to regain Theodore's attention.

"Then who is right, Theodore?" asked Leo, lowering his head to within inches of Theodore's.

"Aristarchus," Theodore replied, not looking up from his project.

"Aristarchus of Samos?" asked Alexander.

"Yes," answered the youngest brother, still not looking up from his work.

"Theodore," Alexander began as he too stuck his face in Theodore's work, "Aristarchus of Samos lived three hundred years before Ptolemy. How could he be right and Ptolemy wrong? I mean his half-baked theory about all of the planets circling the sun and not the Earth is insane!"

Leo laughed. "Little brother, have you learned nothing in all your studies?"

"Aristarchus later recanted his views because his fellow astronomers pointed out that his theory was totally inconsistent with the circular orbits of the planets," Alexander declared with a certain air of intellectual brinksmanship.

Theodore saw that the education of his brothers required a little more of his attention. He carefully pushed set aside his powders and confronted his chuckling brothers.

"Are the orbits indeed circular?" Theodore asked, looking at each of them in turn.

"Most definitely," replied Alexander and Leo in unison.

"What if I could show you that the planetary orbits were, say, elliptical? And that if one considers Aristarchus' observations in light of such a system, then the sun must be at the center of our universe."

Alexander and Leo were dumbfounded but this was not the first time their little brother had shown his superior brainpower. Leo and Alexander looked at each other, smirked, and then turned to Theodore.

"Little brother, your imagination is impressive," Leo sniped. "But, unfortunately your argument cannot be proven. I suggest you give up this fable which goes against all modern perceptions of the heavens."

"If you could allow me some time to find some notes that I have made on the subject and provide me stylus, ink, and parchment, I could easily prove my theory for you," Theodore replied.

Alexander, too, couldn't resist the opportunity to correct Theodore. "Elliptical orbits, how absurd! The whole thing sounds so asymmetric. Look around you, Theodore. There is balance and symmetry in all of nature. The good Lord enjoys symmetry. So it only follows that the universe is symmetric. And being so, the orbits of its planets should be fully symmetric, like circles. Circles are symmetric, even, uniform, harmonious."

Theodore smiled at the simplicity of his brother's argument. "Alexander, look at Leo's face. Is it truly symmetric?"

Leo's facial asymmetry worked well for Theodore's argument. He made certain that Alexander noticed these things, much to Leo's consternation, by painstakingly pointing them out.

"Look at the nose," Theodore said. "Hardly symmetric."

"No, it's rather crooked, isn't it?" Alexander agreed, enjoying his fun at Leo's expense.

"Theodore!" Leo protested.

"And the eyes . . ." Theodore added.

"I see your point; definitely not symmetric," Alexander replied, relishing every minute of this exercise.

"Is this truly necessary?" Leo flared.

"Sorry, Leo," Alexander and Theodore apologized in unison, chuckling as they did so.

Theodore moved on to his next point. "Can you cut a sponge into two identical pieces? Do all trees have the same 'symmetric' distribution of their branches? Is every shore and seacoast regular? Are the mountains truly *symmetric*?" Theodore's incisive questioning left Alexander befuddled.

"Uh, no," Alexander replied, obviously defeated.

"Perhaps you think God enjoys symmetry but can anybody claim to truly understand God?" Theodore stopped, deep in thought.

"Theodore?" asked Leo, reviving his brother from his near trance-like state.

"I don't know what God thinks, nor will I pretend to," Theodore continued. "All I can do is observe His works and try to understand them. One can't put God into a box and say, 'Here He is', and then study Him like an animal and understand Him. The only things we know about God He has revealed to us in Scripture and that is very little."

"You sound like a Bogomil," teased Leo, comparing his brother to a heretic group in the empire who ignored church laws, proscribed marriage and baptism, and disputed much of the Church's tenets.

"Hardly!" Theodore didn't appreciate Leo's jibes. "Leo, you and your philosopher friends scoff at the notion of a 'loving god' who would just as soon send all of his children to hell as look at them. They wonder how 'a wise god' would be silly enough to come to earth as a man and be put to death, knowing the whole time what fate awaited him."

"What?" Leo asked indignantly.

"How can we understand God?" Theodore continued. "How can an ant fully comprehend an elephant? How can a minnow understand a whale? We can't try to fathom Him when we think of Him on our terms."

Leo tried to rebut. "Consider all of the great thinkers of ancient times: Plato, Lucretius, Epicuris, Zeno. These brilliant minds have accelerated human thought. Would you condemn them because their thoughts are not congruent with those of the Church?"

"Perhaps, if these men had heard the Word of God, they would agree," Theodore suggested. "Perhaps they were among those saved when the Lord harrowed Hell."

"Even Lucretius?" asked Alexander.

"Why would a man choose to follow the teachings of another mere mortal when presented with the Word of God?" Theodore was passionate.

Leo asked, "What of the Jews, the Mohammedans?"

Alexander interrupted, "Infidels! To hell with them!"

Leo glared at Alexander indignantly, then continued with Theodore. "Surely the Jews and Mohammedans look at us as infidels and feel that they know the Word of God and we don't."

"Leo, stop this blasphemous talk immediately," Alexander said. "We could be arrested!"

"Alexander, relax," Theodore began. "Perhaps one of them is right, Leo. Perhaps none of us is right."

"This is heresy, I tell you," Alexander protested.

Theodore moved closer to Leo. "One man will look at the world and say surely there is a God and another will look at the same world and declare the opposite, may God's mercy be upon him. I say Jesus Christ is the Son of God, but another would say Jesus was but a man, a wise philosopher, or a prophet, but still only a man. I know that what I believe is true. I have read the Scriptures and know that they are from God. And I know how I have come to believe. Many say they believe but can't say why. How strong is their belief?" He turned and looked directly at Alexander as he said this; the older brother pretended not to notice. Then Theodore looked back at Leo. "But God has left enough room for doubt to allow us to choose. And I know what I have chosen."

Leo was impressed by Theodore's words. His eyes seemed to thirst for more. Theodore saw this and continued.

"Leo," Theodore asked, "when is the last time you read the Bible, not just a verse here and there but a sizeable portion, like, say, one of the Gospels?" Leo couldn't give an answer. "How about the rest of the New Testament? You know, I find it more profound than Plato's philosophy and more beautiful than Pindar's poetry. Try it, Leo. I wish all atheists would read the Scriptures."

"Now wait a minute! I'm no atheist!" Leo protested. "What are you saying?"

Theodore ignored Leo and turned to Alexander. "And when was the last time you read the Bible, yourself, rather than some priest reading it to you and then telling you what it means?"

Alexander recoiled and replied awkwardly, "Hearing an expert opinion can be helpful."

"Yes, Alexander, but you are a well-educated man. Don't let the priests do all of your thinking for you. Use the brain God gave you. Read it for yourself. Explore what God is revealing to you!"

The verbal imbroglio continued. Alexander ranted about how important priests and bishops were for assuring proper interpretation of the Scriptures. Leo sporadically interjected vehement denials that he was an atheist and upbraided Theodore for suggesting such a thing. But Theodore had had enough debating for one day. He sat down at his worktable and returned to mixing the powders before him. Peter and John had been observing the discussion with great enjoyment. They caught themselves laughing under their breath several times.

"Never a dull moment around here," said John.

"I had nearly forgotten," said Peter. "Your Uncle Theodore is quite a tiger."

"Oh, yes. Never argue with him about any subject he loves passionately."

"And what subjects does he love passionately?" Peter asked.

"Why, all of them," John chuckled. "Do you know that *he* studied rhetoric at the university?"

"That fighting skill was not learned. He was born with that," Peter said. "Did you see his eyes when he spoke? They were as responsible for his victory as anything he said."

Justin took advantage of this break in the debate to cross the room and join Peter and John. "Well, that certainly was entertaining," Justin joked.

"Yes, I was totally enthralled," Peter added.

"You two have but half a brain between you!" John sneered.

"Ah, but it's not the size that is important; it's how you use it," teased Justin. "Isn't that correct, Professor Argyropoulos?"

"Most assuredly, Professor Phillipos," Peter replied, trying not to burst out laughing, "most assuredly."

Basilios entered the room with Eleni and walked over to Justin, Peter, and John. "Peter, so good to see you again," he said, extending his right hand and setting his left on Peter's right shoulder. He gave Justin a look that seemed to Justin to say, I hope you've overcome those silly jitters you're having about the upcoming campaign.

Peter straightened his posture, grasped the retired war hero's extended right hand firmly, and pumped it a few times. "It's always a pleasure to see you, sir."

Basilios' three brothers had just taken notice of the Eleni's arrival in their midst. "Eleni! Come and hug your uncle!" beckoned Alexander. Eleni complied with Alexander's request. When she arrived he kissed her three times and hugged her so tight that he lifted her off the ground. Leo and Theodore joined them, each of them greeting her in turn.

"Uncle Leo, Uncle Theodore, Uncle Alexander, you remember Peter," Justin said, his right hand gently pressing Peter forward. They shook hands with Peter and vigorously welcomed him.

"We see that you're continuing to do a good job keeping Justin out of trouble," Leo teased.

"That's no small task, knowing Justin," said Alexander, joining in the fun.

"Oh, he does his fair share of saving my neck, too," Peter replied.

"I wouldn't be so certain about that," Eleni chimed in. "Justin tells me that he still owes you a few."

It was getting difficult for the modest Peter to withstand all of this praise. Justin could forebear the barbs at his expense because the general flavor of the conversation was indeed true. Their conversation continued for some time until Anastasia came to announce that dinner was ready.

As the family gathered around the table Peter pulled Justin aside. "Did you get a chance to talk to your father?" he whispered.

"Not really," Justin answered. "When I told him that we'd been ordered not to discuss our mission, he didn't want to hear any more."

"So you gave up?"

"He didn't want to hear about it. I don't know what he could have done for us anyway."

"He's a soldier, through and through."

"Yes sir." Justin asked, "By the way, who is the patron saint of lost causes?"

"Saint Jude, I think. Maybe it's someone else. Why don't you ask Father Isaiah? He's right there in the hall."

"I think you're right. It's Saint Jude," Justin replied.

The kindly old Father Isaiah was the Phillipos family chaplain. Most households who could afford one had a chaplain. This octogenarian priest was entering his seventeenth year of service with the Phillipos family. He had his own room in the house that Alexander and Leo shared and pretty much kept to himself.

"How did your family find him?" Peter asked.

"He was priest in some small village in the Peloponnesos for many years. The village was decimated by a strange illness; even his wife died. Most of the survivors fled to neighboring villages. Some at the archdiocese placed the blame for the plague on Isaiah. Although the charge was totally unfounded, Father Isaiah was recalled and replaced by another priest. Fortunately, he was able to convince the metropolitan of his innocence and was then sent to Constantinople to serve in a junior capacity at a small church. That was in spite of his long service to the Church and his significant seniority over the other priest at his new assignment. Unfortunately, he made his dissatisfaction known to the wrong people and was discharged from that parish."

"Sounds like the army."

"At about the same time, our chaplain, Father Timothy, died. My father was away in the army so Uncle Alexander went to speak with his parish priest about who might be available. On the way, he saw Father Isaiah sitting, rather forlorn, on a bench on the Mese, sat next to him, and struck up a conversation. Father Isaiah confessed that he was a priest without a parish and Alexander told him we needed a chaplain. The two of them spent the next few hours strolling along the Mese. They walked from the silversmith near the Milion down to the silk merchant by the Forum Tauri and back again."

"And then he accepted the position."

"Only after Uncle Alexander took him to a sweet shop and he had his fill."

"Father Isaiah drives a hard bargain."

"Yes, but he was a quick answer to prayer."

One of the servants walked up to Theodore and informed him that two more guests had arrived. At the front door were two longtime family friends, Senator Gregory Kastros and Giovanni Rossi.

"Welcome Senator," said Theodore. "I'm so glad you could come." He stepped forward and extended his right hand, which the senator took. The two men shook hands and exchanged brief pleasantries. The servant then showed the senator into the great room.

Senator Kastros, a man of great wealth and influence, was tall and gray-haired, his size was commensurate with his rank. For a while he had been Basilios' superior in the army. Kastros had admired the junior officer and kept in touch and their friendship grew quickly.

Theodore greeted Giovanni Rossi as he had the senator. "Giovanni, how have you been? How's your father?"

Giovanni Rossi was a short, thin man who was also a longtime friend of the Phillipos family. His father, Lodovico, was a wealthy silk merchant in Venice who had been poor when he met Justin's father. Basilios had befriended Lodovico when he was serving as military aid to the Imperial Embassy in Venice. Those times were hard for Lodovico; Basilios encouraged the Venetian to send his trading ships to Constantinople. Lodovico agreed and made a small fortune. Soon he was sending his ships throughout the Mediterranean.

Lodovico had done better than most but he was not extremely wealthy. In general, those involved in trade felt lucky to do well at all. Trade routes on land were subject to bandits and the seas were unforgiving when it came to bad weather. When calm, they were rife with pirates, in spite of the imperial navy's best efforts. Few consumers had the buying power to purchase more exotic products from other lands; most cities and regions were fairly self-sufficient in supplying the essentials for the local populace.

Although Lodovico had attributed a great deal of his success to Basilios' encouragement to send his ships to Constantinople, most of his success, he admitted, was due to luck. In one year, storms sank most of the ships of his chief competitors, Venetian or otherwise. This allowed him a significant advantage over his rivals, which he exploited for the next four years.

However, a good deal of his exceptional performance was due to his willingness to try new things, something Basilios strongly encouraged. Typically, the winter was a slow time because mariners refused to brave the rough seas. Conditions on land weren't much better but Lodovico found men willing to brave the elements at sea for a greater portion of his profits. Because he was able to carry this out for six years, this boldness kept him far ahead of his competitors. Soon financial margins were shrinking as more and more traders followed his lead and increased the availability of the merchandise they were selling. And the physical and emotional stress he had endured outweighed any benefits he was realizing, so he returned to more conventional trading methods. But now, thanks to the wealth he had accumulated, it was easier for him to give up the risky endeavors at which he had succeeded so well. Over the years, he had tried trading wine, olive oil, and cotton but his chief success had been with silk, so he stayed with that. It had indeed been good to him. Giovanni was now handling his father's affairs in the eastern Mediterranean from Constantinople. He visited the Phillipos family regularly; he and Justin quickly became friends.

Justin saw the young Venetian and greeted him. "Giovanni, I haven't seen you for quite a while. How's business?" he asked, ushering Giovanni toward the great room.

"The last load of silk I shipped home earned my father a fortune. He was very pleased."

Justin saw Peter and introduced the two. "Giovanni," he began, "this is Peter Argyropoulos. Peter, this is Giovanni Rossi."

Giovanni extended his hand first. "So good to meet you, Captain. Justin has told me much about you."

"Probably more than is true, I imagine," Peter joked. The three of them laughed and proceeded into the great room.

The rest of the family welcomed Giovanni as Justin led him and Peter to the table. Usually the men and women would dine separately but on such a special occasion, all agreed that both sexes would share the same table this evening. Basilios and Theodore led Father Isaiah to the head of the table. Theodore clapped his hands to quiet the conversations taking place around the table and announced that Father Isaiah would lead them all in a prayer.

The old priest gave a brief invocation and followed it with the Lord's Prayer. He finished the prayer by chanting alone, as was customary, the last part: "For Thine is the Kingdom and the Power, and the Glory for ever and ever!"

When Isaiah finished, all of the participants said in unison, "Amen."

"Before we get started," Theodore began, "I would like you to join me in a toast."

Most of those at the table nodded their heads, murmured among themselves, and reached for their goblets of wine, knowing precisely who would be toasted. Eleni and Justin looked at each other and remained politely quiet, anticipating Theodore's words.

As all of those at the table raised their goblets, Theodore began his toast. "My nephew's marriage to his beautiful bride, I can honestly say, truly demonstrates the love that God intended between men and women. Theirs is a love cultivated by friendship and respect and nurtured by trust."

Aspasia's and Eleni's eyes met when Theodore said "trust." The mother projected a stern look at her daughter, as if to say, "Don't forget our little talk on this matter." The look in Eleni's eyes reassured her mother that she would not.

"To Eleni and Justin!" Theodore raised his drink and the others repeated his words.

Hosts and guests had their fill of roast lamb, wine, and other delicacies, including *yuvarelakia*, lamb and herb meatballs simmered in broth; *moussaka,* which is beef, Feta cheese, and eggplant, baked in a bechamel sauce; *pastfeli,* a sesame seed and honey candy.

When the servants came to clear the table, the women returned to the large room in the front of the house while the men went to the rear of the house again. In the front room, the women discussed the goings on at their church. New icons had recently been purchased to replace the old ones on the iconostasis; the older ones were being given to a new church in a village in eastern Macedonia. They also talked about the "excessive" money being spent to refurbish the imperial gardens at the Great Palace Complex and family plans for Easter. Eleni spoke with her mother, Justin's mother, and her sister Eftihia about her young marriage to Justin, which generated a great deal of laughter at Justin's expense.

In the back room, Basilios attacked the government's inadequate military spending. Demetrios joined Basilios in the assault. Leo argued that the money was better spent at the university than on soldiers. Alexander supported Leo halfheartedly.

Senator Kastros seemed detached from the whole conversation, which was most unusual. As a senator, he usually rushed to the defense of the government, especially if the policies it pursued followed his desires. Instead, his mind drifted to a painting hanging on the opposite wall.

Basilios nudged the senator. "The security of the empire is paramount," Basilios declared to Leo as he looked at Kastros, trying to bring him into the conversation. "What good is a university if the city is overrun by barbarians?"

"It would appear that there are barbarians within the city already," Leo smirked.

Basilios glowered at his brother. "Is anyone who is not a student or a sophist a barbarian in your eyes, Leo?" he growled. "Need I remind you that the empire was build by common people: farmers, fishermen—"

"Not again!" Alexander interrupted. "Every time this argument goes down this road, we end up with 'farmers and fishermen'!"

Demetrios burst out laughing, soon to be joined by the younger men and then Alexander and Leo. Kastros remained distracted, something of great importance weighing on his mind. The others saw this but did not intervene in the thoughts of the usually talkative senator.

Anastasia appeared at the entrance to the room and announced, "Senator Kastros, there is someone here to see you."

"Oh, thank you, Anastasia," Kastros stammered, as if he had just awakened from sleep. He followed his hostess out of the room and toward the front door. The other men continued with their conversation but Peter slowly moved out of the room and watched Kastros as he walked to the entrance of the house.

At the door, a young man in the uniform of an imperial messenger dutifully bowed to Kastros and handed him a leather pouch. Kastros dismissed the messenger, turned toward the great room, and hurriedly opened the pouch. From it he removed a parchment and began reading. Peter could see the older man's excitement grow. A more animated Kastros jauntily strutted toward the back room, beaming from ear to ear.

"Gentlemen! Gentlemen!" Kastros declared, as he suddenly transformed back into his usual jovial self. "I have great news!" he added, waving the parchment before them.

"What is it, Senator?" asked Basilios.

"Emperor Romanos has approved the plan!" Kastros replied.

"Plan?" Leo asked, looking at Basilios as if his brother had the answer.

"Trade routes?" Alexander asked, having briefly discussed the plan with Kastros recently.

"Yes," Kastros replied, his eyes wide. "New trade routes to the East!" He quickly sat down and gathered the men around him. He set the parchment on a small table and pointed. "After our campaign in Syria last year, the Caliph of Cairo limited access to markets in Damascus and other cities in Syria. I proposed a new treaty to take to the caliph. It would not only open up Damascus for our merchants but would also allow more goods from the east into Constantinople."

"We already have too many Arab merchants in the city," Basilios grumbled. "They've even built their own mosque!"

Kastros replied, "We have fought many wars with the Mohammedans. Some they have won; some we have won. They will be there a long time. They have goods that we want and we have goods that they want. This new trade agreement will benefit both of us."

Basilios looked skeptical.

Kastros became very frank. "The imperial treasury is seriously lacking in funds. Increased wealth means increased taxes—"

"Which means more money for your army, Basilios," Leo interjected.

"Yes" Kastros agreed.

"So far it sounds like a good idea," Basilios admitted.

"And the new agreement will allow us more freedom to travel in Syria," the senator continued, "and ease some of the restrictions the caliph has placed on Christians living there."

"Was this the emperor's idea?" Demetrios asked.

"Mine, actually," Kastros said, trying to be humble, "but he has given it his full support. However, his enemies are much against it because merchants are still viewed with disdain by aristocrats and, I believe, because the idea came from the emperor's allies and not the Dukas."

"And what do *you* think of the emperor?" Peter asked pointedly. The room became very quiet. "You are known to be a fair man, sir. What do you think?"

The question seemed inappropriate to some of the older men in the room. *How dare a soldier in the emperor's own army ask a senator his opinion of a reigning emperor! Is he insane?* But Kastros calmly answered, "Romanos Diogenes is a good man. He is sincere in his efforts to strengthen our empire."

"Do you trust him?" Peter continued.

"I would trust him with my life," Kastros replied.

"Does Emperor Michael know of this plan? He is, after all, co-emperor."

Basilios raised his right hand as if he were signaling Peter to desist. Kastros repressed Basilios' hand and calmly responded to Peter's question. "Yes, Emperor Michael and all of his family are aware of the plan. Yet they call trading with the Arabs treasonous."

"And what do you think of the Dukas?" Peter asked pointedly.

Basilios rose in protest. "Now that's quite enough, Peter!"

Kastros was not bothered by the question. He motioned to Basilios to be seated and replied, "The Dukas family and its supporters are a malignant growth on the heart of this empire."

Peter was impressed by the senator's candor. He looked at the older men who nodded as Kastros spoke. Apparently they shared his feelings about the empire's most powerful family.

"Under Constantine Dukas, men were promoted or rewarded based on their friendship with or their willingness to pay him. As a result, our government became corrupt and programs necessary for the growth and strength of the empire were gutted. Just look at our army."

"But he was very supportive of the university," Leo added.

"Yes, but even that he did half-heartedly, preferring more to send the funds into the pockets of his cronies than to expand learning in the empire."

Leo did not answer but his face showed he knew that Kastros was right.

Peter was impressed by the senator and his face showed it. Justin leaned toward Peter and whispered, "Sure beats listening to Mr. Handakos!"

"That's an understatement," Peter sniggered. When he noticed that the older men were miffed at their private joke, Peter, desperately trying to atone for his error, said, "Senator . . . thank you very much . . . I truly appreciate your opinion."

The older men were satisfied and drifted into a conversation of their own while Giovanni, Paul, and John joined Justin and Peter.

"You squirmed your way out of that one rather well," John teased Peter. "You do need to show a bit more respect to a man of such standing."

Peter turned to Justin. "Thank you for getting me into trouble."

Justin protested his innocence mutely.

"Come with me, Justin," Uncle Theodore whispered. Justin was enjoying Peter and the others discussing the possibility of mock naval battles in the Hippodrome. Uncle Theodore gently took Justin's arm and led him to the corner where his worktable sat. He picked up a small bowl that contained the dark gray-green mixture of the powders he was preparing earlier. Justin noticed that each of the three bowls left on the table contained a colored powder, one, black, another, yellow, and the third, grayish blue.

"I want to show you something, Justin," Theodore said as he led his nephew away from the table, excitement in his voice. "One of my correspondents knows somebody who has recently been to the eastern end of the Silk Road. He has sent me instructions for the concoction of this most fascinating powder." He enthusiastically pointed to the bowl in his hand.

Justin smiled without saying a word. He didn't have the foggiest idea what to expect from his uncle, but he knew from past experience that Uncle Theodore was capable of the most astounding amusements.

Theodore led Justin into the yard at the back of the house. The older man stopped at a wooden crate in the center and set the bowl on the ground a few feet from the larger container. "Observe, Justin," Uncle Theodore instructed as he walked off twenty paces from Justin. He poured some of the mysterious powder onto the ground and grabbed a flint from his pocket. Theodore squatted down, grinned at Justin as he did so, inviting speculation on his nephew's part, but knowing that the young man couldn't possibly imagine what would happen next.

Indeed, Justin was completely mystified, the purpose of this strange exercise beyond his comprehension. He thought of asking his uncle but didn't want to spoil the mysterial atmosphere his uncle was so artfully constructing. So Justin watched patiently, savoring the intrigue.

Theodore stood before the trail of the magical substance and tried to read his nephew's thoughts. He smiled as he imagined what might be going through Justin's mind. Then he held up the flint, as if to announce that the moment of revelation had indeed arrived.

Justin nodded to his uncle, inviting consummation of his curiosity.

Theodore grabbed a stone from the ground and struck it with the flint. When the waiting powder received the hot spark, Theodore quickly dove away from it. The powder instantly ignited in a luminous flash of white light, the bright flame hissing as it consumed the powder.

Justin gasped and threw his hands up to guard his eyes. The resulting flash caught him completely off guard.

Theodore arose from the ground and brushed the yard's dirt from his clothes. He strutted proudly toward his nephew. "Pretty impressive, isn't it?"

After Justin had reassured himself that the conflagration was extinguished and the acrid smoke produced by the blaze would not kill him, he regained his composure and looked at his uncle in amazement. "What in God's name was that?"

Theodore laughed. "It's quite amusing. Don't you agree?"

"I would say that 'amusing' doesn't quite describe it! That stuff is fantastic! What is it?"

"It's a mixture of sulfur, charcoal, and saltpeter," Theodore replied. When he saw that his description meant nothing to his nephew, he commanded, "Watch this, Justin." Theodore opened the wooden crate and pulled a small cask from it. He made a small hole in the top and sprinkled out a powder identical to the one he had just ignited. He laid the powder out in a straight twelve-foot line. He then set the cask down on its side so the line of powder ran directly into the cask. "Justin," he grinned confidently at his nephew, "this is going to make what you just saw seem like a mere trifle."

Justin was again intrigued by his uncle's surprise. He started to follow the older man but was stopped by a wave of Theodore's hand.

"Go over to that half wall over there," Theodore said, pointing across the yard. "I'll join you in a second." The older man crouched down, lit the powder with a spark from his flint, and ran to the half wall where he joined his nephew. Justin watched his uncle on his knees, his head above the top of the half wall just enough to allow his eyes to see the proceedings.

The ignited powder hissed as the fire consumed it, spewing white light while it burned down the line to the cask. Justin wanted to ask his uncle, who was crouching as he was, what to expect. But he knew the older man wouldn't spoil the surprise.

When the bright flashing reached the cask, a brilliant explosion illuminated the entire compound and the resulting din was almost deafening. The echo reverberated off the walls of the compound and the houses within it. The flash of the explosion temporarily blinded Justin but the young man's eyes recovered quickly and, when they did, he stood and ran through the caustic smoke to the cask and found it reduced to smoldering cinders. Debris had fallen everywhere.

"Good God!" exclaimed Justin.

Theodore stood up and rubbed his hands together, smiling. "Perfect!" he whispered, "Perfect!"

A commotion arose inside the house. A second later, Leo was at the back door with Alexander, Basilios, and Paul right behind him. The neighbors yelled from the other side of the compound walls, demanding to know what was happening.

"What in hell is going on out there?" yelled a neighbor from the other side of the wall. Other neighbors loudly echoed the demand. "I'm calling the constable!" one threatened. "What is it with you people?" asked another irate neighbor. "You're always up to mischief!"

Once Leo saw that his brother and his nephew were unhurt, he reassured the others who returned inside, and went to calm the worried neighbors.

Leo calmly told the rattled neighbors that all was fine and that no further hijinx would occur. Once they were mollified, he marched over to his younger brother. "What on Earth are you doing this time, Theodore?" He didn't wait for an answer. "Is this another one of your attempts to discover the ingredients of Greek fire? It is a state secret, you know, and anyone disclosing its contents can be executed."

"No, no, it's not that." Theodore was irritated by Leo's tone. "It's just a little something I'm showing Justin. Nothing to worry about, I assure you."

"Sounds like you're trying to kill the boy!"

"Leo, Justin is fine," Theodore dismissed his brother with a wave of his hand. "'Kill the boy'," he muttered under his breath. "Your Uncle Leo can be so annoying."

"Someday, you're really going to hurt yourself with this nonsense. Please be certain that nobody else is with you the next time you try to blow yourself up!"

Theodore said nothing but turned to Justin who could imagine his uncle saying, "Maybe he'll go away if I don't say anything."

When Leo was satisfied that he had chastised his brother sufficiently, he returned inside. In truth, though, he was used to Theodore's exotic experiments. This one didn't seem any stranger than the others, but Justin's involvement necessitated his actions.

As Leo strutted his way back inside, Theodore shook his head and rolled his eyes. "I think your Uncle Leo worries too much, don't you, Justin? And besides, I've already discovered the ingredients of Greek fire." When he mistakenly thought that this fact aroused Justin's interest, he added, "You take pine tar, extract—"

"That's okay, Uncle Theodore," Justin said, putting his hands up between his uncle and himself, "you needn't tell me."

Theodore was disappointed. "As you wish."

"What are you going to do with this powder, Uncle Theodore? Sell it to the emperor?"

"I'd sooner sell it to the Turks, or worse yet, the Normans."

Justin grinned at his uncle's defiance.

"No, Justin, I'm just going to enjoy this little secret myself. If the emperor wants it, he can travel to the far end of the Silk Road and get it himself!" They both enjoyed a good laugh. Theodore then reached into the large crate and pulled out another small cask. "Justin, I have some for you."

"No! I can't take it!" Justin gasped.

"Why not? As a soldier, you may find yourself in great danger. This may be useful. Please take it."

Justin hesitated. "It's far too dangerous, Uncle Theodore. I'd probably kill myself trying to use it."

"Justin, it's not dangerous." Justin knew his uncle's skill at stretching the truth. "Just keep it dry and away from fire. It won't cause you any trouble."

Justin shook his head. This volatile substance was beyond him. It could only lead to trouble.

Theodore thrust the cask into Justin's hands. "Take it!" he commanded. "Think of it as a special addition to the weapons you already carry."

"Uncle, I can't! It's too—"

Theodore looked closely at Justin, as if noted something unusual in his nephew. "Justin," he interrupted, "you've never seemed so nervous before about going on a campaign. Something tells me that, for this mission, you *will* require some extra protection."

Justin was surprised his uncle was aware of his discomfort but relieved he didn't inquire further about his inquietude. *What good would it do?* Perhaps this was why he acquiesced. "Okay. I'll take it."

"Good, good, my boy. You won't regret it."

"Thank you, Uncle Theodore."

"Don't mention it. I mean that literally; don't mention it. I want this to be our secret."

"It will be."

Theodore threw his arm around Justin's shoulder and regaled him with stories of his other discoveries as the two of them walked back inside.

CHAPTER 8

Constantine Papakostas awoke slowly from his sleep. His night of passion had exhausted him. He looked around the dimly lit room. Two small candles on nearby sideboard provided minimal illumination. He had been in it several times before but had never noticed the detail in the elegant silk and wool tapestries. The silk tapestry above the sideboard caught his eye: golden griffins on a background of bright crimson bordered with fine Athenian brocade. In the center, one griffin, larger than the rest, had two heads, each attacking the other. Both were seriously wounded and, although neither had the upper hand, neither was about to surrender. This image captivated the young man's imagination and he examined it more carefully.

He was an impressionable young man who had been a monk for three years. His piety had always been genuine and he saw his service in the monastery as his way of thanking God for his life and his many blessings.

Constantine had served his archimandrite well, as if the abbot were God Himself. He had shown himself to be bright and diligent in the execution of the archimandrite's commands and he quickly rose to high favor. In doing so, he surpassed many of greater tenure than himself. He was a layman, as most monks were, and every young monk wanted to emulate his success story but recently Constantine Papakostas had begun to serve the Church in a different way.

"Good morning, Constantine," came a deep, commanding voice from behind him. The room grew light as the entrant lit a large oil lamp in the middle of the room.

Constantine turned around and faced a gray-bearded man in a black cassock.

"Good morning, Your Eminence," Constantine replied, startled by the man's sudden appearance. He could smell alcohol on his breath.

"You were particularly energetic last night." The older man smiled seductively.

"Was it to your liking, Eminence?" Constantine asked, eager to hear a positive response.

"It was perfect," the older man answered, as if there were no equivalent. He walked to the bed, leaned over it, embraced Constantine, and kissed him fully on the lips. He gave him a purse that Constantine opened. It was filled with gold *noumismata*. "It's time to get down to business, my boy," the older man said as Constantine fingered the gold coins.

"Who is the target this time, Archbishop Mavrites?" Constantine asked. This was not the first "business" transaction between the two. It was one of many.

"Strategos Joseph Tarchaniotes."

Constantine's eyes widened.

"My sources tell me that the strategos may be particularly vulnerable to your . . ." the metropolitan paused, "charms."

"I'll do my best, Eminence."

"You usually do but do save something for me, my boy."

The metropolitan leered at the young man with lust, then leaned over and kissed him again. With his right hand, he reached under the bedcovers, caressed the young man's genitals, and gave them a gentle squeeze. The archbishop had been intimate with Constantine for just over six months. He provided the younger man with money and gifts. Constantine provided sexual as well as other services the cleric required, which included espionage and intrigue, a calling to which the young monk was particularly well suited.

"And now you must leave, dear Constantine. The strategos crosses the Bosphorus with the vanguard of the army in a week. You must complete this task before he leaves. Our control of Tarchaniotes is absolutely essential to Caesar John's plan."

"Yes, Eminence," Constantine nodded.

"His son has provided a commission for you," Mavrites continued. "You are now a captain, newly added to Tarchaniotes' staff. Report to him today and get to work." The archbishop handed him a pouch that contained his commission and his orders.

"Understood," Constantine smiled at the older man, more as his lover than as his agent.

Mavrites tolerated this silent breach of etiquette as he remembered the virile young man's dedicated service to him. Ordinarily, he would expect to be addressed "Your Eminence," which was due a man of his rank. Instead, he smiled at his lover and walked back over to him. They kissed one more time before the metropolitan left the room.

Constantine opened the pouch and quickly examined his commission while he dressed in his monk's cassock. Self-satisfied, he grinned and left the bedchamber. "Easiest money I'll have earned this month," he muttered.

On his way out of the door of the metropolitan's residence, he ran into a nun. "Please excuse me, Sister," he said. Upon realizing the woman's identity, he changed his tone. "Oh, it's you," he growled.

The woman returned his acrid greeting. "Brother Constantine, was Archbishop Mavrites in need of your *special* services?" she pried. "Perhaps he needed your help in understanding the story of Sodom and Gomorrah."

"We all must find our own path to heaven, Sister Despina."

"That's strange," Despina countered. "The path you've chosen appears to be going straight to hell!"

Constantine lost his civility. "Since when do whores dispense virtue?"

"Whom are you calling a whore? At least I am involved in no *unnatural* actions."

Constantine narrowed his eyes and raged, "What are you—"

One of Mavrites servants suddenly appeared at the door. "The metropolitan will see you now, Sister."

Constantine's face flushed with anger as Despina followed the servant past him. She saw his reaction and smirked.

Despina and Constantine had been bitter rivals for months. As Mavrites' best agents, they were constant competitors but their competition was anything but friendly. Each loathed the other and would do whatever possible to outdo the rival's accomplishments. The archbishop saw this and exploited their antagonism for his own ends.

"Don't worry, Brother. I'm certain that the metropolitan finds some part of your services valuable," she said.

Constantine turned and left in a huff. How he hated that woman! He prayed for the day when he would hear of her untimely death. *Yes, that would be worth anything! But why was she here?* The archbishop had work for her, he was certain. A competitive surge boiled through his veins. "Do your best, Sister," Constantine said under his breath. "But you'll not outshine this star!"

Elias Mavrites had been born to a poor family, but cleverly realized that poverty was not for him. He was determined to become not only wealthy but powerful as well. Although he was irreligious by nature and far too cynical to take the Scriptures seriously, he was keen enough to see that the church could provide the wealth and power he craved. So, at sixteen, he entered a monastery where he quickly rose to the position of archimandrite. He spent six years in that position and accumulated much wealth, most of it stolen from the coffers of the monastery or extorted from gullible churchgoers. From there, he used his money, influence, and cunning to obtain a position in which he could increase his wealth and power.

However, his self-aggrandizement wouldn't be satisfied with such limited opportunities so he took the Holy Orders and was ordained a bishop nine and a half years after he entered the monastery. Bishops came from monasteries rather than from priests in the community.

Mavrites was not disappointed by the opportunities his new position provided. Later, during the reign of Constantine Dukas, he associated himself with that powerful clan. He used his power to dispatch their enemies and promote their friends. Two years before the death of that emperor, Mavrites was ordained Metropolitan of Selymbria, a position of great authority. It allowed him to stay in Constantinople and serve his new masters, and himself, very well.

Sister Despina loved the archbishop's lavish office. Although she had been there many times before, each trip to this palace-in-miniature fed her avaricious ambition. And indeed Mavrites' office was quite posh, although such richness was not unusual for some one of his ecclesiastical rank. Jeweled icons hung from the walls between expensive wool and silk tapestries. A golden crucifix standing twenty inches high dominated the console behind the archbishop's desk. A mosaic of Christ as Judge dominated the wall behind the console. The room smelled of the most expensive incense the Roman Empire could offer. Despina found him seated in a large cushioned ebony chair at the center of the room's richness. He slowly rose when she entered the room. As he did so, she dropped to one knee, bowed her head, and kissed the back of his outstretched right hand.

"Sister Despina, I'm so pleased that you could see me on such short notice," he smiled. He helped her from the floor with one hand and waved the servant from the room with the other.

"I'm always ready to serve you, Your Eminence."

"And I am happy to direct you in your service to the church."

"How may I serve Your Eminence?" the nun asked. Her manner was superficially dutiful, more a formality in the presence of her employer.

"Are you familiar with Senator Gregory Kastros?" he asked.

"Isn't everybody, Eminence?"

"Yes, of course," he chuckled at the silliness of his own question. "Well, Sister, the senator poses a particular problem to the church."

"And he needs to be neutralized, Eminence?" Despina surmised, not needing or wanting to hear any convoluted justification for a plot against Kastros.

"That's what I like about you, Sister. You grasp the situation so quickly."

"How much time do I have, Eminence?" she asked.

"Oh, there's no rush, my dear," he reassured her. "You may choose to take advantage of the senator for a while but this does need to be done in a reasonable period of time."

"Yes, Eminence," Despina said, appreciating the latitude Mavrites was giving her.

The metropolitan grabbed a leather pouch from his desktop. "This may be of use to you," he said, handing it to her.

"Yes, Eminence. May I ask its contents?"

"Some of the key elements of the defenses of Anazarbus," Mavrites volunteered. "The information's not terribly important but it could be useful under the right circumstances."

Despina turned away from Mavrites and placed the pouch in a secret pocket on the inside of her habit. As she did so, the archbishop picked up a coin-filled purse from his desk, gently shook it to allow her to guess at its contents, and handed it to her. "Spend it wisely, my child."

"Thank you, Your Eminence," said Despina. She again kneeled and kissed the archbishop's hand, then rose and left with a blessing from Mavrites.

As she walked way from Mavrites' residence, she thought it was no wonder that friends and enemies alike referred to Elias Mavrites, this dangerous cleric, as "the Raven." He was cunning, mendacious, and always able to find rotten material in anyone's life. His black clothing only accentuated the moniker.

Eleni watched her silent husband prepare for bed. He was preoccupied again.

"Would you care to share your secret with me?" she asked.

Justin turned to her. "I've left you before to go to serve the emperor . . ."

"Yes."

"But never as your husband."

"Justin, how are things different?"

"I feel some increased responsibility for you now."

"You've known me my whole life." Justin's worrying irritated her. "Do you truly think that I am incapable of this?"

"No, not in the least!"

As Eleni listened to her husband, she heard a familiar voice coming from the back of her mind. With each passing second she heard less of her husband and more of her mother. Aspasia's command for Eleni to trust and accept her husband rang through. Soon Justin's voice replaced that of her mother. Eleni could see that he was doing exactly what she had done to him that morning. He doubted her abilities. *Had the simple fact that they were now married changed the way he saw her, too?* She watched as he struggled to explain himself. He wasn't doing well at all. She took his hands and held them tenderly. "Justin?"

He hesitated. "You are right, Eleni. I'm worrying about you and I shouldn't be. But I can't help but think about your living with the empress. When I've been away before, you've been with your family. Now you'll be with strangers."

"Justin, you worry about the silliest things," she said but with a hint of exasperation in her voice. "Someone talked to me this morning about trust and gave me some good advice."

"Who was that?" Justin asked.

"My mother," Eleni answered, knowing this answer would shock him.

"Really?"

"Yes. She told me to trust my husband and accept him as he is."

"Sounds like you're sharing this with me for a reason. I, too, may benefit from these pearls of wisdom."

"You're much smarter than you look," she teased.

"So now I won't worry about you and the empress."

"You take orders well, Captain Phillipos! And to be honest, I look at this whole thing as a new experience."

"You can't be serious."

"I am. I admit I have no idea what to expect but there's adventure in that, isn't there?"

"My dear, you never cease to amaze me."

"Nor will I ever, Justin, nor will I ever." Eleni gently touched Justin's hand. "Captain Phillipos, you are the one who should occupy our concern," Eleni said, trying her best to sound like someone's commanding officer, "off gallivanting about the Anatolian steppes, sniffing out the elusive Turk . . ."

"Yes, that's right."

"I'm thankful Peter will be there to help."

"Yes, thank God for Peter." Justin tightened his hold on Eleni. "This has been an incredible day." He shook his head slowly as he thought about it.

"I couldn't agree more," Eleni sighed.

"Eleni," Justin's giggling hinted at mischief. "Did your mother also suggest sending Iakovos?"

Eleni's face turned crimson as she pulled herself away from him. Justin's loud laughter relayed his forgiveness but Eleni's embarrassment was complete. "Justin," she began to giggle, "Justin, I'm sorry about that."

"You are forgiven, my dear," Justin said between guffaws. When Eleni smiled at him and looked into his eyes, his laughter stopped. Justin held her tight and kissed her. "I'm exhausted," he whispered. "Let's go to bed."

Each threw on a loose-fitting tunica and approached the bed. Eleni crossed herself in front of the icon of the Virgin and Child on the bedside table, leaned forward, and quickly kissed the images on the icon. Justin followed suit and extinguished the lamp next to the icon.

Eleni embraced her husband and kissed him. "Good night, Justin. I will pray the Virgin keeps you safe."

"Thank you, Eleni. I will pray for your safety, too."

As Eleni crawled into bed and Justin wrapped her in his arms, she ran her hand through his hair and kissed him again. "I love you, Justin."

Justin answered with a passionate kiss, the first of many that night, their last night together for a long while.

Part II

BATTLE

CHAPTER 9

"But I don't recall asking for any new officers," said Strategos Joseph Tarchaniotes to his aide.

"His commission bears the Emperor Michael's personal seal, Strategos."

Tarchaniotes examined the seal closely, hoping it was a forgery. When his hope was denied, he growled, "Oh, very well; show him in."

Constantine Papakostas entered the general's tent, removed his helmet, and sharply saluted Tarchaniotes. "Captain Papakostas, reporting for duty, sir!"

The strategos did not stand. He dismissed his aide and looked at this new captain. Constantine's handsome face and deep blue eyes in the morning light impressed the older man. Tarchaniotes caught himself smiling. "Captain," he began, "Tell me about your previous military experience."

"Sir, I have had no previous military experience."

The strategos snorted. "Another damned political appointment!" he muttered.

"Sir?"

"Captain, what are you doing here?"

"I've come to serve the emperor, sir."

"Yes, we all have." The strategos remained exasperated. "But we don't wish to sacrifice anybody. Our soldiers are well trained. The Turk is a vicious enemy. An inexperienced soldier is a risk to us all. An inexperienced officer is a disaster waiting to happen."

"Sir, I will serve you well."

"We'll see about that," the general sneered. He stood and walked over to the young man. "Now draw your sword."

"My sword, sir?"

"Do you mean to tell me you are unfamiliar with swords?"

"No, sir."

"Draw your sword, Captain!"

"Sir?" Constantine asked, uncertain of his new commander's intentions.

"Draw your sword, Captain!" Tarchaniotes repeated, losing his patience.

"But sir!" protested Constantine.

Tarchaniotes quickly unsheathed his sword and threatened Constantine with it. "Captain, if you don't draw your sword, it may prove fatal. Now draw your sword!"

In one rapid move, Constantine drew his sword and placed the tip of the blade at the strategos' throat. "Like this, sir?" he asked, less than innocently.

This new man's agility stunned Tarchaniotes, who motioned Constantine to resheath his sword. The younger man obliged. "You told me you had no military experience. Where did you learn to do that?"

"Sir, I am as well-trained as any man in your army. I was not trained in the army but one would never know that, would he?"

"You are impressive but clever swordplay doesn't make you an officer in the imperial army."

"What need a captain do other than follow the orders of his superiors?"

Tarchaniotes examined Constantine's commission. "Your commission specifies that you are to be a staff officer." He drew a deep breath and sighed, "Well, do as you're told. Stay out of the way and you'll do well." He inspected the commission one more time before he said, "My staff meets this evening after dinner. Be early!"

"Yes, sir," Constantine said dutifully. Then he added, "What should I do in the meanwhile, sir?"

Tarchaniotes scratched his head. He thought for a few seconds before answering. "Look around the camp. Meet with the quartermaster and discuss our water and food supplies. See how much more we'll need if we have to bring along another five hundred men. Prepare a report to present to me after the staff meeting."

"Yes, sir."

"And I want a comprehensive list of all of our supplies!" the strategos barked. "Dismissed!"

Constantine could see through the strategos. He knew that Tarchaniotes was making work for him but he accepted it as part of his mission and snapped to attention, saluted, turned on his right heel, and left the tent.

As the sixth hour approached, Senator Gregory Kastros left his villa in an extravagant coach. Accompanying him were a driver and two footmen. A morning rainstorm made the country road muddy but Kastros was intent on making good time. He fumbled with the long sleeves of his bright yellow silk dalmatic. The gorgeous, floor length over robe was new; the senator was having doubts about his new tailor's abilities, although he had done a masterly job on his new emerald green cloak.

Trees covered both edges of the road on the tight, narrow turn ahead. There, behind a large beech tree, Sister Despina waited for Kastros' carriage. She was dressed, not in her black nun's habit, but in the black stola of a widow, her head wrapped in a black shawl. This, she had determined, would suit her purposes best.

"Hurry, I don't want to be late," Senator Kastros yelled to the driver.

Choosing precisely the right moment, Despina stepped out from behind the beech tree and into the path of the speeding carriage. The driver's eyes became as large as saucers. He pulled desperately on the reins. The team of horses responded as well as it could but to no avail. The ground was too wet, the turn too sharp, the surprise too sudden. The coach skidded off the road, over a bush or two. It came to rest upright against a second beech tree. The driver and one of the footmen had jumped from the carriage before the impact and found themselves on the ground, ten feet from the coach.

Despina managed to step far enough out of the way to avoid serious injury but close enough to give the appearance that she'd been badly hurt. She fell precisely as she needed to, as she had

122 | *George Vasil*

done many times before, landing on her right side in the soft mud. The bruises and abrasions she had administered by an accomplice before the accident, but no one would know that. The wounds brought some discomfort but nothing she couldn't manage. Once she saw that those in the couch weren't badly hurt, she feigned unconsciousness.

Gregory Kastros was barely injured. He jumped out of the carriage, scolding his driver who lay on the grass to his right. "Christ and Mary! What are you doing, Bartholomew?"

The driver answered but Kastros didn't hear a thing. His eyes fell upon the young beauty in the distance lying on the side of the road, motionless and covered in mud.

"Oh my God!" Kastros screeched. He ran over to her, fell to his knees, and examined her injuries. Despina's face was bruised and bloodied, as was her right arm. Her hair was matted with mud and her clothing was torn in a few strategic places. The senator gathered her in his arms and called to his men. "Help me with her. Let's get her in to the carriage. I'll attend to her there. Spiro, bring me a cloth from the trunk and get me some clean water."

Soon Despina was in the carriage. Kastros instructed his men to continue the journey but at a slower pace. As he gently cleaned her face, hands, and feet, her beauty struck him deeply. He dropped the cloth and gasped. Something about this young woman, he wasn't sure what, was curious. *Very curious indeed.* Despina groaned and turned to her right, exposing her right breast through the torn fabric.

Kastros' first instinct was to turn away from the exposed woman, but something about this enticing Aphrodite made him freeze. Timidly, he reached out to replace the torn fabric, but then reconsidered. He removed his new cloak and carefully placed it over Despina's chest.

Although her eyes were closed, Despina knew she'd registered an effect on the old man. *What's the matter, old man? Been a while since you've seen a tit this good? I'll have you suckling from it like a baby one day and have you remember it forever as you rot away in a dungeon.* She moaned convincingly. *Time to draw you in a little closer to my web.*

Despina slowly opened her eyes and moaned again. "What has happened to me?"

"Madam, I'm terribly sorry. There was an accident. That's a very dangerous part of the road. My coach nearly killed you! Please forgive me." Kastros begged.

Despina was impressed with Kastros' truthfulness. How easy it would have been for him to deny everything, blame an anonymous party. But his honesty would work to her advantage. *Poor sap. I'll have no problems with you, Senator.* Despina laid her head back, closed her eyes, and lapsed into slumber. She hoped the journey would be short, for the carriage was most uncomfortable.

Senator Kastros leaned back but could not take his eyes off this stunning creature. Then he noticed something, something that held a firm grip on his attention. *It's a miracle. It's too much of a coincidence not to be.* His wife had died three years earlier and this poor woman, whom he had almost killed, could have been her twin twenty years ago. Was God letting him have his beloved Demetra back after so suddenly taking her away from him? "Demetra," he whispered to himself. He looked thoughtfully at the young woman. He had only recently embarked on his journey and he had a good six to eight hours more of this grueling carriage ride to go until he reached his destination. He looked again at Despina's face. She let out a soft groan. "Stop the carriage!" Kastros yelled to the driver, almost without thinking.

Bartholomew brought the coach to an abrupt halt. "What is wrong, sire?" he asked.

"I think she's badly hurt. We must return to my villa at once. Have Spiro take one of the horses and ride ahead to Senator Dionysios. Tell him I'll be unable to attend his banquet tomorrow. I'll be in contact with the senator later."

Bartholomew performed his task and Spiro left their company. Kastros was soon on is way back to his villa.

Justin and Peter stood studying the maps of the Anatolian peninsula that lay on the table before them. Their small camp at Gallipoli was quiet. They had been among the first to arrive. Only twenty-five of their heavy cavalrymen had come so far, the others delayed by one bureaucratic blunder or another. Some were sent north to the Bosphorus; others had crossed the strait to Chalcedon and were awaiting further orders there. Some had been told to stand down until further notice. This cavalcade of mishaps was most unusual for the Roman Army; for centuries, it was admired as the most efficient fighting force in the Christian and Muslim worlds.

Peter kidded Justin about their continuing mishaps with this command that neither of them wanted. "If we're lucky, our troops should be here by the time the campaign is over," he laughed.

Justin appeared to be lost in the map but his mind was in Constantinople. His last night with Eleni was more beautiful than he could ever imagine. He could still hear her soft, comforting voice and smell her unperfumed skin. He could see the image of her warm hazel eyes emblazoned into his memory. Although leaving on this campaign was the most difficult thing he'd ever had to do, she had made it easier for him. Eleni set his mind at ease, melted his worries, and thoroughly convinced him they would both be protected. At times like this, she was his strength. To worry would be to doubt her. So he filled his prayers with thanks for her and requests for her continued safety.

"When we cross the Hellespont, where are we to land?" Peter asked.

"Don't know. The navy is responsible for getting us across. They'll know."

"I'll wager that they are not too excited about wasting their time to ferry a mere fifty men and their horses."

"No doubt."

Suddenly a soldier entered the tent and snapped to attention. "A Tribune Zervas to see you, sirs."

"Tribune who?" Justin asked.

Before the soldier could respond, the tribune pushed him aside and entered the tent. Peter could see that this officer was not one to stand on ceremony. He looked more like a master sergeant than a senior officer. Justin unwittingly stared at the grizzled officer. The tribune methodically inspected the tent with his eyes. As they fell on Justin and Peter, he sneered at them.

Justin recovered first. He saluted the man and silently encouraged Peter to do the same.

"Gentlemen," the officer said, before Peter snapped to attention, "I'm here to assume command."

Justin was stunned. *He's taking command?* "But sir," Justin protested, "we were given this command by the emperor himself."

"Yes, but your command falls under the command of His Highness Andronikos Dukas, does it not? Now, His Highness has given the command to me."

Justin turned to Peter. Neither could respond.

"Tomorrow I will review the men at dawn. We will cross the Hellespont by the second hour. I have already notified the navy."

"But, Tribune," Justin protested again, "only half of our force is present. We arrived but two days ago. Some of our men have few or no weapons."

Zervas scowled at Justin and said, "There are two kinds of people in this world; those who are subject to circumstance and those who master it. Gentlemen, you obviously belong to the former group. I, however, will not tolerate any more of your inability. I will lead these troops to Nicaea. Those not present now will be redirected to Constantinople to cross the Bosphorus with the emperor." He didn't wait to hear their response. "It is now the seventh hour. You say that some of your men are inadequately armed? You have until dusk to arm them. I suggest you begin immediately. Dismissed!"

Dumbfounded, Justin and Peter hurried from the tent. "I must have missed something there," said Peter. "Where did this fellow come from? Why would Dukas send a tribune to command a mere fifty cataphract?"

"We still haven't figured out why *we're* here. Anyway, we have no time to discuss this," Justin answered. "We have six hours to find these supplies and return. The quartermaster station is nearly three hours away. We'd better get going."

They found their horses and eight pack mules and began their ride northeast to the quartermaster station.

"Do you think he'll give us our tent back?" Peter asked waggishly.

"Not a chance," Justin replied.

Rain sodden roads complicated the journey. They arrived at the quartermaster's muddy and weary, just over three hours from their time of departure. The quartermaster told them most of the weapons for heavy cavalry had been earmarked for troops near the capital but since they needed to outfit only fifteen, he obliged them.

Within half an hour they had obtained most of the necessary gear for each cataphract, including bows, quivers of arrows, broadswords, daggers, long lances, and axes. To be certain their troops would be fully outfitted, they procured corselets similar to their own, steel shoes, leather greaves and gauntlets, conical helmets topped with tufts of blue horsehair, blue cotton surcoats, and small blue shields. These shields were usually strapped to the cataphract's left arm, allowing him the protection of the shield and the full use of both hands while in the saddle.

The young captains considered bringing horse armor but there was no room for it on the pack mules. They gambled that Zervas would agree that, at this stage of the campaign with their enemy hundreds of miles away, the horse armor would be superfluous. It could always be obtained from other quartermasters once the actual fighting began.

Eleni read the psalm again. It had always been her favorite. In its brevity and beauty, it expressed God's relationship to man and man's to God. She read the last verse out loud. "'Surely goodness and mercy will follow me all the days of my life, and I will dwell in the house of the Lord forever.'"

But was it the psalm or the solitude that comforted her? So far, she was allowed to be by herself in the Palace Bucoleon only when praying or reading. At all other times, she was to be under the watchful eye of Empress Evdokia or, in her absence, one of her trusted maidservants or eunuchs.

Eleni thought of Justin as she admired the tall white marble walls, the beautiful mosaic floor, and the silver door of her chamber. She missed him more than she thought. She could see his eyes and feel the thick, bushy hair of his head as her fingers wandered through it. She could hear his voice and taste his lips. While still thinking about her husband, she returned to the psalm and found what she thought to be an appropriate verse. "'You prepare a table for me in the presence of mine enemies.' Justin . . . Justin . . . what have you gotten yourself into?" She kneeled on the floor, crossed herself three times, clasped her hands together, and prayed silently for her husband. *Justin is Justin. Mother is right. Don't make him change. Only God can do that and only if He sees fit to do so.*

A sharp knock at the door interrupted her prayer. "Madam," said the voice on the other side of the door, "Her Majesty Empress Evdokia requests your company at dinner immediately."

"I'm praying," Eleni protested. "I'll be finished soon."

"Her Majesty is most insistent that you come now."

Eleni arose from the floor, crossed herself, and opened the door. Her escort looked at her impatiently. The tall woman had crossed both arms over her chest. Eleni said nothing and followed.

The empress' apartments were quite extensive, as Eleni was to discover. Their effect was overwhelming. The marble walls of the hallways rose fifteen feet upward. Lamps sparkled from intricate golden wall mounts. Jeweled mosaics, accented with gold or silver, glimmered from the walls. Beautiful silk tapestries hung gracefully from the high ceilings. A troop of servants lined the halls. Each was attired in the most gorgeous of silk and woolen raiment, of a myriad of colors. There must have been a hundred of them; the entire corridor was alive with color.

The walk to Empress Evdokia's personal apartments seemed to take forever. Eleni felt winded when she finally arrived. She couldn't decide if it was the physical exertion that tired her (she thought better of that) or the lofty beauty of this dreamlike existence.

The empress used the three largest of these apartments for her personal use. This evening she was dining alone in one of these rooms. Eleni didn't know it, but she was to be the empress' only guest.

Eleni's escort showed her through the tall pair of silver doors and into the luxurious room. The beauty of this chamber exceeded that of the plush hall from which she had just come. Her eyes widened, taking in the delicious surroundings. Tall mirrors in gilded frames, some six feet in length, were evenly placed around the large room, appearing to double its huge dimensions. Bright light glowed from candles and lamps on golden mounts throughout the palatial apartment, their brilliance magnifying the radiance of the precious stones studded in the intricate mosaics, dominating the walls. A large purple silk tapestry embroidered with fine gold thread framed the empress who sat at a large table. A hint of lilac floated in the air.

Evdokia remained seated in all her glory when Eleni entered. As formidable as the great room was, it paled in comparison to its mistress. Eleni marveled at the purple and red silk headdress, accented with a small golden diadem that adorned Her Majesty's imperial head. Her stola, also purple with red embellishments, had long sleeves, flowing to her fingers, each of which was bejeweled with rings of opulence. A thin pearl-studded golden *superhumeral* gracefully circled her collar.

Eleni looked closely, as closely as she could from the distance that separated them, at the empress' face. She was indeed a beautiful woman, her clothing a mediocre embellishment of her stunning God-given features. Unlike many of the women of her court and most of the noble women of the time, Evdokia wore no cosmetics as far as Eleni could tell, not even a slight powdering of face. Pallor, which was indeed fashionable among the nobility, could be obtained through powdering or painting the face or applying leeches to the cheeks to drain them of blood. Empress Evdokia was known to be a pious woman and the Church officially decried "the painting of the face," although many those who were outwardly pious felt no compunction for committing moral infractions as long as it served their needs.

The empress sat quietly, radiating a palpable imperial presence as she studied her new guest. Eleni's escort bowed deeply to her mistress. She acknowledged her with a nod, facilitating the servant's departure. With a fluid downward motion of her hand, Empress Evdokia signaled to Eleni to be seated at the table. The young guest bowed to the empress and took her seat opposite her hostess.

Steaming fish and meats, venison among them, fragrant breads, and fresh varicolored vegetables and fruits enriched the elegant table. Its ornate covering was of the finest linen and silk. A eunuch steward poured red wine from a tall, ornate, ceramic carafe into each of the golden goblets before Evdokia and Eleni and then left the room after placing the vessel on a side table. After receiving a discreet wave from the empress, the chaplain hurriedly blessed the repast and left, bowing to the empress as he did so.

Evdokia waved her hand over the food. "Please join us, Eleni," she said. "Try the squid. It is our cook's specialty."

The staff deftly served first their mistress and then Eleni before they bowed to Evdokia and left her and her young guest to themselves. Now they were alone, the empress and the young wife of a young soldier. Eleni could easily have been distracted by the rich surroundings but her mind was miles away. She savored the memory of her last night with her husband. Evdokia quickly noticed her guest's disquiet. "How are you faring, child?" Evdokia asked.

Eleni did not answer.

Evdokia was not bothered by this egregious breach of imperial polity. "Do you miss your husband, Eleni?"

Eleni was surprised by the sovereign's informality.

"He is a brave man. The empire needs many like him." After the young woman again failed to answer the question, Evdokia added, "Do you know that the emperor is quite fond of him?"

Eleni, thinking of what Justin had told her about the emperor and empress, was unmoved but she acted grateful. Suspecting treachery at every turn, she wanted to tread lightly.

"Are your quarters adequate?" Evdokia asked patiently. "They must be; we never see you!" She took a drink of wine.

Eleni broke her silence. Whether it was because of her fear of offending her hostess or her slowly growing comfort with the situation, she could not say. "I'm settling in nicely, thank you, Your Majesty. I have all I need."

"Myra is seeing to your needs?"

"Yes, Your Majesty."

Evdokia noticed her continued disquietude. "Myra may seem cold but she has served us well for over a decade." Seeing her guest unmoved, the empress offered, "Do you wish to see your family? We can have them brought here. Your mother perhaps?"

Initially the idea was attractive but Eleni's current unease forced a negative reply. "No, that won't be necessary, Your Majesty."

Evdokia was losing her patience with her reclusive guest but didn't want to show it. Instead, she reached forward and gently grasped Eleni's hand. "Eleni," she began, "you're going to be here for a long time . . ."

"Yes, Your Majesty."

"You're going to go mad if you don't try to enjoy your time here," Evdokia said, half-joking.

Eleni boldly looked the empress in the eye, another breach of imperial polity. The warmth those eyes radiated back eased some of her unrest. She smiled demurely at the empress, trying hard to show her gratitude to her hostess. She was in a beautiful palace, eating superb food, and dining with the empress herself. Eleni knew of many people who would love these circumstances but she was not one of them. No one had asked her if she wanted to come here. And despite all of the heavenly surroundings, no matter how Eleni looked at it, she was a prisoner.

"Have some wine, dear." Evdokia pointed to Eleni's untouched goblet. "It is the finest Attican wine available."

"Yes, Majesty." Eleni slowly reached for the wine. She thought again of her husband, what he might be doing, what he might be thinking. *If only I could see him now!* She reconsidered her hostess' words. She *was* going to be there a long time, but hopefully not too long. With brief reservation and another thought about Justin, Eleni shed some of her inhibition and raised the goblet to her lips.

Evdokia saw this and encouraged her guest with her eyes.

"Thank you, Your Majesty, I will," Eleni said, before drinking and swallowing a pleasant sip of the dry red libation.

The dinner that followed was as exceptional as the empress had promised. The wine loosened their tongues and their conversation flowed freely. Any brief interruption would only coincide with a change of course or a replenishment of wine as Evdokia and Eleni talked for hours. Eleni discovered a certain motherly warmth about the woman.

The older woman spoke longingly of her life as a young woman of Eleni's age. "In life," Evdokia began, "we trade youth for wisdom." Then she sighed and chuckled, "And the further one has gone, the more willing she is to surrender some of that hard-earned wisdom for even a morsel of precious youth!"

Eleni smiled back.

"To be a young child again . . ." Evdokia mused.

"What was it like, Majesty?" The ease with which that question jumped out of her own mouth shocked Eleni.

Evdokia smiled. "Relax, Eleni. You are among friends."

"Thank you, Your Majesty."

Evdokia took a sip of wine. "You might be surprised how often we regret our many duties. Even growing up as the child of a wealthy aristocrat had tremendous drawbacks."

"Your Majesty?" Eleni couldn't imagine what she meant.

"Often, when I was a young girl," Evdokia drew closer to Eleni as if revealing a deep secret, "I would sneak away from my governess to join the children of the street in some game or another."

Eleni's jaw dropped.

Evdokia giggled and raised her hand as if to reassure her guest. "Yes. It is true!" Her smile quickly faded. "But always she would find me . . ." Evdokia didn't notice that she had failed to refer to herself in the imperial manner as she remembered those days. Eleni took another sip of wine and a bite of the exquisite squid as she watched the empress return from her dreamlike reverie.

Evdokia continued her story of her playful indiscretions as a young girl. "We wondered what it would have been like to help the fishermen bring their hard-earned harvest to market, sweep the streets in front of a merchant's shop, or sharpen knives for the woodcarver."

"Does Her Majesty wish her life to have been different?"

"Oh, no, Eleni! Being the daughter of an aristocrat did have its advantages," she replied. "I remember the many tutors my father sent to us. Father paid them well, especially the good ones, so each of them tried to outdo the other."

"Who was your favorite, Your Majesty?"

Evdokia sighed as she remembered her silver-haired favorite. "Without a doubt, Kalabokia."

The name meant nothing to Eleni. "Oh . . ." she said graciously.

"I'm sorry child. To us he was Kalabokia," Evdokia mused. She smiled and continued. "We were his pupil for five years. We loved everything about him, from his toad-like voice to his bushy eyebrows." Evdokia paused as she remembered the man. "He would read *Antigone* to us," she said. "We still laugh at the way he moaned Antigone's lamentation over Oedipus:

*Alas, I only wished I might have died
With my poor father: wherefore should I ask
For longer life?"*

Evdokia croaked as if she were an old poet, her arms held out before her. She looked down at the table as though she were indeed crying over her dead father's body.

*"O, I was fond of misery with him;
E'en what was most unlovely grew beloved
When he was with me. O my dearest father,
Beneath the earth in deep darkness hid . . ."*

Then all signs of her satire dissolved as she slowly, thoughtfully, completed the line.

*"Worn as you were with age, to me you still
Were dear, and will be ever."*

Evdokia sat quietly, staring across the table.

Eleni realized the empress' departure from her intended course but wasn't sure how to retrieve her hostess. She softly said, "Your Majesty?"

Evdokia, once summoned, recovered quickly. "Yes, child," she said with a start. "We are sorry. Old Kalabokia meant a little more to us than we thought." She quickly dried a tear from her eye. "No one has done Sophocles better."

The empress continued her reminiscences of her old teacher and all he had given to her. Eleni laughed as Evdokia remembered Aristophanes, cried as Aeschylus' Prometheus lay bound to Mount Elbrus, and listened with fascination as the empress recited Homer:

*"Such honors Ilium to her hero paid,
And peaceful slept the mighty Hector's shade.."*

Eleni was quite impressed by her hostess. She had often heard the stories of ancient Greece from her parents and her father had sometimes read from the great poets and playwrights. She had even gone to the theater but never had she seen such a skillful rendering of these arts as she had this evening.

The empress continued to speak on a variety of topics, the sculpture of Pheidias and Scopas, the histories of Polybius and Thucidytes, and even the painting of Polydorus with such familiarity that could only be acquired by years of study. She also demonstrated a keen knowledge of laws and government, even medicine and the interpretation of dreams. More importantly, a small bond was forming between the empress and her guest. Evdokia, whether deliberately or not, had shown a likeable side of herself. Eleni nudged aside her cautious nature and allowed herself to imbibe of this most interesting woman.

Evdokia enjoyed herself as well. She admitted that she rarely got the opportunity to speak so freely to any other woman and Eleni had proven to be more than a good listener. The empress was impressed by her astute comments regarding these subjects, some of which she had so recently become acquainted.

"I find it curious, Your Majesty," Eleni began, a thoughtful look on her face, "that the Greeks seemed to have the most undesirable traits: Achilles is proud and arrogant; Odysseus and Diomedes are treacherous liars; Menelaus is hard-headed and dull-witted. Agamemnon is selfish and inflexible, while the Trojans, except Paris and Antenor, are brave and virtuous like all heroes should be. Priam is a great and just king; Hector is a brave and noble warrior; the Trojan women are devoted and pure. Isn't it strange that the more despicable people win the war? Are the Greeks the heroes because they won the war? Or are the true heroes the brave Trojans?"

Evdokia was taken aback. For a moment she was speechless. She had never heard such a question, even from the brightest of her teachers. She smiled and chuckled at her guest. "You are a bright one, dear Eleni, indeed. You have a good point. Homer's Greeks do lack certain *Christian* virtues. We have never considered the Trojans to be heroes." She chewed over Eleni's analysis a second and then a third time. "Indeed, very interesting."

A servant quietly entered the room and informed her mistress of the lateness of the hour. The older woman dismissed the servant and then reached out and gently grasped Eleni's hands. "Eleni, you have been placed here so that we can protect you. But even within the walls of our own palace we are vulnerable." She leaned forward and whispered, "There are spies everywhere. We would appreciate your reporting anything suspicious to me or Myra."

Eleni nodded, astounded by what she was hearing. She had chuckled at Justin's alarm in his dealings with the emperor and empress but now, she could appreciate how her husband was feeling. Like it or not, she was in the thick of it too.

"It is now quite late, my dear. Will join us Sunday morning for Divine Liturgy at the Church of Saint Mary, here on the grounds of the palace?" Evdokia asked.

Eleni nodded. "Yes, Your Majesty."

"And perhaps next week you could join us at the theater? Euripides, we believe."

"Yes. That would be wonderful, Your Majesty," Eleni replied.

The empress smiled at her guest, and added, as perhaps an older sister would, "Sleep well."

"Thank you, Your Majesty," Eleni replied, bowing her head as she did so.

Evdokia winked at Eleni and summoned her servants. Myra arrived and escorted Eleni back to her chamber. Once she was alone, Eleni kneeled before her bed, said a short prayer, and quickly dressed for sleep. She had enjoyed the evening with the empress, much to her surprise. Eleni found herself admiring this woman who had shown her a tender side, in spite of the danger in which the empress and emperor had embroiled her and Justin. As she finished dressing, she wondered how much she was like the empress: trapped by circumstance, mourning her lost freedom. Indeed, the vicissitudes of life, no matter how complex, transcended class. Maybe her time in this gilded cage would be tolerable after all.

Eleni thought again about Justin. "I wonder if he's gotten into any trouble yet," she joked under her breath. She remembered their wedding and how handsome he looked. As Eleni drifted off into this dream, she remembered her mother's words from the day before. Justin was Justin. His flaws were few and now they were miniscule. Why had they bothered her so much yesterday?

Eleni sat on her bed and glanced at an exquisite lily carved from ivory that stood on the table adjacent to her bed. *If I were to choose between being this sculpture, beautiful and timeless yet bound to its base forever, and a genuine lily, wild, free, vulnerable, and perishable, I would choose the live lily over and over again.* As her head hit the pillow, she mournfully compared her hostess to the carved ivory flower.

CHAPTER 10

Joseph Tarchaniotes looked up from the map and addressed his officers. "Tomorrow at the third hour we cross the Bosphorus," he announced, his loud voice rousing the hearts around him as it had done for so many years in his service to the empire. "We are the emperor's vanguard. There have been no reports of any Turkish activity west of Lystra. I don't anticipate any contact until we are closer to Armenia." He looked around the table at the faces of his commanders.

"My aides have informed me that all units of cataphracts, light cavalry, scutati, archers, and light infantry are ready." He looked to his aides as if to demand, "Make it so if it is not already!" Then he surveyed the others, asking in a tone that forbad inquiry, "Are there any questions, gentlemen?" The mutterings among the officers assured him there were none. "Good. I will meet with all officers above the rank of tribune at the first hour tomorrow. Dismissed."

The officers filed out in orderly fashion. Only the staff officers remained. "Gentlemen," the strategos said, "you may leave as well . . . except for you, Papakostas; I need to discuss something with you."

"Yes, sir," Constantine replied.

After the others had left, Tarchaniotes approached his newest staff officer. "I was wrong about you, Papakostas. You are an able soldier and a competent staff officer. You possess good organizational skill and you have performed all of the tasks I've given you well." Then he added with a certain pleasance in his voice, "You are quite extraordinary."

"Thank you, sir, but I'm only doing as you command. You have other capable staff officers as well."

"Yes, but something about you separates you from the rest."

"What could that be, sir?"

Tarchaniotes thought for a minute and redirected his attention to his new aide, taking full measure. Constantine's lustrous blue eyes stirred his passion. The strategos had had a few surreptitious liaisons with men before but he had never with one so sublime. The young man's muscular arms an legs made the fire of passion burn more with every passing moment. *He is Adonis in the flesh!* If Tarchaniotes made his move quickly, he could consummate his passion before the ardor a long campaign demanded his full attention. Although such an interlude between men was not unusual in the empire, it was still proscribed by the Church and not tolerated in the army or the navy. *Tonight. It must be tonight.*

"Sir, I just try to do my duty the best I can. Is there anything else I can do for you, sir?"

Tarchaniotes quickly recovered. "No, that will be all."

"Goodnight, sir."

"Goodnight."

Constantine saluted and left the tent. He had seen the reaction of the older man. It was now time for the critical phase of his plan. He was not surprised by the ease with which he had ensnared the older man. In the last twenty-four hours, he had gone out of his way to be present with his quarry as much as possible. If Tarchaniotes had needed anything, Constantine had made sure he got it for him. He had also been certain to subtly expose the older man to various highlights of his stunning physique.

When he reached his tent, Constantine had his aide rouse a messenger. The mounted man arrived soon after and presented himself before Captain Papakostas. Constantine dismissed his aide and handed the messenger a sealed letter he had written earlier that day.

"To whom shall I take this message, sir?" the messenger asked.

"Archbishop Mavrites," Constantine replied. "And immediately." The messenger departed quickly. Constantine found his way to his bed and waited.

"Bring her into the blue room," said Senator Kastros. Bartholomew and another man carried the sleeping Despina from the coach on a litter. "Lay her in bed, gently. Have Esther wash those cuts and bruises. Dress the young lady in some of my wife's old clothes." As the servants left, Kastros looked at Despina's face. *It's uncanny!* He shook his head as he walked out of the room.

As the maidservants undressed Despina, they did not notice her stola's secret pocket and the pouch it contained. They dressed her, unwittingly, in one of Kastros' wife's blue stolas, the one Kastros had always selected as his favorite.

The senator returned to the blue room and dismissed his servants. He looked at this beauty lying softly on the bed. He recoiled when he saw Despina in his wife's over robe. Visions of his departed wife ran through his head and his heart pounded. Their wedding night was suddenly before his eyes. He saw Despina's angelic face and he gasped. Kastros could feel sweat forming on his brow. Despina's body was well covered now but his imagination and memory filled in what he couldn't see. *Demetra!* Kastros turned away, trying to cool his own passion but he failed miserably. He walked over to her and gently ran his hand over her face, feeling her supple skin. When she began to stir, Kastros retreated, leaving her alone.

Despina awoke feeling hungry. She had been anticipating an excellent meal at the villa ever since she arrived. Kastros' obvious fascination with her made her task easier. And although she might be tempted to get this over with quickly, she knew she had to be patient. If she overplayed her hand, Kastros might get suspicious. Despina knew what she was doing. The senator was not her first victim; she made herself comfortable in bed and took a nap. Give it time, enjoy, she thought, as she lay in the bed. She turned her head toward the door and saw that it was open. "Perfect," she said to herself. She closed her eyes and started to softly groan.

Kastros flew into the room.

Despina turned her head left and right as if awakening from a nightmare. "What has happened to me?" she said, her eyes still closed.

"Madam," Kastros responded gently, "Everything is fine."

She opened her eyes and shuddered. "Where am I? How did I get here?"

"I am Senator Kastros," he said. "You are at my villa." Then he added, quite embarrassed, "My carriage nearly ran you over. I'm very sorry."

"I—I—don't remember," Despina said as if awakened from a long sleep. She looked under her blankets. "Oh, my! What has happened to my clothes?"

"Your clothes were badly torn in the accident. I'm so sorry. My maids dressed you," Kastros quickly added, trying to reassure her he had not taken advantage. "The stola is quite nice, isn't it?"

Despina examined the gorgeous garment. The sensual texture of the soft cotton had an invigorating effect on her skin. The silver brocade across her bust accented her natural beauty. She couldn't have chosen a better accessory herself. "Thank you very much but I must leave immediately. I must return to Saint Martha's." Despina tried to get out of the bed. She slyly collapsed back into the bed once she was upright.

"Madam, you are no condition to travel. You've been badly hurt. You've spent the last six hours in that bed." When Despina seemed alarmed, Kastros added, "Don't worry. I'll send word to Saint Martha's that you are here and will be along when you are better." The mention of the Convent of Saint Martha's roused Kastros' curiosity. "You are living at the convent, Madam?"

"I have been staying there these past two weeks," Despina answered. "I'm on my way to Thessalonika."

"Are you hungry?"

Despina nodded. "Thank you for your kindness."

"I'll have Esther start dinner for us immediately." Kastros called to one of the servants as he escorted Despina to the dining area. They sat opposite each other at a rosewood table. "I'm sorry, Madam," Kastros chuckled, "but in all of the excitement I've been unable to ask your name. Imagine that! You've been in my house for over six hours and I don't even know your name!"

Despina's response was carefully measured. "I am Demetra Georgiou." She turned her head away as she wiped a tear from her eyes. "My husband, Damon, died three years ago." She buried her head in her hands as she wept.

The senator's eyes widened. "Oh, I'm so sorry! You're still in mourning," he said as he stood up, clumsily trying to comfort her. As Despina slowed the flow of tears, Kastros tried to explain himself. "Demetra was the name of my late wife," he said, recalling her memory. "She also died three years ago."

Mavrites had prepared her well: Despina had known this all along. "Oh, Senator, I'm sorry to hear that. It would appear that we have something in common." The prey was one step closer to the trap.

"Yes, we do," Kastros said, a hint of a smile on his face. "She was a good woman. We were married for thirty years."

"It sounds as though you've not gotten over her death."

"I don't know if I ever will," Kastros replied. "Can anyone move forward after such a loss?" He paused thoughtfully. "Welcome to my home," Kastros said as he finally stopped his mind from wandering. "I wish I could have met you under different circumstances."

"Thank you, Senator. You are very kind."

"Tell me about your husband, if you don't mind."

Despina bent her head down as if she were bracing herself for a difficult task. "He was a good man," she sighed. "I still can't believe he's dead."

"His memory has brought tears to your eyes," Kastros said. "He must have meant very much to you."

"We were only married a short time," Despina began. "But I loved him so." She reached up to dry her eyes and continued, "Six months after or wedding, Damon was killed in a raid. He was a soldier, light cavalry. His troop was raiding a village near Antioch when a Saracen lance struck him down. They said he died instantly." Despina reached for a pitcher of water at the bedside table. Kastros quickly grabbed it.

"Allow me, please." Kastros poured the water into a nearby cup and gently handed it to Despina. His eyes drank in her graceful hands and long fingers.

"Thank you, Senator."

"The pleasure is all mine," Kastros said. "Tell me, more about your husband."

"His family was not wealthy. His father was a shopkeeper on the Mese," she continued. "But what his father lacked in money, he made up with his generosity. Once a week he would bring clothing and toys for the children at the Orphanage of Saint Paul. That's where we met."

"You worked there?" Kastros asked.

"No, Senator," Despina replied, "I lived there."

Kastros was astounded. "You are an orphan?"

"Yes, Senator."

"May I ask your age, Madam?"

"I'm nearly twenty."

"And where were you before you were at Saint Paul's? I hope you don't mind my asking."

"No, I don't mind, Senator," she replied. "May I finish my water first?"

"Oh, please do! I don't mean to rush you. You know, Madam, that I am one of the largest contributors to Saint Martha's."

Despina smiled as she swallowed her water. She loved this game; she knew everything about him and he knew nothing of her. "I believe I've heard your name mentioned there before. Yes, the sisters are impressed by your goodwill, Senator." She could see the old man smiling proudly, in response to this imaginary praise.

"I was born in Thessalonika. My mother died while giving birth to me. I was her only child. My father was a good man but he was not prepared to raise a child by himself; so when I was three years old, he remarried. My stepmother was eight years younger than my father and had little interest in raising a child, especially one that was not hers. At first, Father was quite happy with her but soon realized his new wife was no substitute for my mother. They quarreled often. Soon he couldn't sleep. Every morning he would look as though he hadn't slept at all the night before. It was destroying his health. He needed more help than his new wife would give him. He decided we needed to be closer to his parents, so we moved to Constantinople, over my stepmother's strong objections."

Kastros frowned.

"My father's parents were quite old. He was the youngest of eight children. My grandfather was very ill; he coughed all the time. *Papou* was also very thin. He always looked as though he hadn't eaten in weeks. His physician told my father that he could die any day. I remember Papou carrying a small piece of cloth with him everywhere he went. His body would shudder as he coughed up blood. Poor Papou died three months after our arrival."

"That's very sad, Madam Georgiou."

"*Yiayia* was one of the kindest people I have ever known," Despina continued, smiling and acting as if this idyllic grandmother she was creating had actually existed. "She took care of Papou, Father, my stepmother, and me all by herself. She was never cross and always smiled. I used to sit in her lap and she would read to me. When I was sick or afraid, she would hold me close. Then everything was better. I don't think I have ever loved anyone more than my Yiayia."

"She sounds like a saint."

"Thank you, Senator. She was," Despina said, pausing and then sighing deeply. Her tone darkened as her smile hardened into a frown. "Soon my father spent less and less at home and his sleeping problems returned. He would go out at night and not return until the next morning or afternoon. My stepmother constantly argued with him. I don't remember them saying anything nice to each other during the entire time we stayed at Yiayia's. And my stepmother never said *anything* to me. For the most part she ignored me. But once in a while she would glare at me as if she wanted to blame me for all of their problems."

"What kind of work did your father do?"

"Father was a silversmith. He had done quite well until Mother died. When we moved to Constantinople, he bought a shop near the Aqueduct of Valens from an Indian man but he rarely went there. He was very sad. He looked as though he was carrying the weight of the world on his shoulders.

"One day, Yiayia became very sick. Her right arm and leg grew weak and she had a hard time speaking. Walking became very hard for her and washing and cleaning were impossible. I would cry as I watched her struggle. But she insisted on continuing to do all she could to take care of us. My father and I knew that she couldn't take care of herself anymore, let alone my father and me. So Father suddenly found himself thrust into the role of caregiver for all of us. Yiayia finally agreed after a number of painful falls that

Father would take over her duties. Needless to say, my stepmother wouldn't lift a finger to help."

"Despicable creature!" Kastros hissed under his breath.

"Because he had not worked much, "Father's money soon ran out. He couldn't work and take care of his mother and me at the same time. He was forced to sell his shop to pay the creditors. My stepmother continued to refuse to help in any way. She actually made matters worse by spending what little money we had on things for herself.

"Yiayia's condition grew worse. Her eyesight began to fail and she had trouble remembering things. At night, she would forget who we were or where she was. I remember her awakening at night, screaming uncontrollably. Father had to tie her to her bed to keep her from wandering around the house or leaving in the middle of the night. There were many sleepless nights. Father was at his wit's end. One day, the Lord mercifully took Yiayia."

Kastros sighed and shook his head.

"Father now seemed incapable of doing anything. Some days he would not get out of bed and my stepmother began to spend more and more time away from the home. One afternoon, I walked to the market and saw her laughing with another man. I ran home and told my father. He immediately arose from his bed, threw on his clothes, and ran out the door. I ran after him but he ran too fast for me to keep up. I found my way to the market but I could find neither my father nor my stepmother. I held my tears in and ran home, biting my lip the whole way."

"You poor child!"

"I spent the rest of that day and that night in Yiayia's house alone. In the morning I awoke and found some bread to eat. By noon I was still alone. I remember wondering if I could spend the rest of my life this way. Somehow I managed for the rest of that day to stay safe and fed. Just before dusk, some soldiers from the constable's office knocked at the door. I knew they must have bad news. At first I refused to open the door but eventually saw that delaying would not change the news.

"When I opened the door, the soldiers asked for my stepmother. When I said she was not there, they gave a look of consternation. Their leader took my hand and sat down at the dining table with me. I still remember how sensitive and kind he was. He told me he was sorry but he had some bad news for me. My father's body had been found floating in the Propontis that morning. One of the people who found him recognized him but didn't know where he lived. It had taken hours for the constabulary to find the house."

"That's terrible!" said Kastros, on the verge of tears.

"My stepmother was eventually found but to my dismay she was not arrested for adultery. My father was buried the next day. My stepmother and I were the only family members present. She showed no sign of loss but appeared unabashedly relieved. After the funeral, she made it clear that she didn't want anything to do with me. Within a week, she sent me to the orphanage."

"What of your mother's parents?" asked the senator, trying to hide his tears.

Despina coughed and reached for the water again. She had not yet woven this part of her story and her mind raced as she tried to piece together the rest of the fable.

"Of course, I only know of my mother's family from my father. I understand that her father was a sailor in the navy. When she was quite young, her father's ship was lost in a storm at sea. There were no survivors. She and her mother moved in with my mother's grandparents. My mother's mother was quite a bit older than my mother. Even so my mother was her only child.

"Then this grandmother became ill after my mother's birth and nearly died. Her midwife told her that another pregnancy like that would cost her her life. Mother's mother died soon after her marriage to my father. Although tradition would dictate that I should be named for my father's mother, I was named for my mother's; Father did this as a tribute to Mother."

"Madam Georgiou," said Kastros, still fighting back tears, "your story is very touching. I am surprised that, after so many years of sorrow, you have retained such a kind and gracious way about you."

"Thank you, Senator, you too are very kind," Despina said. "At Saint Paul's, I was particularly taken by Sister Elizabeth. She was so gentle. It is her memory that inspires me. If there were ever a woman who approached the level of grace of our Lord, it would be she. I promise you that woman will one day be a saint." She nodded her head and paused as if she were remembering Sister Elizabeth.

"I remained at Saint Paul's helping the nuns with the children until just after my seventeenth birthday." Then she sighed heavily. "That was when Damon and his father found me."

Kastros looked approvingly at this beautiful, kind creature before him. He had been impressed by her story so far and wanted to know more. "And how have you been finding Saint Martha's, Madam?"

"I spend Tuesdays, Thursdays, and Saturdays at the Hospital of Saint Luke helping the nuns care for the sick and dying. On Mondays, Wednesdays, and Fridays, I am a schoolteacher. Of course, Sundays belong to the Lord."

"You are a wonderful woman, Madam Georgiou," Kastros said with sincere admiration.

"Thank you, Senator Kastros."

Esther entered with two other servants bringing dinner, which included fried octopus, Euxine sturgeon, and a selection of Greek cheeses. The senator also served both white and red wines but Despina would not partake of them. A dessert of exotic fruits from the length and breadth of the Mediterranean followed two hours later.

"Senator, you've been so kind," Despina said with the serenity of an angel, "but I really must be getting back. I had hoped to get to Thessalonika before Easter."

Kastros had lost track of time and consulted one of his servants regarding the hour. He raised his eyebrows when he learned how late it was.

"I'm sorry, but it is far too late for you to return," Kastros began. "It is almost sunset. The roads are no place for you at this time. You must stay here tonight."

"But Senator, I mustn't," Despina protested.

Kastros held up his right hand, as if to signal his guest to stop. "I insist, Madam Georgiou. It's best that you stay."

Despina feigned uncertainty.

"Please, Madam, let my servants attend to you. You may have full run of the villa. As a matter of fact, I'll show you around after dinner."

"Thank you, but—" Despina said, still pretending to be hesitant.

"You may sleep in the same room," Kastros continued. "I can have you back at Saint Martha's before noon tomorrow." When he saw that she appeared unmoved, he begged, "Please accept my hospitality. I will send word to Saint Martha's that you've been unavoidably detained. I'm certain they'll understand."

"Well, I am quite tired," Despina said, again feigning reluctance to stay. "I truly have had an eventful day." She smiled at him and concluded, "I will accept your gracious invitation. Thank you very much, Senator."

The senator grinned widely, "Good! Good!" He called his servants who escorted his guest back her room and provided her with all she needed, which was very little.

After she was left alone, Despina took the leather pouch from the pocket in her torn dress and placed it under the bed, to be retrieved when the time was right. She lay down, extinguished the lamp on the bedside table, thought about her mission, and smiled contentedly. Things were going very well. Very well indeed.

Later that night Kastros sat in his bedroom. He thought of his guest's beautiful face. He admitted to himself that there was no bringing his wife back but perhaps the stunning widow Georgiou was God's replacement. She had to be. Why would God send someone who looked so much like his beloved Demetra? He kneeled and crossed himself three times.

"Thank you, dear God, for sending her. Please watch over her tonight and may her wounds heal quickly."

He stood and crossed himself while he did so. He saw his face in the mirror and smiled.

Justin and Peter rode into their camp just after the sunset. They, their horses, and their pack animals were exhausted. Zervas was waiting for them.

"Gentlemen, you are late," he growled. "Did you proceed directly to the quartermaster or did you encounter several detours along the way?"

Justin attempted to answer but Zervas cut him off.

"Never mind, you incompetents," the tribune fumed. "It's a wonder you have survived this long in the army, not to mention achieving the rank that you have." When Justin and Peter didn't respond, Zervas sensed that he had them cowed. "We are crossing the Hellespont tomorrow, in case you've forgotten," he snorted, "and my command consists of twenty-seven barely equipped cataphract, two exhausted junior officers and their equally exhausted horses, and fifteen pack mules, eight of which, thanks to you two, are depleted as well!"

Justin and Peter stared back blankly, unwilling to confront their demonic commander.

Zervas rifled through the supplies on the pack mules. "Where is the horse armor?" he demanded.

"There wasn't enough room," Peter explained. "We felt—"

"Gentlemen, need I remind you that we are a troop of HEAVY cavalry?" Zervas bellowed. He hissed and cursed under his breath and growled, "How many more of your blunders must I tolerate?"

The captains remained silent, their courage having deserted them. Zervas jabbed his finger at them as if attacking them with a sword. "Tomorrow you will dispatch one of the men with enough pack animals to bring the needed armor from the quartermaster," he ordered, his exasperation making itself painfully obvious. He yelled as he thrust his hands on to his hips, "Is that understood?"

"Yes sir!" replied the rattled Justin and Peter in unison.

"Dismissed!"

As the two young captains turned to leave their commander, Justin mustered some of the courage that had left him earlier and asked, "Our tent, sir?"

Zervas smiled. "It would appear that your tent is now occupied," he said calmly but then he roared, "by me! Sleep somewhere else!"

"But we're short on tents, sir," Justin protested feebly, "there's no room."

"Honestly, gentlemen, I feel like the mother of two three-year olds!" Zervas boomed. He wouldn't miss an opportunity to demean them. "Find a tent, find a pile of straw at the stable, find a tree to sleep under but get some sleep! I will see you both at my tent just before dawn. Dismissed." Zervas turned away and headed back to the tent without waiting for Justin and Peter to leave.

The young horsemen looked at each other like two little boys who had been caught stealing coins from the offering plate at church. They didn't speak but each knew the other shared his frustration with this new commander. They made their way to a tall oak tree. The ground was dry and surprisingly soft. The late winter night was fairly warm so their heavy woolen cloaks would keep them comfortable. Both spent, they fell asleep in minutes. The young captains knew their next day would be busy and that Zervas would continue his reign of terror.

Joseph Tarchaniotes could not sleep. As much as he tried, he could not erase the face of his new adjutant from his mind. This young man was a perfect soldier, a handsome man, a veritable Achilles. The strategos arose from his cot. He paced about the tent for several minutes. Then he came to a decision. He had to have Constantine; he had to claim this young man's carnal beauty for himself and the time to act was now. He would charge forward, as if he were leading his troops into the enemy's line, and capture this Adonis to make him his own.

Tarchaniotes wrapped himself in his cloak and headed for Constantine's tent. He had only the day before sent the officer with whom Constantine was sharing his tent across the Bosphorus to "be certain that the ferrying procedure was in good working order." Of course this was Constantine's idea but Tarchaniotes adopted it as his own. He left his tent just after midnight, skillfully evading the camp patrols and finding his way to his destination.

Tarchaniotes knew that the tent would be empty so he directed his attention immediately to his sleeping adjutant. A burning candle in the tent's corner allowed just enough light for the older man to appreciate the handsome young Apollo. The brawny young captain lay across his bunk, asleep, his blanket failing to cover his muscular chest and legs. The strategos slowly approached the cot. He bent down to take in Constantine's sculptured face. As he drew closer, he could smell the musky scent of this perfect male body. He savored the earthy odor as his eyes drank in what the candlelight would allow.

Suddenly Constantine stirred. Tarchaniotes gently calmed him and took his hand. Constantine looked deeply into the eyes of his commander. The older man leaned forward and placed his lips squarely on those of the young officer. At first Constantine offered resistance but soon he gave in. Tarchaniotes was in ecstasy and responded by tightening his embrace of his new lover. He stroked Constantine's full, wavy black hair. Soon his hands found their way to the young soldier's muscular hips and thighs. The younger man remained passive, which excited the strategos even more. Tarchaniotes next moved his head toward Constantine's nearly hairless, brawny chest and found it particularly titillating. His tongue examined the younger man's nipples with wild abandon. Simultaneously, his strong hands caressed Constantine's firm buttocks. After they had had their fill, the right hand slipped forward to find the young man fully aroused; the left had move up the soldier's sinewy back, noting a fine misting of sweat along the spine. He heard Constantine moan his enjoyment. The young buck had been tamed!

Without warning, three armed men burst into the tent.

Tarchaniotes tried his best to recover. He wrapped a blanket around his waist and verbally attacked the intruders. "What is the meaning of this intrusion?" he fumed. "I'll have you all arrested and court-martialed!"

One of the men replied in an annoyingly arrogant tone, "Strategos Tarchaniotes, are you aware that sodomy is a sin and this sinful practice has no place in an army whose patron is the Blessed Theotokos?" The Virgin Mary was the patron saint of the army as well as Constantinople.

Tarchaniotes turned pale. He recognized the voice immediately. This biting indictment was delivered coldly by none other than Andronikos Dukas. The strategos' throat dried almost instantly, preventing him from speaking. And even if he could speak, what could he say?

One of the soldiers lit the tent's only lamp and Dukas sat with commanding presence on the edge of the cot. He displayed a large, self-satisfied smile and slowly ran his left hand over his trimmed black beard as if contemplating what to do next. But Tarchaniotes knew Dukas well enough to know that this oldest son of Caesar John Dukas had planned this entire event from its inception and he, Romanos Diogenes' top general, had easily fallen prey to it.

Andronikos motioned to the two soldiers who had accompanied him; they grabbed Constantine.

"No! What are you doing?" Constantine protested as the soldiers rousted him from the tent.

"Joseph Tarchanoites," said Andronikos Dukas, after Constantine and the others had left, "I believe you have some explaining to do." Dukas spoke with an irritating air, toying with his captive who had no chance of escape.

Tarchaniotes couldn't speak.

"Strategos, are you aware of the trouble you are in? You have been a soldier for thirty years. You have a very distinguished record. You are the emperor's favorite strategos. What would he say if he knew of tonight's escapades? Your career, probably your life, is over."

The strategos remained stoic and defiant in this defeat. He would not admit his crime. He would not admit that his noble career had just been ended by this brief, forbidden sexual interlude.

"The emperor will indeed be disappointed. Now his grip on the reins of power is tenuous at best. Having a lustful sodomite as his best strategos leading the most important campaign of his reign will be intolerable." Dukas waited briefly for a reply. Receiving none, he stood up and turned to walk out of the tent.

"What do you want?" Tarchaniotes muttered.

Dukas turned back slowly. "Did you say something, Strategos?" Dukas asked.

"What do you want?" The guilty strategos spoke more loudly.

"I knew you were a reasonable man," Dukas began, savoring the strategos' vulnerability. "Please sit," he added, motioning to Tarchaniotes. Dukas took his seat again but the strategos remained standing. "I want your complete cooperation. Is that too much to ask to save your career and your life?" Dukas smiled devilishly at his victim.

Tarchaniotes didn't respond.

"Very well then. I'll assume that if you say nothing, then you're in full agreement."

Tarchaniotes remained silent.

"Oh good. Well, let me tell you what you *will* do. You will not move your troops without *my* order. You will respond only to *my* commands. You will act in no way that might raise even a hint of our *new* relationship. As far as anybody knows, you are following your emperor as any dutiful strategos would. If you divulge this secret to anyone, I will share tonight's secret with the world." Dukas glared at Tarchaniotes, waiting for an answer.

The strategos glared back but said nothing.

"Very well then. I'm certain this agreement will work out well, Strategos. I'm assigning Tribune Aristotle Markos to you as my personal representative. And do treat him well, Tarchaniotes." Dukas stood and addressed the strategos one last time. "You will await my orders. Are there any questions?" Expecting none, Andronikos Dukas turned to leave but a question from Tarchaniotes interrupted his departure.

"Why? Why are you doing this to me?"

Dukas turned around. "You will see, Strategos, you will see. However, to show you I can be kind as well as cruel, I'll offer you a more positive incentive to cooperate. My father has a nice villa on the isle of Naxos. I may be able to persuade him to throw that into the bargain."

The strategos was unmoved. He knew that Andronikos was lying, playing with him because he was totally at his mercy. Such prizes didn't interest Tarchaniotes; he was a true soldier and material rewards meant little to him.

"Markos will report to you just after dawn. Strategos, I'm looking forward to our new relationship." Dukas smiled and exited.

Tarchaniotes was stunned. In a brief splash of time he had become Dukas' puppet. A few minutes before he was one of the most respected men in the empire. Now he was but a lacky. Undoubtedly the Dukas were plotting the emperor's demise. How would they use him to betray his commander? His friend. He sat on the bunk, held his head in his hands, and began to weep. There was nothing he could do. He was in bed with the Devil himself.

Adronikos Dukas made his way across the camp toward Constantine, who was now fully dressed, and the soldiers who had dragged him from the tent.

"You do exceptional work, Papakostas," Dukas said. "Tell Archbishop Mavrites the Dukas are again in his debt."

"Yes sir, I will tell him," Constantine replied. Then he added hesitantly, "May I leave now, sir?"

"You may go, Captain, but first," Andronikos began, throwing his arm over Constantine's shoulder, "take this token of my personal appreciation." Dukas removed from his left fourth finger a stunning gold ring topped by a large ruby. He handed it to Constantine.

"No, sir, I can't," protested Constantine.

"Please do," Dukas said. "I would consider it an insult if you would not take it. Please."

Constantine begrudgingly accepted the beautiful ring. "Thank you, sir. Thank you."

"No, it is I who thank you," said Dukas.

Constantine left the other three and made his way to his horse, which had been brought by one of the companions of Dukas. He quickly mounted the horse and went on his way. As he did so, he turned around and waved to the others, wishing to convey his thanks for this precious gift.

Dukas acknowledged Constantine's gratitude with a friendly wave of his own. When Constantine was out of earshot, he turned to one of his men. "Kill him." The soldier acknowledged the order, showing no sign of surprise. "And bring back that ring, too," Andronikos added. "My father would kill me if he found out I gave it away."

"Wake up!" shouted Zervas, jolting Justin and Peter from their restless sleep. They snapped to attention, dropping their wool cloaks. "Argyropoulos! You go to my tent immediately!" barked Zervas. Half asleep, Peter ran forward. "My tent is behind you, idiot!"

"I'm sorry, sir," Peter apologized. He reversed his tracks and ran to the tent.

By now, Justin had realized that darkness still prevailed. It was nowhere near dawn. "Sir," Justin said, "I believe we are a bit early."

"Change of plan, Phillipos," the tribune grumbled. "We're leaving now. Roust the men." When Justin failed to act immediately, Zervas roared, "Do you think you are capable of that, Captain?"

"Yes, sir," Justin replied coolly. He calmly turned on his right heel and went to work. As he went from tent to tent, awakening his men and readying them for their departure, his hate of Zervas grew. This pompous, arrogant, cruel tyrant made his blood boil. In all of his years of military service, he had never encountered such a hellkite.

Gregory Kastros arose unusually early that morning. His excitement about his guest had reduced his usual time of sleep by three hours. As he dressed, he smiled, recalling the vivid dreams of Demetra Georgiou he had had in the night. This woman had a fantastic affect on him. He felt twenty years younger and ready to swim the Bosphorus for her. He sprinted down the stairs to the dining area. There he startled the servants. They were not used to seeing their master awake just an hour past dawn. Word spread quickly to the other servants who left their chores to see this unusual sight. Kastros smiled at them and made his way to the kitchen.

"Esther," he called, seeking his best cook.

The older woman slowly walked out of the pantry. "Senator?" she asked.

"Esther," Kastros asked, finding her at last. "I need you to make the best breakfast you've ever made."

"Sir?"

"Madam Georgiou," he continued, "our guest. I would like you to create something special for her."

Esther smiled. "Yes, Senator," she said, giggling as she made her way back to the pantry. Kastros had to chuckle as he smiled. The reaction of his staff amused him but the chief source of his mirth was his joyful anticipation of this day with his guest.

Meanwhile, Despina was awake and planning her day. She, too, was smiling as she thought of the day ahead. Mavrites had given her plenty of time to complete her mission and she was planning on taking full advantage of that. *He's as good as mine!* The villa's soft bed and excellent food were something she wanted to savor as long as possible. As Despina finished buttoning her stola, she heard a soft knock at the door.

"Madam?" asked a voice on the other side of the door.

"Yes," Despina answered, surprised she would be summoned at such an early hour.

"Oh, thank goodness," said the voice behind the door. "We thought you might still be sleeping."

"No, I am awake," Despina said, still wondering why the servant had come to her door so early in the morning.

"That's good, Madam. Senator Kastros requests your presence in the dining room. Will you be able to come?"

Despina was surprised. She had heard that Kastros was a late sleeper. "Yes, I'll just be a little bit." She hurried over to the vanity, splashed some cool water from the basin on her face, and grabbed a beautifully jeweled silver brush. After a few quick strokes in front of the mirror, she turned and walked to the door.

When she slowly opened the door, Despina saw the servant who announced the senator's invitation. She escorted her to the dining room where Kastros and his chaplain, Father Nicetas, whom Despina had met last evening, were waiting. When the senator saw her, he stood up and beamed. The chaplain also greeted her.

"Did you sleep well, Madam?" Kastros asked.

Despina looked at the table before her. It was covered with foods of all kinds, many of them she knew to be very expensive. In the center of the table was a basket filled with jonquils, crocuses, and daffodils. She gasped as she beheld the beauty before her.

"I am also very fond of beautiful flowers," Kastros said. "Perhaps we can take a walk in the gardens after our meal."

"Yes," replied Despina, still rapt in the beauty of the table.

The chaplain blessed the meal and excused himself to join the staff in the kitchen, per Kastros' earlier instructions. Despina ate her fill of the many sweet breads, cheeses, yogurt, and pastries the table had to offer. The honey was the most flavorful she had ever tasted: sweet yet floral. She found it difficult to contain her greedy appetite. Despina had to remind herself that such overindulgence might betray her mission. Through her strongest efforts, she maintained an air of delicacy.

After the repast, Kastros gently took her hand and led her outside. There, she discovered that the display on the table was but a small portion of the beauty this garden held. The early spring flowers danced gently in the soft morning breeze. Some still held the morning dew, which slowly dripped from their opening petals.

Kastros walked her to the middle of the garden from where she could survey the two acres of well-cared-for plants. "Over there," Kastros pointed to a corner of the garden only ten feet away, "is where we picked our flowers for the table this morning."

Despina drank in the color of the brilliant blossoms. Just beyond them, she saw spring snowflakes, their drooping, bell-like flowers attracting several passing bees.

"In April," Kastros added, "the tulips are up. We've acquired quite a few beautiful varieties over the years."

As the senator led Despina to another part of the garden, she asked, "Do you do much in the garden?"

Kastros smiled and boomed, "Why of course! The gardeners do a great deal of the maintenance but I personally choose the bulbs and seeds. And whenever I can, I come out here and play in the dirt. I designed this garden."

Despina could not hide her amazement. Kastros saw this and took her to another part of the garden. Here were sculpted cypresses, acanthuses, just-blooming azaleas, and hyacinths that had yet to declare themselves.

"They're all so beautiful," Despina said, still absorbing the vibrant surroundings.

"Over there," said Kastros, pointing past a low wall several yards away, "I have built a pond, complete with lotuses, frogs, and fish." He then turned to his right and pointed toward a hill in the distance. "And on that hill, I grow some of the best grapes in Thrace. Last year we had some excellent wine."

Despina looked out over the green hillside, through the morning fog, and sighed, "It's all so beautiful, Senator."

"I'm glad you are enjoying it," he said graciously. "Now if you'll come with me, I will show you the rest of the villa."

As they turned, Despina saw the stunning classical Greek façade of the villa. Its giant fluted Ionian columns were of the purest, whitest marble she had ever seen. Walking toward the building, she felt lost in the villa's magnificence, as if she were in a dream. Suddenly, she stumbled over a small rock in the path. Kastros caught her.

"Are you well, Madam?"

The near-fall awakened Despina from her dreamlike state. A voice from inside scolded her. *Remember why you are here!* Despina felt the senator's strong arms holding her. She saw that this occurrence created a circumstance she should exploit. It was time to act.

"Are you all right?" Kastros asked again.

Despina looked deeply into the old man's eyes. "Why, I'm fine, Senator," she answered. "I dread to think how I'd be feeling if you hadn't caught me."

"Madam Georgiou —" he began shakily.

"Please," Despina said in a breathy voice, "call me Demetra." She saw his jaw open. *Right on target!*

"Of course," Kastros blurted out clumsily, "Demetra." He smiled at her and continued. "May I show you the inside of the villa?"

"Oh, yes," she replied, "that would be wonderful."

Just as the two neared the building, a young Arab man rushed up to Kastros. He was well-dressed, obviously a man of substance.

"Senator! Senator!" he exclaimed, nearly out of breath.

Despina detected the distinct odor of an overheated horse diffusing from the man's soiled clothing. She smiled graciously as he approached. *Who is this fellow?*

"Emmanuel!" Kastros said, extending his hand with an enthusiasm to equal the other man's. "How are you? You look exhausted."

"I've just returned from Damascus!" Emmanuel replied, his face full of excitement. Then he realized that he and the senator were not alone. He turned to Despina. Politely, he bowed and excused himself. "I'm sorry, Madam. I don't believe I've had the pleasure."

"Madam Georgiou," Kastros began, looking from Despina to the newcomer, "this is Emmanuel Ghassani. He's a good friend of mine."

"I'm pleased to make your acquaintance, Madam," he said with a gentlemanly flair. He bowed again before Despina.

"I'm pleased to meet you, too, Lord Ghassani," Despina said, still taking her measure of the man.

"Senator, I believe we need to talk," Ghassani said to Kastros.

"Yes, of course," Kastros replied. He turned to Despina. "We have some urgent business to discuss. Will you please excuse me?"

"Certainly, Senator," Despina replied.

"Thank you, Madam Georgiou," Kastros said. "I'll have one of the servants show you the villa."

"That's very kind of you, Senator, but I believe I'm quite comfortable by myself."

"Are you certain?" Kastros asked, as any good host would.

"Yes, think nothing of it," Despina replied.

"Thank you. I shouldn't be long," the senator said. He turned and threw his arm around the Arab.

As the two walked toward the palatial house, Despina attempted to follow at a distance but she was almost immediately accosted by three of Kastros' well-meaning servants.

"Madam," one of the women asked kindly, "may we show you more of the villa?"

Despina's eyes remained glued on Kastros and his guest as they entered the house and went to the right. When the woman repeated the question, Despina graciously accepted the invitation and followed the two women into the house. Unfortunately, the women turned left as they entered and not to the right, the way that Kastros had gone, the way Despina had *hoped* to go. She shot glances over her left shoulder, down the hallway that Kastros must have taken. He was not in sight.

Despina cursed under her breath.

The Arab's mentioning his return from Damascus certainly raised her curiosity. Arabs in Constantinople were not unusual, but most were traders and kept to themselves. *Why was this one so friendly with a Roman senator?* The empire was currently at peace with its Arab neighbors, but these truces were often tenuous. Something was going on here. But what was it? Could it be useful to her mission?

Eleni had slept well, due in large part to food and wine of exceptional quality plus a growing feeling of comfort with her hostess or, as Eleni jokingly referred to the empress in her absence, her jailer. She arose from her bed quickly. Last night's pensiveness had not abated. She thought of Justin, of course, but today it was her mother who would not leave her thoughts.

Eleni saw that her mother was becoming more important than her father to her. She thought about how unusual it had been for her to seek her mother's counsel about Justin the other day. But, even more intriguing, today she was thirsting for her mother's company more than ever before. Eleni chuckled as she thought of how her independence from her mother had been established years ago, but the need for her at this time had become great. A year ago, she would have consulted her father freely on any issue. Yet, today, her father's opinion meant less to her. Why, she couldn't say. Perhaps she had completely figured him out. Maybe, because of her frequent discussions with him in the past, she had mastered his perspective. And so, as she longed for a new perspective, her mother became the object of her search.

Eleni had to admit she felt strange about the situation. In the past she had, out-of-hand, considered her mother's insight as worthless. Yet her recent conversation with her mother about Justin had shown her a side of her mother fascinated her. Maybe because she was now a wife, the opinion of another wife was more significant. Eleni felt more than a little confused by the whole situation but was determined to speak to her mother again soon.

Myra appeared at the door, Eleni had just summoned her. "Madam, what do you wish?" the servant asked.

"I would like to leave the palace to see my mother."

Myra smiled. "We both know that is against Her Highness' wishes." Eleni sheepishly acknowledged that fact. "Why don't I send for your mother? She can spend the day with you here at the palace."

"That would be very nice. Thank you."

"May I get you something else, Madam?"

"No thank you, Myra. You are very kind."

"Thank you, Madam. It is my pleasure to serve you."

CHAPTER 11

By the second hour of daylight, Zervas, Justin, Peter, and twenty-seven heavy cavalrymen perched on a hill overlooking an isolated wharf in a small harbor near Gallipoli on the west end of the Hellespont. The strait was about a mile wide at this point. Across it, the soldiers could see the western shoulder of Asia. A fierce wind blustered against the faces of the troops with increasing intensity. The wind and overcast sky were daunting. Peter knew it was what Zervas hoped to avoid.

"This is no wider than the Ister," Justin said to Peter. "The crossing should be easy."

"Against the wind and the current?" Peter retorted. "Think again."

Peter watched Zervas wait impatiently. He repeatedly strutted to and fro, as if each step he took would hasten the ships arrival. But the ship that was to ferry them across the channel was nowhere to be seen.

"The dromon is late!" Zervas fumed.

Though it was a galley designed for battle, the dromon had a surprising capacity to carry cargo as well. Peter had captained three of them. The horses as well as the supplies would be carried onboard the ship that was propelled by oars and the two triangular sails. When they embarked they could proceed directly without having to find new horses and equipment.

The tardiness of the ship and the bad conditions boded poorly for their passage. Crossing against a swift current was trying enough, but throwing this hostile wind into the equation heightened the danger. Delaying the crossing would be worth it if it would assure a safe passage. Nothing had gone well since they had arrived at in the area. First, their command was incomplete, almost half of their cataphract being absent. Then, Justin and he lost their command to this minion of the Devil himself. And now, a tardy naval vessel stalled their advance. But he couldn't blame any sea captain for balking at transporting such an insignificant group at the risk of wrecking his ship under these unfavorable conditions.

"Phillipos!" Zervas barked.

"Yes, sir!" Justin replied as he rushed to his commander's side.

"We have orders to pick up additional equipment in Saint Cyril when we land. We will acquire a few horses and some of the supplies of a unit that was badly mauled by a Turkish raiding party last week. Many were killed and most of the survivors are in a field hospital. The rest are being sent back to Constantinople."

"Yes sir."

Zervas bit his lip.

Peter detected the uncharacteristic uneasiness in the despot's voice and watched Zervas carefully. *How will the demon react?* As the wind picked up, Peter wrapped his woolen cloak tightly around himself. He looked out at the rolling strait and crossed himself. "This is going to be fun," he sighed sarcastically under his breath. He turned and looked at Justin, whose eyes were staring into nothing. He knew that his friend must be daydreaming about Eleni. Justin's woes were double his but he was holding up well without his bride.

"There she is!" shouted one of the younger cataphract. Peter peered to the northeast and saw a galley's two lateen sails on the horizon. The unrelenting wind picked up and whipped the soldiers' cloaks and the horsehair tufts atop their conical helmets. The only benefit of such turbulence was that the approaching galley would arrive soon, provided it could dock without incident.

The ship was smaller than Peter had anticipated. It was thirty yards long and about six across. The draft was shallow, no more than five feet. The bottom of the dromon was flat. A keel wasn't needed for a fast ship like this to get around in the Mediterranean Sea. Shields hung on the sides of the ship to protect the sailors from flying missiles. Other areas of the hull were draped with oxhides or covered with lead. A flaming arrow or other incendiary landing on these was much less likely to start a fire than if it landed on the wooden deck.

The dromon had two banks of oars. Fifty oarsmen worked on each side of the upper deck and twenty-five on each side of the lower deck. Once engaged in battle, the sailors on the upper deck would be called upon to defend their ship or attack the opponent. Meanwhile, the oarsmen on the lower deck would continue to power the ship with the long oars. There was usually a contingent of fifty marines on board. They were the vanguard of any attack and the bulwark of any defense of the vessel. Today they were absent to make room for the cataphract and their horses. Typically a dromon could carry twelve horses with its usual crew.

The tall triangular sails were made of linen, although cotton was also used. They were attached to a long, sloping yard arm. One end reached above the masthead and the other nearly swept the deck. The sails actually crossed the ship; if the port side of the sails were above the masthead, the starboard sides would be secured to the rail near the starboard deck. The dromon was steered by large oars, or steering boards, one on each side of the stern. The stern rudder was an innovation that was relatively new and some Roman ships had them, usually the taller cargo ships. The rudder would make its appearance in Western Europe over a century later. These dromons were smaller, lighter, and faster compared to the larger, more cumbersome battle galleys, which were large enough to carry catapults and turrets from which other war machines could fire.

The wind gusted while the galley continued down the Hellespont. The sails came down as the ship continued its approach. The crew struggled against the dogged wind while the galley made its way deliberately toward the harbor entrance off the ship's starboard bow. The titanic swells shoved the galley southwestward with tremendous fury, threatening to push it past the entrance.

"He's in trouble!" Peter shouted to Justin over the howling wind. "He kept his sails up too long coming down the strait and he's picked up too much speed. If he misses the harbor entrance completely, he'll drift past us! If he gets his turn started but can't fully get into the harbor, he'll crash on the rocks at the south end of the harbor!"

Justin looked on in horror. The galley's demise seemed inevitable.

"If this captain has any tricks left, he'd better use them now!" Peter added.

The cavalrymen watched as the crew extended their oars and tried to stop, if not slow, the ship by rowing in reverse. The task at first appeared to be working but soon the forces arrayed against them overtook the harried oarsmen. What the high winds had started, the rapid current seemed intent on finishing as it pulled the galley farther southwestward.

Then one of the crew threw an anchor over the starboard stern.

"What the hell is he doing?" Peter asked.

The galley slowly ground to a halt but its panicked arrest appeared useless. It had stopped but it was still oriented southwest and could not turn west to the harbor entrance. To make matters worse, the galley began to slowly accelerate to the southwest. The swift current nullified the dropped anchor, pulling the ship toward the Aegean, dragging its anchor along the shallow bottom of the Hellespont.

However, the sea captain had one more weapon in his battle against the raging elements. The oarsmen stood poised, their oars held above the water. A second anchor flew over the starboard bow and into the raging water. The ship still slid forward but it slowly rotated to starboard on its bow anchor. As the galley rotated through ninety degrees to the northwest, the portside oarsmen threw all of their effort into their work and the captain cut the stern anchor cable. Simultaneously, some of the crew on the starboard pulled up the bow anchor from the floor of the Hellespont while the others worked their oars for all they were worth.

"How did he do that?" Peter shouted at Justin, throwing his hands heavenward. "That was amazing!"

The dromon moved slowly into the harbor. The oarsmen had defeated the mendacious current. The astonished cavalrymen erupted in wild cheers when the galley neared the dock. Peter shook his head and sighed in relief.

Peter watched Justin inspect the dromon once it pulled close. He turned to Peter like an excited child and asked, "Where are they, Peter?"

Peter could barely hear over the roar of the cheering soldiers. "What?" he asked.

"The fire tubes!" Justin said, still brimming with excitement.

"Look at the bow," Peter instructed, smiling at Justin's childlike fascination with the vessel.

A six-foot-tall green dragon sat poised at the bow. From its red mouth a serpentine tongue projected and two large fangs sprang from the upper jaw and two from the lower. Each five-foot wing spread out thirty degrees from each shoulder. Two tubes, each about half a foot in diameter, projected forward about two feet from the foremost bulkheads, one to the left, under the wing, and one to the right, under the opposite wing.

"There they are!" Justin said, beaming from ear to ear as he nudged Peter in the ribs.

While Justin inspected these wonders of Roman military technology, Peter remembered the history of these deadly weapons. From tubes such as these, Greek fire was pumped onto opposing ships with devastating results. The inextinguishable flames consumed any enemy sailors who could not jump overboard soon enough. This deadly weapon had first been used in the seventh century against Arab warships attacking Constantinople. The tubes decimated the naval assault. Without Greek fire, the Roman Empire, and probably all of Europe, would have drowned in the Muslim tide. It was indeed one of God's many blessings upon the Roman Empire.

Zervas remained taciturn. He walked through the jubilant troops up to Peter and Justin.

"Come with me," Zervas ordered. They followed him to the wharf. Near the galley, they could hear the enthused crew congratulating themselves on their accomplishment. Two sailors jumped from the bow on to the wharf as the ship docked. Sailors tossed lines from the vessel to those men on the pier who promptly secured them and brought the galley to her resting place. The rest of the crew remained aboard except the captain. Once the bow and stern lines were set, his men lowered the gangplank and he stepped off, alone.

The red-haired sea captain swaggered forward confidently. He was in his mid-twenties, over six feet tall, and muscular. He wore a bright green tunic with a black leather skirt and laced-up black boots. He couldn't help but show his pride in accomplishing this difficult feat.

Zervas strutted on to the pier, followed by Justin and Peter, and immediately made his presence known. "Captain, that was quite an achievement."

The captain responded, "Well, it wasn't quite as smooth as I wanted but, given the conditions . . ."

Then Zervas pounced. "Given the conditions, you should have approached the harbor much more slowly! You needlessly sacrificed one of your anchors and put your entire ship in great danger! Your antics nearly sunk your ship and delayed my transport to Asia! I hope that not all of the navy's captains are so reckless!"

"And who are you, sir?" the captain retorted, unperturbed.

"I'm Tribune Zervas. You are to transport my men and me across the strait to Saint Cyril. But I'll not let you endanger the lives of these men with such inept seamanship!"

The sea captain was indignant. "This channel is very unpredictable. I've been sailing for ten years and I know what I'm doing. How dare you tell me how to sail my ship!"

"That ship belongs to the emperor, not you," Zervas countered.

"Then shall we wait for the emperor to come take you across?" the captained snapped back with a sardonic smile.

Zervas had been outmaneuvered. Like it or not, he needed this insolent captain to cross this strait. His berating of the man was not helping his cause. He turned in a huff and stomped off the wharf. He returned to the troops on the hillside, leaving Justin and Peter to deal with the smirking seaman. Justin moved forward toward the captain.

When he approached, the captain glared at Justin who smiled back and said, "Unlike my commander, I think you did quite well, given the circumstances."

The once-threatened sailor cautiously let his guard down. "And who are you, sir?"

"Justin Phillipos. And you are . . . ."

"Andreas Stathopoulos," replied the mariner, warming up to Justin's conciliatory efforts.

Justin tentatively extended his right hand. Stathopoulos did not react but Justin kept his hand extended. Seeing Justin's persistence, the daring seaman gave in and grasped Justin's hand, shaking it vigorously. Seeing this, Peter trotted down to the wharf and joined them.

"This is my associate, Captain Peter Argyropoulos," Justin said, introducing Peter to Stathopoulos.

"Captain," Stathopoulos said, extending his right hand.

"That was quite a landing. Very impressive," Peter said. He shook the mariner's hand. "I've spent a few years at sea but I never saw a move like that one."

"I appreciate that you gentlemen are more gracious than your commander. He reminds me of the back of a mule I once rode."

"Tribune Zervas is a difficult man, to say the least," Justin said. "We just met him. Before he arrived, that small troop back on that hill was ours. We are to cross here and join the main army near Nicaea."

"Pardon my asking, but why didn't you cross up north, at the Bosphorus?" asked Stathopoulos. "It seems a waste to send a ship to transport thirty people."

"Not my idea," Peter answered.

"Unfortunately, my career in the navy has seen stranger requests. I could tell you some wild stories—" Stathopoulos said, warming up to the young soldiers. He walked them down the wharf toward the shore. "I'll hve my crew help you get your men on board and we can get under way."

"What about the wind?" asked Justin. "Shouldn't we wait for it to die down before we cross?"

"You'd have to wait until April for that to happen," answered the captain. "We need to go before that storm comes. Look at that sky," he said as he pointed at the gathering dark clouds, "That will make things even more difficult."

Justin and Peter headed up the hill to report to Zervas. "He's not going to like the fact that we succeeded where he failed," Peter said.

"He couldn't hate us anymore than he already does. What do we have to lose?"

Zervas was stone-faced. He said nothing when his two junior officers returned.

"Sir," Justin began cautiously, "the captain has suggested we board now. He's concerned a storm could be upon us at any moment."

"Very well," Zervas said. "Have the men fall in. Let's get this over with."

Justin and Peter quickly accomplished their task. The soldiers, their horses and their supplies were quickly loaded yet Zervas did not budge from his spot on the hill.

Justin looked up at the liverish tribune. "He's still on the hill," he said to Peter.

"Do you think that Stathopoulos would leave without Zervas if we paid him?"

"He'd do it for free, as a favor," quipped Justin.

"One of us should go get him," Peter noted.

Justin did not respond and Peter was not about to repeat himself.

Justin sighed deeply. "I might as well do it," he moaned. "I'd just as soon take an arrow in the shoulder but I'll get him."

"I owe you for this, Justin."

Justin slowly walked down the gangplank, along the wharf, and up the hill. As Justin climbed the hill, Zervas did not look at him but continued his fixation on the opposite shore. When Justin arrived in front of his commander, Peter saw him salute smartly. Zervas, who didn't break his intent gaze, asked Justin something. Justin responded and Zervas turned toward Justin and nodded.

Zervas reached the wharf, walked to the galley, and boarded without saying a word. He found a place to stand at the port bow, well away from anyone. Stathopoulos stood on the deck just in front of the small enclosure at the stern reserved for the captain and any dignitaries travelling aboard. He looked at Justin who nodded and then joined Peter amidships on the starboard.

The sea captain stood tall on the deck and looked down at his men standing ready in wells in the deck at their oars. He looked up at the two triangular sails. While the catafract were loading he had the crew lift the yard of each sail over the top of each mast, repositioning them so they would be set for a starboard tack.

Stathopoulos barked out his first orders. "Prepare to get under way."

Two sailors pulled the gangplank on board. A third sailor stood at the ready at the bowline while a fourth waited at the stern. The first mate ran up to his captain. Stathopoulos nodded and the sailor ran fore and then aft, yelling, "Cast off the bowline!" The sailor at the bow complied and the bow was freed from the wharf. Stathopoulos looked again to the first mate who ordered, "Cast off the stern line!" The sailor at the stern obeyed and the stern was freed as well. The first mate ran to the bow side amidships on the starboard side, just in front of Peter and Justin, and pushed off the pier with a ten-foot pole. Once the galley cleared its berth, the oarsmen extended their long implements and readied themselves.

Stathopoulos looked to a sailor sitting on a stool at his feet. In front of the sailor stood a drum, two-feet high and a foot and a half in diameter. He was the *keleustes* and his cadence was the ship's heartbeat. "Cruising speed," the captain said. The drummer was surprised by the order but pounded out the tempo necessary to achieve cruising speed. The oarsmen on the the top deck and those on the lower deck below responded by digging their oars into the water and pulling with all their might. Their united rhythmic rowing moved the ship out of the protected harbor. The strong wind whipped through their hair and clothing, doing its best to impede the galley's progress.

"Stathopoulos is really pushing his men to move this ship out as fast as he is," Peter said to Justin. "Jumping off at this speed seems tough but if he doesn't, the wind and the current will send us well south of Saint Cyril."

Their destination, the small fishing village of Saint Cyril, was across the strait to the east-northeast. The dromon shuddered as its bow lunged out of the harbor. "Battle speed!" barked Stathopoulos. The keleustes quickened his pace and the oarsmen followed. The waters grew choppy and the wind continued to blow hard out of the northeast. The ship began a course northeast, almost dead into the wind.

Peter glanced at Justin, who was enraptured by the action. He had never been on a ship before and the mechanics of getting this large wooden creature moving fascinated him.

Stathopoulos continued northeast.

"Why is he heading into the wind?" Justin asked Peter. "His oarsmen will be exhausted before long."

"Watch what he does," Peter answered. He knew well what Stathopoulos was doing.

It wouldn't take long for the galley to lose ground as the wind and the current rallied against her. As she began to drift southeast, despite the oarsmen's valiant efforts, Stathopoulos reacted quickly. "Raise the sails! Hard a-starboard!" he shouted. The helmsman, standing ready behind his captain, pushed the steering board into position while other sailors raised the sails.

Justin turned to Peter. "Why is he putting the sails up?"

"He's going to beat into the wind."

"Beating the wind?"

"We're tacking. These triangular sails help us to do that. As long as the captain keeps the angle of the wind's contact with the sails above about forty-five degrees, the wind will help us move forward," Peter answered. "My guess is that with this wind and current, he knows we can't get across with just oars."

The bow of the galley lurched to the starboard. The sails went up, billowed out gracefully to starboard. The wind grabbed the sails and pushed her forward. Stathopoulos had timed his orders perfectly. The ship headed east-northest at about six knots. The captain ordered the oarsmen to halt and hold the oars out of the water. This would not only rest these oarsmen but it would decrease drag on the ship's hull.

The dromon exploited the wind well but as she passed the midpoint of the crossing, Peter saw that she was well south of Saint Cyril. Continuing this course would leave her almost a half-mile south of the village. Stathopoulos barked out his next command, "Prepare to come about to port!" The oarsmen readied themselves. Stathopoulos looked to the drummer. "Battle speed!" The drummer again began his cadence. As the helmsman moved the portside steering board into position, the oarsmen on the starboard began rowing at battle speed. Those on the port held their oars out of the water. The galley slowly turned to port. The sailors watched the lateen sails luff as the angle between wind and sail fell below forty-five degrees. Having the sailors lift the long yard arms over the tops of the masts to get the best advantage of the wind was impractical at this point. By the time they accomplished the feat, the galley would have been driven further away from Saint Cyril by the raging current. But the captain knew the even if his sails were blowing into the mast, he could still use the wind, although not nearly as well. The wild wind blew into the faces of all of those on board as the bow of the galley turned to the port and came to within forty-five degrees of the wind.

Stathopoulos motioned to the the first mate who bellowed "port and starboard, battle speed!" The galley creaked as she crept forward, resisting the sternward drift that the wind and waves were demanding. Stathopoulos was undaunted. His progress to the north was slow but the captain was patient. He looked toward Saint Cyril and then dead ahead. After what seemed like hours, but fell far short, Stathopoulos ordered, "Hard starboard!" The portside oarsmen renewed their efforts against the unforgiving sea and the starboard oarsmen lifted their oars out of the water and rested. At the same time, the helmsman turned the starboard steering board and the dromon turned sharply to the right. Again the sails luffed halfway throught the maneuver but filled again, this time freely and not against the mast, and the galley sprang forward to the east-northeast, moving faster than she had to port.

Justin looked toward Saint Cyril. The cold salty spray made him cringe. They were closer but still south of their destination. He turned to Peter and asked, "I'm lost. What's the captain doing?"

"He's a hell of a good sailor!" Peter shouted over the deafening din around them. "We're tacking back and forth across the strait, gaining a little ground as we go, but he'll get us there!" Cold spray from the inhospitable sea chilled his face. He licked his lips and remembered what he loved about the sea.

"But we're not going to make it!" Justin declared worriedly.

"We'll make it!" Peter reassured him, patting him on the shoulder.

Peter looked across the galley at Zervas who stoically held the rail with one hand and looked forward over the bow. The wind raged around his face but the crusty soldier remained undaunted.

Stathopoulos looked at the sails and then across the strait to Saint Cyril. "Prepare to come about to port!" he commanded. Then, when the time was right, he ordered, "Come about!" The helmsman pushed the port steering board into position and the dromon slowed in its turn. The portside oarsmen planted their oars in the sea and churned through the resistant water, just as their counterparts on the starboard had done before. Those on the starboard raised their oars. The sails luffed halfway through the turn and then were blown into the mast again by the angry wind. Again, they gained only as much ground as the cruel sea would begrudge them. They won just enough to allow the imperiled vessel to inch northward and complete the maneuver.

Saltwater had drenched everyone and everything on the dromon. Some of the cavalrymen stood amidships, port and starboard, and pronounced unsettling murmurs with each wave that crashed over the side and soaked them and every groan the ship's timbers made as she struggled to complete her task. Other horsemen were below on the lower deck, struggling to adjust to the sudden changes in the ship's attitude that threatened to throw them across the wells where the oarsmen labored and into the soaked walls of the ship. Peter looked east and saw the fishing village. They were definitely farther north than before. "We're going to make it!" Peter heard Justin say.

After five jabs forward to the east-northeast and four backward to the north, the dromon approached the small harbor of the village of Saint Cyril from due west. As if admitting defeat, the fierce wind died down and the galley cruised forward effortlessly. The oarsmen adjusted their oars as they reached the dock. Two sailors jumped from the port bow onto the wharf with the bowline. When the stern neared the wharf, two more sailors left the stern for the pier with a stern line. The four sailors eased the dromon into her berth and tied off the lines. Everyone was exhausted, the crew physically, the passengers emotionally.

Andreas Stathopoulos strutted over to Zervas. "Tribune," he said proudly, "the crossing has been successfully completed."

"Yes," was all he could say and he looked away from the captain.

Stathopoulos turned to his crew. "Prepare to disembark the passengers!" he ordered. He acted as if the events of the last forty minutes were routine to him. Then a large smile overtook his face;

not only was he completely satisfied with his crossing but also with his victory over Zervas.

The crew lowered the gangplank into position. Zervas was the first to leave the galley. He walked to the end of the short village wharf and waited for the others on the edge of a village road. While the soldiers disembarked, Peter and Justin walked over to Stathopoulos.

"From one sailor to another," Peter said, putting out his right hand, "that was very well done."

Stathopoulos grasped Peter's hand and shook it firmly. Then he and Justin exchanged handshakes.

"And I, a confirmed landlubber, was also very impressed!" Justin added enthusiastically.

"Thank you, Captain Argyropoulos, Captain Phillipos," replied the sea captain appreciatively. "I've sailed up and down and across this channel dozens of times and it doesn't get any easier." He paused before asking Peter, "You are a sailor? Why the hell are you in the army?"

"Oh, I've got my reasons."

Stathopoulos recognized the sensitivity of his question and changed the subject. "Where have you sailed before?"

"I sailed for the navy for a few years, a dromon, a little bigger than yours."

"Ever sail this strait?"

"I sailed the Aegean but nothing north of Imbros. Also spent some time in the Ionian and south Adriatic."

"I see."

Peter began to move toward the gangplank but Stathopoulos suddenly positioned himself to block Peter's exit.

"Did you ever know a man named Damon Kasimos?" Stathopoulos asked pointedly. It became apparent the sea captain wouldn't yield until Peter answered.

"Yes," Peter answered.

"I knew your name sounded familiar!"

Justin turned to Peter. "Who is Damon Kasimos?"

Peter didn't hear Justin. He looked into Stathopoulos' stern brown eyes. "How do you know Kasimos?" he asked hesitantly.

"He married my cousin about a month before you killed him," the sea captain said icily.

Justin now surmised that this Kasimos was the sailor Peter had executed. He gently nudged Peter forward, encouraging him to leave.

"The man disobeyed a direct order," Peter responded coolly. "I'm sure you would have done the same in my situation, Captain."

Stathopoulos glared at Peter. Justin again moved his friend forward, more forcefully this time. Peter moved slowly, Justin behind him, and the two left the ship together. Peter could feel the weight of Stathopoulos' eyes on his back as he left the vessel.

"Peter, don't worry about it," Justin reassured his friend. "You did the right thing and that's the end of it. It's not worth stewing over again. It's done. Finished."

Peter demurred.

"Peter, you are a good soldier and a good man. That man was a danger to your crew. You did the right thing. You said so yourself."

"Justin . . ." Peter said, not knowing if he should accept Justin's praise or reject it.

"Stathopoulos knows you're right. That's why he didn't say anything more about it. Peter, listen to me. I'm your friend. You are being far too hard on yourself. First, Kasimos disobeyed a superior officer. How many times have we seen insubordinate soldiers executed? Second, he's dead. You can't undo that. Peter, you've got to accept this or it's going to kill you."

Peter looked at Justin. "You're a good friend, Justin, and I thank you for helping me but I'm afraid it's not so easy to let go."

"You've got to start sometime, Peter. It may as well be now."

Peter hesitated.

"I'll do whatever I can to help," Justin added.

"Thanks, Justin," he said, letting a smile overtake the downturned corners of his mouth.

"You're welcome, Peter. Now let's get the troops together and find Zervas."

Peter, his encounter with Stathopoulos still lingering in his mind, gathered up the cataphract. Justin walked up to Zervas who was staring into the village of Saint Cyril.

"Tribune, the cataphract are ready sir," Justin reported.

"Fine," mumbled Zervas.

The cataphract disembarked their horses and equipment and quickly moved through Saint Cyril. Zervas went with three soldiers to the far end of the village to ask for foodstuffs from the local inhabitants. The poor villagers usually gave without hesitation, though they could scarcely afford to do so. As Zervas sauntered off, Peter and Justin each lashed two empty casks to their horses' saddles and went to obtain additional water from the well in the center of the village.

The opening to the well had a three-foot wall around it to keep animals and young children from tumbling into its mouth. From the edge of this wall, Justin grabbed the wooden bucket at the end of the tether and dropped it into the well.

Suddenly, from a corner of the small village, came a cry of horror. "Don't draw from the well! Don't draw from the well!"

Three men rushed forward as Justin and Peter watched in surprise. Out of nowhere twenty women hurried to the village square but kept their distance from the strangers.

"Don't drink from the well!" said one of the men, a tall, thin, dark-haired man. "The well is possessed by evil spirits!"

Justin turned to Peter who looked back and addressed the men. "What are you talking about?"

"For the last six weeks, six demons have possessed the well. If you listen over the opening you can hear them." He put his hand to his ear to demonstrate how this was to be done. Then he continued, the other men remaining silent. "There are six. We have counted."

The others nodded their heads in unison.

"Anyone who drinks from the well risks possession himself! Dokas' daughter was possessed by them." He pointed to one of the villagers who sadly nodded his head. "They made her arms and legs twitch uncontrollably. Soon she could not straighten her arms or legs. Her jaws would clench so tightly, she'd break teeth. The slightest noise would cause the twitching to become violent. Her muscles became so rigid that we could not open her mouth to feed her. Her breathing grew more and more shallow. She died soon after.

"Giannoulos," he then pointed to a second man, "lost his wife. One of the demons possessed her and made her womb bleed without end. We buried her last week."

"Is there another well here?" Justin asked.

"The next well that is not dry is three miles away in Artemisia," the villager explained.

"You've been carrying water three miles?" Peter asked.

"Yes. But we collect and store rainwater when we can. We are drinking more wine and milk from the sheep and goats. They drink from the streams, which can be murky. Those who have not drunk from the well have not been possessed by the demons."

"We need water. We have a long journey ahead of us," said Peter. "Where can we find enough water for thirty men?"

Another man spoke up. "Sir, perhaps today you are in luck."

"Oh," Peter began, his sarcastic tone bordering on insult, "and why is that?"

"Brother Nathaniel is coming here from the Monastery of Saint Philemon this very day."

Peter looked at Justin as if to say, so what.

"Our own Father Symeon tried to exorcise the demons but he was unsuccessful. Brother Nathaniel is well known in this area for the miracles he can do."

"Where is Father Symeon?" asked Peter.

"About three weeks ago, he tried for three hours to exorcise the demons from the well. Father finally gave up, frustrated by his failure. When he walked away from the well, one of the demons grabbed his leg. The good Father tripped and fell, breaking his left leg. He was doing well for a week or two. We had him resting with his leg held up by a chair for most of the time. But then, one day, it became difficult for him to get his breath. We tried desperately to help him. The men pushed on his chest to help his breathing; the women prayed yet nothing helped. Within an hour, the poor man could no longer breathe. His death was a shock to us. These demons had killed a priest!"

As the surrounding villagers crossed themselves devoutly, their silent murmuring briefly grew louder as they mourned Father Symeon who had served them well.

Justin turned to Peter. "Should we wait?"

"Who knows how long it will take the monk to get here or if he'll be able to do anything about the well," Peter answered. "I think we should tell Zervas we need to move on and get water at the next well we find. I'll attend to — " Peter started but as he spoke, the village erupted in celebration, drowning out first his voice, then his thoughts.

The young captains looked for the origin of the commotion. There, at the edge of the village, was a figure in a black cassock riding a donkey.

"Brother Nathaniel?" Justin asked Peter.

"An excellent deduction," Peter responded. "Shall we meet him?"

Justin and Peter walked through the growing crowd, which had now made its way to the possessed well. The two captains positioned themselves so they could observe the celebrated monk. The monk appeared to be about forty years old, his flowing blond beard speckled with white. He was a good half-foot taller than Justin with large hands and piercing blue eyes. His voice thundered as he spoke.

"Good people of Saint Cyril," Brother Nathaniel began, "God has heard your prayers."

The grateful villagers crossed themselves and breathlessly expressed their thanks to the Creator.

"Please gather around and join me in prayer," the giant man continued.

One of the villagers grabbed Peter's right hand and another grabbed his left. He looked up to find that the same had happened to Justin.

Justin smiled back at him. "Let's see what happens," he whispered to his comrade.

"Holy Father," Brother Nathaniel wailed, "the evil servants of Satan possess this well. Those who have drunk from it have suffered terribly. These, Your loving faithful, beg of You, Lord, to rid their village of this torment. As your Son cast demons out of the many who asked Him and as His disciples did in His name, we beseech You, Lord, allow me, a sinner, in Your Son's name, to cast the demons out!" He paused reverently before adding, "Amen."

The onlookers, Justin and Peter included, echoed the monk's last word.

The monk rolled up his sleeves and circled the well three times. He chanted a hymn as he walked. The hymn, not unlike so many others, praised God, thanked Him for Life and all of its many blessings, bemoaned Sin's hold over Mankind, and asked for His help. Once Brother Nathaniel had completed his third revolution around the well, chanting melodiously, he systematically inspected it. He looked it over thoroughly from the outside. It appeared he had not yet found that which he was seeking. His chant continued as he moved forward to inspect inside of the well. When he leaned over the mouth of the well, a deep groan emanated from it.

"That's one of the demons!" shouted one of the villagers. "I've heard that noise before!" Many of the onlookers became frightened and ran back to their homes.

But Brother Nathaniel was unperturbed. His chanting and inspection of the well continued. He leaned gently against the outside of the wall around the opening to the well and reached down into the well to feel the inside. As he did, part of the wall he was leaning against crumbled. The monk fell forward but he was able to grab part of the wall with his hand. His strength and surprising agility saved him. The remaining villagers shuddered. Would Brother Nathaniel be able to free their well of these demons? Or would he fall prey to them?

The unshaken monk continued about his work. He reached into one of his pockets and retrieved a vial.

"Holy water!" whispered one of the villagers, guessing at the vial's contents.

The monk, still chanting his mellifluent hymn, opened the vial and poured its contents into the well. The groaning from the well recurred. Again the villagers gasped in fear but the monk remained unflappable. He reached into a second pocket and retrieved a small yellow object, made the sign of the cross over it, kissed it, and dropped it into the well. Within seconds, the ground around the well convulsed and a broad tongue of flame spewed from the well. Brother Nathaniel was knocked to the ground, his beard lightly singed. Again, the giant remained unaffected as he finished his chanting and genuflected before the well, crossing himself three times and praying quietly for about thirty minutes.

The villagers prostrated themselves as well, crossing themselves, and joining the monk in prayer as they did so. Justin and Peter had remained upright but as they saw what was transpiring, they joined their hosts on the ground.

Peter had seen an exorcism before and, although he didn't think of it often, he had never forgotten it. When he was seven years old and living in the monastery, some villagers carried in a seven-year-old girl who was screaming and wailing, trying desperately to pull away from the four men holding her. Her cut and bruised body was extremely thin; she looked as though she hadn't eaten for weeks. Her hair was disheveled and large clumps had been pulled out. She spat and retched and cursed all of those around her. When she could pull a hand free, she'd viciously rake her long fingernails across some poor victim's face, causing that person to scream in agony.

What Peter remembered most was the young girl's voice. She shrieked like an animal caught in the throes of death. She cursed the villagers and the monks and ejaculated the most vile blasphemies against the Lord Jesus Christ.

The exorcist was an older man who had been a priest for over two decades and had performed two exorcisms, both successfully. When his wife died, he joined the monastery but continued to study the rite of exorcism. Although his last exorcism had been five years earlier, he appeared confident that, with God's help, he could cast out this demon.

The three monks who were assisting the exorcist chanted while their leader read countless prayers. At certain times, he would dispense droplets of holy water, which caused the girl's shrieking to amplify. Peter shuddered when he recalled that awful sound. The girl spat and snorted at the golden-jeweled cross the exorcist held over her head.

After many hours, the young girl was completely exhausted and taken to the infirmary. There, a physician from a nearby city examined her. Peter, who was the only other person present, watched intently.

"Do you know her?" the doctor asked Peter.

Peter shook his head.

The doctor could see a concerned look on Peter's face and he said reassuringly, "She's going to be fine."

Thirty minutes later, she awoke. She looked around the room and began to call for her parents. Peter stood up and walked over to her. Her face had been cleaned and her hair combed and, to Peter, she looked like an angel. Peter smiled at her and she smiled back. He spoke soothingly and told her that everything was going to be okay. She left the next day and Peter never saw her again.

Brother Nathaniel rose after his half-hour vigil, sighed in exhaustion, crossed himself three times, and announced to the hopeful villagers, "Brothers and sisters, the demons are gone from your well."

Many of the villagers were still incredulous, their low murmurs increasing. The monk heard their rumbling discontent and tried to reassure them. "Your water is safe; the demons are gone. Your faith has driven them away. Come, listen. No more noises."

"Where are they now?" asked one of the villagers skeptically. "What have you done with them?"

Peter turned to Justin and whispered, "What strange people! First they can't wait for him to get here to fix their well and when he does, they doubt him as if he were incapable of doing it."

"Do you think he did it?" Justin asked.

"Do you think the well was really possessed?" Peter asked, smiling at his friend.

"Where are the demons now?" one of the villagers aked Brother Nathanial.

"I don't know," answered the monk. "I asked God to rid your well of the demons; I didn't tell Him where to put them. That is for Him to decide."

"What is to prevent them from coming back and possessing someone or something else?" another villager asked.

"Your continued prayers and trust in God will keep your village safe." And then, as if to reassure them again, the monk dropped the bucket into the well and drew water for himself. He asked for a cup and was given one. He filled it with water from the bucket and drank the cool water eagerly.

This last act dissolved the doubts of the disbelievers and assuaged the fears of the fearful. The villagers went to their homes to get basins for storing the water they could draw from the exorcised well. As they did, Justin and Peter approached the well. There, the towering monk greeted them warmly.

"Good day to you, gentlemen," Brother Nathaniel said. "Don't hesitate to drink from the well. I assure you, the water is safe."

An angry Zervas appeared from nowhere and stormed up to the two captains. Ignoring Brother Nathaniel, Zervas blasted Justin and Peter. "How long does it take you imbeciles to get water? We have a tight schedule to keep if we're going to make it to Nicaea in time. We've got over a hundred fifty miles to go!"

Justin attempted to speak but the monk stepped forward.

"Tribune," he said kindly, "the well has just now been put in working order. I believe you're being awfully hard on these men."

"This is none of your business," Zervas spat back. "These men are under my command. We are on the emperor's business and we don't need your interference."

"Please, be kind. These men are doing as you asked."

"Leave us!"

"Tribune, remember the words of our Lord—"

"Get away, you! We have an important task to complete. We don't need any more useless delays!"

The monk's countenance became stern. He looked Zervas in the eye and said softly, "Your mission will fail."

Zervas shot a sharp look at the monk. The monk's warning grabbed Peter's and Justin's attention.

"You are doomed to defeat," Brother Nathaniel continued, this time in a greater volume. "This emperor will lose his throne this year."

Peter could see Zervas was chilled by the monk's audacious prediction. He was surprised by what the monk said but didn't know whether to take Brother Nathaniel seriously or ignore him. Was this a sign that the Dukas would succeed? Why would such a kind, gentle man say such a thing? And why was Zervas so affected by him?

"Yes," the monk continued, "the emperor will not be on his throne. His reign will end with the summer. And soon after, another emperor will have to call upon the fair-haired nations to save him from the Ishmaelites. And they will. But after one hundred years, the fair-haired soldiers will return, this time to sack the emperor's city and carve up his empire."

Zervas stared back at Brother Nathaniel, visibly mystified by what he was hearing. The monk gently smiled at him, offering friendship but Zervas snorted at him and then growled at the young officers. "Get the water! I expect you to join us outside this village in ten minutes!" He strutted away angrily.

"Don't lose heart, gentlemen," Brother Nathaniel said to Justin and Peter. "The empire will pull herself together after the fair-headed soldiers are expelled but she will be but a shadow of herself."

Peter began to ready the vessels to be filled. However, Justin continued to look uneasily at the monk, hoping to hear more. The monk saw Justin's concern and gave him a reassuring look.

"God will protect you and your friend," Brother Nathaniel said to Justin. "Remember what God has taught you today and do as He commands."

"Yes," Justin said, promising the monk as if he were the Creator Himself, "I will remember."

Peter had overheard the monk and looked up from his work to see Brother Nathaniel smiling at him as well. The monk helped the young captains fill their casks with water from the rejuvenated well. He wished them God's safety and they departed to join their comrades outside of the village. When they were about a hundred feet from the well, Peter and Justin turned around. Brother Nathaniel stood there, smiling and waving at them.

Justin said that this man's presence would be with them for the remainder of their journey, maybe even longer. He again felt reassured. The monk's blessing made him feel as though he were cloaked in the Almighty's aegis.

Peter felt less reassured. The prescience of the anchorite disturbed him. Blessing or not, his life was in danger and the disaster that the monk had predicted for the empire gave him a sense of hopelessness and alarm. If God were to save them from the upcoming debacle, to what kind of empire would they return?

CHAPTER 12

Two hours after being summoned by an imperial messenger, Aspasia arrived at the Palace Bucoleon. Her escort of three of the empress' ladies-in-waiting led her through the busy streets of Constantinople. The Hippodrome was hosting another horse race and was again crowded with men and women hungry for sport. The roars from the stadium punctuated her journey to the palace. The presence of an escort did not discourage the many street vendors from tempting Aspasia. Persian perfumes, Theban silks, grilled octopus, soft ostrich plumes, glittering gold jewelry, and smooth lamb's wool tunicas were among the many things offered for sale.

The palace staff, led by Myra, extended every courtesy to Aspasia as they brought her down the the sumptuous white marble hallway, lined with silk tapestries in a panoply of color, past golden lampstands, whose lamps glowed like the sun, to her daughter's quarters where Eleni eagerly waited. Mother and daughter embraced when they met and continued to hold hands as they faced each other, a subtle scent of jasmine in the air.

"How are they treating you, dear?" asked Aspasia in a worried tone.

"No differently than the Empress Evdokia herself, Mother," Eleni answered, trying to reassure her. "I'm so glad to see you, Mother."

"Your father and I miss you very much," said Aspasia. They hugged and kissed again. "Why don't they let you out?" she added, frustrated by her daughter's confinement. "This whole thing seems so silly."

"Justin said it's for reasons of security. Somebody is afraid I'll be abducted by 'agents unfriendly to the emperor and the empress.'"

"This seems like a lot of foolishness to me," Aspasia said, her frustration not abated. She looked into her daughter's eyes. "Eleni, why did you ask them to bring me here? Nothing has happened to Justin, has it?"

"No, no," Eleni said reassuring her mother. "There is nothing wrong with Justin. I just received a letter from him this morning. He's fine."

"Are you not well, Eleni?" Aspasia asked, looking her daughter over quickly.

"Mother, I'm fine, too," Eleni answered, assuaging her mother's concerns.

Eleni paused. She was finding it difficult to tell her mother what she had been dying to tell her all morning long. She summoned her resolve. "Mother, I just needed to talk to you," Eleni began slowly. "I know that I've never been like this before but since Justin and I were married, I've felt this strong need to talk to you, to get your advice, to be closer to you."

A maternal smile crossed Aspasia's face. "Like the other day . . ."

"Yes, when we talked about Justin."

She reflected on the past eighteen years. *After all this time, Eleni needs me.* She gracefully accepted the role she had waited to play for so long. "Eleni, you've always been the different one. You were weaned before any of your sisters. You talked and walked earlier than they did. By the time you were five, you were ready to leave the house and strike out on your own. I felt that I could never reach you. After you were married, I thought you had taken another giant step out of my life."

Eleni smiled at her mother and hugged her.

"And now, when I thought you were beyond my influence, you tell me these things." The older woman began to cry tears of joy. Eleni held her tightly in her arms. "The other day when you asked me to brush your hair, I was surprised by your coming to me and I thought it would not happen again. And now this . . ."

Eleni released her mother and looked her squarely in the eye. "I guess I finally realized how important you are to me. You know, I *have* been listening to you and watching you all of these years. I haven't completely taken you for granted. I just didn't want you to know that you had any say in the way I was going to run my life. And now that our separation is greater, my need for you is greater. It is time to be honest with you, and myself."

"Eleni, you have always been full of surprises," she said softly.

They heard a knock at the door. Myra and two other servants entered with the early afternoon's repast. Aspasia's eyes consumed the roast lamb, orzo, ocra, grapes, and freshly baked bread. The look on the older woman's face showed approval of the sumptuous meal before them.

"Are you hungry, Mother?" Eleni asked, knowing the answer.

"This looks wonderful. The empress is taking good care of you."

One of the servants poured two goblets of red wine that Aspasia and Eleni gratefully accepted.

"Does Madam need anything else?" Myra asked.

"No, but thank you, Myra," Eleni replied.

Two of the servants bowed and departed but Myra remained.

"My, this is impressive," said Aspasia, overwhelmed by the luxury of her daughter's situation.

Myra summoned a chaplain who blessed the meal and left, followed by Myra. Aspasia's eyes surveyed the room, itself a visual feast. A large mosaic spanned almost the entire wall behind Eleni. It showed Artemis, goddess of the moon, the hunt, and chastity. This black-haired beauty had steel gray eyes as cold as the moon itself. She wore clothing, as was appropriate one blessed with eternal virginity. But her attire consisted of a draping so thin it barely obscured the landmarks beneath. Artemis rode a majestic, muscular brown stag who carried his mistress effortlessly. Directly behind the goddess a pale, yellow-white full moon silhouetted the goddess and her mount in a striking profile.

"It's beautiful, isn't it, Mother?"

"I've never seen anything like it before."

"The palace is full of such beautiful things. Look to your left."

The image was all too familiar: the Virgin Mary, the Theotokos, holding her infant son, whose young face was resolute but reassuring. Even in His infancy, the Savior knew of the fate that awaited Him and His face showed it. The Virgin's robe and head covering were a deep azure blue, her skin a rosy flesh tone, her lips straight and thin and only slightly darker than her skin. The background was of minute gold stones tightly arranged—a regal presentation of the young mother of Heaven's King.

To her right Aspasia saw a red silk tapestry, hanging from the twelve-foot ceiling. Heracles battled the Amazon Queen Hippolyta, with a dozen Amazons looking on. This hero of many of the old myths found his adversary formidable, as revealed by the surprised look in his eyes. One would assume that Hippolyta was the victor, not Heracles.

The dining table was a fascinating marriage of ash and ebony. The high-backed chairs were constructed in the same way. The arms, legs, and backs were ebony, the seats ash. A blue velvet cushion covered each seat. Eleni noted that the surroundings were overwhelming her mother. She pushed her plate aside. "Let me show you the palace and the gardens. We can talk there."

"No, Eleni," said the older woman, regaining her concentration and her appetite. "Let's finish our meal." She again looked at the food on the table. "It's all so delicious!"

When they were satisfied, Eleni told Myra they wished to tour the palace. Eleni led her mother down a marble staircase directly to a colonnaded marble wharf. From it, they could see imperial navy vessels moving adroitly through the harbor. At its eastern end they saw one of Emperor Romanos' personal galleys. The three hundred foot vessel gracefully pulled out of its dock.

"It's magnificent!" Aspasia gasped. "Look at all that gold!" She pointed to the lavish gold ornamentation that glowed from a structure the size of a house at the stern of the galley, over the decks, and down the sides of the vessel. Its sailors, more than three hundred in number, were dressed in gold too. Its brilliance intensified as it pulled out of the pink marble-roofed home and into the middle of the harbor. Its radiance likened it to the sun as it moved across the water.

Eleni and Aspasia spent their remaining hours together touring the palace, its gardens, and the church of Saint Mary. Empress Evdokia was with her court entertaining the ambassador from Kiev for the day, so a meeting with her was not possible. Two servants guided the women through the many buildings and gardens as mother and daughter continued their conversation. When the afternoon was spent, they returned to Eleni's quarters.

"Mother, I am so glad you came," said Eleni.

"May I see you again soon?" asked Aspasia, as if she were a child asking for an extra pastry.

"Please, come anytime. I'll send a messenger every day, and if you wish to come, just return with the messenger. If you don't, tell the messenger and he'll report back to me."

"That sounds easy enough. I'll be here tomorrow for certain!"

The two women hugged tightly and held hands while saying good-bye. They savored the feeling of warmth and closeness that had stolen into their relationship.

"I can't wait to tell your father!" said Aspasia.

Eleni smiled and she watched her mother leave. The rebirth of her relationship with her mother held new hopes for her. Indeed she wished it had happened years earlier. Justin's situation was the catalyst. Had it not been for that, how could she have accomplished this new rapport with her mother? Perhaps this perturbation had a greater purpose.

That night as Eleni retired, her thoughts returned to her husband. In her prayers, she asked for intercession by the Blessed Virgin. When she finished, she slipped into her bed and dropped into a deep slumber.

After five days of hard riding over the well-maintained roads on the southern shore of the Propontis and through the coastal mountains, Zervas had brought the cataphract to Andronikos Dukas' camp outside of Nicaea. The emperor and most of the army were camped on the opposite side of the city.

By the time the sun set, men and beasts of burden alike were exhausted. Sentries met Zervas' cataphract and promptly notified the officer of the guard. Zervas ordered his men to dismount. Soon they were billeted to their tents and Zervas led Justin and Peter to their new commander's tent. Andronikos Dukas and the rest of the Emperor Romanos' army had crossed the Bosphorus just two days earlier, during the first days of the second week of March.

Justin marveled at the grand size of Andronikos Dukas' tent. The center pole rose twelve feet in the air and was supported by eight one-inch thick ropes held to the ground by twelve-inch stakes. Four shorter poles, only nine feet each, supported the center pole.

Two guards stopped the three soldiers as they entered Dukas' tent. Zervas told the guards his identity and one left to inform a senior officer. When he returned, the three cavalrymen were ushered into the tent where Tribune Azarius, an Armenian who was a longtime friend of the Dukas, greeted them.

The inside of the tent looked like a small palace throne room. The ground was covered with beautiful wool rugs. Sashes of red silk ran from ceiling to floor around the periphery of the well-lit tent interior. Candles burned from four gilded lamp stands. A silk tapestry hung from each of the three sides of the tent. Three large gilded icons, one of the Virgin and Child, one of John the Baptist, and one of Saint George, presided at the base of each tapestry. A large table contained enough food and wine to feed fifty people. *His baggage train must be a mile long. What would the emperor's tent be like?*

Dukas and seven of his officers peered over a map when Azarius interrupted them and announced the arrival of Zervas and his two junior officers. Andronikos Dukas raised his head from the table. He looked to be in a foul mood, but quickly changed his demeanor. He strutted over to Zervas, grabbed his right hand, and gave him a hearty greeting. "Tribune Zervas, welcome!" Dukas said with a commanding smile. "I trust your journey was safe?"

"Yes, sire, it was," Zervas replied.

"Oh, and you've brought two of those brilliant young officers that Emperor Romanos honored last week!" Justin could see through his feigned kindness and knew he had nothing but contempt for them. "Well, it is an honor to meet you," he added. He moved over to shake their hands.

Justin noted that each of the prince's fingers was adorned with a beautiful, jewel-studded ring except one, his left fourth digit. Justin found this curious because that finger was usually reserved for the most impressive of rings, other than the wedding ring, that traditionally claimed the right fourth digit.

Andronikos Dukas was dressed in a bright scarlet tunic and dark blue skirt with gold trim. His greaves were gold as well. Over his tunic he wore a corselet covered with one-inch by three-inch golden shards. His fine leather boots were laced over blue silk stockings.

"Tomorrow we will meet the emperor," he continued. "The senior officers and I have just finished reviewing our plans. You gentlemen must be very tired after your long and rapid journey. You will need a good night's sleep; so you can be ready for the emperor tomorrow. Sergios will show you two to your tent. Tribune Zervas will need to review with me your group's role in the upcoming campaign." He then motioned to one of the junior officers in the tent.

Just as Sergios arrived, two impressive figures burst into the tent. One was darkly complected and looked much like Andronikos Dukas. His attire was similar to that of Andronikos' but with more subdued greens and light blues. The other soldier was tall and brawny with long, thick blond hair and a bushy blond beard. His armor was unlike any that Justin had ever seen. Over a woolen brown tunic, he wore a long-sleeved chain mail shirt that reached down to his middle of his thighs. Over this, he wore a loose-fitting linen forest green vest. His legs were covered with leather trousers and his feet with leather boots. In his left hand, he cradled a conical helmet with a one-inch-wide metal appendage that projected over and protected his nose. Peter recognized him as a Norman, probably from southern Italy or Sicily.

"Brother," began the darker man enthusiastically, "this is Lord Roussel de Bailleul."

A look of disapproval appeared on Andronikos Dukas' face. He glared at the dark-haired man and again motioned to Sergios to escort Peter and Justin from the tent. The young officer hurriedly complied, leading Peter and Justin to a small tent on the opposite side of the camp. He showed them in.

"Gentlemen, I'll have an aid bring your gear. His Lordship Andronikos Dukas has instructed me to inform you that you are to be ready by dawn tomorrow to receive further orders. Good-night," he said curtly then turned on his right heel and departed.

"Quite a welcome," Peter noted. "I'm surprised they are being so kind to us."

"Well, this is better than sleeping under a tree," Justin responded with similar sentiment. Then he changed the subject. "Who were those two that came into Dukas' tent as we were being rushed out? Was the dark-haired fellow his brother?"

"He must be Constantine Dukas. The family resemblance is strong. I've heard of him but never had the pleasure of meeting him."

"Is he coming on this campaign, too?" asked Justin. "I would think Andronikos would be enough to keep an eye on."

"I agree. I don't think the emperor would risk having both of them to deal with but what concerns me is the Norman."

"Why is that? Our army has always employed mercenaries. I hear that the Normans are fierce heavy cavalrymen."

"Yes, but why would the emperor use Normans? We've just lost all of southern Italy to them. Justin, I used to fight against these men. Now they are in our army."

"There are Pechenegs in our army as well," Justin said, trying to reassure his suspicious comrade. "We spent a lot of time chasing them down when they were our enemies. Now many serve the emperor. You must admit, Peter, they are excellent light cavalrymen."

"Yes—"

"So what's the difference between using Pecheneg mercenaries and using Norman mercenaries?"

"What was this Norman doing in Dukas' tent?"

"Maybe he's under Dukas' command as well. He needed to be there to plan the campaign."

"If so, he was late. Why didn't Dukas' brother bring him there before the meeting started? Remember how Andronikos reacted when the two of them came in? Something's not right here. Dukas is hiding something. Why would he want to keep one of his commanders a secret?"

"Peter, you worry too much."

"And you, my friend, don't worry enough. This Roussel de Bailleul is trouble."

"Since this whole episode began, I don't think we've met anyone with whom we're particularly enamored. I say we get some rest and re-examine the situation in the morning."

"Best idea I've heard all day. But I still think that Norman is dangerous."

Justin and Peter were ready the following morning at dawn. They were ready by the time the sun cleared the horizon but no orders came from their new commander. Their gear arrived in a big heap in the middle of the night so they decided to sort it until Dukas made his will known to them.

Around them, the camp stirred like an anthill. Infantrymen and mounted cataphract hurried by. All were heading to this end, the eastern end, of the camp. About thirty yards away a baggage train was forming. Carts, wagons, mules, oxen, and horses were moved into position and their cargoes readied. Tents were dismantled, water and food supplies secured, and weapons of war checked and loaded.

Andronikos Dukas had some fifteen thousand men camped here. As the army began to form ranks, the young captains could appreciate the impressive size of the endeavor. In their previous military experiences, they had never been part of such a large mobile force. Later that morning they would join the other forty-five thousand men under the emperor's command.

Suddenly, they heard an all-too-familiar grumbling behind them.

"Do you blockheads think you are ready to go yet?"

The sound of Zervas' voice felt like a bucket of ice water poured down their backs on a cold winter morning. They shot up and stood at attention. Behind them, Zervas had assembled all of their troops, mounted and ready to go. The young captains could hear their men snickering at them. This premeditated humiliation in front of their own troops left them angry, yet again, with their commander. Zervas' presence in any capacity was becoming increasingly unbearable.

"Sir," Peter said, "we were awaiting further orders."

"Further orders?" fumed Zervas. "I'll give you further orders. You *will* be mounted and ready to move out in fifteen minutes. Meet us at the head of the baggage train. We'll move into position from there." He circled in front of them and added malevolently, "Will that be too difficult for you two clowns to accomplish?"

"No, sir!" Peter and Justin shot back crisply.

"Phillipos!" Zervas barked.

"Yes, sir!" Justin responded with a hint of reservation in his voice.

"You two will disassemble this tent and load it on the last cart of the baggage train immediately. Move!"

Justin and Peter began their task as Zervas led the smirking cataphract forward. It was quite an insult to have men of their rank do something as menial as loading a tent. The last of the cavalrymen led their horses before them and handed them the reins.

Once the troops were out of earshot, Peter tied the reins to a tree trunk and grumbled to Justin, "I wonder what the likelihood would be of his getting hit right between his eyes by an errant arrow in the heat of battle."

"Pretty high if he's anywhere near us."

As they organized their gear, they saw that they'd need to leave some of their supplies behind. Zervas' early morning surprise had deprived them of the chance to load those things they couldn't carry on their horses onto the pack mules. When Justin came across the wooden cask Uncle Theodore had given him, he thought it would have to be left behind but then he remembered the magic of this grayish powder. Perhaps he could take some of it. He found a cotton sack and poured about three quarters of the powder into it. He threw in a couple of small flints, bound the sack at the top, and tied it to his saddle. Justin emptied out the rest of the powder, taking care to disperse it evenly in the tan soil in front of their tent. No one must know he had it.

When Peter saw the sack, hanging like a large melon from the saddle, he looked at Justin inquisitively. "What's that?"

Justin grinned back at him. "Nothing," Justin answered, ineffectively deflecting Peter's question.

"Whatever it is, it sticks out like a whore at communion!" Peter sighed when he saw that his comment made no impression on Justin. "Well at least try to cover it up!" he added as he threw a saddlebag to Justin.

"Thanks, Peter," Justin replied without another word.

The captains finished their task and joined Zervas with only a second to spare. They had carried out all of his orders and he was surprised to see them there on time, but his face did not betray him. When they saluted him, Zervas returned their salutes without looking at them. Thereafter, he gave the order to move out. The small group of cataphract rode forward from the baggage train and took their place among the other cataphract, some five thousand of them. Within an hour, they caught sight of the emperor's larger force and joined it.

This huge army was indeed impressive. The sixty thousand included a majority of troops from the empire and a smaller number of mercenaries, which ranged from Kipjack and Pecheneg light cavalry to Uz and Armenian infantry. Following the infantry was a large train of seige engines: catapults, giant crossbows on wheels (*balistae*), giant battering rams, and all of the makings for great seige towers.

Andronikos' force integrated itself into the larger force with some difficulty. This delay gave Justin and Peter time to observe the spectacle a hundred and fifty yards before them. After about half an hour, Andronikos, and five of his staff officers rode forward, away from the confusion, toward a group of ten mounted officers who had come from Emperor Romanos' portion of the army.

Four of the newly arrived group of five saluted the tallest man in the larger group, Romanos Diogenes. But Andronikos Dukas paid no homage to Romanos. The prince merely rode up to the emperor and began speaking to him as one would do with someone of equal rank. Yet the emperor didn't seem to mind. Strategos Joseph Tarchaniotes was to the right of Romanos Diogenes. He wore a distinctive bright green cloak over his uniform and a golden helmet, which had a tuft of black horsehair projecting from the top. After a long twenty minutes, Andronikos and his men rode back to their troops.

Upon Andronikos' return the enormous army moved forward along the road to Ancyra, leaving clouds of dust behind them. Most of the heavy cavalry followed the emperor and his entourage. Light infantry, the archers and then the scutati, the heavy infantry, followed the main body of cataphract. Behind the scutati was a small rearguard of more cataphract. Light cavalrymen preceded the column by several miles and acted as scouts. One of them returned to the emperor every hour with a report of what lay ahead. They were still in Roman territory, so the attitude of the force was relaxed.

They had heard no reports of any raids in the area. The location of Alp Arslan and his Seljuk Turks was unknown but the soldiers were confident that Romanos Diogenes would soon find them.

During the first week after their departure from Nicaea, Justin and Peter found themselves busy with their group of cataphract. It had doubled to its originally intended size and was quite uncoordinated, despite the arduous efforts of Zervas, Justin, and Peter. The new arrivals had been pulled from other commanders and different units. They resented their reapportionment to this new, motley group. Even their uniforms were different. Some wore red overshirts and had red horsehair tufts on their helmets; others wore yellow or green colors versus the blue of the original troops.

After six days, the hard work of reorganization was complete. The fifty were forged into a cohesive unit. This was no small task because their retraining occurred while they were moving eastward with the army. They were now familiar enough with each other to perform among the best of any unit of their size. The rigorous training they'd received years ago when they were enthusiastic adolescents had hardened them into Roman cavalrymen; the last six days made them comrades. When the quartermaster provided new blue overshirts and helmet tufts, their assimilation was complete. Zervas' crack force boldy rode east, ready to smash the Turk and send him back to the steppes of Central Asia from whence he'd come.

CHAPTER 13

Despina continued to enjoy the luxurious life offered by Senator Kastros and his sumptuous villa. Her sojourn now exceeded three weeks. She had sent several letters to Archbishop Mavrites' agents at Saint Martha's in the guise of notifying the nuns of her continued delay at the villa. She nurtured Kastros' affection for her as they dined together, eating the most sumptuous of meats and fruits of the land, and drinking the best wines the empire could offer. They spent hours alone walking the grounds of the estate, strolling down its majestic marble halls, and relaxing in its heavenly rooms while musicians brought lyre-like *pandorion* to life. Kastros had fallen in love with "Demetra Georgiou" and Despina was not surprised how easily it had occurred; but that was not important. Most significant was that she had gained his confidence. And she needed to exploit that to uncover what the senator and his Arab friend were up to.

Emmanuel Ghassani arrived from Damascus one day later than expected. Ghassani quickly found Kastros and Despina in the garden and greeted the senator as he had done the last time. He took note of Despina and smiled. "It is so good to see you again, Madam Georgiou."

Despina replied, "It is a pleasure to see you again as well, Lord Ghassani."

"Madam Georgiou has agreed to spend some more time with me," Kastros told his friend.

"Then you are truly blessed, my friend, truly blessed."

Kastros noted Emmanual's eagerness to discuss his journey and nodded to him.

As Ghassani turned and walked back toward the house, he said to Despina, "I look forward to seeing more of you, Madam Georgiou."

Despina smiled back. "Thank you."

Kastros gently grasped her hands. "Demetra, Emmanuel, and I have some business to discuss," he said. "I'll have Alexandra show you the new tapestries I bought yesterday for your room. I hope that you'll like them."

Despina tried to refuse his offer but knew to do so may cause suspicion. "Thank you, Gregory. I'm certain that they're beautiful."

As Despina said this, the servant arrived to take her to her room. She walked hesitantly inside the villa. As she walked to the room, she saw Kastros and Ghassani go into the library. *If I could only get in there!*

Most of Andronikos Dukas' command was comprised of the Levies of the Nobility, essentially the personal armies of the great landowners. Some of these nobles were among the officers of his command. Many of them had holdings in the area and asked their commander to send troops to visit their estates. He wanted to make certain they had not been victims of any recent Turkish raiding parties. Andronikos gave this menial duty to Zervas. He certainly did not want Justin and Peter anywhere near him.

Zervas reluctantly complied. His hard work of the past week seemed, for the short term at least, wasted. His crack unit of cataphract was to be used as mere errand boys. However, the tribune knew his commander's wishes were to be followed without question. So Zervas and his troops spent the next five months shadowing the gigantic army as it moved east. They called upon any estate within twenty miles of the army's path. Their excessive riding was tiring and direct contact with the main army was minimal. Whenever the troop would attempt to link up with the army, a messenger would intercept them on their way and, without fail, present them with new orders to visit yet another estate. Finally, by the middle of August, they were allowed to join the main army.

Justin found the army in worse shape than when he had left it. The mercenaries were slovenly. Some had left. Those that remained were often insubordinate to their Roman commanders. The rank and file soldiers began to show their lack of training. They griped about the cold when it was cold and the heat when it was hot. Some of the scutati left their heavy weapons behind rather than care for them. Interaction with the local populace had been rough at times and in some instances created friction between the army and those it was sent to defend. In short, the army no longer resembled a coordinated collection of trained professionals.

One night the army set up camp in western Armenia about two miles east of Erzurum. Peter and Justin slipped away from the watchful eye of Zervas. Any soldier caught leaving camp could face serious consequences. They walked with torches in hand to a large rock three hundred yards from the edge of camp. Each planted his torch in the soft sand around the rock and walked a few yards ahead. There they sat and looked up into the star-filled sky.

"I never thought I'd be spending my time on this campaign running around to check on the estates of this prince or that duke or some count," Peter lamented, his eyes glued to the heavens. "We're nothing but glorified messenger boys. What a waste of fifty cataphract."

"Dukas is definitely going out of his way to keep us away from him," Justin added. Then he pointed to the sky and asked Peter, "Isn't that Jupiter?"

"Mars," Peter replied. "Well, Dukas has certainly accomplished his goal. What use are we to the emperor doing this?"

Justin sighed heavily.

"Wondering about Eleni?" Peter inquired, still drinking in the sky above.

"How did you know?" Justin asked, turning to his friend.

"Just call it a lucky guess," Peter answered, his gaze still cemented upward.

Justin stretched out on his back and rested his head on his hands. "I wonder what she's doing almost every minute of the day. I miss her voice, the smell of her hair, the look in her eyes . . . ." Justin's voice quavered.

But, Peter didn't respond. His thoughts were lost above. The brilliant stars reminded him of his days at sea. He enjoyed beholding this celestial splendor from solid ground, but he remembered how much more he appreciated it from the deck of a dromon or a larger galley. It was imperative for any sailor to be familiar with the celestial activities of all five of the known planets, as well as the moon and the sun, the constellations, Polaris, and other key stars. Peter had not only acquired the necessary familiarity; he had also formed a deep love of their beauty.

The moon, now in its second quarter, shone through that clear sky of August 20, 1071. A summer night in the Aegean was the most beautiful sight Peter had beheld as a sailor. He would imagine God, at the dawn of Creation, holding all of these celestial bodies in His two hands. After giving them His blessing, He tossed them into the heavens for the delight of all.

Suddenly a vaguely familiar voice broke the silence. "Are you gentlemen alone?" it asked, its volume just above a whisper.

"Who's there?" Peter demanded. He spun around to the direction of the voice and drew his sword.

"Are you alone?" the voice asked again, this time more forcefully.

"I think I know that voice, Peter," said Justin, whose initial response was the same as Peter's but delayed by a few seconds. "Yes, we're alone," he answered.

Peter looked at Justin curtly and made it clear he disagreed with Justin's communication with this stranger. They could trust no one.

A lone figure stepped out from behind the rock and came forward. The stranger's identity was still unclear to them.

"It's Tribune Michael Attaleiates," the figure proclaimed as he walked toward them.

The young men were stunned. They had never imagined they would see Attaleiates again at all, let alone here in the middle of the high steppe of Armenia.

"Tribune," Justin began, "We—"

"Never thought you'd see me again?" Attaleiates said with a smile.

"No sir," Justin replied.

Peter said nothing. Attaleiates sudden appearance was both welcome and unwelcome. Contact with the tribune was equivalent to contact with the emperor, which should have conveyed a sense of security. But it was the emperor and his lieutenants, Attaleiates and Alexios Comnenos, who had thrown them into the middle of this tangled web of intrigue.

"Gentlemen, please be seated," Attaleiates asked, motioning his hands downward.

The two captains complied, Justin eagerly, Peter with reservation.

"What of Andronikos Dukas?" Attaleiates began. "Feel free to speak openly," he added as he sat down.

"Sir," Justin replied, "we've haven't been around him enough to notice much of anything. He's had us running hither and yon since April. We've been in the saddle constantly."

Peter sat quietly as Justin recounted the events of the last four months. Meanwhile, he stewed about Attaleiates, the emperor, and Comnenos. His thoughts of the latter dredged up an irritating uneasiness. He had to remind himself that if he and Justin were going to get out of this campaign alive, they needed the protection of the emperor and his men.

When Justin finished, Peter added, "Sir, we did see a Norman mercenary, Roussel de Bailleul, in Andronikos Dukas' tent when we arrived in Nicaea." He hoped to infect Attaleiates with his suspicion of the Norman.

The tribune didn't appear to be impressed. If anything, he dismissed Peter's concern out of hand. Something weightier was on his mind.

Peter saw this and suspected that all was not well with the emperor. "Tribune," he began, "how is the campaign going so far?"

Attaleiates was caught off-guard by the question. "Umm, fairly well, so far," he replied.

"Any contact with the Turks?" Peter asked, picking up on Attaleiates' uneasiness.

"None to speak of," Attaleiates replied, still unable to shed his discomfort.

"And the army?" Justin asked pointedly.

"Now gentlemen, *I'm* the one who should be asking the questions." His feeble attempt to regain control of the conversation was fruitless. The scholarly soldier lacked the ability to think on his feet, which his two opponents had mastered.

"Something is wrong, isn't it?" Peter probed.

Attaleiates tried in vain to maneuver his way out of the situation. "No, no, that's not true." His pathetic denial fortified the two captains further.

"Something's wrong with the emperor," Justin said in a demanding tone that bordered on insubordination.

Attaleiates' face hardened as the two angry young men demanded the truth. "Yes," he admitted at last. "There is something wrong with the emperor."

"What is it? Tell us!" Peter demanded.

"The emperor is well, physically, and I thank God for that," the tribune continued. "But there is something within him that has changed. He is not his usual self."

"What do you mean?" Justin asked.

"Rather than being in the midst of the army as he had been on previous campaigns, the emperor has isolated himself. He has set up his own camp and surrounded himself with excessive embellishments: thickly padded chairs, golden food service, musicians, and silk adornments for his tent. This is most unusual for the Romanos Diogenes I have known for so many years."

Peter remembered the ostentatiousness of Adronikos Dukas' tent.

Attaleiates continued, "When the army crossed the Halys River, the emperor didn't accompany it. He stayed several days at a nearby fortress, which he had recently built. Soon after his belated crossing, he ordered his officers to separate his private possessions from those of the army. He is acting more like his predecessor, Constantine Dukas, than the soldier Romanos Diogenes.

"And His Majesty has become ill-tempered. Whenever even his most trusted commanders offer advice, he rejects it out of hand and flies into a rage." Attaleiates looked down and shook his head. "Only yesterday His Majesty had one of his soldiers mutilated for stealing a donkey from one of the local people."

"Mutilated?" Justin asked in horror.

"One of the commanders brought the scutati before the emperor. The heavy infantryman was accused of stealing the donkey from one of the nearby farms. When His Majesty heard of the offense, he immediately ordered the soldier's nose to be severed."

"But Tribune," Justin cried, "that practice was stopped over three hundred years ago!"

"What's worse is that the emperor upheld the sentence even after the soldier invoked the intercession of the icon of the Holy Virgin of Blachernae. Even the clergy present could not dissuade the emperor."

Peter and Justin looked at each other. "Dear God! What's happening to the man?" Peter exclaimed.

Attaleiates continued as though Peter had said nothing, "I've witnessed bad omens as well. The center pole of the emperor's tent snapped spontaneously one evening. One of the stables burned down; no one knows why. And two weeks ago, some of the mercenaries attacked Emperor Romanos."

"Lord Christ preserve us!" Justin groaned.

"Please pray for the emperor, gentlemen. The intercession of our Lord now is crucial."

Justin and Peter nodded and agreed to do as the tribune requested.

Attaleiates collected himself and slowly stood up. He motioned to the captains to remain seated. "I will tell the emperor what you told me about Roussel de Bailleul," he said, trying to be reassuring. Then, before he departed, he asked one more time, "Please pray for our emperor, gentlemen."

"We will, sir," Justin replied. But Peter was silent.

Then the tribune disappeared into the darkness.

"It just keeps getting more and more strange, doesn't it?" Justin said as he picked up the torches and handed one to Peter.

"Yes, it does," Peter sighed. His doubts about his commanders swirled with increasing velocity through his mind. Again he had to remind himself of the more undesirable alternative: the Dukas.

The two of them found their way back to camp, extinguished the torches thirty yards from the nearest tent, and inserted themselves into their tent undetected. That night they slept soundly in spite of the foreboding news Attaleiates had brought them.

The next morning was Sunday. The soldiers would attend the beautiful Divine Liturgy service as they did every Sunday, for clergy were always available. However, this was the first opportunity Justin and Peter had had in three months. Today the emperor was to pray before the entire army, asking God to grant His holy empire victory over its Turkish enemies. Aggressive war was a sin but going to war to take back what had once been yours was considered a defensive war and certainly within the rights of a Christian king.

Reveille woke them at dawn and the captains readied themselves for worship that Sunday morning. As Justin finished dressing and left the tent, he discovered Zervas had other plans for him. The tribune ordered him to obtain some additional food rations from the quartermaster. Zervas suspected that Andronikos Dukas was going to send them on yet another special mission and wanted to replete their food supply for such a contingency.

Justin grabbed two pack mules and rode for two hours to the rear of the army without objecting. It was, after all, another opportunity to be away from Zervas.

Peter and Justin had obtained supplies they needed prior to crossing the Hellespont from this same quartermaster. When Justin and the quartermaster recognized each other and noted they were alone, they easily struck up a conversation.

"We've been detached from the army off and on for the past four months," Justin began. "We're starved for information. What's happening?"

"It's become quite complicated," the quartermaster replied. He walked back and forth getting Justin the food rations he needed. His wide brow and prominent nose revealed that he was not a Greek but a Slav. Indeed, most of the enlisted men in the army were not Greek. "At the end of March, we received word that the Turks were about to besiege Edessa. You know they took Manzikert and Archesh at the end of last year, even though there was a truce between us. Filthy pigs!"

Justin nodded his head in confirmation.

"Well, the emperor sends word to the king of the Turks to renew the truce," the quartertmaster continued. "The emperor asks for the return of Manzikert and Archesh. In return, he gives the Turks Hieropolis in Syria, which we captured three years ago. Their king agrees to this. He leaves Edessa and heads south to Beroea, which he besieges. Then, almost six weeks exactly after the new truce was accepted by the Turks, the emperor sends another envoy with the same offer but for some reason the offer is submitted in a much more threatening fashion." He drew near to Justin and whispered, "I hear that their king didn't like that at all. He became angry and forced the envoy to leave immediately. Rumor has it that the Turkish king — sultan, they call him — is on his way to Armenia right now."

"That means we'll be fighting them soon," said Justin. He asked, "Have you been with the emperor on campaigns before?"

"I was with him last year. We chased the Turk all over Anatolia: a couple of victories here and there, a minor setback occasionally, but no pitched battle. The Turk hates that. You see, his troops are lightly armed. But the Turk is a great horseman. He can shoot the bow while riding his horse and from a variety of positions. But if he ever stands fast, our cataphract will squash him."

Justin tried to imagine this new enemy as the quartermaster finished getting his supplies. He bade the man good bye and headed for his tent. Peter would be interested in the news he had obtained. The possibility of an upcoming battle against this new kind of enemy excited him but when he recalled Attaleiates' revelations, his enthusiasm cooled.

In the afternoon the priests with the army blessed the battle flag of each unit. Some soldiers drilled and practiced the art of war and others fortified the camp by digging a six-by-eight foot trench around the encampment, heaping the divested earth on the inner rim of the trench and punctuating this barrier with sharpened wooden stakes. Romanos Diogenes called all of his senior commanders to his tent. Diogenes made certain everyone entering his tent would know immediately that he stood in the tent of the Roman emperor. The interior walls of the enormous enclosure were purple silk interwoven with golden thread. Chains of pearls and diamonds followed the ceiling from end to end. Exquisite mosaics stood on porphyry pedestals and jewelled silver caskets rested on those of green marble. The imperial dinnerware, nothing but the finest gold, was displayed on tables covered in the most opulent silk and linen weave. In comparison, Andronikos Dukas' tent was that of a mere provincial governor.

Diogenes stood over a map table lost in its detail when the first of his officers began to arrive. He had dismissed all of his aides so that he was alone in his tent.

The first through the door was Nikephoros Bryennios. Close behind him was Basilacios, an Armenian, and Michael Attaleiates. The three men came to attention. A few minutes later, the Cappadocian commander Alyattes came in.

Romanos, however, was a thousand miles away. Attaleiates couldn't determine if the emperor was deliberately ignoring them or truly unaware of their presence. Romanos looked restless. Later Attaleiates discovered that the Diogenes had not slept well for the last few days but he wouldn't admit that to anyone.

Bryennios broke the silence. "Your Majesty . . . ."

"Hmmph!" Romanos snorted, acknowledging this interruption but failing to look up. He stroked his dark beard firmly with his left hand while he traced a path on the map with his right index finger. After a full two minutes, he looked up at his commanders. He said nothing but looked sternly at each of them, showing his fear and anger. Those present could see he lacked his usual strength.

Just then, Joseph Tarchaniotes entered the tent and saluted Romanos Diogenes. The emperor's face brightened. "Welcome, Tarchaniotes! Come over here," he said excitedly, gesturing with his left hand. "I have something to show you."

As Tarchaniotes walked to the map table, Andronikos Dukas entered with Roussel de Bailleul but Romanos and Tarchaniotes failed to notice their entry. The late arrivals slowly walked to where Bryennios and the others were standing. Bryennios and those near him, who shared the emperor's distrust of Andronikos Dukas, cooly acknowledged his presence.

Roussel de Bailleul was relatively unknown to them. Attaleiates knew of him only because Peter had mentioned him. He surveyed the other commanders. Bailleul's association with Dukas appeared to arouse their suspicion of him.

Having just started with Tarchaniotes, Romanos then called his other commanders to the map table. "My lords, take note of the map." He pointed to it with his right index finger. "We are currently here, at Erzurum." He lifted his finger off the table. "I believe that Alp Arslan will arrive in Armenia soon, so the time for action is now." He returned his finger to the map. "The Turks have fortified Khelat, here, close to the north shore of Lake Van." He moved his finger westward on the map. "And here is Manzikert, another fortified town. With these two targets subdued, we will secure a significant advantage in Armenia."

"What is your plan to take these cities, Your Majesty?" asked Nikephoros Bryennios.

"To make certain we take both fortresses before Alp Arslan arrives, I will divide our force into two groups."

Tarchaniotes looked uneasy. Romanos ignored the strategos' look of apprehension and spoke directly to him. "Joseph, I am giving you command of twenty thousand scutati and fifteen thousand cataphract. You will take Khelat. With the remaining twenty-five thousand men, I will take Manzikert."

Tarchaniotes was apprehensive. "Majesty, I feel this is a grave error! You should not divide your army!"

Romanos snapped back, "You will do as you are ordered, Strategos!"

"Sire, this will certainly lead to disaster. The Turk is very mobile and we don't know where he is —"

"That will be enough of your insolence, Strategos!" Romanos thundered.

Tarchaniotes again tried to raise his objection but the emperor stopped him with a penetrating glare.

Tarchaniotes backed down but Attaleiates could tell he hadn't changed his opinion. The strategos was humiliated. Never had any emperor been so rude to him.

Andronikos Dukas broke the brief silence that followed Romanos' berating of Tarchaniotes. "His Highness' plan is ingenious," he declared.

Not having detected Dukas' arrival, Romanos was surprised to hear his voice and doubly so to hear Dukas' support of his plan. Joseph Tarchaniotes turned pale.

Tarchaniotes grew bolder and regrouped, determined to convince Romanos Diogenes that his plan would lead to disaster. The emperor's tongue-lashing had hurt his pride but his life and reputation were at stake. "Your Majesty, we don't know how many men Alp Arslan can muster. By dividing our forces we provide him with an opportunity to defeat us piecemeal. It is better that the army remain intact."

Surprisingly, Romanos had cooled down and seemed willing to listen to his most experienced commander.

Dukas glared at Tarchaniotes but the strategos continued to press his case. "Please, Majesty, choose the more important of the two fortresses and take that one."

"But Joseph, they are of equal importance." Romanos turned away from the map. "We will execute the plan as we have discussed."

"Majesty," Andronikos Dukas began in a conciliatory manner, "perhaps the strategos would feel more at ease with his new orders if an expert cavalryman were to accompany him."

Romanos recognized Roussel de Bailleul standing next to Dukas and excitedly agreed. "Yes, that is an excellent idea." He turned to Tarchaniotes. "You will be in command of the attacking force and Roussel de Bailleul will lead your cavalry. Such a formidable force and extraordinary leadership will be unstoppable."

Tarchaniotes was silent. He looked helpless, defeated. But Andronikos Dukas was smiling ear to ear.

At dinner, Justin and Peter joked with their men as they ate lamb, vegetables, and bread. Soon after dinner, three horns blew and the men sang the Trisagion hymn: "Holy God, holy strong one, holy immortal one, have mercy on us." The exhausted soldiers, their days spent continuously marching, drilling, or preparing camp, easily fell asleep.

The morning of August 22ⁿᵈ was cooler than most summer mornings in Constantinople. Eleni walked unattended through the gardens of the Palace Bucoleon, a woolen shawl around her shoulders. She had just finished breakfast with the empress who was spending the rest of the morning on official court business. As she strolled, Eleni thought of this person she had come to know over the past five and a half months. She was truly an intelligent woman that Eleni respected. But beyond the intellect, the empress possessed warmth and an inner strength that was equally bona fide. It was obvious to Eleni that Empress Evdokia cared for her. It was evident in their discussions of everything from the mundane to the miraculous. She knew the empress, too, enjoyed this new relationship. They would spend hours laughing about events from both of their lives. What a strange miracle: Evdokia, Empress of the Romans, treasuring her time with a young commoner. Perhaps, Eleni thought, it was because Evdokia could trust her, unlike the women of her court and her servants. Yes, Justin had been wrong in his assessment of this woman but perhaps the circumstances of his interactions with her were to blame. Indeed, Eleni considered the empress a friend and she felt certain the feeling was mutual.

Aspasia arrived to visit with her daughter one hour later. Eleni was pleasantly surprised and ran to hug her mother when she saw her, although it had only been two days since they had last enjoyed time at the palace together.

"Your father was sorry he couldn't come. He really misses you," Aspasia began. "He truly enjoyed coming with me the last few times."

"I thought he seemed out of place," Eleni responded. "He didn't say too much. I think he's changed a little. He just seemed different."

"Oh, he's no different, my dear," Aspasia said. She took her daughter's hand and walked with her toward her favorite part of the garden.

"What do you mean, Mother?" Eleni asked. "Are you telling me that *I've* changed?"

"That was very clever of you to figure out so quickly," Aspasia answered. "But, then again, you are your father's daughter."

"Yes but over these past five months, I've also discovered that I'm my mother's daughter," Eleni said, smiling at her mother.

"Yes," Aspasia agreed, "you are. It's funny how we both came to realize that." Aspasia stopped and held her daughter's hands. "I've enjoyed coming to visit you here but I do so look forward to seeing you at home. Why does the empress still keep you here?"

"She has always said it is for my protection—" Eleni replied.

"Oh, posh!" Aspasia interjected in a huff. "I still don't believe that excuse. I think Justin was right. You are her hostage!"

Eleni was not going to let a disagreement interfere with this time she loved so much. She walked with her mother to a hedge of red and yellow rosebushes. "She's a very good woman, Mother.

And if I'm being held hostage, I don't mind much. I do so miss Justin, though."

"We all do, Eleni," Aspasia said, holding her daughter close to her. "We all do." The two continued their walk past the cypresses and pines to a large grassy area. "Isn't it wonderful?"

"Yes, Mother," Eleni admitted.

Aspasia grew sober. "Your father has heard that the army has yet to find the Turks."

Eleni looked back at her mother, her eyes begging Aspasia to say more.

"He says that the campaign may drag on through the fall," Aspasia added as she saw tears welling up in her daughter's eyes. "I'm so sorry, Eleni." She held her daughter closely and added, "I hope to God his information is wrong."

CHAPTER 14

After the early morning cool had cleared, Despina left the library to join Senator Kastros for a midday repast. Emmanual Ghassani was again with them, having arrived earlier that morning. But instead of rushing off with Kastros to the library upon his arrival, he had promised the senator to relax a bit and share a meal with him and Madam Georgiou before discussing the events in Damascus. This last voyage had been particularly rough with unexpected summer storms making their presence known and increasing numbers of bandits along the roads, extracting what they could from unwary travelers.

This visit was Ghassani's sixth since March. Over time, Despina and he had become more acquainted. As much as either would be hesitant to admit, each had grown to enjoy the other's company. She found him to be a clever, witty man who was clearly well-bred and her deceptions gave him the impression that he was dealing with a kind, pious woman who was beyond suspicion.

However, Despina had still never been able to eavesdrop on their conversations in the library. Despina was now obsessed with this. She knew this was the key to removing Kastros from the game. Her last two messages from Mavrites demanded action. Luckily, the emperor's prolonged campaign gave her more time to discover what was happening in the library, and decide how to eliminate Kastros.

The chaplain blessed the meal and then excused himself. Kastros, Despina, and Emmanual Ghassani shared wine from Kastros' vineyard as they ate stuffed grape leaves, cheese, and olives, followed by *kakavia*, a delicious seafood soup. Despina played the role of Madam Georgiou with consummate skill. She was particularly charming toward Ghassani who couldn't help but take notice of the young widow. Perhaps her efforts would be rewarded with the information she so dearly needed.

After the meal, Kastros and Ghassani excused themselves and went directly to the library. But something different happened this time; something very significant. Despina was left alone. The servants busily rushed from kitchen to the dining area and back again. Others returned to work in the bedrooms and in the gardens. Madam Georgiou had been overlooked.

Despina looked around slowly. Nobody was in sight. Without another thought, she slid out of her chair and hurried to down the hall where she stopped to reconnoiter. The hallway was empty. *The library is just down the hall. How can I get in without their seeing me? I know there has got to be a way. They were just a few minutes ahead of me. Can't have discussed much. Almost there. Right over – damn!* One of the maids shot out of nowhere right in front of her. Despina slammed herself up against the wall. Luckily, the blankets the maid carried blocked enough of her view to prevent her from seeing Despina.

After the maid passed, Despina sighed deeply, her heart accelerating in her chest. Used to danger and intrigue, she found the moment exhilarating and moved quickly onward to the library. The beautifully carved ebony library doors inlaid with ivory and gold stood before her. As she approached them, beads of sweat formed on her forehead. She wiped them away as she contemplated her clandestine ingress. Despina slowly, silently placed her hand on one of the delicate gilt bronze handles, relieved to find the door unlatched when she depressed the cool hilt.

Excellent! So far, so good. Slowly, so as not to disturb even the smallest fleck of dust, Despina pushed the door open. She leaned forward and slid half of her face past the open door to find a small vestibule. *Perfect!* Twenty feet ahead, she saw Kastros and Ghassani inspecting a document and discussing their thoughts. She quickly slid into the vestibule, unnoticed by the two men. From there she easily heard them. She didn't need to see anything. She settled onto a small bench and patiently took in the intelligence coming from the library.

"So the Caliph of Cairo is satisfied?" Kastros asked.

"Yes, Gregory," Ghassani answered. "His representative in Damascus tells me the caliph has agreed to keep the four principal roads into Damascus open to all traffic from the empire, not just to pilgrims travelling to Jerusalem. The caliph also promises to keep the ports of Jaffa and Tyre open to our ships and, perhaps, he will open Acre and Tripoli as well."

"And your people?" Kastros asked.

"If the empire accepts the plan, he will lighten proscriptions on all Christians living under his power. He even promised to allow the repair of many of our churches in the caliphate," Ghassani replied, his voice full of hope.

"Complicity with the infidel Arabs," Despina whispered softly. "Sounds like treason to me. Senator Kastros arrested for treason. That will suit me very well."

"Emmanuel," Kastros began, "I, and I'm certain Emperor Romanos Diogenes, appreciate all of your hard work. You've done a great deal of riding back and forth from Constantinople to Damascus for the last six months. Thank you." He reached across the table and shook Ghassani's hand.

"It could not have been done without your influence, Gregory. The fact that you have the emperor's ear was the key to our success. Otherwise, the caliph wouldn't have bothered with me."

"So we're a good team, my friend," Kastros said, smiling broadly. "A damned good team!"

"Praise Christ for that," Ghassani added.

"Yes, of course. When will you head back to Damascus?"

"As soon as possible," Ghassani replied. "When will the emperor see the proposal?"

"I'll show it to him as soon as he returns to Constantinople. I'm certain he will be eager to complete this endeavor."

Despina grew anxious as she thought of a way to extricate herself from the vestibule without leaving a trace. In the corner, she spotted a black leather pouch. She knew that it was Ghassani's. She had seen him take it off of his horse and carry it into the villa enough times to be certain of that. Then she thought of the tool that Metropolitan Mavrites had given her. *Plans for the defenses of Anazarbus in Emmanuel Ghassani's pouch, found on him as he rides back to Damascus! Oh, I couldn't have planned this better! Ah, but how to get the plans into the pouch? There has to be a way.*

The two men stood up. As they took their first steps away from the table, Kastros stopped Ghassani.

"Emmanuel," the senator began, "there's one more thing I need to talk to you about."

"Yes, Gregory," Ghassani said, without attempting to hide his curiousity. "What is it?"

"It's about Madam Georgiou," Kastros replied with a boyish grin on his face.

Despina froze when she heard her pseudonym mentioned. She redoubled her efforts to hear what Kastros was saying.

"Yes . . ." Ghassani said, smiling at his friend, very interested in what he was about to say.

"Well . . ." Kastros found himself tongue-tied. "I've really gotten to know her these last five months . . ."

"Yes . . ." Ghassani said again, anticipating his friend's announcement.

"She's quite a beautiful woman . . ." Kastros continued, finding it hard to get to the point of his announcement and almost hoping that Ghassani would finish his sentence for him.

"And quite charming," Ghassani added.

Despina listened intently, fearing where the senator was going with this.

"The next time I see her . . ." Kastros continued, still faltering.

"Yes . . ." Ghassani said, his smile growing ever wider.

"I'm going to ask her to marry me," Kastros blurted out.

Despina gagged after she heard the senator's declaration. She held her hand over her mouth to stifle a cough and then said under her breath, "He must be joking!"

"I want to spend the rest of my life with her," Kastros said, speaking much easier now that the news had broken.

Despina rolled her eyes. *Rich or not, I'm not going to spend the rest of my life with that old fool!*

"That's fantastic, Gregory!" Ghassani said, grabbing and shaking his friend's hand. "When will the wedding be? I'd love to be there."

"Well," Kastros began slowly, resuming the same meandering speech with which he had started the conversation, "I've spoken to Father Nicetas, my chaplain . . ."

"Yes yes . . ." Ghassani said, his friend's sudden change in speech pattern making him uneasy.

"Tonight!" Kastros blurted out.

Despina grabbed her forehead with her hands and squeezed, "Oh, God!" she sighed under her breath.

"That seems a bit sudden," Ghassani said gracefully, so as not to offend his friend.

"Why not?" Kastros asked, trying not to be defensive. "We've been living under the same roof for the last five months. She's a widow; I'm a widower. We both long for companionship . . ."

"Does Madam Georgiou have any inkling that you're interested in marrying her?"

No! Despina bit her lip.

"No," Kastros admitted, "but I know she'll say yes. I know because of the way she looks at me when we speak, the feel of her hand in mine as we stroll through the gardens . . . ."

Despina rolled her eyes.

Ghassani looked back at his friend, his face reflecting his doubt.

"I'm going to ask her, Emmanuel. And I want you to be my Koumbarro."

"It would be an honor." Ghassani smiled as he accepted the request to serve as Kastros' best man.

As the discussion in the library continued, Despina's mind raced. *The old man is determined to have me and if I say no he may be hurt, enough to send me packing. Then I won't be able to plant the evidence on Ghassani and Kastros will still be able to lead his allies on Romanos Diogenes' behalf. I've done worse for the archbishop. I'll go through with this wedding, teach the old boy a thing or two on our wedding night, and then watch the Mavrites' men haul him off to the dungeons the next morning.*

Despina stealthily poked her head around the vestibule wall and saw both Kastros and Ghassani talking and looking out of the library's only window, their backs to the vestibule. Seeing this, she slipped out of the vestibule, past the ebony doors, and into the vacant hallway. Despina smiled as she let herself relax. She would send a message to Archbishop Mavrites, via Saint Martha's, immediately. *In two days I'll be done with Kastros. Too bad, though. It's been quite fun.* Then she dreamed about how she would spend Mavrites' gold.

Why, Gregory," Despina said, appearing to be surprised, "I don't know what to say!"

"Does that mean you won't marry me?" Kastros asked.

"Oh, no!" Despina replied. "Ever since I met you, I have dreamed that someday you would ask me to marry you. And now that day is here! Oh, I just can't believe it!"

Kastros' expression rapidly changed from disappointment to delight. He held out his arms and hugged his wife-to-be. "And you don't mind that the wedding is this evening?" Kastros asked gently.

"Oh, if it were possible, I would wish it to happen now!" Despina was enjoying her role as the giddy bride.

"I do too, my dear Demetra!" Kastros said hugging her again. "I do too!"

The villa's chapel stood on the opposite side of the entry hall from the library. The nave could easily accommodate forty people. Ornate porphyry columns flanked the nave on each side. Outside of the columns on each side were narrow galleries with stunning jeweled mosaics adorning the walls. The vault over the nave was painted a brilliant blue. Four large lighted chandeliers hung from this celestial loft, spreading their bright light over the nave and sanctuary. Beyond the nave was a gilt bronze iconostasis with icons, from left to right, of Saint George, the Virgin Mary holding the Infant Christ, the Lord Jesus Christ, and John the Baptist. Beyond the discrete double doors, placed between the Virgin and the Christ, Father Nicetas waited in the sanctuary. In front of the iconostasis, Kastros waited with Ghassani at his side.

The ecstatic groom was wearing a fine cotton tunica under a vivid green silk dalmatic, which was studded with sapphires from India and pearls from Crete. The sleeves were long and flared at the ends. A fine border of golden thread circled the neck. Fine white silk hose covered his legs.

Ghassani wore a simpler dalmatic that he borrowed for the occasion from one of the groom's valets. It was light blue with small gold medallions at the hemlines. His face showed how happy he was for his friend.

Despina stood at the entrance to the nave with Esther. She wore a stunning ivory-colored silk stola over a sheer cotton tunica. The stola, discreetly accented with rubies, had fine gold thread stitching at the hemlines and golden silk brocade around the ends of the long, bell-shaped sleeves that covered her wrists. Despina's hair was a work of beauty. Kastros' servants had worked for hours to create this triumph, reminiscent of the styles that embellished statutes of ancient Greek goddesses. Esther wore a simple rose-colored stola that Kastros had made for her in anticipation of this wedding. The old woman beamed as she remembered Kastros' wedding to his first wife. She looked at him now; that first wedding was the last time he looked this happy.

Despina drank in the beauty of the chapel as she and Esther walked through the nave to where Kastros and Ghassani awaited them. She glanced up at the gracefully domed vault just before she began the walk to her future husband. Despina had been there with Kastros many, many times before, celebrating the Divine Liturgy on Sundays, all of the holy days and saints' days, and the tremendous spectacle of events that Holy Week and Easter brought. Yet tonight, the chapel looked more stunning than usual. Kastros had added more candles to increase the chapel's brightness and he brought in large earth-filled pots, brimming over with Madam Georgiou's favorite flowers.

It's all so gorgeous! The flowers in particular caught Despina's eye. *The old fool must be pretty excited about this. It will be a shame to spoil it.*

Upon the women's arrival at the front of the nave, Father Nicetas walked from the sanctuary through the double doors that separated the Virgin and Christ, and took his position with the groom and best man in front of a small cloth-draped table. A young altar boy stepped out from a door on the right side of the iconostasis and joined him at his side. As the women arrived, the priest invited the presence of the Father by invoking the name of the Son. The wedding party followed the lead of the priest as he crossed himself, led them through several prayers, and exorted the bride and groom to strive for perfection in their marriage. He cited several examples from the Bible and church history: Abraham and Sarah, Issac and Rebecca, Joachim and Anna.

The altar boy handed Father Nicetas an exquisite golden bible, which was covered with precious stones and small hand-painted icons. The priest read the story of the Savior's first miracle at the wedding in Cana from the Gospel of Saint John. Next he turned to Saint Paul's Epistle to the Ephesians and urged the bride and groom to heed the apostle's advice regarding the proper conduct of husband and wife.

After the bride and groom exchanged rings, the ceremony moved on to its most important segment. The bride and groom faced Father Nicetas. He held in each hand a golden crown, each crown joined to the other by a fine white silk ribbon. The priest raised the conjoined crowns into the air, signaling Ghassani to move behind the bride and groom. As the priest lowered the crowns onto the heads of the wedding couple, the best man assumed their care. When Nicetas made the sign of the cross, Ghassani lifted each crown above the head where the priest had laid it to rest and crossed his wrists, thereby transferring the crown of one to the head of the other. After this was done three times, the priest led the wedding couple around the covered table behind him, chanting hymns and prayers. The altar boy remained closely at his side, holding a censor. Fine incense burned within in it. The priest would stop at regular intervals and gently swing the censor before the wedding party, sending the fragrant incense their way, as if he were the Father Himself sending the Spirit to bless the wedding.

As Father Nicetas led the procession around the table, Ghassani held the silken strip between the golden crowns with his right hand. The crowns rested solemnly on the heads of the bride and groom. As he did so, Esther dutifully followed the bride. When the procession was over, the priest announced that "Demetra" and Gregory Kastros were now married. He presented them with a golden chalice from which they each took a sip of red wine, the senator first and then his wife. When Despina had finished, Kastros surprised her and kissed her fully on the lips.

Father Nicetas and the young altar boy joined the wedding party for a celebration at the villa. The servants had been hard at work preparing this dinner for their master and new mistress. They had been told only four hours earlier that the senator was getting married that evening.

"I haven't seen him this happy in years," said Father Nicetas to Ghassani as both of them watched Senator and Missus Kastros accept the congratulations of their servants.

"Nor have I, Father," Ghassani said. "Nor have I."

Kastros accepted the hands of each of his servants, treating them more like friends than servants. He introduced to Despina those few whom she had not met.

Soon after, Ghassani toasted the new couple. All of those present, even the servants, raised their goblets and wished them well. The kitchen help brought out a sumptuous feast of venison; *keftedes*, meatballs of beef and herbs, dredged in barley flour and fried in olive oil; *dolmades*, stuffed grape leaves; exotic fruits and vegetables; four types of bread; three different kinds of cheese. Father Nicetas led everyone, servants, masters, and guests, in a prayer of thankgiving. Once everyone, including the servants, was seated, the wine began to flow. With it came a seemingly boundless river of love and good feeling that bathed the hearts of everyone.

Despina found herself thrown off-balance by the evening's events. She had never been part of such a joyous happening. Her new husband laughed gleefully as Ghassani and he talked about this sudden good turn in the senator's fortunes. She watched him. *The poor bastard has no idea what he's in for.* Yet there was something about Kastros, something she had never seen in him before. She had always thought him to be a doddering old fool and she took great pleasure in thinking she would to be the instrument of his destruction. However, now Despina had to admit she found something intriguing about him.

Kastros was certainly a kind man but that didn't make him much different than most. She looked at his face and saw something in his eyes, something she had never seen, or had never noticed, before. She felt a warmth in her heart, a soothing, comforting warmth. Esther, who was seated at her side, spoke to her but Despina didn't answer. She was totally and inexplicably entranced by her husband.

Perhaps this is how the lioness feels before it pounces on a deer and tears it to pieces. But she had played the lioness many times before and never felt like this.

The evening continued and, with it, the mirth and merriment, dancing and more wine. No one showed signs of tiring, least of all the groom. Kastros, his goblet replenished with wine, stood and urged Despina to do the same.

"Demetra and I," the senator began, "would like to thank each of you for making this day so special for us." Kastros looked at Despina as if to ask, "Am I right?"

Despina saw his eyes as she had never before seen them. That same feeling of warmth bathed her heart again as she smiled at her husband, answering his unsaid question in the affirmative. As she did so, she suddenly shuddered inside. *What are you doing? Tomorrow at this time, he'll be on his way to prison and you'll be busy counting your money. Don't get soft! You've done this dozens of times before. Don't let all of your hard work be for nothing!* She braced as if she were suddenly inundated with icy water. *Finish the job! Be done with him!*

The wedding festivities ended just after midnight. Kastros ordered the servants to bed; the debris from the celebration could be cleared away the next day.

Emmanuel Ghassani wished his host and hostess a goodnight. "I am very happy for both of you," he said as he hugged each of them.

Father Nicetas, who had fallen asleep hours ago, snored in a dark corner of the room. Kastros walked over to his chaplain and gently roused him. "Father, it's time for bed."

"Oh?" The old priest, who had not quite awakened, stumbled forward. Kastros asked one of the servants to help the chaplain to his quarters and then walked across the empty dining area to his wife.

Despina watched Kastros like a hawk watches an unsuspecting rabbit. She had exorcized the demon that was compromising her mission. She had overcome that fleeting moment of weakness and was resolved to send the senator to his doom. Despina would clench her teeth when she reminded herself that she had nearly faltered.

A professional of your abilities? Who would have thought . . . Despina imagined the senator languishing in a dark prison, Metropolitan Mavrites' minions torturing his bruised body, Kastros' cries for mercy going unheeded.

Despina looked into Kastros' eyes, thought again of the condemned man's fate, and smiled. *Time to get to work.* She kissed him, holding him tightly. She slowly opened her mouth while their lips were still together and soon felt Kastros do the same. When their lips parted, she could hear him gasp and pant. Knowing that his passion had been stirred, Despina's lips at once descended upon his again. This time she grabbed his head and held it firmly against her lips, opening her mouth every so often, leaving her quarry to wonder what to expect next.

Kastros' heart pounded wildly in his chest. He had never known such passion and he wanted more. He surprised his wife, and himself, by lifting her off of her feet, their lips still joined in their torrid intercourse. He carried his bride to his bedroom, a stranger to this kind of commerce for too long.

As Kastros carried her, Despina's mind coolly calculated her next moves. The game was coming to its end and she would need to be careful that everything went perfectly. But then, out of nowhere, she again felt that gentle tugging at her heart. She angrily tried to expunge it. What on earth was she thinking? She thought of living a leisurely life with Kastros but she knew that was impossible. Kastros was a marked man. If she refused or failed to complete her mission, Archbishop Mavrites would just send another. He probably had someone waiting in the wings already. She knew that the metropolitan had a large network of spies and assassins; there was no escaping him. Not even the wife of an imperial senator could elude his grasp. To betray Mavrites was to sign her own death warrant. Was she willing to do that? *Certaintly not! Enough of this foolishness! Do the job, collect your money, and enjoy it while you can or die!*

This last thought was enough to cleanse the realistic Despina of any thoughts that would distract her. Mavrites, or at least his money, had always been good to her.

Once in the bedroom, Kastros laid his bride on the silk bedspread. He stood by the bed in the dark room as if he were trying to remember what to do next. Despina reached up from the bed and gently pulled Kastros onto her. She slowly kissed his lips and then suddenly opened her mouth, again electrifying her husband with her erotic antics. Despina continued on and on, feeling Kastros' robust heart beating furiously against her breast.

Despina sent her skilled hands to work, surreptitiously peeling Kastros' clothes from his impassioned body. By the time he realized his own nakedness, his wife had slid out of her wedding gown. Their steaming, naked bodies pressed up against each other. She could hear his rapid short breaths as he floated, wonderfully intoxicated, into this sexual paradise. She lifted her right breast to his lips, inviting him to partake of this sensual ambrosia.

Their bodies writhed together, each enveloped in the other, the volume of their sexual furor deluging the room. Despina welcomed his pumping and thrusting by pulling him deeper and deeper inside her. Kastros acknowledged his wife's silent requests by mustering every last ounce of his strength to satisfy her. Each of them prayed that this pleasure would not end. Yet, as always so soon, this sensual exclamation reached its zenith, its convulsing climax and sent them tumbling from this mountain of passion to the valley of exhaustion below.

Hours later, Despina awoke in her husband's arms. She didn't remember how exactly she had arrived there but she did remember the remainder of that voluptuous voyage. She sighed as she thought of the night's passion. *Too bad. The old fellow was fun.* Despina gently rolled out of her sleeping husband's grasp and went back to sleep.

Daylight brightened the bedroom as Despina awoke. She was surprised to find her husband gone. She went through the wardrobe of Kastros' first wife and found a white linen tunica. She threw it on and then pulled on a gold stola and rushed from the room. Outside she found Kastros and Emmanuel Ghassani, who, with his cloak around his shoulders, held his baggage under one arm.

"You're not leaving us?" Despina asked, just catching her breath.

Kastros was surprised by his wife's urgency. "Emmanuel will return in two weeks, Demetra."

Despina's mind raced a mile a minute. If Ghassani were leaving, then she would have to make certain he left with the Anazarbus defense plans. Mavrites would not wait two more weeks. Despina clenched her fists, determined to see her plan through.

"Emmanuel," Despina said, as she moved toward the door, "I have something to give you before you go."

Despina ran to the room and grabbed a small ornate silver casket. She opened it to find the defense plans hidden exactly where she had planted them. She ran back outside to Ghassani and gracefully presented it to him. "Emmanuel, please accept this from Gregory and me," Despina said as she held it out to him.

"Oh," Ghassani stammered, "Thank you. I'm very surprised." He carefully examined the outside of the casket and turned to Despina. "Thank you, Demetra. It's beautiful!" Then he looked at Kastros who was as flabbergasted as he was. "And thank you, Gregory."

"Oh, you're welcome, Emmanuel, but this gift is all Demetra's doing." He beamed as he saw how thoughtful his new wife was. He lovingly put his arm around her shoulder.

"Good bye, Demetra," Ghassani said, reaching for Despina's hand. He gently held it and added, "Until next time."

Despina smiled back at him. "Until next time," she replied, thoroughly enjoying the deadly irony of the situation.

"Good bye, Emmanuel," Kastros said, taking Ghassani's hand after Despina had released it. "Have a safe journey to Damascus," he said. "We'll see you in two weeks."

"Until then, my friend," Ghassani replied. He turned and mounted his horse.

Despina waved as the Arab rode away. She knew she would never see him again; his fate was sealed. Despina softly grabbed Kastros' hand and walked with him back inside the villa. Once inside, she smoothly excused herself from her husband, found a messenger, and sent him to Saint Martha's with a message for Archbishop Mavrites: "The quarry has been released."

In the late afternoon, Gregory Kastros looked carefully at the documents that Ghassani had left with him. "This is a work of beauty," the senator noted. "The emperor will want to see this as soon as he returns from his campaign." He sat back and smiled. Members of the Senate and the emperor would indeed be appreciative. No doubt Kastros would be richly rewarded but any money the senator received he would give to the monasteries and convents to help with the poor and sick.

Kastros walked to the chapel and kneeled before the icon of Jesus Christ on the iconostasis. He crossed himself three times and bowed his head. "Dear Lord Christ," he prayed, "I thank you for the successful conclusion of this task. May Your glory, the glory of Your emperor, and the glory of Your holy empire be increased by this work." Then he thought of his new wife. "And also, thank you for Demetra. She's—"

"Senator Kastros!" a loud voice boomed from the narthex.

The senator slowly rose, crossed himself three times, and turned around. He was exasperated by the interruption. "What do you want? Can't you see that I'm praying?"

The man who had interrupted him was a captain of the heavy cavalry. He was accompanied by three fellow cataphract. "Senator," the cavalryman said, lowering the volume of his voice, "I have a warrant for your arrest, sir."

"What is this?" Kastros demanded as he walked toward the soldiers. "What on earth are you taking about?"

The captain hesitated. He knew of the senator's sterling reputation and closeness with the emperor. "I am here to arrest you, Senator Kastros," he said cautiously.

"What is the charge?" Kastros demanded, his eyes burning in anger.

The captain froze. His comrades were equally intimidated.

"Treason!" said a cold voice from behind Kastros.

Kastros spun around to find Metropolitan Mavrites standing by the iconostasis.

"What is this, Mavrites?" Kastros growled.

"Do I need to repeat myself?" asked the archbishop as he walked toward Kastros. "Treason," he repeated when the senator didn't reply.

Kastros took a breath to deliver a loud retort but Mavrites cut him off.

"Do you know a certain Emmanuel Ghassani?" Mavrites asked.

Kastros' heart sank. He knew well of the treacherous churchman and to hear him mention his good friend's name meant that the Raven had ensnared him. Again, he did not respond.

"Of course you know him, Senator," Mavrites said acridly. "He is a good friend of yours."

Kastros silently glared at the mendacious Mavrites.

"Ghassani has been riding from this villa to Damascus with frightening regularity."

"He has been assisting me in negotiations with the Caliph of Cairo," Kastros responded.

"I have many friends at court and I am not aware of any negotiations with the Infidel."

"These were secret negotiations," Kastros said, his anger with the archbishop growing.

"Oh, I see: *secret* negotiations," Mavrites returned mockingly.

The archbishop walked to within a foot of the senator, reached into his cassock, and pulled out a parchment. "Do these secret negotiations include passing defense plans for the city of Anazarbus to foreign governments?" he asked as he shoved the document into Kastros' face. "This was found among Ghassani's possessions."

"What?" Kastros roared. "What is this treachery?" He grabbed the document from Mavrites and quickly read through it.

Mavrites smiled as he witnessed the anguish on the senator's face. "You obviously supplied the document. Who else but a senator has access to state secrets? I guess the only question is whether Ghassani was working for the Caliph of Cairo or you."

"This is insanity! Where's Ghassani?" Kastros demanded.

"On his way to the darkest jail cell in Constantinople," Mavrites smirked. "Where you will certainly join him."

"Mavrites," Kastros began, "you'll regret this. I'll appeal directly to the Emperor Romanos!"

"Emperor Romanos is hundreds of miles away," the metropolitan shot back. And then, as if he were anticipating what Kastros was going to say, he added, "and the empress will be hard pressed to pardon a traitor without the agreement of the Emperor Michael."

Despina then ran into the chapel. "Gregory," she cried to her husband, "What is this?"

"Your husband, madam" — he winked at Despina — "is a traitor!" Mavrites ordered the senator shackled.

"No!" Despina screamed. "Gregory! It's not true!"

Kastros looked at his new bride lovingly. "No, my dear. It's not true."

"Let him go!" Despina yelled, attacking the soldiers who were leading her husband away. "He's not a traitor!"

Despina followed the soldiers and Mavrites outside as Kastros was forced to mount a mule. She yelled at them and swung her fists. "Let him go! My husband is innocent!"

Soon, servants came from all directions to watch the commotion. The soldiers held them at a distance with their lances. Kastros saw Esther crying and asking him what was happening. Father Nicetas ran to Mavrites, begging to know why Kastros was being taken away.

Mavrites pushed him away. "Stay away from me or you'll be arrested as an accomplice!"

The soldiers were soon on their way down the road with Kastros. The servants and Father Nicetas ran behind them, hoping for a miracle that would bring him back to them.

As the servants ran to Kastros, Mavrites walked over to Despina and whispered to her, "Well done, my child! You played the role of the faithful wife very well."

Despina, tears still streaming from her eyes, didn't answer. Her eyes remained on the soldiers and the senator, now just small silhouettes on the horizon.

The archbishop nudged Despina with his elbow. "Good work my child," he whispered again.

Despina turned and looked at Mavrites. "Oh," she said uneasily as she wiped her eyes, "thank you, Your Eminence." Her gaze returned to the horizon.

The metropolitan could see that Despina was preoccupied. "I'll send a carriage for you in the morning," he added.

"Yes," Despina said, her eyes still fixed on the horizon.

Mavrites stepped into his carriage. As it sped away, Despina's eyes filled with tears.

Mavrites caught a glimpse of her as he left. "She'll get over this," he reassured himself. He pulled a flask out of his cassock, opened it, and sipped some of the wine inside. He watched the scenery go by, and thought of Constantine Papakostas. He had always liked that boy. It was too bad he had to be sacrificed. Mavrites sighed. He would miss Constantine but the archbishop knew there were still plenty of other young virile men in Constantinople to be had.

CHAPTER 15

Two days after that fateful meeting in Romanos Diogenes' tent, both parts of the imperial army left Erzurum. Tarchaniotes and Roussel de Bailleul led thirty-five thousand men toward Khelat while Romanos Diogenes led twenty-five thousand toward Manzikert, including Nikephoros Bryennios, Basilacios, Michael Attaleiates, and Andronikos Dukas.

Tarchaniotes' massive column of twenty thousand infantry and fifteen thousand cavalry moved slowly eastward through Armenia toward Khelat. The men marched throughout the daylight hours. At dusk, it was still moving, searching for a bivouac for the night. Two cavalrymen rode side by side, speaking quietly in the low light.

"Have you found the strategos in a most peculiar humor these past two days?" whispered one to the other. Both were junior officers who had served with Tarchaniotes for the past year.

"Yes," replied the other. "He's very sullen. Acts as if someone close to him has died."

"The senior officers are avoiding him, or so it seems to me," the first one added.

"I've seen that as well. Except for the new tribune, Markos. Sent by Emperor Michael himself, they say. He is constantly at the strategos' side."

"I get the impression that the strategos would sooner be rid of him but Markos is as tenacious as a well-bred hunting dog."

"That Norman who is commanding our cavalry —"

"Roussel de Bailleul. A savage, like all of those barbarians."

"He has been with the strategos quite a bit as well."

"You know, the more I think about it, the old man hasn't been himself for the past several months."

"Has he fallen out of favor with the emperor?"

"I doubt that. They've known each other for years. Would the emperor trust over half of his army to someone who had fallen out of his favor? Our mission to take Khelat is probably the most important segment of the campaign thus far."

"You're right," the second one admitted, "but I still would like to know what's bothering him so much."

The column came to a halt and the troops set up camp. The first horseman tried to renew the conversation with his mate but by the time he found him, he was asleep in the tent.

Reveille sounded at dawn the following morning. The cavalry and infantry were on the move within an hour. Again, the two young junior officers found themselves riding next to each other yet they did not resume the previous day's conversation. Today they would arrive at Khelat. They were saving their mental strength for this first battle with the Turks.

By the fourth hour of the day, Tarchaniotes and his commanders could see Khelat. They stopped their horses and inspected the prize ahead of them. The town was heavily defended but the Roman troops were eager and confident. Tarchaniotes turned in his saddle and looked back at his army. He could tell they were ready. At his left side was Aristotle Markos, the puppeteer Andronikos Dukas had sent to oversee him. At his right was Roussel de Bailleul, commander of his cavalry and second watchdog of the Dukas.

The strategos was taciturn. This is a battle he could easily win and with half as many troops as he was given. He wanted to give the order to attack but the presence of Markos and Bailleul reminded him that to do so, even if he were victorious, was inviting a disaster he could not withstand. He'd sooner be the first to die in this battle than to bow to the Dukas.

Yet there would be no way the men at his sides now would allow him to do that. If he gave the order to attack, they would expose him then and there, before the attack could be launched, if they didn't kill him first. Who could know the torture that awaited him. His death would be neither quick nor painless. What bothered him more was that he was betraying Romanos Diogenes, a man he admired. To save his own reputation, and life, he was willing to play false with his homeland and his sovereign. But he had made his choice, despite the guilt that came with it.

One of his senior infantry commanders rode over to him. "Strategos, may I offer some suggestions for the use of my infantry in taking this fortress?"

The strategos didn't answer.

The commander repeated his request.

Again Tarchaniotes was silent. He wanted to answer. He wanted to send those men on to victory but he couldn't. He wasn't going to sacrifice himself for Romanos Diogenes. Tarchaniotes was quietly blunt. "There will be no attack."

Roussel de Bailleul and Markos looked triumphantly at one another.

The infantry leader was shocked. "There will be no attack?" he asked, being certain he'd heard Tarchaniotes incorrectly.

"The fortress is too heavily defended. There will be no attack," Tarchaniotes replied.

"But sir, we have more than enough men to take this fort!" the commander objected.

"There will be no attack," the strategos shot back, increasing the volume of his voice.

"Sir, the emperor's orders?" The man was practically begging Tarchaniotes to attack.

Tarchaniotes turned to Markos. His infantry commander had become an unpleasant irritant to him. "Have this man arrested. Bind him, gag him, and place him on a cart in the baggage train."

As the infantry commander was taken away, the strategos began to rationalize: Romanos Diogenes was doomed; the Dukas would take over and he would be on their side. True, he had betrayed the emperor but he was aiding in the stabilization of the empire under the powerful Dukas family. So he was actually doing the empire a great favor. He felt the corners of his lips curling upward. He would probably be considered a hero when he returned to Constantinople. His reputation would be enhanced and his secret would die with him. As the minutes passed, he thought about the island of Naxos and the villa Andronikos Dukas had promised. It sweetened his disposition. With this thought, Joseph Tarchaniotes turned his army around. They continued to Militene on the Euphrates River, more than two hundred fifty miles to the west.

On the same morning Joseph Tarchanites led his troops away from Khelat, the Turkish garrison at Manzikert gave up without a struggle. Many of the Turkish prisoners were released. The officers who could prove useful in future negotiations with the Turks were detained, though there were only a handful of them. The emperor inspected the prisoners with only a small fraction of satisfaction. As long as Alp Arslan and his army were freely roaming the countryside, Romanos could not rest.

Peter and Justin were able to see their new adversaries. Both found them a most curious lot. These men were short with narrowed eyes, black hair, and yellow-brown skin. They wore pointed woolen caps with appendages that covered the ears. Their long-sleeved shirts were partially covered by wool or leather vests. Each wore a thick leather belt around his waist and covered his legs with a woolen skirt. Knee-length leather boots were worn over those parts of the leg not covered by the skirt. The prisoners were, for the most part, quiet. When they did speak, their words were guttural and rather unpleasant to Roman ears.

Justin examined some of the prisoner's weapons; he and Peter found them very interesting. The swords were double-edged and razor sharp. Most of the prisoners carried a mace with a bone or iron end for striking. Justin picked up one of the Turkish bows, short and difficult to shoot. The tightly scrolled ends held the leather string taut. Peter could see how such a small, powerful weapon would be useful to a soldier who spent a great deal of time on horseback. The Turkish horsemen rode small, quick mares. He knew that a direct attack by the rugged stallions the Romans used would crush the lighter enemy.

That evening, Justin and Peter were invited, with the officers, to the emperor's tent. Although they were Romanos' guests, Justin and Peter received no special treatment and sat with all of the other junior officers. One might think that after being singled out by the emperor as exemplary soldiers, Justin and Peter would receive some privileges. However, *not* receiving them didn't bother them one bit. The further away from the center of this hornet's nest they were, the better.

The mood of the gathering was one of cautious celebration. Romanos was quiet and almost unapproachable. Nikephoros Bryennios had become his principal commander since Tarchaniotes was assigned Khelat. Peter watched him approach the emperor.

"Your Highness," Bryennios began, "it is unusual for a commander to not be happy with a victory."

The uneasy Romanos seemed ready to attack Bryennios verbally but caught himself and maintained his civility. "Alp Arslan is out there, somewhere," he mused. "We have no idea where and we have had no word from Tarchaniotes."

"Your Majesty, I cannot imagine the strategos failing to take that fortress. He is your ablest general and his troops are among your best. I'd be surprised if you don't hear from him by morning, sire."

"If I've not heard from him by midday, I'll send someone to Khelat," Romanos said decisively, regaining his imperial presence. "We'll bring this Turk to heel yet."

The following morning, Justin and Peter were sent with twenty of their cataphract to forage for food. The Romans didn't know that the Turkish troops were also down to the last of their victuals. It was no wonder they had surrendered without a fight.

The Armenian steppe, arid and nearly flat, had little to offer on this summer morning. The local farms grew mostly wheat, root vegetables, and various nut trees but most of these were not ready for harvest. Goats, sheep, and chickens were plentiful and, therefore, so were cheese, milk, eggs, and yogurt. Typically, the locals were reluctant to surrender their hard-earned produce to army foraging parties.

Although they were Christian and part of the Roman Empire, the Armenians were less than loyal subjects. For most of the last century and many times before, the Romans saw fit to persecute them because their view of Jesus, being more divine than human, did not match the view of the Orthodox patriarch in Constantinople: Jesus' divinity and humanity were of equal measure.

Justin and Peter broke away from the larger group, leading five other cataphract due east until they came across a small farm. The farmer came out of his house when the cavalrymen approached. His wife came a little later, accompanied by their prepubescent daughter and two small boys. Each of the males wore a woolen cap and the black-haired females wore white cotton scarves.

The family stood silently in front of their home, watching the thundering horses come to a halt. They looked up at Justin who was leading the column. He looked back and, for a minute, didn't quite know what to say. He dismounted and walked over to the father. Doubting he would get a response, he asked the family patriarch for some food. The farmer did not answer. He didn't even move; he just looked Justin straight in the eye.

"He probably doesn't speak Greek," said Peter, still mounted on his horse.

Justin responded to Peter without taking his eyes off the deep dark brown eyes of the Armenian farmer. "Do any of the men speak Armenian?"

Peter turned and asked among the cataphract if any of them could translate, but none could. Their horses whinnied at random and took a step forward or back, impatiently waiting for this work to be complete. The horsemen began to murmur among themselves, echoing the sentiment of their mounts. Justin continued to stand speechless in front of the farmer. Neither of them moved. Justin knew he could demand whatever he wanted and take it with impunity. Foragers were known to take entire holdings of farms, livestock and crops, and kill anybody who got in their way. However, Justin couldn't. The farmer knew he was winning this battle with Justin but his hold on victory was tenuous. He was aware of that, too. Peter remained silent but tried to support Justin without usurping his authority. The mutterings among the cataphract grew louder. It was obvious they had been kept waiting too long.

Justin reached into his purse and retrieved a gold noumisma. He held it up for the farmer to see and nodded his head. Again the farmer wouldn't budge. What use was the emperor's money to him? The situation was growing tense. Justin felt compressed by the army on one side and this poor but resolute man on the other.

Three soldiers dismounted and began to walk toward the farmer, their frustration with the matter driving them toward desperate action. Peter quickly spotted them and barked, "Remount those horses immediately!" The stunned cavalrymen stopped in their tracks. They believed they were trying to help their commander and Peter's response confused them. The fracas caught Justin's attention and he freed his eyes from the grip of the recalcitrant peasant. He turned toward his men but didn't have to repeat Peter's order. The cataphract returned to their steeds and remounted begrudgingly.

When Justin turned back to the Armenians, the mother stood in front of him, replacing the father. She held a young lamb in her arms. Behind the mother, the daughter held a large basket containing bread and cheese. The woman's face was expressionless but her actions seemed to say, "Please take these and leave us alone."

Justin was only too willing to accept her unspoken offer. He smiled and turned to his troops. "Manelis, Kusulos, take care of these!" He held the coin up again but the family walked away. Relieved that the situation was over and a satisfactory ending had been found, Justin thanked them. The farmers stared back coldly as they continued to walk away.

"Justin," Peter said, "It's time we go."

Justin agreed and pulled himself away. At his order, the cavalrymen proceeded southward.

As the morning's event at the farm began to sink in, Peter heard some of the men describe Justin as weak and less than admirable. He became angry and wanted to set the men straight. They didn't know him like Peter did and they hadn't seen him in battle. But Peter knew Justin didn't need his defense. As soon as the battle came, these young horsemen would see what their commander was made of.

The next farm was about a half-mile to the south. Justin wanted to get back to the camp by midday so his troops could be fed. Peter feared they would return to camp with inadequate results and suffer Zervas' wrath for doing so.

The second farm showed no signs of life. Four of the cavalrymen were ordered to dismount and search the grounds. They reported that all of the livestock were gone and the small hut was empty: no food in sight. Justin and Peter dismounted and went inside the hut. The hearth was cold and the walls were bare. There were no blankets, kitchen implements, or even a bucket for water; the previous occupants had taken everything. "Why would they leave?" Peter asked.

Justin's reply was cut short by a sudden commotion outside. One of the cataphract screamed in agony. Another yelled, "We're being attacked!"

Justin and Peter ran outside to find two of their command dead from arrows through the back. The rest of the men were circling their horses around the hut, yelling for Justin and Peter to come out. Arrows filled the air as Justin and Peter leapt onto their chargers.

"Let's get out of here!" Peter exhorted.

"Follow Captain Argyropoulos!" Justin enjoined his men. He turned to Peter. "I'll cover the rear." He caught a look of protest in Peter's eye. "That's an order, Peter!"

Peter knew that this was not the time to question Justin's judgment. He slapped his stallion on its rump and dug his spurs into its ribs. The muscular horse bolted forward.

As the troop followed Peter, more arrows found their marks. One of the cavalrymen was hit in the shoulder but could still ride and was able to keep up with Peter. A second soldier was hit twice in the back. He fell backward off his horse and landed on his buttocks. He bounced and as he did so, Justin, who was right behind him, scooped him up with his left arm without breaking his horse's stride and pulled him toward his saddle. The grateful soldier groaned as Justin hoisted himself up over the front of the saddle.

Justin looked behind him and could see at least fifty Turks giving chase. They amazed him by accurately firing arrows from their bows as their small horses charged forward. One arrow hit his helmet but bounced away harmlessly. Another arrow struck the rider ahead of him under the right ear. That man collapsed like a little girl's doll, dying before his body hit the hard ground below. Justin saw that the Turks were gaining on them. Another arrow flew toward him. As an involuntary reflex, he threw up his right arm and the small shield strapped to it deflected the oncoming missile. The enemy horsemen continued to gain ground.

The wounded cataphract lying astride Justin's saddle looked up at him and, in a panic screamed, "We're not going to make it back to the camp!" Justin did not reply but pushed his horse to increase its speed.

Justin could see a Turk out of the corner of his right eye, not less than one hundred yards away. Soon, a second appeared in his peripheral vision on the left at the same distance. Justin looked at the cataphract ahead of him. Two more fell from their horses. A chill went up Justin's spine. Peter was no longer at the front of the troop. Had he been killed? Where was he? An arrow struck Justin's chest but it landed on one of the small iron plates on the back of his corselet and fell harmlessly away. Justin sighed in relief and wondered how much longer his luck would last.

Then Peter appeared about twenty yards ahead of him. He had slowly drifted backward to get close to Justin. Just as he saw Peter, a bold Turk moved his horse within a few yards. Peter waved to him and pointed at an attacker gaining on him. This man did not have a bow but rode toward Justin brandishing a mace. Justin grabbed his short sword with his right hand and prepared to meet the attack. He leaned forward to warn the wounded cavalryman he carried, but to his surprise, the man was dead. Two new arrows were lodged in his right side.

Justin looked back at his attacker who was rapidly approaching on his right. When the oncoming Turk was within striking distance, Justin slid the dead man up and over his saddle, and quickly rotated his body to his right as he leveled a slashing blow with the sword in his right arm. The enemy horseman never saw the sword coming. His head tumbled off his body. For a second, his horse carried a headless rider, stunning those Turks who had witnessed their comrade's demise.

Now Peter was riding at Justin's right side. "What are you doing here?" Justin yelled, infuriated with Peter.

"I wasn't about to leave you alone," Peter responded, an arrow just missing his right cheek.

"I ordered you to get the men out of here, Peter!" Justin snapped, still irritated at his friend's disobedience.

Just up ahead, a fourth cataphract succumbed to a hail of Turkish arrows but the remaining cavalrymen had added distance between themselves and the onrushing enemy. But from behind, four Turkish cavalrymen were gaining on Justin and Peter. As one loaded his bow with an arrow, Peter yelled to Justin, "Separate!" Justin veered to the left and Peter to the right. At that exact moment, the enemy bowman loosed his arrow, only to have it fly harmlessly over Peter's left shoulder. Two of the Turks chased after Justin and the other two tailed Peter.

Justin's pursuers were armed with short lances and short, double-edged swords. At a distance of twelve yards, one of them launched his lance toward Justin. It struck him in the left shoulder. The iron blade burned as it broke the skin but it's penetration into the underlying muscle was superficial. As Justin's stallion galloped forward, the lance bounced up and down, ripping the tissue in Justin's shoulder. Though the pain was tremendous, Justin knew if he surrendered to it and fell from his horse or slowed down, he would be dead. He bit his lower lip and concentrated on riding as fast as he could back to the Roman camp.

The bowman pursued Peter. He was fifteen yards from his target and Peter knew he wouldn't miss from this range. He feathered the arrow and drew back on the bow. His partner riding next to him watched in anticipation. Peter looked back, terrified, but before the Turk loosed his arrow, he was struck in the eye by an arrow that came from a hundred fifty yards in front of Peter. Although the Turk's arrow flew forward, it had lost guidance from the bowman and flew over Peter's head. Three seconds later, the bowman's partner shared the same fate.

Peter spun his head forward to see a small Roman column led by Bryennios rushing headlong at Peter, Justin, and the Turks. Seeing his rescuers ahead of him, Peter crossed himself, thanking God as he did so.

The Turks chasing Justin saw the oncoming cataphract, many armed with bows, and pulled back to the main body of the Turkish force. Peter raced over to Justin and looked at the wound in his shoulder. Bryennios rode over to them and urged them to the back of the attacking formation. Bryennios had only twenty-five men with him and only ten of Justin's men had survived. This left the Romans with a force of thirty-seven. But Justin was wounded. Bryennios realized they were outnumbered and ordered his two fastest riders back to the camp for reinforcements.

Continuing to run played to the Turk's advantage. So Bryennios formed the rest of the men into a circle, riding counterclockwise in single file. Soon the Turks had them surrounded. Their commander halted his troops as he looked for a weak spot among the Roman cavalrymen. After a moment's deliberation, he reformed his men into a standard line of battle and ordered the right wing of his command, about twenty men, forward toward the Roman troops. The Seljuks whooped and hollered as they charged.

Bryennios realized what the Turkish commander was doing. He adroitly moved twelve men to meet the attack and left most of his men in a static, crescent-shaped position with the convex aspect projecting toward the Turks. Justin watched as the twelve cataphract smashed into the oncoming Turks. The armor of the Romans and their larger horses made the difference. At close quarters, the Turkish archers proved ineffective; their clubs, swords, and battle-axes were light and easily deflected. The armored Romans could sustain several blows before being weakened, whereas the unarmored Turks could be dispatched by one or two well-placed blows from Roman swords or lances. Within minutes, ten Turks lay dead on the field. Two Romans were badly wounded but not killed. The Turkish commander abruptly called off the attack and his men fell back.

Bryennios remained cool. His men felt jubilant but he knew the battle was far from over. The frontal attack the Turks had attempted was not their usual tactic. It was no surprise to him the enemy had been routed, but the situation was still tenuous. He was still outnumbered. The Turkish commander reformed his men who surrounded the Romans again. Bryennios pulled back the force that had broken the last Turkish assault and reformed his men into a circle rotating counterclockwise. He rode in the center, issuing orders to his men.

The Turkish commander returned to more conventional Turkish tactics by sending his archers around Bryennios' rotating circle. The

Turks rode parallel to the Romans and in a counterclockwise motion as well. Bryennios grew uneasy. He didn't like what he saw.

The Turkish archers drew their bows and launched their missles. The first wave of arrows had a devastating effect on the Romans: Four men fell dead and two were wounded. Three or four more attacks like this would seal the fate of his force and Bryennios knew it but he doubted he could launch another effective charge against the circling Turks.

The Turkish commander realized he had the upper hand and slowed the pace of his attack. A moment's rashness could cost him this victory that was within his grasp.

Just then, one of Bryenius' men grabbed the general's arm and pulled it like an excited child. With his other hand, he pointed to the west. A large column of Roman cataphract was minutes away. The Turks hadn't noticed it yet. Bryennios ordered all of his men, even the wounded, to be ready to ride to the west at his signal.

Peter wondered what Bryennios was planning but when he saw the relief column in the distance, it became clear what was on Bryennios' mind: surprise the Turks with his attack and occupy their attention while the relief force smashed it from the rear. Then, not only would he ensure the escape of his troops, but he could also turn this setback into a victory.

"Charge!" Bryennios ordered. The newly invigorated heavy cavalrymen stormed westward. The Turks were confounded by what they saw. *Why was the trapped quarry attacking?* The Roman cavalrymen tore through the Turkish line, killing nine and wounding a dozen others. Justin, with Peter at his side, was in the middle of the Roman line, as were the other wounded.

One wing of the Turkish cavalry disengaged and waved frantically at their commander. He cursed them until he looked to the west and saw the large Roman force closing down on his rear. He immediately ordered his troops to disperse and head back to their camp. Within minutes, the Turks disappeared.

The liberated cataphract cheered as the relief force rode after the retreating Turks. The commander, the impetuous Basilacios, made a slashing movement across his throat, as if to say, "We're going to wipe them out!" The cheers turned into roars of approval.

Bryennios remained sober. He was not about to get caught up in the zeal of the moment. His troops had narrowly escaped slaughter and were exhausted. He ordered them back to the camp at Manzikert with all possible haste.

The Roman soldiers cheered when Bryennios' force entered their Roman camp. Bryennios and Peter helped Justin off his horse and into a tent. Other men joined them to see how Justin was doing. Within minutes a stern-faced Romanos Diogenes loudly entered. "In the name of all of the saints," he growled at Bryennios, "what is happening out there? I send you to dispatch a small band of Turks and then half of my cavalry leaves camp to save you!"

Bryennios could see there was no soothing Romanos' ire. He acknowledged the emperor's concern with contrition but then, to justify his actions, he gave an accounting of his brave troops. "The Turks were fifty strong and we were but half that. The men fought well—"

"That will be all!" barked the emperor. The other men present recoiled. Romanos' abusive treatment of Bryennios left them cold. "You men are dismissed!" Romanos shot back when he saw their reaction. As the others left, Diogenes reeled on Justin and Peter and snapped, "Not you two!" He was totally oblivious to Justin's wound. "Into my tent!"

Peter and Bryennios helped Justin into the emperor's tent. Romanos showed the three of them to a table and moved to take the seat at the table's head. Justin quickly looked at his wound. The bleeding had stopped but it would need medical attention.

Romanos collapsed into his seat and let out a deep sigh. "Nikephoros," he said calmly, as one old friend would say to another. "I've received no word from Tarchaniotes." This news squelched any thoughts of a quick victory. "I'm sending Tribune Volas and Captain Iatrelos with a detachment of Pechaneg light cavalry from Dukas' rearguard to Khelat to find him."

He dropped his head into his hands, sighed, and then looked up again, his hands still supporting his weary head. "Our first contact with the enemy in weeks, more than half of my army is missing, and half of the cavalry I have left is off chasing ghosts," he added with surprising calmness. He grabbed a small bell from the table and rang it. A servant appeared with four golden goblets filled with red wine.

"Please join me, gentlemen," the emperor said, his offer sounding more like an order. He raised his goblet as each of the officers received his wine. "To victory!" he declared boldly. The others repeated, in a less enthusiastic tone, "To victory."

As they imbibed the wine, a harried messenger rode into camp. The commotion he caused brought Romanos, Bryennios, Peter, and even Justin out of the tent. "He's been surrounded!" the messenger cried breathlessly. "Cut off! Won't make it without help!"

"Who?" demanded Romanos, "Basilacios?"

The rider nodded as he struggled to catch his breath.

"Damn! My army is disappearing before my eyes!"

"Sir," implored Bryennios. "Let me rescue him. Let me have the right wing's cavalry."

"And then lose even more of my cavalry?" bellowed Romanos. "I won't permit it!"

"Basilacios is a good commander. And he saved my life. Let me save his."

Romanos knew he couldn't deny Bryennios. "All right, go," he said with a tone of both hope and frustration. "And take Argyropoulos with you."

Peter shot up and showed his readiness. Justin grabbed his hand. "Be careful, Peter."

Peter nodded and saluted the emperor.

"You won't regret this, sire," the general promised his sovereign.

The emperor soberly returned their salutes. "I will pray for your safe return, gentlemen."

Bryennios thanked the emperor, and he and Peter quickly left the tent to organize the relief force. Romanos sat down, put his hands up to his face, and cast a deep sigh. This precarious position left him deep in thought.

Justin rose slowly, wincing from the pain in his shoulder, and requested permission to retire to his tent and have a physician sent to tend to his wound. The emperor merely nodded without looking at him. As Justin went to exit the tent, two soldiers entered and Diogenes' spirits lifted.

"Volas, Iatrelos!" he smiled. He stood to greet them, immediately forgetting Justin, just ten feet away. "Gentlemen, gentlemen!" he said excitedly, reaching forward and grabbing their hands. "I have a very important task for you!"

The two new arrivals were taken aback by the emperor's sudden informality. This behavior was certainly not worthy of a man of his rank. Justin, intrigued by Romanos' sudden effervescence, remained in the room. Romanos told them their orders with great enthusiasm. Justin studied the faces of these two would-be heroes and wondered if they would be up to the task. Before long, he left the emperor's tent, found his own, and dropped his exhausted body on to his cot.

The growing din outside of Justin's tent awakened him from the most restful sleep he'd had in a week. Alarmed, he awoke and made his way out of the tent as fast as he could. He saw Peter ride up with Bryennios. The strategos had obviously been wounded several times but appeared as strong as when he had left the camp several hours before. The rest of the cavalry from the relief force slowly filtered into the camp. There was no sign of Basilacios.

As Justin walked over to Peter and Bryennios, Romanos Diogenes ran out of his tent and began interrogating random soldiers. Upon seeing Bryennios, the emperor shot straight to him and demanded an account of the mission. Romanos was initially oblivious to Bryennios' injuries, perhaps because of the latter's stoicism. As Bryennios began to explain, Romanos realized the strategos' state and called for assistance. Against his wishes, Bryennios was carried into the emperor's tent.

Justin nudged Peter, silently demanding an accounting of the assignment. With his head, Peter motioned toward Justin's and his tent. The two of them slipped away as the commotion of the relief force's return continued around them.

"What happened out there?" Justin asked. "Where are Basilacios and his men?"

"There must have been ten thousand of them," Peter began, trying hard not to exaggerate. "As we rode up, we could see Basilacios and his men in the middle of them. But there was no way we could get to them. Bryennios led four charges into the

Turks but we couldn't break through. We got some of them out but most . . ."

"Bryennios was wounded," Justin interjected, impatiently seeking answers to his questions.

"Two arrows in the back, a lance wound in the chest," Peter began, "and one Turk slammed a mace against his left shoulder. That nearly unhorsed him! Fortunately, the wounds were all superficial. You should have seen him, Justin! He fought like a lion, slashing through Turks with his sword, blocking their blows effortlessly, easily dodging arrows—"

"Were you hurt, Peter?" Justin asked, quickly looking his friend over.

"Not a scratch, Justin," Peter replied before he returned to his description of Bryennios. "The man fights like Heracles! I'll bet he killed thirty of them single-handedly! But there were just too many of them . . . far too many of them." Peter's voice trailed off, recalling the hordes of enemy soldiers that had opposed them.

"Well, how did Basilacios end up in such a mess? Couldn't he see what was going on around him?"

"I spoke with some of the men we had managed to save. They said that for three miles, they chased the band that had attacked us. Suddenly Turks began appearing out of nowhere, attacking them ferociously. They must have ridden into an ambush."

"The Turk's an expert at that, I keep hearing," Justin added. "So what happens next?"

"I don't know but I'm beginning to appreciate the emperor's dissatisfaction with the whole affair."

CHAPTER 16

That moonless night, August 25, the Turks surrounded Romanos' camp at Manzikert and filled the pitch-black sky with a constant hail of arrows. Most of the Roman soldiers sought cover that wasn't available. The officers had a difficult time keeping the camp's defensive perimeter manned. The unremitting deluge and chaos made sleep impossible and the profound darkness only made the matter more onerous.

It had been five hours since sunset. Andronikos Dukas had summoned Zervas two hours before and the tyrant had left Justin in charge. He and Peter sat with the thirty men left in a command that had originally totaled fifty. They had stabled their horses in a hastily built wooden structure on the other side of the camp. The cavalrymen crowded near four stunted pine trees at the center of the camp, taking whatever meager protection the trees could give from the endless Turkish darts.

"They're attacking the west palisade! The west palisade!" The panicked cry came from the western end of the camp.

Peter flew from his position toward the origin of the alarm. Before he had gone twenty feet, the alarm was rescinded. Two other men had followed Peter, and on their way back to the pines, they fell victim to the Turkish arrows. One was killed outright and the other sustained a serious wound to the thigh and couldn't walk.

"That's the fourth alarm tonight," Justin noted. "The Turk is wearing us down. These men will be in no condition to fight tomorrow."

"You're right, Justin. The Turk is very clever," Peter said. "He saps our strength a little at a time."

"Only four hours till daybreak. I pray the Turk has grown tired of his mischief," Justin added. Noting the dead quiet, he suggested the unthinkable to his men. "Let's try to get some sleep."

Justin was the only one of his command who was able to do that. The barrage of arrows soon returned and continued through the night. Yet Justin managed to sleep through them. Peter willingly took over for him, realizing his wounded friend needed more rest than he did.

By dawn, the weary soldiers were invigorated by the fact that the camp's perimeters had held. The casualties that night had been surprisingly light. A new confidence seemed to grow inside the Roman camp. Justin remained asleep; Peter was in no hurry to wake him. Their command readied itself for the day ahead.

Peter watched Romanos Diogenes patrolling the camp, evaluating the fitness of his men and their spirits. He appeared to be happy with what he saw. He saw the emperor headed toward them and gently awakened Justin. Justin jumped to his feet.

"Thanks for letting me sleep," Justin whispered.

"You needed it," Peter responded as the emperor arrived and the soldiers snapped to attention.

"Gentlemen, I pray this morning finds you well," said Romanos Diogenes jovially, as if he were oblivious to the past evening's goings-on. He held out his hand as he surveyed the troops. "The Roman army is still the most powerful fighting force the world has ever seen. I am confident that the men are up to the challenge before them." He added without waiting for a response, "Are these cataphract ready to smash the Turkish menace today?"

Peter nodded to Justin. "Yes, Your Highness," Justin replied eagerly. "We are ready."

"They're gone! They're nearly all gone!" A junior officer came running across the camp bearing bad news. "Your Majesty," he said as he stopped and saluted the emperor. "They're gone! Nearly all of the Uz have left! They must have snuck out last night."

"Damn!" Romanos said under his breath. "How many remain?" he asked out loud.

"Maybe a hundred, Your Majesty."

"Have them form ranks with the Thracians."

"Yes, Your Majesty. It will be done," said the young officer and he sprinted to the other side of the camp.

"Maybe by redistributing the remaining Uz, we can obscure their defection from the others," Romanos confided to Justin and Peter. "Can't really blame them for leaving," he mused. "We've been on this campaign since March. It's a wonder the Armenians and Pechanegs haven't joined them, not to mention the Cumans." He turned to Justin. "How is the shoulder coming, Captain?"

"It's coming along well, Your Majesty." Justin stretched the truth a bit.

"Any news of Strategos Tarchaniotes, Your Majesty?" Peter asked.

"None," the Romanos Diogenes answered. "But I expect to hear something today."

"And Strategos Bryennios, sire?" Peter wondered.

The emperor's face brightened. "It takes a lot more than a few flesh wounds to disable Nikephoros Bryennios. He's a good man and a superior commander." Romanos paused and repeated, "A superior commander."

The three other foraging parties had managed to secure a great deal of food without encountering the enemy. Romanos was content to rest his army today. He would send out scouting parties but otherwise would undertake no major efforts. He reiterated his confidence that Tarchaniotes' force would be found and brought to him.

Before the emperor left them, a group of six horsemen, not Turks but not Greeks or Armenians either, rode into Romanos' camp. Ten Roman light cavalrymen escorted the strangers. The commander of the Roman squad dismounted and told the emperor that the six strangers said the Caliph of Baghdad had sent them with a proposal for a truce between the Romans and the Turks.

Romanos was dubious. "Since when does the Caliph of Baghdad have any interest in the quarrels between the Roman Empire and the Seljuk Turks?" Peter heard him say under his breath. Then the emperor told the commander, "Show them to my tent. Get them some water. I'll be there shortly."

After the guests had been led away, Romanos Diogenes spoke to Justin and Peter quietly. "This 'delegation' comes from Alp Arslan, not the 'Caliph of Baghdad.' I don't need a truce; I need a victory. I cannot return to Constantinople without one. That would incite more intrigue by the Dukas. I haven't spent the last five months chasing Alp Arslan across Anatolia and Armenia to come home with a truce. No, no, no, gentlemen; victory is the only option.

"Perhaps this offer of a truce is a sign of his own weakness," Romanos hoped, speaking more to himself than to Justin and Peter. "No. No, this Turk is far too clever to try that. He wants a fight and a fight he's going to get." The emperor turned and left the two captains and headed toward his tent.

Justin and Peter watched Diogenes' tent from across the camp. Within five minutes, the six delegates left the tent. They didn't appear happy. They mounted their horses and were escorted out of the camp by light cavalrymen.

Justin turned to Peter. "Looks like we'd better get the men ready."

As Justin moved, Peter stopped him. "How's the shoulder? Don't lie to me, Justin. We could be in for the fight of our lives."

"It's sore but much better than yesterday. I know I can use it." He started to put the extremity through its paces. Peter could see the pain he was in and stopped him.

"Save your strength, Justin. Do as little as you can with that arm. I'll help you as much as I can."

"Thanks, Peter," Justin said, relieved at his friend's offer.

Romanos Diogenes flew out of his tent, shouting orders left and right, demanding the presence of Nikephoros Bryennios, and readying himself for battle. Alyattes, the Cappadocian, was the first commander on the scene. He received his instructions from the emperor and rushed away, barking out orders of his own to his junior officers following him. Bryennios appeared next. Romanos grabbed the strategos' hands and held them as he spoke to the gallant commander. He slapped him on the shoulder and sent him away as he moved on to another commander.

Peter looked for but could not find Andronikos Dukas. "Where's Dukas?" he asked.

"He's just leaving his tent," Justin noted.

Peter turned his gaze to the other end of the camp and saw Dukas lethargically mustering his officers. Zervas was with him.

They spoke briefly and then Zervas headed toward their position. "He'll be here soon. I'll see to the men." He added as he disappeared among them.

"Ah, well. It was nice while it lasted," said Justin, savoring their last few seconds of separation from the Devil's own. "I'd almost rather take another Turkish lance in the shoulder."

"Why aren't the men ready, Phillipos?" the tribune screeched from forty feet away. "Can't you witless toads see we're getting ready to move out? I leave you alone for two days and the whole command goes straight to hell!"

Justin didn't try to interrupt. Bearing these assaults was by far easier than trying to interrupt Zervas, justify one's existence, and then suffer another hail of degrading maledictions. "Where the hell is Argyropoulos?" Zervas roared. He pushed Justin aside to seek out his next victim. "I swear the man has the brain of a goat!"

Peter heard the insults and realized he could hide no longer. And what kind of friend would he be to leave Justin alone with the "Terrible Tribune". So he followed the sound of Zervas' voice and found him. "You called, sir?"

Zervas bellowed, "Are the men ready, Captain Nitwit?"

"Yes, sir!" He too had no option but to bear the tribune's affronts.

Zervas found his captains' complete compliance and lack of resistance unnerving. He wanted to get a rise out of them and his current tactics were failing. He mellowed his tone. "Form the men at this spot," Zervas ordered. "I'll return in five minutes. We'll be marching in the rear guard with Prince Andronikos Dukas."

Justin and Peter formed their diminished ranks and awaited Zervas' return. The despot returned, mounted his horse, and with one word, "Follow!" he ordered his group forward.

Romanos Diogenes had formed his army by the book, placing himself in the center at the head of the scutati, which were several ranks deep. The cavalry assumed the flanks. Bryennios was sent to the left and Alyattes to the right. This vanguard of seventeen thousand men would lead the attack. The rearguard, commanded by Dukas, had just over eight thousand men. They were mostly scutati but contained a small contingent of Pecheneg light cavalry as well as Justin and Peter's meager number of heavy cavalrymen.

The army moved to the east where twenty thousand Turks waited for them in a formation that resembled a crescent. Its open end was toward the Romans. Romanos Diogenes began the attack about midday. At his signal, his men advanced forward across the flat tableland. They looked magnificent, unstoppable.

However, the Turks would not engage. They fell back slowly in the center. Only the mounted bowmen on the wings attacked, harassing the Roman cavalry on the flanks by firing wave after wave of arrows into their midst. The Roman archers returned volley for volley but their effect on the mobile Turks was minimal. The Romans kept advancing. The Turks kept chewing at the flanks and then falling back.

Justin imagined how frustrated the emperor felt as he wached this scenario from the rear. The enemy's center seemed invisible. All he could see were the marauding horsemen at the Roman flanks and then the Turks were suddenly gone. Romanos would not get his quick victory by chasing this uncooperative foe across the Armenian steppe forever.

After enduring the tenth or eleventh barrage of Turkish arrows, some of the cataphract on the right flank, under Alyattes, broke ranks and chased the Turks. Their commanders tried in vain to deter them but the headstrong cavalrymen shot forward. Justin watched them pursue the wily Turks who retreated into the nearby foothills. Within minutes, those Roman cavalrymen who gave chase were in trouble; their impatience had led them into an ambush. Within minutes, dozens of fresh Turkish cavalry sprang forward from their hiding places in the hills. The Roman cataphract turned and ran when they saw they were outnumbered. Justin squeezed his hands together in frustration when he saw the trap sprung.

"That's how they got Basilacios!" Peter said.

Turkish arrows and lances had similar results on the Roman left flank. Small groups of cataphract shot forward to meet their attackers. Bryennios cursed their lapse in discipline and left the ranks to bring them back. He rode quickly and brought back some but the others were too far ahead. These impatient soldiers rode hard into the foothills that were studded with drawf pine trees. Again the Turks used surprise to their advantage and sprang another ambush. Their arrows cut down most of the Romans. Those who were wounded were finished off by infantry lurking in the scrub vegetation or by riders wielding maces or lances.

Justin watched in anguish. His view of the battlefield from the second line gave him the perspective those at the front couldn't see. If only he could help them.

In the center of the vanguard, Romanos Diogenes made his displeasure known. Justin could see him waving his arms to and fro, wildly gesticulating at the unfortunate junior commanders near him. He was frustrated with his undisciplined cavalry. Such spontaneous forays were very costly. He sent messengers to Alyattes and Bryennios.

This game of martial cat-and-mouse continued, hour after hour, through the rest of the afternoon. The Romans continued their advance; the Turks continued their withdrawal. The Turkish strikes on the Roman flanks continued but lost their effect. The rearguard continued to follow the vanguard, precisely as the military manuals specified. Justin watched patiently, waiting for the battle to unfold before them but the battle he waited for would not come.

Romanos Diogenes pointed to the larger foothills ahead.

"We've got them cornered!" Justin said to Peter.

"They have no choice but to fight now," Peter declared. "And this fight will be on our terms."

But the enemy still refused to cooperate. The Turks dissolved into the foothills and, for a moment, seemed to completely disappear. Justin looked up at the sky. The sun had nearly completed its diurnal course and darkness loomed. The vanguard suddenly halted. The emperor struck his thigh with his gauntleted right hand in frustration.

"Looks like victory has eluded us today," Peter declared.

"Tomorrow will be different," Justin added. Maybe he'll choose different tactics, free up the cavalry."

Justin looked back at the commanders of the second line, who were ten yards behind. Andronikos Dukas gave a nod to Zervas who was at his right hand. Zervas rode forward and shoved a leather pouch in Justin's hand. "Take this to the emperor immediately!" Zervas barked. Then he turned to Peter. "You go with him! Now!"

They spurred their horses forward and, within minutes, had reached the vanguard.

As Justin and Peter arrived at the vanguard, Romanos turned to the aide at his left. "Reverse the standards," he ordered. This was the usual Roman signal for withdrawal. The junior officer relayed the order to each of the imperial standard-bearers and the emperor's order was broadcast to the troops. The Roman troops realized the signal's meaning and prepared to comply. However, many of the non-Roman mercenaries in the vanguard were unfamiliar with the significance of the reversed standards. They remained facing the foothills, awaiting further orders. Some of them saw what the Roman troops were doing and tried to follow their lead but the effect was piecemeal. Still other mercenary groups thought that the reversal of the standards meant some tragedy had befallen the emperor. Many of them turned and ran back toward the Roman camp at Manzikert. As a result, most of the mercenary units were a shambles.

"Get those men into position," Romanos yelled to the junior officer. As the emperor gave the order, Justin and Peter rode to his side. "What in Christ's name are you two doing here?

As Peter tried to answer, hordes of Turks poured out of the foothills. The emperor saw the onslaught and didn't wait for an answer. He wheeled around on his horse and took in the action around him. Thirty thousand enemy fighters, twenty thousand of them on horseback, fell on his disorganized imperial troops. Their cavalry shot through the fissures in the Roman line caused by the fleeing or discombobulated mercenaries. Within minutes, the Turks had surrounded a good part of the imperial center, including Romanos Diogenes, Justin, and Peter.

At first, the surrounded troops responded well. The scutati assumed defensive positions around the emperor. Those few horsemen who were trapped with the emperor, including Justin and Peter, formed with him behind the infantry. A group of archers was among those in the imperial salient and they, too, mechanically assumed their positions.

The Turks threw two hundred cavalry and three hundred infantry against the isolated Roman center. They were thrown back with heavy casualties by the dogged defense of the scutati and the precision shots of the Roman archers. The Turks broke off the attack and returned to their customary tactics of wearing their opponent down with deadly discharges from their mobile mounted archers. Turkish horsemen rode wildly between cut-off Roman units, randomly shooting arrows at imperial troops with devastating effect. Other horsemen threw their lances over the heads of the infantry, killing unsuspecting archers and horsemen.

Some Roman units, notably Bryennios' left flank, valiantly struck back at the Turks as Bryennios tried to break through to the emperor. Peter and Justin could see Bryennios slashing to his left and right, leaving dozens of Turks in his wake.

However, the Turks sent more men in to fill the gap created by the gallant strategos. All too soon, the counterattack lost its impetus. This was complicated by the fact that Bryennios was surrounded as well. He looked longingly toward the emperor's position. The titan fought bravely. But Bryennios' continued attacks were futile and continuing to do so risked the loss of his entire force. He reluctantly ordered his men to halt their effort to break through to the emperor, reform, and effect a breakout to the west, and to safety.

Romanos coolly directed those around him in the fight of their lives. His confidence was infectious. When a gap would form in the perimeter, he would rush forward himself to fill the hole. Romanos personally dispatched no fewer than thirty Turks in fifteen minutes' time. But the Turkish enfilade was beginning to take its toll. More than a third of the men within the Roman perimeter were dead and the Turks showed no sign of slowing their attack.

Romanos yelled at Justin, "Where the hell is Dukas and the rearguard?"

Justin rode fifty yards to the west to find the rearguard disintegrating. It wasn't even retreating in good order; cavalry and infantry ran in complete disarray. "What are they doing?" Justin said. The ten-thousand-man force could have easily stormed forward and saved Romanos Diogenes and his army, but only if the commander would give the order. Justin frantically opened the pouch that Zervas had given him.

It was empty.

Justin's heart sank. Andronikos Dukas had condemned them all to death. Justin returned to the emperor.

"The second line is retreating in total disarry," Justin reported to Diogenes.

Romanos cursed under his breath and grabbed Justin by the shoulder. "You and Argyropoulos have got to get out of here! Get back to Constantinople, find Comnenos, warn the empress!" When Justin hesitated, he yelled, "Go! Now!" Romanos rode over to another part of the shrinking perimeter, slashing at four Turks who had just broken through.

Justin found Peter who was trying to reorganize the decimated archers.

"Peter!" Justin interrupted him. "The emperor has ordered us to break out! Get back to Constantinople!"

"What? Justin, just how the hell are we supposed to do that?" Peter shot back.

Justin dismounted and desperately looked around for anything that could deliver them from their doom. Just then, a Turkish arrow glanced off the top of his helmet and he craned his head forward, continuing his mad search. *Nothing! Absolutely nothing!* Frustrated, he slammed his fist onto his saddle. It struck the cotton sack filled with his uncle's powder. Justin looked at the sack, remembered its contents, and said out loud, "God bless you, Uncle Theodore!"

Peter heard Justin's exclamation. "What did you say?"

"Take the armor off of our horses! Now!"

Peter saw that the situation would not permit debate. He leapt off his horse, stripped off its armor, did the same to Justin's, and then ran at top speed to his comrade. Meanwhile, Justin set a stream of the explosive powder away from his former position toward western end the perimeter. There he left the sack open and on its side, allowing the gray powder to flow uninterrupted into the cloth container.

Peter looked at Justin as if to say, "So now what do we do?"

Justin grabbed the flints from the sack. "Get on your horse!"

Peter complied without question.

Justin crouched down and held the flints together. He looked back at Romanos Diogenes. The embattled sovereign continued his futile efforts. Less than half of the encircled Roman soldiers were alive but he fought on with inspiring heroism. Justin knew he would never see Emperor Romanos Diogenes again.

He looked forward and saw that the Turks were advancing through the western perimeter. He waved at Peter who acknowledged his readiness to try this stratagem. Justin shouted, "Clear the perimeter!"

As the confused Roman troops before him followed his command, he struck the two flints together and produced a large spark that instantly ignited Uncle Theodore's magical concoction. Justin leapt onto his horse as the conflagration flared brilliantly toward the waiting cotton sack. The luminescent blaze amazed Turks and Romans alike. When the glowing trail reached the cotton crucible, a loud, bright explosion blinded those nearby. At that exact instant, Justin slapped his horse on the rump and shot through the opening with Peter right behind him.

The enemy troops froze as Justin and Peter escaped through the amaroidal smoke. This allowed them a good head start but the Turks reacted nonetheless. Within seconds, fifteen horsemen were chasing the two captains.

Peter shot a glance backward and saw the oncoming enemy. "Trouble!" he yelled ahead to Justin.

Justin didn't have to look back to know what was happening. "Stay on my ass!"

Peter followed as Justin headed for the distant foothills. They could use the trees and rocks ahead to lose their pursuers. The two of them moved as one. When Justin cut left, Peter did the same a half-second later. They swerved left around a small pine tree. The Turks followed. Ahead, Justin saw another pine tree with low-hanging limbs. The newly arrived dusk would help them.

"Remember Vidin?" Justin yelled, without turning back.

"Yes!" Peter said with a delirious enthusiasm. They both remembered encountering a similar predicament in Bulgaria.

"Thirty yards!"

"Right!" Peter said, preparing himself.

When he reached the tree, Justin ducked under the low limb. So did Peter. The approaching nightfall obscured the limb sufficiently to eliminate the first three Turks who fell headlong from their horses. This befuddlement slowed the remaining horsemen enough to allow Justin and Peter to put another fifty yards between them and their pursuers.

Peter shot a glance over his shoulder. "We've picked up some ground but they're still coming."

Justin looked ahead. "We're running out of foothills. We'll be back on the open steppe soon."

"Any ideas?" Peter asked.

"Just one," Justin replied over the noise of his horses thundering hooves. "See those rocks up ahead?"

"Yes, barely."

"We'll swing hard to the right once we've passed that tall one. Then we'll jump off our horses, to the right. With any luck, the horses will keep going and the Turks with them."

"And how will we get home without horses?"

"I'm open to other suggestions," Justin said with surprising calm.

Peter hesitated a second. "Okay. I'm game."

The tall rock loomed ahead. Peter quickly looked behind. The Turks had not gained much ground and were still a good hundred yards behind them.

As they rounded the tall rock, Justin yelled, "Now!" and launched himself out of his saddle. Peter followed without a second thought. Luckily, they landed, unhurt, in long, soft grass and their luck held. The horses continued forward without hesitation. The loss of their riders allowed the horses to move away from the Turks with even greater speed.

Justin and Peter hugged the ground in the tall grass as the enemy cavalry rode past. The obscuring darkness would make it difficult for the enemy horsemen to make out the shapes of the horses, let alone see if they had riders. Their pursuit continued uninterrupted.

Justin and Peter lay still in the grass. They had to be certain the Turks had long passed. Justin slowly got up and walked over to a cluster of rocks twenty yards to their right. Peter cautiously followed. The growing darkness protected them but also hid any potential dangers. Justin knew they couldn't stay out in the open, so he trotted toward the rocks.

After ten yards, the ground beneath his feet vanished. He fell eight feet into a hole. He yelled as he fell to warn Peter of the new hazard but Peter was too close behind and fell victim to the same pitfall.

When he had recovered, Justin called through the blackness, "You all right, Peter?"

"Yes. I'm okay."

"Where do you suppose we are?"

"Sinkhole. Cave, maybe. Could be a good place to stay for a bit, sleep, let the dust settle up there."

"You're right, Peter. We could use the rest."

Justin lay on the soft dirt and sighed. "Do you remember what the monk said?"

"That fellow in Saint Cyril?" Peter replied. "Brother Nathaniel, I believe . . . ."

"Yes. Do you remember what he said . . . about the emperor and all that?"

"Monks always spread gloom. It's part of their job," Peter joked.

"But he wasn't just spouting off randomly. He was very specific. 'Your mission will fail. You are doomed to defeat. The emperor will lose his throne.' That's very precise if you ask me."

"Hmmm," Peter grunted, his exhaustion catching up with him.

"'And a new emperor will ask the fair-haired nations to save him from the Ishmaelites.' What do you think that means?"

But Peter was now fast asleep.

"'And the fair-haired nations will return one hundred years later . . . .'" Justin continued, more for his own benefit. "'To sack the emperor's city and carve up his empire.'" What could it mean? Who were the fair-haired nations? Certainly not the Turks. Could it mean the Normans? Justin's head swam as he contemplated the prophecy. He remembered the monk's final words: 'God will protect you and your friend. Now remember what God has taught you and do as He commands.' Justin felt a sudden warmth in that cool, black hole, the same warmth he had felt when the monk first spoke these words.

Justin thought of Eleni. Was she safe? When would he see her again? Had she become involved in the viperous schemes of the imperial court? He was ashamed he had not thought much of her in the last few days but, given the circumstances, most husbands wouldn't have been so hard on themselves. He could see her long auburn hair, blowing in the cool wind coming off of the Propontis. He heard her soft, strong voice, reassuring him. This vision of his wife, undoubtedly sent to him by God, was a revelation that he and Peter would return home again. He would soon see his parents. All of the joy that filled his life before would return. Justin felt certain of it.

The sun's rays slowly crept into the cool hole. Justin and Peter continued to doze despite the gleaming orb's gentle efforts to arouse them. By the time the first hour of day had passed, Peter began to stir. More and more light seeped into the cave. Peter sat up and stretched. He had slept well, despite their precarious circumstances. He glanced over at Justin whose sleep remained uninterrupted. He looked up and saw a cloudless blue sky. Peter quickly studied the rocky walls of the hole and then climbed out. He stayed close to the ground and surveyed the immediate area. No sign of anyone.

Peter returned to the hole, deftly let himself back down into it, and looked beyond where he and Justin had spent the night. This was no mere hole but a cave, most of it situated beyond where they had slept. As more light entered the cave, Peter explored it. He slowly moved past Justin, being mindful of every step. The deeper recesses of the cave were still dim. Cautiously hunched forward, he walked ahead. Then something caught his attention. He got on his hands and knees and crawled to it. The object ahead was disturbingly familiar. Peter recoiled as he realized what he had found. He braced himself and slowly reached forward. He placed his hand on the bare foot he saw in front of him. Its coldness confirmed its owner's death. Peter pulled the foot toward him and its lifeless body followed. The wretched soul wore the uniform of a Roman tribune. His hands were bound behind him and his throat was bloody. Peter didn't recognize their new companion but he knew his presence was foreboding. He crawled over to Justin and roused him. "Justin! Justin! Wake up!"

Justin, now aware of the sunlight penetrating the cave, slowly opened his eyes. "What is it?"

"Come with me!" Peter ordered.

Justin quickly followed.

"Ever seen him before?" Peter asked pointing at the body.

Justin cringed as he looked at the corpse's face and then his uniform. "I saw him in the emperor's tent, after you and Bryennios left to rescue Basilacios. He's a tribune, all right." Justin thought for few seconds. "Volas, Tribune Volas," he added. "The emperor ordered him and some captain to lead some light cavalry to find Strategos Tarchaniotes. Iatrelos, I think . . . Yes. His name was Iatrelos."

Peter inspected Volas' body. "Hands are bound behind his back with leather . . . sword wound just under the breast bone . . . deep sword wound. His chest and belly are covered in blood."

Justin crawled over to inspect Volas' body. As he did, he saw something in the dim distance and quickly climbed over Volas. "Peter, I just found Iatrelos."

CHAPTER 17

Peter followed Justin over Volas' corpse. "Wound is the same. Hands bound with leather straps." The second corpse was as cold as the first.

Justin looked up from the corpse. "Who did this?"

"Look at the leather straps." Justin examined the straps carefully. "Do those straps remind you of something?" Peter continued. "How about those knots? Rather peculiar, don't you think?"

Justin recalled where he had seen the knots before. "No one ties knots like the Pechenegs. And I've never seen this kind of red leather anywhere but among those very same Pechenegs." He looked up at Peter. "So our friend Andronikos Dukas not only withdrew the rearguard at the battle's most critical moment, but he also made sure no help would come from Tarchaniotes."

"He's probably on his way back to Constantinople to tell about the 'unfortunate disaster' which has befallen the emperor."

"The Dukas will take over the capital and make Michael sole emperor," Justin concluded.

"And the empress—"

"And Eleni!" Justin grabbed his friend's hand. "Peter! We've got to get back!"

"Justin," Peter said, "calm down! We'll get there, I promise! But we're not going anywhere without thinking this through."

"I'm sorry, Peter. I'm asking you to risk your life to help me. You don't have to do this."

"I know that, Justin," Peter responded. "But I must help you. You won't make it by yourself. I'm your friend and I give myself no other choice."

"Peter, I'll never forget this."

"Well we're not there yet. We still have several hundred miles to travel. I just wonder how we're going to get back."

"Do you think that there is anything left of the army?" Justin wondered.

"The only effective force is commanded by Dukas. Something tells me he wouldn't be too interested in helping us."

"We might as well ask the Turks!" Justin added. "What about Bryennios? I thought I saw his wing withdraw intact."

"That may be but where did they go?" Peter replied. "I imagine every Roman unit is on its way back to Constantinople by now."

"As are we," Justin added.

"True," Peter said. "Although I doubt we'll find many friends there."

"What about Alexios Comnenos?"

"Not even he could help us, Justin. Comnenos is going to lie low. He won't dare get in the middle of this. The Dukas are too strong. They now control the army, the aristocracy, and, if they've planned as thoroughly as I suspect, they've eliminated any political opposition in the Senate—"

"Quiet!" Justin hissed. "Did you hear that? Someone's coming this way!"

Peter followed Justin into the deepest, darkest recesses of the cave as the sound of voices outside the cave grew louder.

"Let's see if our friends are still here," a voice said in Greek. Justin looked at Peter. They knew too well to whom that voice belonged. A second later, Zervas lowered himself into the cave. Three Pecheneg light cavalrymen slid down after him. The tribune looked into the recesses of the cave. He couldn't see Justin or Peter but he could tell that the bodies of Volas and Iatrelos had been disturbed. He whispered something to one of the Pechenegs who relayed the message to the others in the cave and then to others outside. One of those dropped into the cave with a torch. Justin felt his heart accelerate. Zervas grabbed the torch and moved deeper into the cave.

At first Zervas, was shocked to see them but he quickly recovered. "Well, look what we've found!" he declared with delight. "It's those two villains who betrayed Emperor Romanos." Justin and Peter were defenseless. "We've done the Roman Empire a great service by finding these dangerous traitors!" Only one of the Pechenegs spoke Greek and he hurriedly translated Zervas' words so his comrades could enjoy the fun. "And look!" Zervas added. "They've killed Tribune Volas and Captain Iatrelos!" The Pechenegs exploded in laughter as their interpreter finished. Justin and Peter had never seen Zervas more happy. "We'd better get these devils back to Constantinople to account for their treachery."

Peter and Justin looked at each other. They didn't want to return to Constantinople as prisoners.

Zervas and his minions hurried the two captains out of the cave. The Pechenegs allowed them to mount the two extra horses they had with them, obviously those belonging to the dead men. One bound their hands in front of them while a second and a third took the reins of each horse.

"I'd like to thank you both for making your own arrest so easy," Zervas said with biting sarcasm. "This is the first thing you've done right since I've known you!" Zervas nodded to one of the Pechenegs and continued, "When Prince Andronikos saw your shameful betrayal of the emperor on the battlefield, he felt compelled to have you two declared outlaws. Your murder of these other two brave soldiers makes your apprehension even more significant. Perhaps His Highness will increase the bounty he has placed on your heads!" Zervas exploded into a sinister laugh and the Pechenegs joined him.

Zervas and his five henchmen headed west with their captives. The tribune had hoped to be in Nicopolis with his prizes by the middle of the coming week. As the ride entered its fourth hour, Zervas ordered his men to look for a place to rest the horses. One of the Pechenegs spotted a small grove of trees and led the rest of the men to it.

When they arrived, Zervas told the Pecheneg leader to dismount his troops. The commander turned around to relay Zervas' order but, as he did so, two arrows suddenly appeared in the front of his neck. The stunned cavalrymen whirled around to see six mounted

Turks closing in on them. In another second, the horseman holding the reins to Justin's horse grabbed at his chest and fell over dead, a Turkish lance in his back.

Zervas unsheathed his sword and tried to rally his remaining men but they froze when they saw the death of their comrades. Justin seized the opportunity and dug his spurs into his horse's ribs. The animal cried and then bolted forward. Peter smashed his guard's face with his two bound hands, knocking him off of his horse. As the man fell, the agile Peter nabbed the short sword from the Pecheneg's outstretched hand. Zervas lunged at Peter with his sword. Peter tried to dodge the blow but it grazed his left shoulder. By then, Zervas was off balance and Peter was able to shove him off of his horse with his two hands. In a flash, he spurred his horse forward and took off. He soon caught up with Justin, who was waiting for him behind a tree a quarter of a mile ahead.

"Koumbarro," Justin quipped as Peter rode up, "you're getting a little slow in your old age." He saw the sword in Peter's hand. "Well done!" He held his bound hands in front, inviting Peter to sever the leather bonds. Peter obliged him, handed the sword to Justin, and retorted, still winded by his narrow escape, "I'd say, the task, I undertook, was a bit, more challenging, than yours." Justin returned the favor as Peter urged his horse forward and said, "Come on, let's get out of here!"

But Justin didn't move.

"Justin! The Turks! Let's go!" Peter knew what his friend was thinking and didn't want to hear it.

"We can't leave him, Peter," Justin said.

"The hell we can't!" Peter fumed. "Need I remind you that devil was going to have us killed?"

"I'm going back," Justin said, not waiting for Peter's opinion. "Care to join me, Koumbarro?" he asked as he sped back toward Zervas.

"He's probably already dead!" Peter shouted as Justin left. He knew Justin wasn't changing his mind. "Justin!" Peter yelled. "Lord Christ, help us all!" He quickly crossed himself and dug his spurs into the horse's sides.

The two captains returned to find, much to their surprise, that Zervas was still alive. The last Pecheneg had succumbed to the

Turks and three Turks lay dead on the ground. The remaining three harassed Zervas, who was giving a good account of himself. He successfully dodged a blow here, smashed a Turk over the head there, and wheeled his horse to the left to land another blow but the Turks could tell that Zervas was tiring. So could Justin and Peter.

"Follow me!" ordered Justin as they galloped forward. The young captain laid into the unsuspecting Turks with the purloined sword. Peter, although unarmed, was right behind him. The enemy horsemen were confused at first, uncertain how to deal with this new threat. One of them ordered the other two to go after Justin and Peter while he finished off the beleaguered Zervas.

The larger of the two charged toward Justin. This Goliath must have been six and a half feet tall and nearly three hundred pounds. He swung a large mace at Justin's head. Justin ducked and slashed ineffectively at the giant with his sword. The Turk recovered and backhanded his mace into Justin's chest. The mighty blow knocked the wind out of him but Justin could see that the horseman, being at the end of his stroke with the deadly instrument, exposed his huge unarmored chest. Justin saw the opportunity and lunged forward with every last bit of energy he possessed, holding the short sword with both hands. The blade dove deeply between two of the Turk's ribs and buried itself to the hilt in his right lung. The colossal warrior tried to scream but the violation of his chest collapsed his lungs and rendered him mute. Justin retrieved the sword and the giant Turk fell dead.

Peter, being unarmed, had a greater challenge. When the Turk who faced him saw Peter's perilous predicament, he raced toward his opponent. The attacker slashed and hacked at him continually. Peter kept his horse moving, turning left, then right, spinning around, but never turning his back on the enemy horseman. The Turk parried and then suddenly jabbed his sword toward Peter's chest. The blade broke through the bony carapace of Peter's corselet and continued through to the skin. The wound drew blood but was superficial.

Encouraged by his success, the Turk attempted the same move again. The result was the same.

Peter realized the urgency of his situation. If he tried to disengage his enemy, he would risk getting a greater wound to the back or perhaps the arm. If he could keep his assailant in front of him, he could hold out until Justin could help him.

The Turk pressed the attack once more. His parrying tactic had borne fruit twice. A third, more forceful blow, would end this combat.

This time Peter was ready for him. The Turk parried twice and then lunged at the left side of Peter's chest. When he did, Peter lifted his left arm straight into the air and rotated his right shoulder forward. The Turk's blade hit Peter's chest tangentially, causing little injury but, more importantly, for a few seconds, the blade hung up in the bony armor of Peter's corselet. With his assailant overextended and temporarily snagged, Peter summoned all of his strength and, with his clenched right hand, landed a crashing blow on the Turk's left jaw. The man was stunned but still very much in the fight. Peter delivered three more blows, the last of which knocked the Turk off the right side of his horse. Peter leapt on top of the man's chest and savagely beat the horseman with his hands. The Turk attempted to use his sword but Peter knocked it out of his hand. Both of them wrestled for the sword but Peter grabbed it first. His attacker had enjoyed three opportunities to kill him; Peter was not about to give him a fourth. With the agility of a cat, Peter swung the sword across the Turk's neck. Blood spewed wildly and seconds later, the man was dead.

Zervas was in trouble. His attacker had just inflicted two sword wounds. Before Justin and Peter had arrived, he had sustained two arrow wounds in his left thigh and a lance had torn open the back of his left shoulder. The tribune desperately used every last ounce of his strength to defend himself. He lacked the strength to attack, and his ability to resist was near its end. The Turk's jab opened a new wound in Zervas' chest. Totally exhausted, he groaned as his assailant prepared to do him in. The Turk wound his arm back to ensure the power needed for this final blow. He started forward and then suddenly stopped. He looked down at his own chest and saw the bloody tip of a Pecheneg short sword poking through it. Zervas saw it, too. As the dead man fell forward, Zervas saw Justin standing a few feet behind the dying Turk. Zervas realized what had happened but said nothing. He stared apprehensively at Justin.

Justin stared back at him with a glint of self-satisfaction in his eye. Then Zervas saw Peter.

The exhausted tribune was silent. He had escaped death at the hands of the Turks, only to fall victim to the two captains who undoubtedly would complete the work the Turks had begun. Justin stared at Zervas and turned to Peter and then back at Zervas.

"Poor bastard," Justin said to Peter.

"He'll be fine. A Roman patrol will find him."

"Or a Turkish patrol."

"One can only hope."

"Let's go."

Peter and Justin mounted their horses and rode off without a word. The exhausted and confused tribune watched in amazement and then collapsed.

Justin and Peter rode hard the rest of the day. Their situation was impossible. Odds were that every Roman soldier they came across knew of the bounty on their heads. Marauding bands of Turks roamed the countryside and they would find two Roman soldiers a fun martial diversion. Yet the two captains knew they had to return to Constantinople. There was no other option. As night fell, they dismounted and sat under a sycamore tree.

"Any idea how we can get back?" Justin asked.

"Going dressed like this won't do at all," Peter answered. "We need disguises of some kind." Peter looked out over the arid Armenian steppe. "I'm open to any ideas but I think traveling in the daylight and on the main roads will make it easier to be found out. Better to travel at night and stick to the back roads."

"That's probably the safest way but it will take us over a month to get back. We need to get there sooner, Peter." Both of them thought for a moment. "How about going by sea? Make our way to the coast."

It was obvious that Peter didn't favor that course. "Pirates," he said matter-of-factly. "The imperial navy will be looking for us as well. And there is the small matter of obtaining an ocean-going vessel. That's not quite like stealing a horse or an ox cart."

"We stillhave a lot of ground to cover," Justin argued. "Which route is best, Nicopolis to Ancyra, then to Nicaea? Or traveling to Trebizond and then Sinope, along the coast?"

"Let's stay away from the coast, head for Nicopolis. We'll stay on the main road but travel only between the twelfth hour and dawn." Their chances were bad either way. Nicopolis was a good two hundred miles to the west. They would have to ride hard to make good time.

Justin and Peter rode for nearly six hours, the last three in the dark. A thin crescent moon gave dim light to the clear sky. Justin spotted a camp in the distance. A group of men gathered around a fire that burned in the center of the camp. There were four tents and several horses and pack mules. The captains had not eaten since the day of the battle at Manzikert, two days earlier, and their stomachs were getting the better of their judgment. They quickly dismounted and tied their horses to a shrub. They stole forward silently. When they were two hundred yards from the brightly burning campfire, they could hear the men talking.

"That's Arabic," Justin whispered.

"Who do you suppose they are?"

"They're not locals," Justin began, scrutinizing the situation closely. "Looking at the tents, the horses' tack, and their clothes, I'd say they are visiting from Syria or Egypt."

"Where do you suppose they keep their food?" Peter asked, smiling, his stomach now growling.

"Your guess is as good as mine," Justin replied. "Let's start looking."

They crawled silently over the cool grass to the tent nearest them. There they found silks and jewelry, but no food. They furtively crept to the next tent. This tent contained wool, large urns, presumably for olive oil, and blocks of ivory. Peter looked at Justin in frustration. *Where is the damn food?*

Justin pointed to a tent on the other side of the camp. They would have to circle around the men at the campfire to avoid detection. Horses and mules were tied to the right and left of the tent, so getting inside would not be easy.

Peter opted to circle wide to their left and approach the tent from the rear. They slowly moved forward over the flat terrain. They circled past the men at the campfire and the beasts of burden to the left of the tent. The back of the third tent lay ten feet ahead of them. Justin looked at Peter, who nodded his head in encouragement. Justin crawled forward toward the tent. One of the horses startled, so he stopped immediately. But the horse soon calmed down and Justin continued. When he was about halfway there, Peter followed. Justin reached the tent, slid under the rear flap, and was in. Peter was a few seconds behind. Inside, they found bread, salted meats, pistachios, and a myriad of fruits. They fought the pressing urge to fill their bellies immediately and stuffed whatever they could under their corselets. Each shoved a handful of sustenance into his mouth as they prepared to exit.

"May we help you gentlemen?" said a man in perfect Greek. He stood before them at the tent's entrance. Behind him were seven other men; two held torches, the other five were armed with wickedly curved Damascene swords.

Peter scurried out the back, only to find others. The leader said something in Arabic to two of the men. They grabbed Justin and Peter who offered no resistance. They were disarmed and made to sit in front of the leader, who, himself, was seated. One of his men sat at the leader's left, another at his right. The remaining seven stood behind the captives.

"Please tell us who you are," said the leader. There was no response. "What were you doing?" he continued. Again, there was no response. The Arab shooed a fly away from his face. "Why were you stealing from me?" he asked. Justin and Peter still gave no response. "Very well," he said. "What if I start the conversation? That might make it easier for you to speak. I am Rashad ibn al-Faisal. My companions and I are from Damascus." He stopped and waited for a response. None came.

The man's name was familiar to Justin but he couldn't tell why. He racked his brain trying to remember why he remembered this name.

Faisal was losing his patience. He tried another tack. "You men are soldiers of the Roman Empire." Justin and Peter nodded slowly. "Ah, that's much better," he said with a grin. "You men are obviously hungry. Have you been separated from your command?" The young captains did not respond.

The man sitting to Faisal's left studied the swords taken from their captives. He leaned toward to Faisal and said something while he pointed at the captured swords.

"My friend Omar informs me that your weapons are most unusual for Roman soldiers." He grabbed the Turkish sword and held it up. "This one, for example, is a weapon of your enemy, the Turks." He then held the Pecheneg sword in his other hand. "This sword comes from I know not where but it is definitely not Roman." He glared at his captives. "Deserters?" he asked, the term obviously repulsive to him. "Perhaps you are not Roman soldiers. Perhaps you have stolen those clothes and these swords just as you intended to steal from me."

Faisal stood up. "In my country, we have an effective way of punishing thieves." He said something to the men standing behind the captives. They rushed forward and grabbed Justin and Peter. Two of them held each captive and two others grabbed Peter's right arm and held it outward. Faisal came forward, pulled a sharp curved knife from his waist, and moved toward Peter. Peter resisted as best he could but could not escape. He looked over to Justin, his eyes imploring his friend to do something. Faisal slowly drew the knife across Peter's wrist, just enough to leave a thin trail of blood.

Suddenly Justin remembered where he had heard Faisal's name before. In broken Arabic, he begged Faisal to stop. Faisal looked at him with contempt and smirked. "Do you think your friend can escape punishment because you know a little Arabic?" He returned his attention to Peter's hand.

"You are the brother of Najib ibn al-Faisal!" Justin shouted out in Arabic.

This time, Faisal stopped. He turned toward Justin and glared. "How do you know that?"

"I am Justin Phillipos," Justin began, expecting Faisal to react to his name.

"That means nothing to me," Faisal replied as he returned to his knife.

"I lived in your brother's house four years ago."

Faisal looked at Justin again. Now Justin's name was striking a chord in his memory. "Justin Phillipos . . ." he repeated. "Justin Phillipos . . ." he said again. Then he smiled. "Of course, the Greek!" He grabbed Justin's hands and shook them as he ordered his men to release the captives.

"Rashad!" Justin embraced his host and silently thanked God for their deliverance.

"You've changed a lot in four years, Justin." Rashad hugged him tightly.

The circumstances of this meeting weren't a complete mystery to Peter. He knew that Justin was captured by the Arabs and held as the slave of an officer, presumably this man's brother, for a year but he certainly wasn't treating Justin like a slave. He looked to Justin for an explanation.

"Peter Argyropoulos," Justin began, "this is Rashad ibd al-Faisal."

"Please, call me Rashad," their captor-turned-host begged as he shook Peter's hand.

Justin continued, "Rashad is the older brother of Najib Ibn al-Fiasal, the Arab officer who captured me during the siege of Antioch. Do you remember my telling you I was the slave of an Arab officer for a year?"

"Slave?" thundered Rashad Ibn al-Faisal. "You were his guest! Najib treated you very well! He gave you a servant of your own, access to his most excellent library, and the run of his lands. By the way, you should practice your Arabic more."

Things were falling in place for Peter. Except one thing. "Justin, what about your . . ." Peter hesitated to finish his sentence. He moved his hands like water forming waves, trying to communicate with Justin.

"Water?" guessed Justin. "Oh, the ship!"

"Are you talking about your *miraculous* escape? When you swam to the Roman ship from the beach?" Rashad asked jokingly. "Najib told me about that."

"You did escape, didn't you, Justin?" Peter asked, hoping the answer was "yes."

"It was an escape of sorts," Justin began. "But I wasn't escaping from Najib."

"My brother saw that Justin was growing homesick," explained Rashad. "We were still at war with the Romans at the time so the release of any captive was forbidden. Najib devised a plan and took Justin to the seaside to execute it. Justin, Najib told me that it was a very touching moment."

"But the emperor called you a hero, Justin."

"He was a hero for saving his men," Rashad explained, "not for jumping into the sea and swimming to a Roman ship."

"Do you ever write to Najib?" Peter asked Justin.

"My brother died of scrofula two years ago," Rashad interjected soberly yet courteously.

"I'm very sorry," Peter said.

"He was a good man," Justin added. "I cried when his servant sent me the letter that Najib was writing when he died."

"But that has passed," Rashad concluded. "You are hungry. Please, join us for a meal."

Throughout that night, Justin and Peter enjoyed Rashad's generous hospitality. They were fed until they could eat no more. They explained their current predicament to their host who was both entertained and concerned. A trader by profession, he and his men were on their way to Trebizond to conduct business. From there, he was going to Constantinople by his own ship for more transactions and, from the capital, he would return to Syria via Cyprus.

Surprisingly, Rashad took an interest in helping the two captains. He remembered his brother's close friendship with Justin and felt that this is what Najib would want him to do. He proposed disguising Justin and Peter as Arab traders. "We'll sneak you back right under their noses!"

"Good idea," Justin said. "We see Arab traders all the time in the city."

"But I don't speak any Arabic," Peter noted.

"I can teach you," Justin replied enthusiastically. "As Arab traders we'll be free to move about the city to find Eleni and my family."

"I agree. It will work," Rashad added. "And to ensure that it does, you two need sleep." Rashad called to his men. A new tent was set up for Justin and Peter. Sleep overtook them the minute their heads touched the soft ground.

"A great tragedy has befallen the emperor," said Archbishop Mavrites, not attempting in the least to sound concerned. He walked back to his desk, opposite the person he was addressing, and slid into his great chair. "We believe there are traitors in our very midst who may be responsible. I will need your help in subduing one of them."

"Why don't you just arrest them, Eminence?" asked Sister Despina callously.

"I'm afraid it's more complicated than that, my child," he explained. "This malefactor has corrupted the empress and obtained her complete trust. We believe that she may have convinced the empress to betray her own husband."

Despina hesitated. "Certainly your Eminence has others who can—" Despina began.

"Sister Despina," Mavrites interrupted impatiently. "Have you grown weary of working for the Church?"

Despina's heart jumped at Mavrites' words. He had not forgotten the tears in her eyes the day Kastros was led away. "Why, no, Eminence, I do so enjoy the work you give me."

Mavrites grinned. "The woman must die, Sister Despina."

"Die?" Despina's mouth dried quickly; it was hard to swallow. Mavrites had never asked her to murder anyone before.

"She has been living in the empress' apartments at the Palace Bucoleon. She is a young woman, eighteen."

Despina thought desperately while Mavrites spoke. To snub him was suicide. Murder or not, this was her only chance to retain Mavrites' favor. "What is her name?"

"Eleni Phillipos," Mavrites replied. "Her husband was a soldier in what is left of the Emperor's army. He and another officer betrayed the emperor on the field of battle and then deserted. Being the wife of a coward by itself would be sufficient reason for her execution."

Despina nodded as she eyed the bulging purse in the metropolitan's hand. "Where do you want me, Eminence?"

"Start at the Palace Bucoleon. Wear your habit. My people there will know who you are."

"Yes, Eminence."

Mavrites stood, reached forward, and handed the purse to Despina. "For your trouble, Sister."

"Thank you, Eminence." Despina bowed and humbly received her wage.

"And Sister," the archbishop added, "please, do be discreet."

Although the battle had taken place nearly two weeks ago, news of the disaster had just arrived early that morning. The Palace Bucoleon was in chaos. The incessant chattering and moving about awakened Eleni from a deep sleep. She arose from bed, threw a robe over her tunica, and rushed to the door to open it. She accosted one of the empress' attendants as she scurried down the hall.

"Marina," Eleni called, "what's happening?"

"Terrible news!" Marina replied on the brink of panic. "Terrible news!"

"What?"

"The army has been defeated!" Marina shouted, "The emperor has been captured!" Then she ran off down the hall crying, "Oh Blessed Theotokos, what has happened to your army?"

"Defeated?" Eleni wondered, thinking of Justin. "The emperor captured?" she added, thinking of the empress. She closed the door and walked slowly, as if she were in a dream. She kneeled beside her bed and placed her hands over her face. Eleni began to cry but after a moment, she stopped and placed her hands together. She lowered her head and prayed as she sobbed. "My God, how could this happen? Oh, please let Justin be alive!"

Eleni held her hands together tightly. She wept sadly as she continued beseeching the Almighty. She said a prayer she had learned when she was young but found it hard to remember the words. Eleni's constant thoughts of Justin made the prayer impossible to say anyway, so she stopped. She thought of their last days together. She remembered her anger toward her husband and her frustration with his forgetfulness. Why had she been so hard on him? He may be dead! Eleni clenched her hands together, tighter than before. "Lord Jesus Christ, don't let it end this way!" She closed her eyes tightly, so that her tears could barely trickle through the lids. "Dear Lord Christ, let me see my husband again!"

Eleni felt something warm on her shoulder. She immediately rose to her feet, convinced that someone had touched her. Yet she saw nothing. She knew that she should be alarmed but something told her she need not worry. Eleni thought of Justin again. The fear that she felt moments ago had disappeared. A strong feeling now grew in her heart: She would see Justin again. He was coming to her.

Eleni couldn't say why things had suddenly changed. Was her prayer answered already? Eleni didn't know what to think but she knew what she had to do. She had to get word to her parents and to Justin's. She dressed herself and returned to the hall. She hoped to find someone who could help her but the surrounding hysteria wouldn't allow that. Eleni thought about sneaking out of the palace but the guards were probably aware of the news and were on alert. Eleni wrung her hands in frustration. What could she do? Then it came to her. "The empress," she said. "The empress can help me." She ran to the empress' apartments but something was very wrong. Two of the Varangian Guard stood at the door to her apartments denying access to all who dared ask for it.

Eleni ran up to one of them. "I must see the empress!" she demanded.

The burly blond with cold blue eyes did not answer. When Eleni pressed him again, he growled, "No one may pass!"

Eleni turned away in frustration. "I must get to her!" she said to herself. Her quick mind began constructing a scheme to get past this guard. She was about to implement her strategy when she heard a familiar voice calling her.

"Eleni." It was the prioress of Saint Barbara's convent. "Eleni, my child."

Eleni turned to the older woman. "Mother Ioanna," she said, desperately hoping the older woman could lead her to the empress.

"Eleni, my dear," the doughty, gray-haired woman began very somberly. "You must not have heard the horrible news! The emperor has been captured, the army defeated! And . . ." The old nun would have run on forever had Eleni not skillfully interrupted.

"Mother Ioanna, I've heard," Eleni interjected. "Yes, it's terrible. My husband is with the emperor."

"You poor dear!" Mother Ioanna cried. "You must be very upset."

"I want to speak to the empress," Eleni said, changing the subject as tactfully as she could. "I must get word to our families."

"The epress left the palace very early this morning. Nobody has any idea where she is."

"Left? What will I do now?"

"That's why I'm here," the nun began. "Her Majesty sent word to me before dawn today. She wants you to stay with me at Saint Barbara's. I'm certain one of the sisters could get a message to your family."

"And what of Her Majesty?" Eleni asked with concern. "Will I ever see her again?"

"Only the Lord knows, my child." The old woman gently took Eleni's hand. "But come with me now. We'll take good care of you."

As the two women rushed out of the palace, Eleni saw Myra and stopped. "Mother Ioanna," Eleni said to the prioress, "I must speak to Myra. Perhaps she knows where the empress is! Myra!" Eleni ran to the servant before Mother Ioanna could respond. "Myra!"

Myra was surprised to see Eleni running toward her. "Eleni!"

"The empress is gone!"

"Yes, I know. I saw her leave this morning."

"Where has she gone?"

"I don't know but you must return to your chamber."

Mother Ioanna gently tugged at Eleni's arm. "Come along, my dear."

"Where are you going?" Myra asked. "You must return to your chamber!"

"Remember, Eleni, this is the empress' order!" Ioanna hissed under her breath.

"Yes, Mother," Eleni replied. "I must go, Myra."

"No!" Myra protested. "You must return to your chamber!" she added as she tried in vain to grab Eleni's arm. "The empress said nothing to me about this!"

Mother Ioanna stepped between the two women and shoved Myra away with surprising force. "Leave Eleni!" When Myra lunged toward Eleni again, the old woman threw her to floor. "Now, Eleni! We are leaving!"

As Myra got up from the ground, grimacing in pain, and saw Eleni and Mother Ioanna running out of the palace, she looked as though the Gates of Heaven had just been closed in her face. She placed her hand over her mouth and ran down the great hallway. She turned into a large room and threw herself on the floor at the feet of three men.

"Sire," Myra wailed, "I have failed you! Please forgive me!"

Before her stood Caesar John Dukas, dressed in the splendor reserved for one of his rank. To his right stood Patriarch John Xiphilinios and to his left, Dukas' son, Andronikos, just back from Manzikert. Her interruption turned his face to stone.

"Who is this?" asked Andronikos.

"I am Myra, sire, the empress' servant," she said into the floor.

"And one of my best spies," John Dukas' added. "You say you have failed us? What have you done?"

"The Phillipos woman, sire" she replied. "She has left the palace!"

"When?" the Caesar demanded sharply.

"Just now, sire, with Mother Ioanna."

John Dukas looked to Xiphilinios.

"The prioress of Saint Barbara's, Caesar," the patriarch said.

John Dukas looked to his son and nodded. Andronikos immediately departed through an archway door behind him and entered a small alcove. There he found a young soldier who snapped to attention. Standing beside the soldier was Sister Despina.

Andronikos Dukas leered at the comely nun. "Sister Despina?"

Despina bowed. "Yes, sire."

"Very good. Archbishop Mavrites has told you of a young woman . . ."

"Eleni Phillipos, sire."

"Yes. She is now on her way to Saint Barbara's convent. Do you know it?"

"Yes, sire."

"Then go. Do your duty. I will make the necessary arrangements."

Despina hesitated momentarily, then left without a word.

Eleni and Mother Ioanna arrived by carriage at Saint Barbara's. The prioress led Eleni to a small cell within the convent. She opened a closet, took out a nun's habit, and handed it to Eleni. "This was Her Highness' idea. We want to be certain you blend in with your surroundings."

Eleni look with apprehension at the habit. "Very well," she said, "If the empress thinks it should be done, I'll do it."

"While you're here you shall be called 'Sister Eleni.' I don't want to make this too complicated for you."

"How can you keep me safe?"

"We'll find a way. Right now you don't have any other choice."

"Thank you, Mother. Thank you for taking such good care of me."

"Think nothing of it, dear." The old woman walked to the door and turned around. "Oh, Sister Eleni," she said, winking, "I'll send one of the sisters here to help you get a message to your parents."

"Thank you, Mother Ioanna."

"And I'd love to see you at vespers this evening," the nun suggested.

"Yes, certainly."

CHAPTER 18

The voyage from Trebizond had gone smoothly. In exceptionally cooperative weather, Rashad's ship had made excellent time. Unlike most cargo ships of the time—round and bulky—she was built for speed. The sacrifices she had made in capacity proved worthy when she outdistanced deadly pirate ships. She boasted two high masts with white cotton lateen sails that powered her sleek bow through the surrendering sea. Like many Roman cargo ships, she had a stern rudder.

Justin looked out over the bow at the Bosphorus. He was dressed in flowing dark blue robes and a red turban, looking every inch an Arab. Justin had never seen the strait from this viewpoint before and was impressed. Before him were two rugged land masses, Europe from the west and Asia from the east, stretching outward to touch each other, only to be frustrated by this sleeve of the sea. Peter joined him a few seconds later and shared his fascination with this strait. He wore a plain black robe and a small red cap.

As the ship breezed through Bosphorus, they could see the Golden Horn and Constantinople. The city looked majestic, like a gentle giant, welcoming mariners coming from the north and the south. From the deck, all could see Saint Sophia, the Church of Holy Wisdom, dominating the city, its dome shining like the sun and spreading its life-giving warmth over the entire city. Peter pointed out the Great Palace Complex and the Hippodrome. Justin could see the Gate of Neorian near his home. He grew quiet as he thought of Eleni and their parents.

Rashad came up from the hold and found Justin and Peter. "Quite a sight, isn't it? I believe it is the most beautiful city in the world."

The ship made its way through the overloaded shipping lanes and glided into Harbor of Julian at the southern end of the city and docked effortlessly.

Rashad escorted Justin and Peter down the gangplank and took them aside as their feet hit the pier. "My business here is brief," he began. "But I wish to make certain that you find your wife and family. It sounds to me as if this city will not be a safe place for any of you. Justin, if your family were to leave the empire, where would they go?"

"I don't know," Justin began. "Venice, perhaps. Ludovico Rossi is a merchant from there. He and my father are good friends."

"I will have my associate Omar take care of my business here. I will go with you. We can return here after we find your family."

"We? Rashad, you needn't come with us. You've done a great deal already," Justin protested. "I don't want to involve you in this."

"You already have, Justin," Rashad replied jovially. "And besides, my presence will enhance your disguise."

"I think he's right, Justin," Peter added.

"All right," Justin agreed. "Thank you, Rashad."

"Think nothing of it."

"Where to first?" asked Peter.

"Eleni's likely at one of the palaces with the empress," Justin responded. "Let's try finding our parents first. We're probably closest to my parents' home since we're on the south end." Then he remembered something. He turned to Peter and asked, "Didn't Lord Comnenos tell us if we returned to Constantinople under dire circumstances, we should find Simon the Jew and he could help us?"

"Justin, I can't believe you still trust those people!" Peter barked. He calmed down when he saw the surprise in Justin's eyes. "I'm sorry, Justin, but believe me, they're both gone. We're going to have to find them by ourselves."

"I wouldn't be so certain about that, my friend," Justin said calmly. "Something tells me we're going to get some help. Let's go to my folk's house first and see what we find."

"All right, Justin," Peter acquiesced. "We'll see what's out there."

"Very well, then," Rashad added, "I shall follow you, Justin."

The three of them proceeded through the main gate of the massive stone wall that surrounded the harbor. As they walked east along the wall, ahead they could see the empty Hippodrome and in fifteen minutes reached their goal. They walked through the gate at the front of the compound. But something was not right. They saw no sign of Justin's family at all. The servants were gone as well, as were Basilios' horses.

"I wonder where they've gone," Justin asked as he looked around. He stepped toward the front door. "Let's go in."

The inside was empty as well. They walked through the great room and into the kitchen. No sign of people. Justin cried out, "Anyone here?"

A soft rustling came from the bedroom. All three of them ran, expecting to find at least one family member, but all they found was a little old woman sleeping on the bed.

Justin slowly walked up to her. He nudged her gently with his hand. When she didn't awaken, he yelled, "Hey, you! What are you doing here?"

The old woman awoke with a start. "Oh, you startled me!" she said in a deep, masculine voice.

"Who the devil are you?" Justin asked, holding his right fist menacingly over the woman's head.

"Captain Phillipos?" the old woman asked in that same deep voice and not one bit intimidated by Justin's threatening.

Peter reached down. He grabbed the woman by the throat and shouted, "Identify yourself!"

"Now that's no way to treat a priest," the old woman said calmly.

"Priest?" Justin and Peter asked simultaneously.

"Captain Phillipos, Captain Argyropoulos," the old woman began as she slid off her gray wig and peeled away a false nose and eyebrows. "Don't tell me you don't remember."

Justin figured it out first. "Simon?" he said, still a little unsure.

Simon continued to remove his disguise and said, "Yes, it is Simon." He freed his face from the rest of his disguise and added with a dire sense of irony, "Welcome back to Constantinople."

"Where is everybody?" Justin asked impatiently.

"You'd better sit," Simon advised. "I've a lot to tell you, some of it good, some not." Justin, Peter, and Rashad found chairs and sat down. Justin introduced the Arab to Simon and explained how he came to be with them. Simon greeted him cordially but quickly returned to Justin. "I'll start with the emperor. He has been captured by the Turks."

"We expected as much," Peter said, recalling the chaos on the battlefield and Romanos Diogenes in the middle of it.

"It's difficult to believe," Rashad added. "A Roman emperor captured by the enemy—"

Simon agreed. "Hasn't happened in eight hundred years." Then he put his arm around Justin. "Captain, your wife is safe."

"Thank God for that!" Justin sighed. "Where is she?"

"She was moved by the empress, this very morning, to the convent of Saint Barbara in Blacharnae. As I said, she's safe for now but I'm afraid that the Dukas will find her."

"And our parents?"

"They left the city early this morning, two hours before dawn. My agents informed me of the disaster at Manzikert yesterday morning. I immediately came to your father and told him of the debacle and that you had escaped the Turks and were probably headed back to Constantinople."

"But how did you know?" Peter asked.

"I have ears throughout the army," Simon answered. "I advised your father it would be best for your family, Justin, aunts and uncles included, as well as Eleni's entire family to leave the city as soon as possible. I told them if they chose to stay within the empire, I could not guarantee their safety. Your father suggested going to Venice to stay with some friends there."

"The Rossi," interjected Justin.

"Exactly," Simon continued. "It turned out that Giovanni Rossi had just arrived in the city from Venice two days ago. He was to return today with a large cargo of silk. Needless to say, when your father presented his predicament, Giovanni eagerly offered his services. He ended up leaving half of his silk to accommodate your families."

"They left without Eleni?" Justin asked.

"Initially they refused to leave without her but I told them their continued presence acted as an impediment to her freedom. I promised them her release was of paramount importance to me. They were most reluctant to leave but they finally agreed."

"So how do we get Eleni out of the convent?" Justin asked.

"It's going to be difficult," Simon admitted. "Since the news broke this morning, the whole city has been in upheaval. The worst part, as you may know, is that the Dukas have taken over. Caesar John Dukas has returned from his exile to Bithynia. The Varangian Guard came to the caesar's side once the news of the emperor's defeat had been made known. Andronikos Dukas took half of the guard and charged through the Palace Bucoleon, proclaiming his cousin Michael emperor. None of the aristocracy will recognize Romanos as the ruler because of his defeat. The empress was arrested this morning, in her own apartments, by the Varangian Guard. She'll probably be exiled to a convent, far away from the city, and forced to take the veil."

"Where is Tribune Attaleiates?" Peter asked pointedly.

"He somehow managed to escape capture by the Turks," Simon explained. "My sources tell me he's in hiding on one of the estates of Nikephoros Bryennios."

"And Alexios Comnenos?" Peter continued.

"His mother, Anna Dalassena, has been arrested by the Dukas," Simon replied. "She may be bound for a convent as well. It seems that the Dukas are sending a clear message to the Comneni that they'd better cooperate."

"Will Alexios do that?" Peter asked.

"He is a very shrewd man," Simon replied, his loyalty obvious. "He'll do what is expedient but he did tell me to make certain you and your families got out of Constantinople."

Justin and Peter were stunned by the news. The Constantinople they had left six months ago had been turned upside down.

"Eleni," Justin reminded Simon. "How are we going to get Eleni out of the convent?"

"One of my agents has provided me with information about Saint Barbara's that will be useful to us." Justin, Peter, and Rashad began to see a ray of hope in this dark dilemma. "It seems that when the convent was built, His Majesty Romanos Lekapenos, the emperor at the time, had formed an 'attachment' to a certain nun. He worked with her and the builders to create a series of secret entrances and passageways by which he could slip into the convent and meet with his lover for their forbidden forays. Romanos Lekapenos meant to have these passageways and secret doors sealed after his fascination for the young woman waned some eight years later. However, the man in charge of completing the task, a certain Tribune John Zanos, had been using the passageways in much the same way as that emperor had. He was not about to give up that privilege. He told his master he had fulfilled his duty by sealing all of the secret doors and passageways. The emperor had no reason to disbelieve him so he assumed the secret features of Saint Barbara's were a thing of the past. Zanos continued his liaisons with various nuns at Saint Barbara's until he was ordered to lead a *numerus* of four hundred men into battle against the Bulgars. However, as Fortune dictated, he did not survive the campaign and his secret died with him."

"Until your friend rediscovered them," interjected the ever-skeptical Peter.

"But of course," Simon replied with a mischievous grin. He was about to elaborate on the discovery when Justin sharply cleared his throat.

"Could you continue, please?" urged Justin.

"Oh, please forgive me, Captain," Simon said, returning to the subject at hand. "We should get to this right away." He looked at the other three men in the room. "The Arabian clothing may have gotten you this far but the sight of Mohammedans congregating around a nunnery will generate suspicion."

"It looks like it's up to me to provide the disguises now, Rashad," Justin said.

Justin, Peter, and Rashad were able to find the clothes they needed in Basilios' closet. Justin directed Simon, who was shorter, to Leo's home to find what he needed. Simon added a couple of decades to each of them by mixing some white chalk into their hair and beards.

The convent was in the northwest part of the city, next to the Church of Saint Mary Blacharnae, so they had quite a walk ahead of them. They split into two groups to avoid arousing suspicion,

Justin walking with Simon while Peter traveled with Rashad. They left about fifty yards between the groups, when they could, and sometimes traveled on opposite sides of the street.

"Have you determined how we are to escape from the city?" Justin whispered to Simon as they walked down the street.

"Once we've freed your wife, you'll go by galley to Venice to join your families," Simon answered.

"Our friend Rashad has a ship and he is ready to take us," Justin interjected.

"I mean no disrespect to your friend," Simon began, "but the waters of the Ionian and the Adriatic are rife with pirates from Norman Italy. You need someone who knows those waters well."

"Something tells me you have someone in mind."

"Of course."

As they got closer to the convent, the city streets were filled with soldiers randomly accosting passersby. Justin whispered in Simon's ear, "This doesn't look good."

Simon, without turning to look at Justin, calmly replied, "My people tell me it's been like this since early yesterday morning. The closer we get to the Blacharnae, the worse it will become but if you ever want to see your wife again, there's no other way."

Fifteen yards ahead, a group of four soldiers and an officer were stopping everyone who walked down the narrow street. Ten people were ahead of them waiting to clear the checkpoint. As they drew closer to the soldiers, Justin glanced up at the soldiers and the officer. *Good. I don't know any of them.* He calmly walked up to the soldiers with Simon.

"Good morning, sirs," the officer said politely, which sounded most unusual given the circumstances. "Please excuse this inconvenience. We are looking for someone who may do harm to our empress."

"We are happy to cooperate," Simon said smoothly.

A fifth soldier came out of a nearby house and whispered something to the officer. "Please wait in there, sirs," the officer asked politely, pointing to the door of the house next to the one that the fifth soldier had exited previously. Simon and Justin had to comply. There were now six soldiers around them and any attempts to flee could have disastrous consequences. Besides, they had no clear indication they had been found out. They had noted the same thing happening to others in front of them, being briefly detained and then released. They entered the house to find two soldiers who urged them to sit in the small vestibule of the house.

Peter and Rashad were too far behind to see that Simon and Justin had been detained. When they reached the soldiers, that same fifth soldier exited the house and spoke to the officer. Soon Peter and Rashad were escorted into the same house. When Justin saw his friends walk in, he knew something had gone wrong. He looked at Simon in a panic as Peter and Rashad were seated and four more soldiers entered the room.

Justin's heart leapt into his throat when he saw a familiar face enter the vestibule: Zervas. Justin could hear Peter gasp when he recognized the demonic commander. Did he recognize them?

"You," Zervas said as he pointed his finger at Justin. "You come with me."

Justin turned pale as he stood and walked toward Zervas.

"And you," Zervas continued, this time pointing at Peter, "you come too."

Peter followed Zervas and Justin into the next room. The three were alone.

Zervas face was as cold as a statue's. "You gentlemen probably never thought you'd see me again." He silently waited for them to speak although he knew they wouldn't. "Gentlemen, these are treacherous times. It can be difficult to tell one's friends from one's enemies."

Justin wrinkled his forehead. *What the devil was that supposed to mean?*

"Gentlemen," Zervas continued. "I always repay my debts." He held out two small parchments and gave one to each of them. "These passes will get you safely out of the city. I suggest you leave before they expire." His face was as granite-like as ever.

Justin and Peter froze in disbelief. Zervas, their hell-sent nemesis, had them in his sharp-clawed hand and *he was letting them go*. This couldn't be.

"If I need to remind you, I may change my mind."

"Yes, sir!" Justin wheezed. "We're leaving!"

Peter nodded nervously as he followed Justin out of the room and into the vestibule. He and Justin filed out quickly, beckoning Rashad and Simon to join them. After they were out of sight of the checkpoint, Justin and Peter turned around and smiled at the oncoming Rashad and Simon. They were positively bursting.

"Do you mind telling us what this is all about?" Simon asked.

Justin replied, "That tribune at the house, my friends—"

"Yes," Simon interjected, growing inpatient with Justin.

"Was Tribune Zervas!"

"Do you mean the one who—" asked Rashad.

"Yes," Peter interrupted.

"Why didn't he arrest you? He had you in the palm of his hand," Simon wondered.

"Let's just say he was returning a favor," Justin replied. He smiled at Peter to remind him of his objection to rescuing Zervas.

Peter smiled back and shook his head.

Sister Despina handed a note of introduction to Mother Ioanna. The prioress read through the letter quickly and looked up at Sister Despina. "I'm so happy you could join us on such short notice, Sister Despina."

"Think nothing of it, Mother Ioanna," Despina said. "I am always happy to serve wherever the Lord wants me."

"According to Metropolitan Mavrites' letter, you have provided great service to the Lord in the past. We are not only fortunate that you have come so quickly, but also that you come with such exceptional credentials."

"You are too kind, Mother," Despina added, wondering what Mavrites had put in the letter.

"It was indeed strange the way that Sister Evangelia became ill so suddenly," the prioress continued, "but I shouldn't be too concerned. Fortunately, the physician has said that not much should come of this. Again, I'd like to thank you for coming."

Mother Ioanna showed Despina to her quarters but instead of staying there, Despina continued to follow the prioress, saying she wished to start helping right away. She offered to help the prioress with that morning's matins, hoping to meet Eleni at that point. The prioress accepted. They heard the bell announcing matins twenty minutes later.

Soon all of the nuns filed into the chapel. As they came in, Mother Ioanna introduced each of them to Despina who pretended to be genuinely interested in each of those that she met. However, none of the sisters was young enough to be Eleni Phillipos. All of these women were over thirty. Then at last, a sleepy Eleni, wearing an ill-fitting habit, strolled into matins. Despina quickly spotted her and realized she must be the one.

"And this," said Mother Ioanna, her left arm outstretched to greet Eleni, "is our newest arrival, Sister Eleni. She came just this morning."

Despina smiled and her anticipation grew, like that of a lioness that had just spotted a lame zebra. "Sister Eleni," she said graciously, "I'm Sister Despina." Despina took her hands and held them. "I understand that you're new here." Eleni nodded. "I'm new, too. Well, actually I've been a nun for some time but this is my first day here. Come, let's stand together for matins." Despina gently took hold of Eleni's hand and walked with her toward the iconostasis.

After matins, Despina walked with Eleni in the convent's courtyard. Eleni found her new friend charming. Despina insisted Eleni join her for the midday repast. Eleni, impressed by the attention that Despina was showing her, felt comfortable with her and enjoyed her company. After the meal, Despina asked if she could join Eleni in her room for prayers. She graciously accepted and anticipated what she believed would be a meaningful experience.

Simon led Justin and the others to the southeast corner of the convent. It was shaded by a cluster of cypress trees and obscured from any scrutiny by overgrown shrubs. Simon pulled a small cloth out from under his tunic and studied it. He moved ten paces northwestward and looked down at his right foot, then up at the cloth, then back at his right foot. He squatted down at the wall and began to run his right hand over the surface of the wall. Then he stopped and looked at Justin. "I've found it!" he whispered excitedly.

Simon examined the mortar on the outside wall of Saint Barbara's. He found loose bricks in the wall and clawed at them to free them from their place. Justin offered his help and, soon, four one-by-twelve-inch bricks were extracted. Simon stuck his right hand into the hole left by the bricks and felt for something. He applied both hands and began to pull it. After a while, the smaller man was exhausted.

Justin again offered his help. "Simon, please let me try," he whispered.

Simon nodded. "Inside there is a lever. By pulling it down," he instructed, "we should be able to open a secret door in the wall but a hundred years of lack of use has made the mechanism a little rusty."

Justin moved into position, found the lever, and jerked with all of his strength but the lever wouldn't budge. Justin tried to move the lever forward. Again he had no luck. Justin tried to pull the lever back and then push it forward but again failed. He looked back at Peter and signaled for him to join them.

Peter hurried forward. Justin and Simon apprised him of the situation. Peter took Justin's place, spat on his open palms, grabbed the lever, and gave it a mighty tug. Justin also spat in frustration when nothing happened but Peter continued pulling on the lever. When still nothing happened, Justin swore under his breath and started to whisper something to Peter. Peter didn't wait to hear; he just pulled vigorously once again.

"Nothing's happening," Justin said in frustration. "What are we going —"

Simon spoke up. "Quiet!" he said. "I hear something moving!"

Encouraged by Simon's report, Peter redoubled his efforts. Justin and Peter could now hear the noise that Simon had heard. Simon followed the sound about ten feet forward and saw a portion of the wall, about three feet by two feet, slipping forward an inch or so with each of Peter's forceful efforts. However, after it slid its inch, the secret door would retreat back to its original position.

Simon and Justin analyzed the stuck secret door carefully.

"Peter," Simon whispered. "Get Rashad." He turned to Justin. "The door may be jammed but at least we know where it is. Perhaps the four of us can get it open."

Peter returned with Rashad and a branchless tree limb.

"Justin," Peter whispered as he returned to the lever, "Wedge it in the opening. We'll use it to open the door."

Justin and Rashad crouched ready at the secret door while Peter found the lever. He pulled with all of his strength and again the door opened an inch. Rashad jammed the end of the limb into the door opening. Justin joined him and they pried and rocked the immobile door as Peter continued tugging the lever. After ten minutes of tugging, rocking, and prying, the opening grew from one inch to two, then to four.

"Keep going! It's working!" Simon cheered.

The secret door's ancient mechanism creaked and groaned with each effort to overcome it. After another five minutes the door was six inches ajar, enough for them to sneak through. The four of them sat down, exhausted, and caught their breath.

Simon stood up and announced, "I'll be back." He ran across the street to a small church and returned with a lit torch. "We're going to need this."

"Where did you find *that*?" Peter asked.

"Captain Argyropoulos, I knew it would be dark in there so I prepared," Simon answered with a wink as he crawled into the passageway.

Eleni kneeled at her bedside in prayer. "Holy God, Creator and Keeper of all, please bring my husband back to me. I know you would not send him to his death when we are but newlyweds. Watch over him and his friend Peter. Keep him alert to danger and strong enough to withstand it."

For a few seconds, she imagined Justin's happy, handsome face. And although her eyes were closed, as she prayed, she smiled. He seemed to be saying to her, "I love you." She opened her eyes, anticipating seeing her husband before her. Eleni sighed, closed her eyes again, and silently finished her prayer. She said softly as she crossed herself three times " . . . in the name of the Father, the Son, and the Holy Spirit."

As Eleni arose, she heard a knock on her door. She opened it to find her new friend, Sister Despina, waiting outside, eager to enter. "Sister, please come in," Eleni welcomed Despina with a smile.

"Shall we sit?" Despina suggested, pointing to the bench near Eleni's bed.

"Certainly, Sister," Eleni agreed.

"Sister Eleni," Despina noted as she set her hand on Eleni's shoulder, "you look troubled. What's the matter?"

Although Eleni was eager to share her troubles with Despina, she knew she couldn't divulge the entire truth. "I have a friend who may be in danger," she began. "I'm deeply concerned about her." Eleni almost ended her sentence with the male pronoun but caught herself just in time.

As they sat Despina asked, "Is your friend in some kind of trouble with the constable?" When Eleni shook her head, Despina asked, "Is she ill? Tell me why your friend is in danger."

"She traveled to a distant corner of the empire and now she is lost. No one knows where she has gone." A few tears streamed from the corners of Eleni's eyes. She reached up to wipe them away.

"Oh my, that is not good," said Despina sympathetically. "Are you and your friend close?"

"Very close," replied Eleni. She gazed outside of the window. "I can't bear the thought of never seeing her again." Eleni put her hands over her face for a few seconds, then took a deep breath and tried desperately to recover. "We've known each other since we were children."

"I lost a close friend, too," Despina interjected. "Christina and I were almost like sisters. Our fathers owned shops next to each other in Smyrna. Every day, except Sunday, of course, I would go with my father to his shop in the middle of the city. And Christina was always there with her father. We would spend hours playing in and around the shops. Our poor fathers indulged us terribly. When we were older, they'd let us walk around the city. We had all kinds of fun, running in and out of mischief. And then one day, Christina's family went to Samos to see her grandmother who was ill and dying. The short crossing by ferry was usually routine, but that day, a terrible storm struck soon after their embarkation. The boat never made it to the island."

Eleni shuddered. "Oh my! What a tragedy!"

Despina wiped a tear from the corner of her eye. "When my parents told me what had happened, I refused to believe it. I prayed three times a day that Christina would return. I had convinced myself that I would see Christina walking into my house or standing in front of me at church one day. After two years, I finally accepted her death yet I still catch myself looking for her among the crowd in the market or thinking that I see her off in the distance when I take my morning walks."

"You must have been very close," Eleni said.

"Yes, we were," Despina added with a tone of finality in her voice. "And do you know what saw me through those difficult times?" She didn't wait for an answer. "Prayer. I believe that through my constant prayers, the Lord finally allowed me to accept Christina's death. I believe such intensive prayer will help you, too."

"I prayed before you arrived," Eleni explained.

"*Constant prayer*. Yes, Sister, it will help," Despina spoke as if she were ordering Eleni to get on her knees to pray right away. She produced a small icon and handed it to Eleni. "This belonged to the prioress of my previous convent. She was a pious woman and used this often when she prayed. I'd like you to have it."

Eleni not only felt compelled to take the gift, but now she felt that she needed to start using it immediately. She looked at the icon and then at Despina. "Thank you very much," she said. She dropped to her knees, closed her eyes, and began to pray aloud a prayer that the empress' chaplain had taught her just a week earlier. As she prayed, her thoughts returned to Justin.

The deep, dark tunnel was made for someone of diminished height. Simon had the least trouble getting through but Justin, Peter, and Rashad found themselves constantly knocking their heads against the low ceiling. Simon tried to read the crude cloth map he had pulled from beneath his tunic. But the low light and the simplicity of his map made it extremely difficult.

"Damn," Simon swore under his breath as the tunnel reached another dead end. He backtracked, the other three following him without comment, and returned to the last fork they had encountered in the tunnels. Then he muttered excitedly as he compared his map to the tunnel ahead of him, "Yes, yes. This is it."

Justin didn't question Simon's ability or his methods. He had led them this far; Justin prayed that the diminutive master of disguises would be able to complete the task, and soon.

Simon stopped after going about a hundred paces. He turned to Justin and held the torch out in front of him. "Do you see that?" he asked, pointing to a small alcove off the main tunnel. Justin nodded. "Let's see where that gets us. According to the map, this would be an area used for grain storage." The four of them moved forward to the wall. "There should be a release lever up along the top here. He ran his right hand over the top most bricks. A minute later he declared, "Found it!" He pulled hard on the aged lever. Justin saw a portion of the wall quiver. His excitement grew. Soon he would be united with Eleni! Simon pulled again and a panel in the wall opened forward about a foot. Justin looked at Simon with even more excitement. Simon nodded in encouragement and Justin poked his head through the open panel.

"Is this the granary?" Simon asked.

Justin pulled his head back quickly. His face looked like he had just inhaled the contents of a ripe compost pile. "No."

Simon then poked his head through. He was surprised to see two young nuns bathing one of the more senior residents of Saint Barbara's. The old nun's skin was so pale and wrinkled that her appearance was more akin to a baby elephant than a woman. Simon quickly withdrew his head and looked at Justin's contorted face. "Sorry," he whispered. "Obviously the purpose of this room has changed in the last hundred years." Peter and Rashad shot forward to take a look. "I would advise against that, my friends," Simon said, shaking his head as he and Justin closed the portal. Simon reexamined his map and led onward.

"What was in there?" Peter asked Justin. Rashad, too, was eager for a description.

As the three followed Simon, Justin turned and said, "Imagine your grandmother's grandmother still being alive . . ." Peter and Rashad still appeared interested, " . . . and taking a bath before your eyes . . . Need I continue?"

"No!" Peter and Rashad answered together.

Meanwhile, Simon had found something. Again he compared the map to what was ahead. "I think this is what we need." The others raced forward. "I'll bet this is the granary," Simon said, pointing at the wall ahead of them. Again he found a lever near the topmost bricks in the wall. With some help from Peter, he pulled the lever back and, as before, a passageway in the wall revealed itself.

A bright light shone through the door into the dark tunnel. Justin didn't wait for any invitation from Simon. He peeked through the open portal and found the source of the bright light. "Simon!" he groaned as he turned back into the tunnel.

Simon nudged past Justin and looked through the door. He sighed as he looked out into the convent's central courtyard. He saw twelve nuns working in the convent garden and a second dozen carrying gardening tools, books, candles, and bags of flour across the busy courtyard.

"Now what?" Justin asked.

Simon didn't respond but continued down the tunnel, encouraging the others to follow.

Eleni continued to pray aloud, closing her eyes tightly. She spoke each word softly but intently, as if the energy she put into the prayer equated with the likelihood of its acceptance by God.

Despina saw Eleni's tightly drawn eyes. She slowly, silently moved toward the door. When she got there, she quietly turned the lock, sealing the room from any unwanted intrusion. She listened at the door for a few minutes to make certain no one was outside then she glided over to the kneeling Eleni. She stood over the younger woman and thought briefly about what she had to do.

She took a leather strap out of her pocket and held it in her right hand. Despina listened to Eleni, and every now and then, would join her in the long prayer's recitation. She examined the leather strap closely. Despina tried to avoid thinking about the task at hand. Her misgivings about committing murder mounted. Yet Mavrites seemed intent on the death of this young woman. The money he gave her suddenly was not an issue. Despina remembered that if she failed or refused to complete this mission, Mavrites would extract his vengeance. It was Eleni's life or her own.

Eleni suddenly opened her eyes. Despina calmly patted her on the shoulder and encouraged her to continue her prayer and Eleni complied.

Despina realized that the time had come. The nuns would soon be gathering for the midday meal. Any further delays would invite interruption, or worse, she could be caught in the act.

She held out the leather strap with her right hand and grabbed its dependent end with her left. Then she pulled the instrument taut, parallel to the floor and pulled on the ends a few times, trying to secure the grip of her moist palms. Despina hesitated again, relaxing her tight grip. *Kill the girl and leave!* She was losing patience with herself. *Be done with this unpleasant task!* She gathered her courage and prepared to lunge forward and garrote Eleni.

Eleni continued to pray with her eyes closed.

The time to act had come. Despina lurched forward, attempting to throw the strap around Eleni's neck. At the same instant Eleni lunged away from Despina and opened her eyes. Despina was surprised and irate that she had missed her quarry. She cursed and glared at Eleni's trembling eyes.

"The wife of a traitor . . ." Despina said cryptically to Eleni, trying to unnerve her. Despina held up the leather strap and moved toward Eleni who backed up slowly, knowing soon that she would be against the wall. Despina advanced and quickly closed the distance between them. She jumped forward but Eleni quickly moved away. Despina tried again and again but Eleni was too fast.

This line of attack was fruitless. Despina quickly looked around the room for another weapon. A three-foot iron rod, used to hold the room's solitary window open on hot days, rested in the corner. Despina ran toward it. Eleni, too, saw the rod and broke for it, but Despina got there first. She grabbed the rod and brandished it dangerously close to Eleni's head. She twice jabbed at Eleni's chest and then swung again at her head. Three times unsuccessful, Despina grew more aggressive. She rushed toward Eleni, swinging the deadly rod but Eleni always managed to stay beyond injury. Despina swung wildly, smashing the lone chair in the cell, tearing into the wooden frame of Eleni's bed, and scarring the plaster walls with the vile implement.

"Help me!" Eleni screamed.

The yelling enraged Despina and increased the urgency of completing her task. "You little bitch!" she spat, racing toward Eleni and swinging with all of her might. When she missed, she swung again, and again. Her heart pounded in her chest. "You're dead!" she shrieked. She attacked again, like a woman possessed by a demon.

Eleni screamed again but her dry throat produced a weak result. Despina rushed forward and jabbed, striking Eleni's left breast. The pain burned sharply and made Eleni cry out in pain. Seeing her success with this tactic, Despina tried it again, this time just below Eleni's ribs on her right side. Eleni's reaction time was a slowed by the previous blow but she managed to move backward enough to lessen the impact of the well-aimed poke. Despina moved as if she were going to jab again, then suddenly wound the rod to her right and swung it into Eleni's left shoulder, knocking her to her knees.

"Help me!" Eleni cried in anguish.

Despina smiled devilishly. "Nobody can help you, Missus. Phillipos," she taunted, preparing to strike another blow with her unstoppable weapon.

Eleni looked desperately for anything with which she could defend herself. Despina swung at her head, just missing. Eleni's relief was brief. The indefatigable Despina swung again and again. Eleni try to move left, keeping Despina in front of her but the nun wouldn't allow that. Despina jabbed and swung at Eleni's left shoulder or abdomen. Eleni shifted to her right but encountered the same resistance.

Despina heard someone walking in the hall. *I've got to finish this!* She saw Eleni drop her guard and rushed at her, wielding the iron rod back over her head and preparing to land a devastating blow. But Eleni dodged Despina and shot past her to the other side of the room. Eleni grabbed the back of the broken chair and held it in front of her. She smirked at the surprised Despina, who realized that her advantage had shrunk considerably.

Despina knew, however, that she still had the better weapon. With a few well-placed blows, she could smash that shield to kindling. She tightened her grip on the iron rod and rushed at Eleni.

Simon led his followers forward through the seemingly endless tunnel. He found yet another alcove and bade his weary followers to accompany him. The four of them went through the all-too-familiar machinations, Simon again referred to his cloth map as the others pried open the stone panel.

Peter quickly snatched it from him and snapped, "This cursed thing hasn't been right yet! Why do we need it?"

Simon snatched the map back. "It got us in here, didn't it?" he barked back.

Justin looked at Peter as if to scold him. "We're here to save Eleni, remember?"

Simon and Rashad opened the passageway and Justin rushed in. He quickly returned with a smile on his face. "I think this is what we want."

"Are we in the granary?" asked Simon.

"No," Justin replied. "Some place better." He turned around and proceeded back through the door. The others followed.

"This must be the laundry," Simon noted, sounding confused. He looked at his map and said to Justin, "I don't see this room on the map at all. How is this better?"

"I'm sorry, Simon, but it could take us weeks to find Eleni if we keep using the tunnels," Justin said. He picked up a worn nun's habit from the floor and put it on over his clothes. "Find yourselves one of these. I prefer to continue the search from here."

Peter and Rashad needed no convincing. They, too, were tired of the endless dark tunnels. They dug through the piles of clothing around them to find something that came close to fitting them. Simon eventually came around and joined the others.

The new disguises were less than perfect. Justin's habit ended somewhere above his knees. Peter couldn't find a habit big enough for his shoulders; he had to slit the back open to allow it to cover his muscular chest. Rashad's hairy forearms projected far beyond the ends of the sleeves. Only the small Simon's habit fit well. And to makes matters more complicated, the chin wraps of the habits covered most but not all of their beards. The four men looked at each other as if they were admitting that there was no way this masquerade would work. But Justin, sensing the desperation of their plight, assumed the lead, although he had no idea where to go. The three others obligingly followed him out of the laundry.

As they made their way into the hall, they saw two nuns ahead of them walking up the stairs. Justin whispered to Simon, "Let's follow them. They may lead us to the dormitory."

Simon agreed but as the troop set out, he reminded them that they were supposed to be nuns and their discovery would dash Eleni's chances. Stealth was more an asset than speed at this point. He stepped past Justin and led the way. Justin, Peter, and Rashad tried to walk daintily. On seeing them, Simon could only shake his head and hope they didn't come across many nuns.

The staircase that the two nuns had taken brought them to a hallway directly across from the dining hall. From this vantage, they could observe those entering or in the great room with little exposure.

The great room was empty except for the two nuns the men had seen going up the staircase. As more and more nuns filed in to the dining hall, Justin and Peter waited to find Eleni. As the last pair of nuns entered, someone closed the great doors. Simon looked to Justin who shook his head in disappointment. Eleni was not in the dining hall.

Simon whispered to Justin, "This is just as well. Now we can search the convent unhindered."

"But only until the meal is over," Peter interjected. "They'll be all over this place after that."

Simon agreed and the four of them hurried up the stairs to the next floor. "The nun's cells should be up here," Simon said. This time Simon was right. As they entered the long hall at the top of the stairs, they saw nothing but two rows of doors. Justin rushed to the first door and knocked: no answer. He proceeded on to the next door without waiting for Simon's order to do so. Peter followed Justin's lead and knocked on the doors across the hall. Rashad and Simon ran halfway down the hall and began knocking on other doors.

At the eighth door, Peter got a response. He whistled to Justin who joined him immediately. Peter tried to force the door open but it was locked. They heard someone opening the door from the other side and looked at each other excitedly. This was what they had been waiting for. "Eleni!" Justin whispered loudly. "It's Justin!" From the other side of the door, they heard some unintelligible muttering that confused them. Then the door slowly opened.

A small white-haired, hunchbacked old nun who, Peter later remarked, "must have been around one hundred and fifty years-old," appeared in front of them. A look of utter joy came to her face as she saw that two of her "sisters" had come to visit.

"Welcome, sisters, welcome," the nun's voice quivered. "It's so nice of you to come see me! I don't get many visitors." She slowly stretched out her creaking right hand and clutched Justin's surprised left hand.

Justin shuddered when he realized the predicament he was in. He was trapped. He didn't dare push the old woman away but he had to find Eleni. Peter quickly moved down the hall to the next door and continued knocking. Justin looked to Peter as if to beg him, "Get me out of this!"

The old woman showed surprising strength as she jerked Justin into her cell. "I was just reading Solomon's Proverbs," she croaked. "I do find so much wisdom in God's word." She pulled Justin over to a chair, "Sit down Sister—" The old woman looked at Justin, encouraging him to tell his name.

Justin's mind fumbled for a name to give to the old nun. In desperation, he blurted out, "Eleni."

"Oh, that's right, Sister Eleni," the old woman said. "It's so nice of you to come down to see me especially since we just met this morning. I don't remember you being this tall, though."

Justin suddenly realized he was on to something. "Come down, Sister?" he asked. "Down from where?"

"From your cell, silly young girl," the old woman laughed.

"My cell," Justin repeated, hoping for the answer he needed.

"Your memory is worse than mine, child. Don't you remember?"

"Remember?"

"You are directly above me," the senior nun laughed.

"Directly above," Justin stammered, glassy-eyed, not quite grasping what she had told him.

"Let me get you a pillow. You look tired my dear." As the old woman turned around, Justin shot out of the room. "Peter, upstairs!" he yelled loudly as he ran up the stairs to the cell directly above.

Peter yelled to Rashad and Simon down the hall. "Upstairs!" And he raced up to join Justin. Rashad and Simon were not far behind.

Despina charged forward again and swung the iron rod at Eleni's head. Eleni adeptly blocked the blow with the broken chair's back. Despina recovered and delivered another blow aimed at Eleni's chest. Again the assault was frustrated by the younger woman's defense. She resumed, this time jabbing at Eleni's face. Another failure.

Despina lowered the iron rod. She needed a new tactic. Her eyes searched the room for anything she could use. She picked up a prayer book, then the Psalms, and launched them at Eleni in rapid succession. What Eleni couldn't evade, she knocked out of the way. Now Despina threw anything: a stylus, icons, pieces of the broken chair. Then she saw something in the corner. She looked at it with pleasant surprise. "Why didn't I see this before?" she said under her breath.

A candle burned in front of the icon of the Virgin and the Christ child on the night table by the bed. Beneath it was a plain linen cloth. Despina quickly made her way over to the bed. When she was between Eleni and the candle, she slowly backed up to it.

Eleni shuddered when Despina reached for the candle and the cloth. Eleni jumped forward to attack Despina, who jabbed her in the chest, forcing her away. Despina grabbed the cloth, wrapped it around the end of the iron rod, and lit it with the candle.

Eleni attacked again but Despina was ready. She jabbed the torch at Eleni's face. Eleni retreated immediately, holding the back of the broken chair tightly in her hands.

Despina now had significant advantage and intended to make the most of it. This time she was more direct. She didn't taunt her victim, but pressed immediately. She forced Eleni back again, jabbing the torch at her face. She thrust the torch forward again, forcing Eleni up against the wall. Despina looked down at the floor and noticed that Eleni was standing on a wool rug. Despina smiled malevolently as she slowly bent down, picked up the end closest to her and ignited it with her torch.

Eleni leapt to her left off the burning rug. The stench of burning animal hair soon filled the room. Eleni tried again to cry out but again her voice failed her. Despina jabbed the torch at Eleni's habit. It seemed inevitable that the long habit would catch fire. Surely Eleni couldn't hold out for long. Despina lunged forward and parried the torch at Eleni's feet again. But this time Eleni quickly moved to her left, and jabbed down with the broken chair's back and pinned the torch to the floor.

"Damn you!" Despina yelled as she tried unsuccessfully to pull her weapon free. "Damn you to Hell!"

Eleni then swung the chair back upward and out, striking Despina squarely in the jaw and momentarily knocking her senseless. Eleni turned toward the door but Despina recovered quickly, striking with her touch. Eleni ducked, spun to her right, and clubbed the nun in the jaw again, knocking her to the floor. Eleni again turned toward the door. Despina pulled herself up and desperately grabbed Eleni's ankle, digging her nails into Eleni's flesh, nearly sending her to the floor. Despina struggled to get up and launch herself at Eleni again. She lunged forward with her torch but Eleni easily dodged her and, almost without thinking, slammed her weapon into the back of Despina's skull.

Despina's body lay lifeless on the stone floor. The burning torch remained locked in her right hand's grasp. Eleni cautiously approached the body. It didn't move. She quickly grabbed the flaming rod with her left hand, stifled the flame with the blanket from her bed, and dropped the iron implement to the floor. As she looked at the lifeless nun again and saw blood trickle from Despina's right ear, Eleni dropped the back of the broken chair onto the floor, fell to her knees, held her hands up to her face and gasped.

A loud pounding on the door broke the silence. "Eleni!" the voice screamed.

Eleni sprang to her feet. It was a miracle! "Justin! Justin!" she yelled, half-unbelieving, running toward the door.

Justin tried to push open the locked door. "Eleni, are you hurt?"

"Justin, how in God's name did you find me?" Eleni cried as she opened the door. They embraced immediately. She squeezed him as hard as she could and he pulled her up to him. They kissed and the last six months vanished from their memories.

"Missus Phillipos, I presume," Simon said dryly, looking at them from outside the open door, Peter and Rashad standing at his side.

Peter ran forward and embraced Eleni. "Good God!" he shouted when he saw Despina's lifeless body. He also saw the burning rug and ran toward it. "Simon! Get me something . . ."

"Certainly, Captain," Simon answered as he surveyed the room for something to extinguish the fire. He grabbed three thick blankets from the closet and threw one to Peter. Within a minute, the two of them snuffed out the flames.

"She tried to kill me!" Eleni cried as the others rushed forward.

"Christ and Mary save us!" Justin gasped as he held her tightly.

"Captain?" Simon gently intjected, "we must leave this place now."

"Yes, of course." Justin quickly introduced his wife to Rashad and Simon as the quintet ran toward the stairs. "How can we get out of here?" Justin asked Eleni.

"Down two staircases, turn right, and then out through the main entrance."

"We can't go out the front door," Simon protested.

"I'm not going back in that tunnel," Peter shot back.

"Nor am I," added Rashad.

"Is there another, more discreet way out?" Simon asked Eleni.

"Follow me!" Eleni ordered.

The five of them descended to the main floor and left the stairwell in front of the dining hall. The huge doors at its entrance opened as they ran by. The midday meal had just ended. The nuns looked on in confusion as this strange-looking group ran down the hall in from of them.

"I think the small one is Sister Eleni," Mother Ioanna said to one of the sister's beside her. "I can't place the others but you can be certain they'll all be punished severely for this type of behavior!"

Eleni led them to the library. As they ran in, a tall thin nun asked if she could help them. Justin thoughtfully said, "No thank you," as they sped by her. At the end of the library, Eleni turned to her left and led them into a small chamber. At the back was a door. "This is it!" Eleni said, racing toward it. Eleni pushed her way through it, followed by Justin, Peter, Rashad, and then Simon.

The bright sun was a welcome sight. They could feel its pleasing warmth permeate their clothing and their skin. A ten-foot wall surrounded the convent. Twenty yards straight ahead was one of its few gates. The men peeled off the nun's habits and ran for the gate with Eleni as fast as they could. Beyond that, they could lose themselves in the gigantic city, make their way to one of its many harbors, board a ship, and be gone from this nightmare.

Eleni was first through the gate. Justin and Peter were next, followed by Rashad and Simon. Those on the street outside the wall were only momentarily disturbed by the sudden appearance of this strange-looking fivesome. These farmers worked the open fields between the old Walls of Constantine and the gigantic ninety-foot Theodosian Walls that formed Constantinople's western boundary.

"Where to now?" Justin asked Simon.

Simon collected his thoughts and then said, "There is a pier across from the Gate of the Phanar. I've got a man there who can take you to Venice." Simon took the lead with Peter at his side. Within five minutes, they could see the gold domes of Saint Mary Pammakaristos less than two hundred yards away. As they arrived at the front door of the church, Simon stopped and gathered the troop together. He gave them a few seconds to catch their breath before continuing.

The road to the Gate of the Phanar grew more and more narrow. This area of the city was usually quiet and lacking in foot traffic but today its activity was increasedf significantly. Farm carts, oxen, and donkeys, among other things, impeded their progress toward the Phanar. They picked up their pace for a few minutes before shepherds running a herd of goats across the road blunted their progress. Once the animals had passed, Simon encouraged his charges onward. Justin tripped over one of the shepherds' dogs that got tangled in his feet but managed to avoid falling.

The tall gate was directly ahead of them. Simon whispered to Justin, "Almost there." Simon quickened the pace but then stopped. Ahead were four soldiers and they were looking for someone.

Simon spun around. "This way!" he said excitedly to Justin. He turned right and led them toward the Church of Christ Euergetes.

They hurried through the small gate into the church's north courtyard and ran into a pair of heavily armed soldiers who ordered them to stop. They turned around only to find three more infantrymen just outside the gate behind them. There was no way out. Justin looked to Peter for any ideas. Peter shrugged his shoulders.

"Kidnapping a nun is a very serious offense," said an unfamiliar voice, as if out of nowhere. They spun around to find Archbishop Mavrites standing in front of them. Peter did not know this man but the look in his eye and the tone of his voice let them know he was not looking out for their best interests. "But this crime cannot compare . . ." Mavrites continued with both anger and satisfaction in his voice, "to treason!"

Peter looked for a way out. There was no use in fighting; the soldiers were well armed. Justin reached into his pocket, retrieved the document Zervas had given him, and handed it to Mavrites. Peter was not optimistic.

The pass left Mavrites confused at first. When he finished reading the note, the archbishop cackled in a most sinister way. He turned to one the soldiers, handed the document to him, and joked, "Captain Phillipos, it was very kind of you to give this to me. My bird's cage can always use something to line its floor." He laughed even more robustly. As he continued to howl, he motioned to the soldiers to move the prisoners on to their destination. Between guffaws, Mavrites added, "Remind me to have this Zervas fellow killed." He turned to his prisoners. "We are taking you to the Praetorion. I am sure the eparch has room for you in his jail!"

Peter knew the note was worthless. Mavrites didn't seem like the kind of man who'd follow orders with which he didn't agree. The captors shoved their captives roughly forward, moving east, through a gate in the old Wall of Constantine and past the Church of the Holy Apostles, the resting place of many of the Roman emperors, including Constantine the Great.

Peter shuddered at the thought of the eparch. He was one of the most powerful men in the city. He not only served as chief magistrate and chief of polce. His duties included supervisor of immigration and trade commissioner. The eparch kept track of the city's sixty thousand foreign merchants and set prices on everything from gold to honey. This top civil servant and his army of helpers tracked down the cities criminals and flogged, blinded, or executed them, depending on their crime. They enforced a strict curfew on the Mese and any man unfortunate enough to wander out of a tavern and on to the boulevard after hours would soon regret his mistake.

Mavrites clutched Eleni's wrist tightly. Walking directly behind him was Justin, followed by Peter, Rashad, and then Simon in the rear. One soldier followed Simon and the remaining four flanked the male prisoners. Justin stuck as close as he could to his wife without alarming the guards. Peter kept a close eye on the soldiers around them.

They moved from the square around the church and entered into a densely peopled urban area of the city via the Mese. As usual, the Mese was loud and quite crowded with people moving in and out of the hundreds of shops. The dozens of varieties of scents and sounds was distracting. The presence of the soldiers and their prisoners was not unusual, so the group attracted little notice by the crowd. The Mese merchants in particular took little notice, continuing their sales of everything from alabaster to yeast in the shops and booths under its arcades.

Peter glanced around and noted that the soldier to the right of Simon had disappeared. He then looked at the other soldiers, who appeared to be unaware of this development. Peter kept this finding to himself but increased his surveillance of the other soldiers.

Looking to the northeast, up and over the roofs of the shops, Peter could see the Aqueduct of Valens. This emperor built this huge structure in the fourth century to bring water to the city. Peter had long admired its engineering marvel but now was not the time for casual wonderings. Did it offer a place to escape? Could he hide in the arches? No. Such thoughts were fruitless. He couldn't desert his friends.

Peter quickly took another look around. Now the soldier to the left of Rashad was gone. Both Rashad and Simon looked at Peter as if to say, "Now's our chance; let's run for it." But Peter's stern look back at them informed them of his disapproval. The conditions were still far too dangerous. There were still three other soldiers who could easily cut one or two of them down and Mavrites still had a vise-like grip on Eleni's wrist. Yet this gradual dissolution of the guard unnerved him. *What was happening to these soldiers and who was responsible? Would they be next?*

Ten minutes later, they were walking through the Amastrianum, in the middle of the city. From this square, a turn to the right went to the Forum of the Bovis and later to the Forum of Arcadius. The Aqueduct of Valens continued to flank them on the left. Peter looked up again at Valens' masterwork and again surveyed the group. The soldier to Rashad's right was now gone. Peter was perplexed. Three soldiers had vanished silently and left no trace.

The Mese east of the Amastrianum narrowed because of an especially large crowd. The soldiers were having a difficult time keeping up with the prisoners. The one to Peter's right was pulled westward by the flow of the immense crowd. Peter felt an elbow in his back. He turned to his left to evaluate the disturbance: nothing there. When he turned to his right, the soldier that had been there was gone, again without a trace. Peter thought he may have disappeared into the crowd but it would be unlikely that a fully armed soldier would not be able to push his way back to join them. He continued to look for that soldier in the crowd but his efforts were unrewarded. He sighed and then glanced to his left. That soldier was gone, too!

What the Devil? Peter was flabbergasted. In the space of three quarters of a mile, the five-soldier escort had disappeared. While Peter continued to ponder this conundrum, a tall man wearing a black cowl slipped past Simon, then Rashad. As he moved past Peter, he turned his head and gave Peter a stern but reassuring glance. *Now who's this?* Perhaps this was the man responsible for the soldiers' diappearances. If he were, then he may be a friend. He had disposed of the soldiers but had left the prisoners alone. Yes, he must be there to help them.

But who was he? He was too tall to be Alexios Comnenos and he didn't have Attaleiates eyes. *Who else could he be?*

Peter watched closely as the black-cowled man glided past Justin and then took a dagger from his pocket and moved up behind the archbishop. Mavrites, unaware of the new presence behind him, continued his tight grip on Eleni's wrist. Justin moved to accost this new interloper but Peter stopped him with a tap on the shoulder and a brief whisper of reassurance. Peter turned around and signaled Rashad and Simon to come closer. Soon, the four of them were close behind the stranger, Eleni, and Mavrites.

The stranger quickly looked around him. He saw that all of the prisoners, except Eleni, were behind him. He nodded to Peter who nodded back. The stranger moved up to Mavrites' back and jabbed the dagger into the archbishop's flank. Mavrites gasped and immediately, almost reflexively, released Eleni's hand. "You will turn down that alley to the left," the black-cowled man said to him. The metropolitan obeyed. He moaned softly and the stranger jabbed him again. The once arrogant Mavrites was now quite timid and he trembled as he moved.

Peter's curiousity was piqued. *Who was this savior? What would he do with the archbishop?* Peter led the group to follow the stranger. When they were about thirty yards down the narrow alley, the black-cowled stranger spun Mavrites around and pushed him against a wall. The archbishop cowered in front of the mysterious man as Peter and the others watched from directly behind the stranger.

Mavrites mustered all of his courage, stood tall, and demanded, "Who are you? You are interfering with the execution of orders from His Highness Emperor Michael. If you desist, I will recommend a pardon for you—"

The tall stranger began to laugh. His deep, sonorous voice filled the alley. Mavrites' voice faltered. He had heard that laugh before. He knew this man but couldn't place him. "Who are you?" Mavrites demanded.

"So you want to know who I am?" the stranger began. "Let me show you." He pulled back his cowl to reveal his stunning black hair and blue eyes.

Mavrites turned white, as if he had seen a ghost. "No, no! It can't be! You're dead! His Highness the Prince—"

"Do you mean the man who gave me this?" The man held up the fourth finger of his left hand, on which was a beautiful gold ring, topped by a large red ruby.

"Constantine!" Mavrites pleaded. "I knew nothing about this! Please, you must believe me!"

Constantine calmly turned to the Peter and said, "I think you people should leave now."

"Certainly," said Peter, as if he were in someone else's dream. He motioned to the others that they had to leave. "And, thank you for—"

Constantine held up his hand and sternly said, "Go!"

As Justin, Eleni, Peter, Rashad, and Simon hurried out of the alley, they could hear Mavrites pleading for his life. These calls for mercy were soon replaced by muffled cries of agony as Constantine Papakostas thrust his dagger into the archbishop's abdomen and slowly extracted every ounce of revenge from his betrayer and former lover.

Once they had cleared the alley and found themselves on the edge of the crowded Mese, the five gathered together. "Where do we go from here?" Justin asked of no one in particular.

"I'll take you back to the Phanar. My captain will be waiting with a ship," Simon began.

"Justin, we can't risk going back across the city," Peter interjected. "I say we head for the Harbor of Julian and find Rashad's ship. We're practically there now."

"You need a captain who knows those waters," said Simon, objecting to any variance from his original plan.

"I've sailed in the Adriatic," Peter retorted.

"Have you ever sailed to Venice?" Simon asked.

"It's at the north end of the Adriatic. How could I miss it?"

Justin stepped between them. "Calm down. Let's not attract attention." As Peter and Simon cooled down, he continued, "Simon, I think Peter is right. It's too dangerous to stay in the city. We must leave immediately."

Eleni and Rashad expressed their agreement but Simon wouldn't give up so easily. "You could sail from the Harbor of Julian to the Golden Horn and change ships there."

"If Rashad and his men are willing, I think that it's best that they take us to Venice, straightaway," Justin said, looking at Rashad.

"We would be honored to take you," said Rashad.

"What about the pirates in the Adriatic?" Simon continued, now addressing Rashad. "Those Normans would delight in capturing Arabs. It would be a great risk to you and your men."

"That is a risk we're willing to take," Rashad replied.

Simon turned to Justin. "Captain," he protested, "Lord Comnenos has charged me with your safety. I'm not about to fail. If you were to be captured or die—"

"We'll reach Venice safely," Justin interjected. "I'm certain of that, Simon."

The others expressed their agreement.

Simon saw that further discussion was useless. Peter's plan wasn't a bad one. And he was right that time was of the essence. "Very well then," he said with a smile. "Let me see you to the ship."

"Thank you, Simon," Justin said.

"And might I suggest a change of clothing for Missus Phillipos?" Simon added.

"We can stop at my father's house again. It's on the way," Justin replied.

Knowing that they were far from out of danger, the five moved quickly east, down the Mese, through the forums of Tauri and Theodosius, and to within a block of the Forum of Constantine. They could just see the Milion, the prime mile marker for the empire. All roads started there. The Milion was also where the bodies of traitors were left to rot.

They continued south, through the narrow streets to the houses of Basilios Phillipos and his brothers. There they all found fresh clothes and from the Phillipos' home, they continued south, through the streets, past the imperial warehouses, and to the walled Harbor of Julian.

Rashad's men had been worrying about their leader. His return was long overdue. Omar paced the deck nervously. When he had concluded Rashad's business for him and had returned to the ship, Omar expected Rashad to be there and ready to depart. That was hours ago. He'd begun to fret for his safety. Constantinople was a foreign city to him. He had never felt comfortable trading with the empire. He did not trust Christians, not even those in Damascus. The fact that he had to wait for Rashad and may even have to go find him in this "sea of infidels" was unhinging to him.

One of the men began to stare at something on the pier. He walked to the stern of the ship, never taking his eyes off what he saw.

Omar noticed and ran to the stern. "What is it?" he demanded.

"Four men and a woman coming this way!" the man said.

"Four?" Omar asked. "Who is the fourth?" he asked. "Is one of the four Rashad ibn—Faisal?"

"Maybe. I don't recognize the clothes."

As the five drew closer, Omar recognized his friend. He jumped to the pier and ran to meet Rashad and the others. When he got to Rashad, he gave him a gentle scolding. "Where have you been?"

"We encountered a few difficulties," Rashad said. He introduced Omar to Eleni and Simon.

"We're ready to get under way," Omar informed Rashad, letting him know of his impatience.

"We're eager to leave as well, Omar," said Rashad. "But we now have a new destination. Let's talk in my cabin." Omar strutted away. "Justin," Rashad said, looking at Eleni, "I hope your wife will be comfortable on board."

"I will be fine," Eleni said to Rashad. "Thank you so much!"

"Good! Good! You're welcome. I'll get the final preparations completed." He turned to Simon. "Will you be coming with us, sir?"

"No, thank you," Simon answered. "My mission requires that I remain here."

"I thought your mission was to get us out. You've done that," Peter said, hoping the diminuitive master of disguises would join them.

"Lord Comnenos will certainly have other things for me to do."

Peter grimaced when he heard Comnenos' name.

"Thank you, Simon," Justin said, offering the small man his hand. "We owe you our lives, as do Eleni's parents and mine, too."

Eleni, Peter, and Rashad enthusiastically agreed. The men shook his hand and patted him on the shoulder. Rashad boarded the ship, taking Peter on board to join the other two dozen men of the crew. For the time being, Justin and Eleni remained on the wharf with Simon.

Eleni offered him her hand, which he graciously kissed. Eleni looked Simon in the eye. "How can I ever thank you for bringing my husband back to me and saving my life?" Justin stood by silently, but his face showed he was in complete agreement with his wife.

Simon smiled, childlike. "I do this kind of thing all of the time . . ."

"We will always remember you, Simon," Eleni said, "always." She hugged him tightly.

Justin grabbed Simon's hand again as Eleni released him. "Thank you again, Simon. You'll be in our prayers."

Peter came over to them and announced, "We're ready to leave, Justin. Don't worry, Simon. I'll get us there."

Simon nodded his head, half-agreeing with Peter. He still had his reservations but there was no stopping them. As the ship pulled away from the wharf and moved out of the dock, Justin, Eleni, and Peter waved to Simon. Rashad was busy shouting orders to his men. Every now and then, he would look over to Simon and wave. The ship cleared the harbor wall and sailed south into the Propontis. Soon they could no longer see the small man on the pier.

Part III

ODYSSEY

CHAPTER 19

Justin, who had been wrapped in Eleni's arms since they boarded the ship, looked into his wife's wondrous hazel eyes. It had been six long months since he'd seen that perfect green but his memory had not betrayed him. They were as vivid as he had remembered. Her face and lips beckoned to him. The events of the last half-year vanished from their minds. The six months may have just as well been a week or even just a day.

The sailors around them worked busily around them. They shouted orders and reports back and forth. Ropes whined a high-pitched song as they slid through pullies and block and tackle. Extra cords plopped on the deck when not needed. Hammers rapped on nails and wood as spot repairs were quickly completed. The hull creaked and groaned as plowed through the sea. It would ride up on a wave and then thud onto the water, sending spray over the bow.

Justin turned to Eleni and fell into those lustrous eyes again and, this time, he stole a kiss. Eleni's lips welcomed his. She tightened her grip around him. The world around them disappeared. They couldn't hear Rashad and Peter shouting orders to the crew, or the cawing of the sea birds as they hovered and dove around the ship, or the vessel's rhythmic churning through the water. When the crew saw Eleni and Justin, they would think of their women at home. It gave them brief pause before they returned to their work.

Eleni was deeply saddened to hear of Evdokia's arrest. Tears slowly filled her eyes as Justin tenderly told her. She was soon overcome with grief and she buried her head in his chest and wept.

O mighty queen! First of all of God's handmaidens! My dearest friend! Why were you forsaken?

Later, Eleni and Justin spoke of their time apart. Eleni was particularly amused by Justin's story about Zervas. She was perplexed as to why Justin made Peter go back to rescue the tyrant from the Turks. "I would have left him to die after what he did to you two," she said. When Justin reminded her of Zervas' return of the favor at the checkpoint in Constantinople, she shrugged, "I still would have left him."

Eleni's stories of the empress fascinated Justin. He was surprised that such a stern political animal could be so kind and generous. He was also glad to hear that Eleni had become closer to her mother in his absence. "I knew you would eventually," he teased, acting as though, being older, life had supplied him with a few more answers than she had. She gently elbowed him in the ribs and smiled.

As the setting sun cast a fiery hue in the western sky, the sleek vessel glided smoothly through the even waters of the Propontis. Peter and Rashad joined the wedded couple and they all celebrated their recent adventure. With nightfall came a sudden chill in the air. Rashad escorted his guests to the small cabin below deck at the stern.

"I hope that you and your lovely wife will be comfortable here," Rashad said warmly to Justin.

"Rashad," Justin protested. "We can't. This is your cabin."

"It's the only one at the stern so you will have all the privacy you need."

Eleni joined Justin, "We can sleep on deck with the crew—"

"Take the cabin, my friends," Rashad insisted. "I will share Omar's cabin at the bow. Please."

"Thank you, Rashad," Eleni and Justin said.

"Peter, you will share a cabin with Amin, my physician."

"Thank you, Rashad," Peter replied. There was no use objecting.

"Before you retire for the night, I want to discuss with you what Peter and I have determined about our trip to Venice," Rashad began. "We've decided that it is best not to dock anywhere until we are well away from Constantinople. We will keep moving. A stop in any port could invite capture so we'll stop only when we need water, food, and the like. When we're in port, it's probably best for the three of you not to leave the ship."

"The prevailing winds blow eastward in the Mediterranean and they may be unfavorable for most our voyage. Ships have travelled west in this ocean for centuries. It just takes longer. Rashad's ship is sleek and built for speed. I estimate that we'll be at the Hellespont in two days," Peter said. "If all goes well, we'll be in Venice in two-and-a-half to three weeks."

"What sort of problems might we encounter?" Eleni asked. She was excited by the prospect of her first voyage by sea.

"Pirates, storms . . ." Rashad began.

"And the imperial navy," Peter continued. "We may have difficulty avoiding their patrols."

"God help us," Justin sighed as he, Eleni, and Peter, crossed themselves. As Justin finished he looked at his host, hoping he wasn't offended.

"You are right, Justin." Rashad smiled reassuringly. "We will definitely need the help of Allah."

"Rashad," Justin began, "we can't thank you enough for what you are doing. You and your men are sacrificing a great deal to take us to Venice."

"It's nothing."

"I would think they would be angry," Justin continued. "They're risking their lives for three people they don't know. Weren't they upset when you told them?"

"Omar expressed his disapproval but I was able to convince him and the others that it would be worthwhile. We still have room for cargo and Venice may have precious goods to offer."

"You're being very kind," Eleni interjected. "Please pass on our thanks to the entire crew."

"I will do that and you are most welcome."

They exchanged "goodnights" and Rashad and Peter left the cabin.

Eleni looked at her husband's face. In many ways, he was still the little boy she played with all of those years ago. But he was also a strikingly handsome man she looked to for comfort and understanding. She reached up and rested her hands on his thick black beard. She combed her fingers through the soft, thick hairs.

She gazed into his deep dark brown eyes and heard her heart sing. *At last! You're back!*

Justin placed his hands on her shoulders and slowly gently, moved them over her perfect skin up to the base of her neck. He was captive to her eyes, looking at them as if he'd never seen anything like them before.

Neither of them spoke. They didn't need to. They told each other how much each had missed the other, how much they loved one another. Eleni moved her hands past Justin's ears and pulled him to her. Their wet lips met and locked in bliss but rather than sate their hunger, their kissing merely encouraged it. They fell side by side, slowly onto the captain's bed. Still kissing her tender lips, he moved his hands to her head and ran his fingers slowly through her beautiful auburn locks.

Eleni felt her husband's muscular shoulders. Each movement of his strong hands sent sensuous ripples through those strong sinews. She clutched them with her small hands, tightly at first, but then gradually caressed his brawn. The heat between them mounted. A thin film of sweat covered their skin.

Eleni slid Justin's tunic over his head. She admired her husband's firm pectorals and buried her head in his chest. He held her tightly, as if he were protecting her. Justin slid his arms down to the small of her back. He could feel her ribs tapering inward and then her hips beginning their outward curve. He pulled them slowly but firmly toward his. She quickly shot her hands downward and pulled him toward her hips. Their pelvises met and gently ground against each other. Each groaned in ecstacy. Justin could feel his musculature contracting with every grind of his hips against hers. Eleni pulled away the remainder of Justin's clothing and stroked him, measuring his response to their foreplay.

Justin's arousal intensified. He tugged clumsily at Eleni's clothing. She stopped and patiently helped him undress her. He looked up at her, drinking in all of her incapacitating beauty with his eyes. They rejoined their kissing with renewed fire. Justin caressed her hips and slid one hand down her inner thigh. Eleni's reaction was intense. She rolled her husband onto his back and engaged his sexual readiness.

Their erotic gyrations continued, seemingly without end. The rhythm of the ship plowing through the passive sea stimulated their energetic thrusts. Sweat dripped from them as they rolled and turned in ecstacy. The complement of their intercourse had a protracted course and each was physically exhausted by the time their love was consummated, too spent to move their bodies.

Justin found a blanket in the closet and threw it over them. He spread it over them without disturbing Eleni. He looked at her slumbering face and again thanked God for their safe return. Even if they were to die tomorrow, he could pass happily, knowing he had been reunited with the woman who meant so much to him.

The next morning, Justin emerged from the cabin to find the ship's deck buzzing. Over the stern, he could see the sun piercing the scant overcast, painting the eastern horizon with indigo and coral. Justin breathed deeply and tasted the salt in the air. He walked toward the bow and met Peter amidships.

Peter smiled at Justin when he saw him. He could only imagine Justin's reunion with Eleni. "Good morning, Justin," he said. "I trust you slept well."

"Yes, Koumbarro, I slept very well, thank you. And yourself?"

"Best sleep I've had in weeks," he answered with a big smile.

Rashad hurried over to Justin. "Good morning, Captain. Did you sleep well?"

Justin grinned. "Like a baby, Rashad, like a baby."

"Oh, that is good." He directed Justin's attention to the bow. "We're making good time."

Eleni appeared on deck and immediately Peter and Rashad walked toward her. Peter wanted to hear about her confinement with the empress. To Justin, she looked particularly radiant this morning but he chose to consume that radiance from where he was. He relaxed as he listened to the sounds of the busy crewmen. He looked upward and saw, and heard,the triangular white sails fill with a fresh gust of wind.

The day went smoothly, with no signs of imperial vessels. The weather was exceptional. Other than the magnificent scenery, the journey was uneventful except for the five daily prayers to Allah observed by Rashad and his men. The Christians saw these five-time-a-day rituals as opportunities to worship as well, invoking Father, Son, and Holy Spirit, and did so. They would gather in Rashad's cabin to chant prayers they learned in their youth.

The crew worked hard; when they had time to relax, they spent it singing songs, or just passing time in conversation. Occasionally Justin would test his Arabic by joining the conversation. For the most part, his efforts failed miserably but the crewmen were understanding and happy to help him improve his fluency of their tongue.

Their course hugged the northern edge of the Propontis. By nightfall, they were headed west. Peter said he hoped to be as far as Rhaedestum by the next evening. The moderate wind continued out of the northeast. Eleni enjoyed the light chill of the night air, the scent of the sea, and the rhythmic movement of the ship through the peaceful Propontis. Justin sat beside her and he too imbibed in this sensory cornucopia. Peter had fallen asleep in a corner of the deck; his day had been very busy. His experience as a mariner had been invaluable to his Arab comrades. Rashad busily readied the crew for the next day and then came over to speak with his guests. The conversation was brief as Rashad's exhaustion soon became evident. He excused himself and retired below.

"Do you think he's dead, Justin?" Eleni asked.

"Who?"

"The emperor."

"The Turks are vicious, Eleni. It wouldn't surprise me." He paused for a few seconds. "I wonder how our families are doing. Can you imagine your mother on a ship?"

Eleni smiled. "Strangely enough, I can."

"Really?"

"Yes. These last six months I've learned a great deal about my mother, and myself."

Justin held her tightly and kissed her cheek. "It's getting late."

"I could sit out here all night."

Justin stood. "As you wish, my love. I'm going to bed."

"I'll be along soon, Justin. Goodnight."

"Goodnight my dear." Justin bent over, kissed her and went below.

Eleni looked out over the dark sea and saw a lighthouse in the distance. Its light shined brightly in the clear night. She kept her eyes on it and held her hands out in front of her, as if she were receiving something. "What more do You have planned for Lord? What other trials must we endure?" She admitted to herself that she was angry with the Almighty. She thought of David's psalms of anguish and despair and she recalled the last several weeks. All the while, she kept her gaze on the lighthouse. How wretched this dark veil of life could be. Slowly, the light appeared to grow brighter and larger. Eleni suddenly saw her mother in the light, speaking to her. She couldn't hear the words but this vision calmed her impatient heart. Her once-agitated heart warmed as she realized that they were alive and had the chance to see their loved ones again. Their lives had been shattered by this cataclysm. How wretched this dark veil of life could be. And yet, how beautiful. A gentle wind blew into her face and she bowed her head. "Dear Father," she whispered through joyful tears, "the winds obey Your word. Help me to do the same, for as is the wind, so are You with me."

By the end of the next day, they had reached Rhaedestum. This port on the north shore of the Propontis was booming with maritime trade. Here, the crew quickly reprovisioned the ship and got under way.

At dawn on the morning of the third day, they had arrived at the east end of the Hellespont. Justin was the first to emerge from the cabin.

Peter greeted him from amidships. "We're at the Hellespont," he said. "It will be interesting to see how our passage goes this time."

"Indeed," Justin agreed, vividly remembering their crossing of the strait six months earlier. "Do we still have a good wind?"

"Yes and it's even picked up a little for us. We're making nearly ten knots."

Eleni appeared at the stern and Justin, Peter, and Rashad joined her.

"What do you think of the sea?" Rashad asked Eleni. "Isn't she beautiful?"

"This is a different world," Eleni replied. "It's wonderful!"

Justin smiled and gently collected her hands, kissed them, and brought them together in his.

"Many a wonderful day at sea remain etched in my memory," Peter added.

"I can see why," Justin added as he took in the scenery.

One of the crew called to Rashad. He muttered something to Peter who motioned to Justin and both followed the captain. Eleni looked around her in awe at the high cliffs around this legendary strait. She looked down at the water and felt the cool northeast wind at her back. She remembered stories her father told her about the young Leander who used to swim across the fast current at night from Asia to join his lover Hero on the European side, until one night his strength failed him and he drowned. Eleni used to cry when her father would tell her of Hero's grief at finding the drowned body of her lover on the shore the next day.

At the bow, Peter, Justin, and Rashad inspected the map and reviewed the plans for the voyage. "Yesterday was a good day of sailing," Rashad said. "Do you think we can reach Imbros today?"

"Perhaps this afternoon," Peter replied. He looked out over the water as they left the Hellespont. "Then from Imbros, we'll go to Lemnos."

"How are the crew?" Justin asked.

"They're doing well," Peter answered Justin. He turned to Rashad. "They're good men."

"Yes, they are. I've known most of them for five years or more," Rashad beamed.

The next morning dawned clear and sunny. Justin got up early with Peter and Rashad. Eleni remained in bed until the first hour. The cadence of the prow slicing through the glassy sea was hypnotic and kept her sleepy for hours. She awakened slowly, dressed herself, and brushed her hair. She reached into the water basin and splashed cold water onto her face, then fell into a chair and thought about her parents and her sisters. How good it would be to see them again!

On deck, Justin was enjoying another morning at sea. The clear blue waters of the Aegean shimmered in the morning sun. Dolphins chased the vessel. Gulls flew overhead and occasionally lighted on the tops of the masts. The sea fascinated him. He tried to imagine

Peter's service in the navy. He found himself envious of his friend's maritime experiences. Suddenly his reverie was cut short.

"Roman galley, about three hundred yards off our starboard bow," Peter announced as he grabbed Justin's shoulder. "You and I will have to hide in the cabin with Eleni. I've spoken to Rashad. He'll take care of it."

Justin didn't waste any time getting into the cabin. Peter was directly behind him. Eleni buckled as they rushed in.

"What is it?" she asked.

"Roman ship," Justin answered. "We must hide."

Rashad poked his head in the door. "They'll be here soon."

"I think we're ready," Peter responded. He pointed under the bed. "This will be a good spot for you, Eleni. It's too small for Justin or me."

In the corner of the cabin, a large, dark blanket hung from the ceiling to the floor from three wooden brackets. This makeshift closet could hide at least one of them. Justin stepped into it as Peter looked for a third hiding place. "Nothing," Peter grunted. "There has to be something!"

On deck, Rashad watched as the Roman galley approached. He looked warily at the fire tubes jutting from the bulkhead at the bow. A discharge from even one of these deadly cylinders would incinerate his ship and his crew in a matter of minutes.

Rashad knew he had no choice but to cooperate. He waved courteously to the Roman captain, a commanding redhead who stood atop the starboard gunwale. Rashad studied the man carefully and thought of how to appear obsequious, yet keep him away from his fugitive friends.

Peter redoubled his furious efforts to find a place of concealment. When he heard a commotion outside, he rushed to join Justin. He apologized when he saw Justin's surprised face. "Sorry. There's nothing else in here," he explained.

Outside, things were getting loud. The captain of the Roman vessel was aboard with twelve of his men. Peter and Justin could hear the conversation. "Who are you and what are you doing here?" the Roman captain demanded in Greek as he jumped on deck. He knew he was dealing with Arabs but he arrogantly assumed that any civilized man would speak Greek, even an Arab.

Rashad was courteous but very wary. "We are from Damascus. We've just come from Constantinople. We're bringing some of your beautiful silks to our markets."

"Where is your cargo?" the Roman demanded.

"Below," Rashad said, pointing to the stern. "Would you like me to show you, Captain?"

The captain didn't wait for Rashad. He strutted down to the hold.

Peter and Justin could hear Rashad, the captain, and two others walk by their door to the hold.

"What's in here?" the captain grunted as he pointed to four large crates.

"Over four hundred yards of silk and some brocade as well." He opened one of the crates and showed them to the Roman.

"What's in these others?"

"Oil, wine—"

"Wine?" the Roman asked suspiciously. "You people don't drink wine."

"There are Christians in Damascus, too, sir. And we also trade the wine with other peoples for gold, jewels—"

"What about that cabin we passed on the way down here?" the Roman captain asked.

Peter studied the voice he perceived to be that of the Roman captain. He knew it from somewhere. He nudged Justin and pointed outside with his eyes. Justin listened more acutely and realized he also recognized the Roman captain's voice. The answer flashed into Peter's mind. "Stathopoulos!" he whispered. They both recalled Peter's last encounter with that sea captain and recoiled. If they were found, Stathopoulos would kill them then and there. After all, he had just found two dangerous traitors.

They could hear Rashad and he was doing well keeping Stathopoulos happy and away from them. However, Stathopoulos kept revisiting the subject. Rashad soon realized that further diversions away from the cabin would only inflame the visiting sailor and double his interest in exploring it. He thought he had given Peter, Justin, and Eleni enough time to hide so he took the captain and one of the Roman sailors to the cabin. He made certain to make as much noise as possible so that his friends would be alerted to the approaching danger.

The cabin door flew open, banging the wall behind it. Rashad apologized to the Roman captain for his clumsiness. Peter spied through a small hole in the blanket and realized that his suspicions were correct. The tall, redheaded seaman was definitely Andreas Stathopoulos. He nodded silently to Justin who bit his lower lip.

Rashad continued his distractions. He moved Stathopoulos from this side of the room to that, keeping him off balance, showing him this, telling him about that. "Captain," he would say, quickly lifting a Corinthian pitcher from a nearby table, "have you ever seen finer pottery than this?" "Look at the workmanship in this ivory cask. We found it in Trebizond." Then he lifted the edge of the linen cloth covering the bedside table. "No one makes better linens than the Lydians. Wouldn't you agree?"

Seeing the treasures only momentarily diverted the Roman captain. Stathopoulos left Rashad and walked over to the closet and looked closely at it. Rashad's eyes followed him over. An attempted diversion at this time may heighten the captain's curiousity. Stathopoulos raised his hand to pull the blanket aside and inspect the contents of the makeshift closet but his inspection was cut short when the sailor with him knocked over the bedside table, sending the wooden basin on top of it crashing to the floor and spilling all of its contents.

"Christ and Mary!" yelled Stathopoulos at the clumsy sailor. "What are you doing, you oaf?" The sailor frantically looked for something to clear the mess. Stathopoulos continued to curse him. "You clumsy bastard!"

Another Roman sailor abruptly appeared at the cabin door. "Captain, sir," he announced, "the first mate reports that the leak in the port stern quarter has worsened. We're taking on more water."

"Damn!" Stathopoulos decided that he had seen enough. "Tell the first mate to make for Imbros. We can repair there." Then he said to Rashad, "Your ship will follow us to Imbros. If my ship develops any more trouble, I may need your help."

Stathopoulos said something to the sailor at his side and the man left the cabin. "I'm taking three of your men with me. You seem like an honorable fellow but I prefer to have a little more than just your assurances that you won't abandon us. Once we are in port, I will return them to you." He left the cabin and boarded his vessel, randomly choosing three of Rashad's crew and ordering his sailors to bring them on board.

Rashad followed Stathopoulos out onto the deck, assuring him he had every intention of helping the Roman. Justin and Peter sighed once Rashad had left the room.

"That was close," Justin whispered.

"We're not out of this yet," Peter reminded him. "Don't forget the hostages."

"I don't think Stathopoulos will come back onboard. He's more concerned about his ship. Once he's in port, he'll send them back and we'll be on our way."

"I wouldn't be so sure of that, Justin. I won't relax until he's going one way and we're going the other."

The Roman galley eased away from the Rashad's vessel. Peter made for the door as Justin rushed over to the bed and helped Eleni out from under it. "That was close, wasn't it?" she remarked.

"Yes, even closer than you think," Justin replied. "That was Stathopoulos, the sailor who ferried us across the Hellespont."

Eleni held up her hand up to her mouth and gasped. She crossed herself quickly. "My God!" she said, remembering what Justin had told her about that crossing and Peter's encounter with the red-haired mariner.

On deck, the situation remained tense. Rashad carefully watched the Roman ship. Omar walked over to him. "Now what?"

"Patience, Omar. We can only wait."

"Rashad, why do we risk our necks for these infidel Greeks?"

"Is that why you have been so sullen these past days? I am disappointed, Omar. Surely you understand the bonds of friendship. Justin Phillipos is a good man. I am certain he would do the same for me—or you, for that matter."

"I sincerely doubt that."

"Well you can stop your grumbling because as long as I am in charge we're going to get them to Venice. Understood?"

"Understood," he muttered begrudgingly.

"We follow them to Imbros. We're going there anyway. And now we have an imperial escort." Over the next few minutes, he skillfully, unobtrusively worked his way down to the cabin. He opened the door and slid inside.

Justin and Eleni turned to him. "Rashad, I'm sorry he took your men," Justin began. "I didn't want you to get caught up in this."

"Justin, my men and I knew what we were in for." He patted Justin's shoulder. "And I'm certain nothing will become of this. We'll follow them to Imbros, my men will be released, and you'll be back on the way to see your families."

Justin smiled. "Thank you. I wish I shared your optimism."

"That was beautiful. You manipulated them like sheep, Rashad!" Peter said, as he shook Rashad's hand. "But something tells me that this will not be the last time this happens."

"We'll just have to face the troubles as they come," Rashad replied. He turned to leave the cabin and said, "I'll have more water and some food brought in. It's best for you to stay in here until we are free of them."

The western sky turned a flaming red with accents of orange and yellow as the two ships sailed into the harbor at Imbros. The Roman ship had taken on quite a bit of water and was listing to port. Its sailors were bailing furiously as it settled into the dock. Rashad's vessel docked in front of the Roman ship, as Stathopoulos ordered. The red-haired mariner shouted some orders to his crew. Two of them jumped onto the wharf and ran into the town. A quarter of an hour later, the two returned with three other men, naval stores, wooden planks, and various tools.

The fifteen minutes that it took to get help for the Roman galley seemed like an eternity on board Rashad's ship. Justin held Eleni's hand tightly. They dared not speak above a whisper. Justin turned and looked into her eyes. She smiled at him and he returned her smile.

"This is just like when we were children," Eleni whispered. "You, Athanasiou, and me," she continued, remembering her capers with Justin and her brother. "Do you remember when you were almost caught stealing that silver chalice from Mr. Manolakos' shop?"

"As I recall, you stole it and gave it to me to carry!" Justin protested. "You told me you had bought it for your mother!"

Eleni sniggered. "Justin, you've always been so gullible!"

"We were lucky that we outran the constable."

"Well, the hiding place I found was what really saved us."

"That was rather clever, hiding in the scaffolding at the Capitol. We were lucky plenty of drapes were hanging over the scaffolds."

"You were lucky Athanasiou was willing to take the chalice back and convince Mr. Manolakos you weren't really stealing it."

"I wasn't!"

"Keep quiet!" Peter whispered as he peeked out of a small hole in the cabin's stern wall.

Eleni giggled as she remembered the story. Justin looked back at her with mock vengefulness but soon smiled. *How good it was to be with her again!*

Eleni asked Peter, "How long will it take them to fix the ship?"

"Depends how bad the leak is," Peter replied. "Judging by the distance we had to go to get here and the current condition of the ship, I don't think it will take that long."

Peter watched as the sailors continually bailed water from the ship. Then he saw Stathopoulos disappear from view. Most of the sailors left that area of the vessel, presumably to give their captain room to work. After five minutes, he rose. This time he had a hammer in one hand and a brush coated with tar in the other. One of the sailors wiped the captain's brow with a clean white cloth. Stathopoulos disappeared from view once again but it wasn't long before the captain was standing again. This time, he dropped the hammer and brush and stretched. The sailors returned to the area with buckets and bailed with renewed vigor. Peter could hear jubilation coming from the Roman ship.

"They've finished!" Peter announced as he cautiously left the cabin. He slowly made his way toward the deck and poked his head outside.

The three Arab hostages left the Roman galley and Stathopoulos was right behind them. Peter quickly returned to the cabin and warned, "We could have trouble! Stathopoulos is on board!"

"Do we hide again?" Eleni asked.

"Quiet!" Peter commanded, listening intently.

After several seconds, Justin asked, "What do you hear?"

Peter smiled, "Nothing! I think they're gone!"

Justin and Eleni smiled warily.

"I'm going up there," Peter said after listening for a few more seconds and hearing nothing. He moved to the door of the cabin and slowly crawled up the stairs to the deck. He slowly craned his head forward and looked to his left. He stayed hidden behind the stair railing. At the starboard gunwale amidships, he saw Stathopoulos shake Rashad's hand and the hands of the hostages he had returned. Then he saw him go back to his ship.

Peter silently scurried down the stairs to the cabin. "Now we can relax!" he whispered as he opened the door.

Rashad wasn't far behind. "It's over, my friends," he announced with a great deal of relief as he opened the cabin door. "Their captain has decided to stay here tonight. He has invited us to do the same but I have told him we must return to Damascus and we are behind schedule."

"Let's leave now! It's not safe! How is the wind?" Peter asked.

"Perfect," replied Rashad. "The waters are smooth and we still have the wind. We will be at Lemnos by tomorrow morning if we leave now."

"That's wonderful!" said Justin and Eleni together.

"Give us a few minutes to clear the harbor and then come join me on deck."

"Right," Peter replied.

Justin, Eleni, and Peter listened in excitement as they heard Rashad's ship pull away from Stathopoulos' galley. As Rashad issued their orders, the crew raced about the deck, shouting the orders back to their captain for confirmation. The pullies creaked as the sails were rigged and the hull groaned as the sailing ship caught the wind and lurched forward. Before long, Rashad appeared at the cabin door and invited his guests up to the deck. Astern they could see Imbros progressively shrinking in the fading twilight. Eleni hugged her husband tightly and he gently kissed the top of her head.

CHAPTER 20

A light rain fell at dawn the next morning but it stopped within an hour. The ambient temperature rose to above sixty degrees as the sky cleared. Since they had not reprovisioned at Imbros, as they had planned Peter and Rashad chose Lemnos as the next stop. After an hour in port, the ship was restocked and was again under way.

Justin walked with Eleni on the deck. The crewmen were, as usual, impressive in their arduous tasks. Omar shouted to two men in the rigging and they immediately implemented his requests. The sight and sound of these men functioning together to propel this vessel to their destination amazed them. The wind shifted and was coming from the north. This favorable change allowed the sails to work more effectively, granting the ship more speed.

Eleni lost herself in the clear blue Aegean Sea. The dolphins were again their companions. Two or three would leap out of the water, to be followed by others, never tiring of their playful pursuit. The sublime combination of warm sun, cool sea breeze, and beautiful vistas intoxicated them. Eleni turned to her husband. "It's so beautiful." He agreed and held her closely.

In the early afternoon, they passed the island of Saint Evstratios. By dusk, they approached Skiros and the crew prayed to Allah. Justin, Eleni, and Peter listened quietly to the sacred words and prayed silently.

Later, more clouds gathered in the western sky. Blues and purples dominated the sunset. Eleni and Justin sat on the deck with Peter and Rashad. As they finished a dinner of salted mullet, olives, flat bread, and water, a crewman ran up to Rashad and whispered something to him. It wasn't long before a look of concern came over Rashad's face.

"What is it?" Justin asked, having caught bits and pieces of the Arabic conversation.

"Omar has fever," Rashad replied soberly.

"He looked fine this morning!" Justin exclaimed with concern.

"My physician reports that the fever began very early this morning, just after the third call to prayer," Rashad reported. "Omar has become delirious in the last hour and he isn't responding to the treatments thus far."

"What is he giving Omar for his fever?" Peter asked.

"Various herbs, I suppose. Perhaps white willow bark. I have seen him use that before for fever but I'm no physician. Amin is a good man and a well-qualified physician. He has studied with many great physicians in Baghdad and Damascus. He has an impressive medical library."

"My Uncle Alexander is a physician," Justin volunteered.

"Amin has told me that most of what we Arabs know of medicine we've learned from the old Greek texts. We've had our great contributors as well, Ibn Sina, and Al-Razi, but the root of their learning was from Galen, Soranus, Dioscorides, and others. We are surprised that you Greeks haven't used your own medical knowledge as well as we have."

Justin chuckled, "I believe my uncles would take exception to that, Rashad. Our physicians are quite good."

"Then I stand corrected," Rashad replied cordially.

Peter stood up and pointed over the starboard bow. "There's Skiros." The setting sun behind the island gave it a pink-indigo halo. As a few small fishing boats headed into port, the friendly fishermen waved as Rashad's ship passed.

"I'm amazed at your vessel, Rashad," Peter continued. "She is so sleek and speedy. She uses every bit of power the wind gives her."

"Thank you, Peter," Rashad beamed. He didn't have to remind him what great sailors the Arabs were. They dominated the southern Mediterranean and their ships ruled the Indian Ocean, moving goods from the Indies and Persia to East Africa and the Arabian Peninsula.

"The wind is still with us, Rashad," Peter added. "If it doesn't fail us, we'll make good time and arrive off the coast of Euboea by midmorning."

"The weather has indeed been kind to us," noted Rashad. "The winds have been exceptionally favorable and the sea calm."

"We'll pray it stays that way," interjected Eleni. She crossed herself. Justin and Peter saw her example and followed her lead.

"Yes, of course," Rashad added. Then he paused. "I'm going to see Omar. Then I shall retire."

"Rashad," Justin began, "Eleni and I would like you to sleep in the cabin tonight."

"That is not necessary. You are my guests. Please stay in the cabin tonight."

"No, we will stay on deck with Peter. Omar needs his rest. Amin will be in and out of that cabin all night. You'll never sleep. Go and enjoy your cabin." Eleni echoed her husband softly.

Rashad was about to insist that his guests follow his request but Justin and Eleni wouldn't budge. "Very well. But just for tonight."

Justin smiled back at him. "Certainly, just for tonight."

Eleni watched Justin and Peter gather blankets as Rashad circulated among the crew emitting a few last instructions. The final call to prayer two hours after dusk had come and gone and most of the crew were already retiring. Those who remained on duty checked the rigging and enjoyed the cool night breeze as it blew over the blue-black sea. Eleni saw Rashad find Amin and immediately engage him. The good doctor smiled as he spoke, whereupon Rashad let out a burst of jubilation and hugged him. Then he jauntily perambulated around his ship. When he came by the Greeks, he bid them good night.

"How's Omar?" Eleni asked.

"He's sleeping. Amin thinks he may be better tomorrow!"

"Good!" Eleni said. "That's very encouraging!"

Justin and Peter echoed her words.

"Indeed," Rashad replied. "Good night. Sleep well."

"Good night, Rashad," the guests replied.

The graceful churning of the ship through the calm sea helped Justin and Eleni to fall asleep easily. Peter held out for about an hour. He sat quietly on the deck and consumed all of the sensations around him. Earlier in the day, the crew caught sea bass. The cook grilled the fish and seasoned it wth thyme and black pepper. The taste was fantastic and complemented the ripe oranges, tabouli seasoned with spearmint, and jasmine tea that composed the rest of dinner.

Peter truly loved the sea and regretted having to leave her. If only his experience in the navy had been different. If only he'd never had met Damon Kasimos, let alone ordered his execution. He tried to evade those thoughts but they always managed to catch up to him.

They arrived off the eastern coast of Euboea just before noon, precisely as Peter had predicted. The morning's crew yielded to their replacements when Rashad received word from the ship's physician: Omar was no longer responding to the medicine. Rashad ran to the cabin and went inside. Amin, who was dutifully attending Omar at his bedside, failed to hear him enter. The patient looked as if Death were about to claim him.

"Is he making any progress, Amin?" Rashad could see how bad Omar looked but he couldn't think of anything else to say.

The physician did not leave Omar's side, nor did he turn to look at Rashad. He maintained his gaze upon his afflicted patient, who lay in his bed, sweating, and groaning in torment. "No progress, Rashad. If anything, he is worse." Finally, he looked up at the captain. "The effect of the white willow bark is only temporary. I've bled him three times now but that's not doing anything."

Rashad walked over to Omar and tried to comfort his friend by placing his hand on Omar's leg. Rashad could feel the heat radiating from it. *He's burning up!* Sweat covered the patient's groin, navel, and armpits. Amin replaced the cloth over Omar's forehead with a cool, wet one.

"He is exhausted!"

"Any rest he gets is interrupted by paroxysms of wailing and thrashing," the doctor added.

"Omar," Rashad said soothingly. "Omar, how are you feeling?"

His mouth, opened wide, issued a ghostly, dry moan, as if he were seeing his Maker in all of His glory.

Rashad recoiled as Omar arched his back and then collapsed as if all of the life within him was instantly drained. As this paroxysm subsided the sweats returned.

"He's been like this for the last two hours," Amin noted.

"Is there anything else you can do?" Rashad asked gingerly.

Amin sighed deeply and buried his face in his hands. He closed his eyes and rubbed his beard. "Perhaps a different poltice. I'll have to find some other herbs . . ." Amin replied. Then in frustration he exploded, "There must be something!"

Rashad put his hands on Amin's shoulders. "I know you're doing the best that you can, my friend. Don't be so hard on yourself." Then he added under his breath, as if Omar could hear them at all, "Perhaps it is the will of Allah."

"Perhaps," Amin admitted somberly. He walked away from Rashad and suddenly turned around. "But perhaps it is the will of Allah that Omar shall live."

"Yes." Rashad walked over to soothe the worried physician. "Perhaps it is." He hugged Amin and added, "Go on my friend. Practice your art."

Amin smiled briefly at his captain and returned to his work. Rashad took another look at Omar and left the cabin.

Peter accosted Rashad as he left the cabin. "How's Omar?"

"About the same," Rashad answered sadly. "Amin is doing all he can."

"We still have the wind."

Rashad made no response, his mind on Omar.

Peter continued, hoping to enlist Rashad's attention. "The crew is doing very well. I'm sure we'll pick up some extra time. We'll pass Andros before sunset and then Serifos by morning."

Rashad only grunted in response to Peter's report.

Peter looked Rashad in the eye. "Omar is worse than you're telling me, isn't he?"

Rashad sighed and confessed. "Yes, Peter. Amin has done all he can. I am afraid my friend will die."

"Can I see—"

"Amin says Omar must rest," Rashad interjected, "if he is to have any . . ." Tears formed in his eyes.

"I'm sorry, Rashad. I wish there were something I could do."

"Thank you, Peter," Rashad said quietly as he wiped his eyes. Rashad cast his glance up to the stars. He and Omar had known each other since they were young. *What will I tell his mother?*

Justin and Eleni came from the bow where they had been enjoying the smooth ride and fresh sea air. He said jovially, "I should have been a sailor, Peter. I love this!" Then Justin saw Rashad's furrowed brow and knew things were not right. "Rashad, what's wrong?"

Rashad hesitated. Peter detected his uneasiness and spoke up. "Omar is dying."

Eleni gasped and crossed herself. "I'm sorry, Rashad!"

"Amin has tried everything," Peter continued.

"We must see him!" Eleni cried as she turned toward the cabin where Omar lay.

Peter grabbed her arm. "Amin forbids it. Any disturbance may worsen his chances."

The words stopped. Eleni wiped away a tear as Justin held her closer.

Rashad's face had none of its usual vigor. Hope had left him, or so it seemed. Yet he surprised the others by asking, "Peter, are we far from Athens?"

"Athens?" A contorted look overtook Peter's visage. "What's in Athens?"

"Physicians . . . hospitals," Rashad said bluntly, uncertain of himself. It was apparent to all that Rashad had asked out of desperation. He didn't want to see Omar die.

Peter knew that a detour to Athens was a risky proposition. Imperial galleys regularly patrolled the waters around Piraeus, Athens' port. Carrying a dying Arab sailor through the streets was bound to attract attention. If they were exposed, they could all face death or a life in the darkest prison the Roman Empire could offer. Yet here was a man, a friend, who needed them. Hadn't the Lord said that there was no greater thing that a man could do than give his life for a friend? And wouldn't God protect them on this mission of mercy? But was it wise to risk *everyone's* life for a mere flicker of hope for Omar? He sighed and calmly spoke. "Amin is an excellent physician, Rashad. You told us so yourself. He's studied with some of the greatest physicians in the world. No Athenian physician can do more for Omar." Peter's words were cold. His brain had one its argument with his heart.

"So we let him die?" Eleni cried.

"Peter is right," Justin interjected. "I don't think that there is anything more that can be done for him. His life is in God's hands."

"No, now it is in our hands!" Eleni shot back. "We can't let him die without doing all we can for him!"

"Like what?" Justin demanded, raising his voice.

"Take him to a hospital in Athens!" Eleni countered.

"And risk *all* of our lives?" Peter screeched.

"Rashad and his men have been going in and out of ports since we left the capital with no problem. Why is this different, Peter?"

"They will not be simply buying goods and leaving an hour later. They will have to take Omar into Athens and find a hospital. That will arouse suspicion. People will ask questions. We'll be docked for days or weeks. That will give the port inspectors ample opportunity to search this ship."

"Doesn't the love of Christ demand that you take those risks to save Omar?" Eleni's words were incisive.

The silence that followed was broken by Rashad. "I fear that Peter is right," he said softly. Then he spoke up, as if in protest. "But he is my friend! There must be something more that I can do for him! Surely Allah will not abandon such a good man!"

"He is a friend to all of us," Justin added. "We all want him to live."

"But I will not risk the lives of the rest of you for Omar," Rashad concluded in resignation. He turned to Eleni with a tear in his eye. "I thank you for your compassion but I will not take the risk. Peter is correct when he says that Amin's care has been as good as anything Athens could offer. It is the will of Allah, praise be to His great and holy name."

"I am so sorry, Rashad," Justin offered as he grasped his friend's hand. "I wish it were otherwise."

"The ways of Allah are strange to mere men," Rashad added as he wiped the tear from his eye. "Look where He has taken us. And now Omar . . ."

Justin threw his arms around Rashad and pulled him close. "Dear God, if it could only be otherwise!"

Peter glanced at Eleni as Justin and Rashad embraced. Her face suddenly developed a peculiar look, as if she were listening intently to a soft voice coming from behind her.

"Eleni?" Peter asked. "Are you well?"

But she was lost in thought. "Therapeftikos," she whispered to herself.

"What?" Peter asked.

Then she said it louder, "Therapeftikos."

The other men heard her and immediately gave her their full attention.

"Therapeftikos!" Eleni said again. When Justin and Peter looked at her blankly, she added, "My father always used to talk about a man who had a gift, a gift of healing." The men remained silent, inviting further explanation. "There is a man, a monk, who lives in a monastery on one of these islands. He's a healer. God has blessed him with that gift. People are brought to him from all over the empire to be healed."

Rashad went to her and softly inquired, "Where is this man?"

"Delos, I believe," she answered softly.

"Delos? It's been abandoned for centuries," Justin interjected incredulously.

"Is that true?" Rashad asked.

"Well, for the most part that's right," Peter added. "There's a small fort near the harbor."

"And the monastery?" Eleni asked hopefully.

"I've never heard of one there," Peter answered. "But I don't think going to Delos will help Omar."

"I'm sorry, Rashad," Justin added.

"I can't believe you two!" Eleni cried. "Are you just going to let Omar die?"

"Do you think a wild goose chase to Delos will save him?" Peter shot back.

"Eleni," Justin said firmly as he reached out to hold her, "Peter is right."

"No, he's not!" Eleni responded, pushing Justin away.

Rashad stepped closer to Peter. "Delos is close, is it not, Peter?" His voice was full of hope.

Peter opened his mouth to protest but the look in Rashad's face stopped him cold. "About a day," Peter replied somberly, "to the southeast."

Amin ran up onto the deck and headed toward them. Rashad turned to him. "Omar?" he asked, almost not wanting to hear the answer.

"He's vomiting bile," Amin replied. "Yesterday it was yellow. Now it's black." He said "black" with a distinct ring of finality. Rashad looked at him, almost begging him for better news. Amin shook his head and went over to the port side and leaned on the gunwales. Rashad rushed down to the cabin with Peter close behind.

Omar lay quietly on the bed. He was uncovered and absolutely still. Rashad at first thought that his friend had died. His shallow breathing was almost undetectable. His lips were dry and cracked. The corners of his mouth showed traces of dark brown vomitus, as did his pillow. Rashad walked over to him slowly. He picked up the dying man's right hand with both of his. Omar's skin was warm but dry. "Omar," Rashad said gently, hoping with all his will that Omar would respond. "Omar, it's Rashad," he said in his native tongue. Still no response. Rashad gently set Omar's hand back on the bed. He bent his head into his hands and covered his eyes. Tears formed in the corners of his eyes and he noiselessly began to weep. His attempts to muffle his sobs were soon overwhelmed and he wailed for his friend.

Peter, who had followed Rashad and watched the whole scene from the door, turned and walked back to Justin and Eleni. "I'm going to have the first mate change our course for Delos."

By sunset, the ship had nearly negotiated the entire length of Andros, to the east. The wind blew out of the northeast. Peter stood at the bow. The sky was overcast, muting any colorful sunset they might see. Rashad had still not left the cabin. He stayed with Omar, as if his presence could save his friend.

Justin sat quietly with Eleni. Each of them felt helpless in this atmosphere of slow, unstoppable death. Justin held out his hand

and Eleni softly grasped it. She pulled herself closer to him. They held each other tightly as the sun sunk below the horizon and the temperature dropped. Eleni was angry with Justin for doubting her about Therapeftikos and she had made her thoughts known. To her Therapeftikos was no legend or old wives' tale.

Justin clumsily broke the silence between them. "If you are right about Therapeftikos, then you will have saved Omar's life."

Eleni was annoyed by Justin's simplistic view of the situation. She pushed him away from her and scolded him. "Justin, where is your faith?"

As happened so many times, she had caught him off-guard. He couldn't think of a response.

"Why do we pray, Justin?" Eleni continued. "Don't you see God working in your life?"

"Of course," Justin stammered. "Just look at the last six months." How many times had he seen God's hand deliver him from impossible situations? How many times did he pray and beg God to save him . . . and Peter? Was this situation any different? "Of course, Eleni, God has blessed me many times over."

Eleni looked at her husband, as if to make certain of his sincerity. Then she slipped her arms around him and kissed him.

She has taught me so much, most of it about myself. Justin held his wife tightly. He thought about her as a young girl and chuckled. He whispered something to Eleni but got no response. He looked at her face and saw that she had drifted off to sleep. Justin sighed and smiled. Before long, he too succumbed to the pleasures of sleep.

Peter remained awake through the night, guiding the ship to Delos. *Dawn in another hour.* Ahead, he could see the few lights from the small harbor of Delos. He thought about his response to Eleni. Why had he doubted her? He was a faithful Christian, as Orthodox as Emperor Romanos and the patriarch. He attended church whenever he could. Why did this "healer" stir contempt and disbelief in his soul? Peter thought of his last visit to Saint Sophia. He remembered how that beautiful cathedral made him feel. Why was believing in something presented in a church so much easier than a deeply spiritual event that took place in everyday life? He thought of Brother Nathaniel. Did he have a divine gift as well? His predictions had been correct up to this point. Peter could feel doubt crowding its way into his heart. He realized that *his* faith, taken out of the safe setting of the church, was difficult to sustain and understand. *Was this true faith?* His thoughts left him unsettled.

Peter was at the bow when the ship pulled into the harbor of Delos. *Delos. Home to Apollo, the Greek god of the sun and music, as well as healing. How ironic.* He awakened Justin and went below to get Rashad. Justin gently roused his wife. "We're here." The island was dark, save the torches around the harbor.

Peter and Rashad emerged from the cabin carrying Omar on a makeshift litter. Amin stood behind them with a torch. Eleni gasped when she saw the dying man. By the torchlight, his face was pale and dark blue circles surrounded his closed, sunken eyes. She could barely discern any breathing.

Justin asked Peter, "How are we going to do this?"

"You and I will carry Omar. Eleni can lead the way to the—"

"Wait, Peter," Eleni broke in. "Those monks are not about to let a woman into the monastery."

"She's right, Peter," Justin added.

Peter looked to Rashad. "No!" Rashad demurred. "I can't. They'll know I'm not one of you. I would be arrested for violating—"

"You must," Peter said calmly, yet forcefully.

"There's no one else, Rashad," Justin added.

Rashad stared at the dying man who looked very little like the Omar he had known for so long. He looked to his guests and opened his mouth to issue a second protest, but the compassion on those Greek faces and the image of Death on Omar's face left him no other option. "Very well," he conceded. "I will go."

The crew eased the ship into the dock. Five of them helped Peter and Rashad bring Omar ashore.

"Go with Christ," Eleni whispered to Justin as she kissed his cheek and crossed herself.

Amin handed Justin the torch. Justin proceeded down the gangplank ahead of the others toward the gate of the small fort a hundred yards ahead of them. There was no sign of anyone else around the harbor.

As Justin neared the gate, he heard a small door in the middle of the gate open. Three imperial soldiers stepped out. Justin immediately balked. He and Peter were still outlaws. They could be captured. He turned away but then thought of Omar. There was no alternative. Justin stiffened his resolve and accosted the soldiers.

"Good evening, sirs," Justin began politely.

"Good evening to you, sir," replied the leader with equal cordiality. "What brings you to this island?" We don't see many visitors."

"I'm looking for the monastery. I have a very sick friend —"

"Plague?" the soldier asked gravely.

Justin didn't know what to say but wagered that an affirmative answer may have undesirable consequences. "No," he assured the soldier. "The physician said it definitely was not that."

The soldier's face showed his relief. "Any idea what ails the man?"

"No, but he's very ill. He may die. That's why we're going to the monastery, to see Therapeftikos."

"Poor soul," the soldier said compassionately as he crossed himself. "This is his last chance." Justin nodded his head. "Follow that road up the hill," the soldier said as he pointed. "Saint Luke's is at the end of it. It's about an hour walk, maybe less."

"Saint Luke's. Thank you. Thank you very much, sir."

"My pleasure, sir."

Justin ran back to Peter and Rashad who had set down Omar's litter. "I've found it!"

Justin's optimism was contagious. Peter and Rashad looked at each other excitedly.

"It won't be long, Omar!" Rashad said to his friend's lifeless body.

Forty minutes later, they could see dim torchlights outside the monastery. In the interim, Justin traded places with Peter and later Peter relieved Rashad, who was uneasy about taking the lead. They arrived at the walls of Saint Luke's in another fifteen minutes.

Rashad turned back to Justin, his discomfort obvious. Justin gladly agreed to the change and stepped forward to ring the bell that hung beside the gate. When this failed to generate a response, he rang it again. Soon after, a short, white-bearded monk in a black cassock opened the gate.

"He's dying," Justin explained, pointing at the litter.

The monk stepped out toward the others and inspected Omar's face. He touched the black matter in the corners of Omar's mouth. "Hmmm," he said. "What treatment has he had so far?"

"Are you Therapeftikos?" Justin blurted out.

"No," the old monk said patiently. Then he repeated his question.

Justin looked to Rashad for the answer. Rashad became uneasy but he knew he was the only one who could give the information. He told the monk about the willow bark, the poltice, and the bloodletting.

"Hmmm," the monk said, approving of what had been done thus far. He took another look at Omar. He examined his eyes and felt Omar's neck, chest, and belly. When he had finished, he instructed them to follow him. "Leave the torch," he told Justin. There will be plenty of light inside."

They proceeded through the gate, which the old man closed behind them. Peter led the way, carrying the foot of the litter. Rashad carried the head while Justin followed. As they walked through a small courtyard, Rashad noted a small well to his left. He felt something curious about this well and, as he started to wonder why, the door to the monastery opened in front of them. A young monk emerged from behind the door and welcomed the visitors. The vestibule was dark, save a hundred votive candles blazing in front of dozens of icons, some hanging from the walls and others standing on small tables lining the hall.

As they proceded down the hall, Rashad looked warily at the icons around him. The sterile images stared eerily forward, their eyes blank and lifeless. He felt his teeth clench as he passed each of them. He dare not look at these *idols* that the Prophet himself had condemned. Yet to not glance at them was close to impossible. His eye caught a glimpse of one, then another. Each time his eye would spend a fraction of a second more on each successive image until each furtive glance became less secretive and more deliberate. The stone-faced saints pictured in them seemed inhuman. However, as he advanced down that endless corridor one set of eyes awakened. They were looking at him! Then another pair! The lights of the votive candles suddenly flickered wildly. He looked to the opposite side of the corridor. *A sudden breeze? No.* He felt his heart accelerate. He directed his eyes to the end of the passageway. *Still a long way to go!* Rashad now *felt* the idols staring at him. His dry tongue stuck to the roof of his mouth. The weight of their unholy eyes pulled him down. He jerked his head left and right, as if that would scatter them, yet their surveillance continued. Their cold eyes looked through him. The flickering light intensified their power. *I must leave this place!* He gasped for air and turned to look for a door, a window, anything. But then he saw Omar's face. His thoughts of escape vanished. *Omar, my friend, if there were any other way . . .* It was difficult enough being in a house of Christian holymen, but to have one's soul violated by these penetrating images was almost unbearable. Yet, he could not give up.

Ahead, a larger icon on a small table grabbed Rashad's attention. It depicted a balding, gray-haired man with cold, dark brown eyes. His dour mouth was flat and featureless. His right hand was raised with his ring finger flexed over the palm, the thumb flexed over it, and the other three fingers extended heavenward. The severe face of the image forced Rashad to falter. He stumbled but quickly recovered. *Demon!* He looked away to the other side of the corridor only to have another image confront him. This one took the form of a young woman, her head covered in white. Her trance-like glare sent a chill down Rashad's spine. *Cursed she-devil!* Her cold grip squeezed his heart. He jerked his head away to avoid her captivating glance and, as he did so, he nearly dumped Omar to the floor. Only Peter's strength avoided catastrophe.

"Rashad!" Peter whispered to him.

"I am fine," Rashad said.

Justin saw what had happened and offered to spell his friend. Rashad resisted at first but Justin's gentle persistence prevailed and he assumed the position at Omar's head.

The old monk stopped and pointed to a spiral staircase to his right. "This way," he announced. He started up and the others followed. Dozens of candles illuminated the way. The pitch of the staircase was fairly gradual so Peter and Justin had an easy time transporting Omar. Rashad looked over Peter's shoulder at his friend's face and shuddered. The light revealed a wretched creature that Rashad could not recognize. *How could these changes have come on in such a short time?* Death's grip on Omar had tightened.

When Rashad looked up, he gasped quietly. To his disgust, the stairwell was inhabited by more of the damned idols. The first image pictured the Nativity: golden angels flying over an open cave, trumpeting the birth of Jesus. In their eyes, Rashad saw not the same sterness of the saints in the hall but a gentle joy. He was momentarily relieved but he reminded himself that this idolatry would lead him away from the Prophet Muhammed. He wanted to look away but his curiosity forced his eyes to the next icon, which showed Jesus as a small boy teaching in the synongogue. Again the soft eyes of the icon reached out to Rashad. He turned away and, as he did so, he saw Omar's face. *He's dead!*

CHAPTER 21

Rashad had probably been hearing the chanting for some time but only now did he recognize it. It was followed by men singing in response to the cantor's exhortations to God. Peter and Justin heard them as well. The singing grew louder as they climbed the spiral staircase. Rashad cautiously looked back at the wall and its images. These icons told of the Passion: Christ's arrest in the Garden of Gethsemene, His trials before the Sanhedrin and then Pilate, His scourging by the soldiers, the Crucifixion, and the Descent from the Cross. *No! These were untrue! Lies!* He wanted to look away but the icons held his gaze. The singing grew louder.

Rashad was petrified. The overpowering imagery shook him. And then, the face of the dying Christ gently reached out to him. *No!* The votive candles flickered and Rashad raised his left hand. These were the fires of Hell itself. He was alone. He had disobeyed and would be condemned. Why had he agreed to come into this place?

He looked at Peter and Justin. They now were alien to him. Their faces were different. The irregular undulations of the dancing candle flames threw bizarre shadows around these two men. Or were they other than men? For they had grown horns, like the minions of Dis itself, and they were leading him to his destruction!

Yet Rashad proceeded with the others, involuntarily, as if his legs now belonged to the Devil. They reached the top of the spiral staircase. The singing was deafening. The last icon was that of the Resurrection. The candlelight around it leapt wildly on its images. Justin and Peter bowed their heads in reverence as they passed the holy image. The singing crescendoed. Rashad saw the image of the Risen Christ. Bright light radiated from the resurrected man, His life-filled eyes demanding Rashad's attention. He felt heaviness in his chest, faltered, and nearly fell. *Blasphemy!* Rashad's eyes blurred as if the icon were bewitching him. At first, he felt nausea but then a strange feeling of comfort invaded him. As his heart tumbled into this spiritual abyss his mind precipitously recovered. *No! This infernal image was an abominable adulteration of the True Faith! There was no Resurrection! Jesus was not divine but a lesser prophet who prepared the way for ultimate prophet! There is no god but Allah and Muhammed is His Prophet! Muhammed is His Prophet!*

The singing ended when they reached the top of the stairs. In front of them, forty monks dressed in long black robes, their heads covered with cowls, stood in an open semi-circle. In the center was an old man seated in a simple wooden chair. The white-haired monk led Rashad to him. The old monk sensed Rashad's presence and held out his right hand. As Rashad placed his hand inside that of the old monk, he looked at the old man's faded eyes. He was blind. The old monk took his left hand and covered the top of Rashad's hand. Rashad's uneasiness grew. He looked back at Omar. Was he dead? The old monk bowed his head and said a prayer under his breath. He raised his head and turned it toward Rashad. "Your friend is dying," he said gently.

Rashad hesitated before he answered. "Yes, he is."

"Why have you brought him here?"

Rashad was perplexed, if not insensed, by the question. *Why was the old man asking? We brought Omar here to be healed. Isn't that why anyone brings anybody here?* Rashad overcame his anger and replied soberly, "I have brought him to you to be healed."

"To be healed?" the old monk asked. "I cannot heal him."

Rashad's heart sank. "But you are Therapeftikos!"

"That is what they call me," the old man chuckled, "but I prefer the name I received when I first came here: Silas."

"Brother Silas," Rashad said, trying to maintain his composure and yet encouraging the monk to act, "the man is dying! Can't you do something?"

The old man took his time in replying. "Take your friend to the courtyard," he said. "Give him a drink from the well there. I imagine he's quite thirsty."

"Thirsty?" Rashad tried to ask the old man how that would help Omar but the old monk raised his hands, which still were wrapped around Rashad's right hand. He started a prayer and the monks began to sing, quietly at first, but then crescendoing loudly as they did before. Rashad was lost. They had come all this way and his friend was still dying, if he weren't dead already. *This old man is a charlatan! He can't even cure his own blindness! How could he heal anyone else?*

Rashad looked to Peter and Justin for help but they had set Omar's litter on the floor and were on their knees praying. The monks continued their hymn. Rashad looked around in exasperation. Wasn't anybody going to help him? His friend was dying! He was ready to give up the struggle, leave his friend to be buried by the monks when the old monk released his right hand, reached up, grabbed Rashad's right elbow and pulled it down to him, bringing his head to level of the old monk's mouth. "Peace be with you," said the old monk in perfect Arabic. "Your faith has saved your friend's life."

Rashad was stunned. What had just happened? He looked over at Omar. He looked no better. The white-haired monk took Rashad by the hand as Justin and Peter lifted Omar off the floor and led them down the stairs.

A tempest of anger raged in Rashad's mind. *Omar is no better! He's dead! That man is a fake!* He felt his teeth bite his lower lip. *How did the old man know I was an Arab? That devil probably knew that I am Muslim as well! And if he did know, why did he not tell the other monks?* Rashad yearned to scream his indignation out loud but he didn't dare upset the monks. *Liars! All of you! Allah's curse be on you!*

Rashad braced himself as they descended the spiral staircase. The icons were there and he was certain they would once again slide their steely grips through the windows of his soul and crush his weakened spirit. He redoubled his resolve and kept the cursed images from his sight. "Diabolical idols!" he screamed deep in his soul. "Betrayers of faith! Agents of evil!" But this time they did not torment him. The reprieve perturbed Rashad. *The devils are toying with me! Allah, save your faithful servant!*

When they reached the bottom of the stairs, the white-haired monk led them down the long, candle-lit hall. The shadows of the flames still darted furiously against the walls and icons. Rashad prepared himself to run this second gauntlet. *Pagan images! Tainted religion!* He automatically held his breath as he completed the perilous walk, as if the icons were capable of spraying poisonous gases into his face. When he saw the door to the courtyard ahead, Rashad's heart accelerated. *Soon I'll be out of this hell!* He shot a quick glance at the icons but this time they indolently stared blankly ahead.

The young monk appeared at the door and opened it for them. As he did so, the golden sunshine streamed over them as the white-haired monk led them to the well. The light of the new dawn bathed their bodies in maternal warmth.

"Peter! Rashad!" Justin shouted. "Look!"

Peter, who was carrying the head of the litter, ordered Justin to set the litter down. "There's color in his face! His lips are moving!"

"Omar?" Rashad said gently to his friend. He saw Omar's lips move very slightly. The darkness around his eyes had faded.

"He is healed! Thank God!" Peter and Justin gasped and kneeled down beside the litter.

Rashad fell to his knees opposite Justin. He could not believe what he was seeing. The white-haired monk came to him and suggested, "Perhaps your friend would like a drink."

Rashad quickly remembered what Therapeftikos had instructed him. He shot up and went with the white-haired monk to the well and lowered the bucket into it. It seemed to take forever.

The monk sensed Rashad's impatience and looked reassuringly into his eyes. "It's full."

Rashad tugged upward to confirm the monk's pronouncement and raised the bucket as fast as he could. When the full bucket reached the well's edge, the monk calmly handed Rashad a wooden cup. He filled it with the clear cool water and ran to his friend, trying not to spill a drop.

As Justin cradled Omar's head and gently bent it forward, Rashad slowly poured the water over Omar's parched lips. Omar jerked as the water wet his tongue. He struggled to sit up by himself and Justin helped him. Omar reached up and grasped the cup, and poured the water down his throat.

Rashad hugged him as he finished and held him tightly. His eyes filled with tears of joy. "Omar!"

"Rashad?" Omar slowly acknowledged his friend, as if he had awakened from a long sleep. He hugged him back. "Rashad! Rashad! Praise be to Allah!" he added in Arabic.

"Yes!" Rashad replied, also in his native tongue. "Praise be to Allah!"

Peter turned to Justin and embraced him. "Dear God! It's a miracle, Justin!"

"Thanks be to God!" Justin cried. "Thanks be to God!"

"Thank you, Justin!" Rashad said tearfully as he layed his arm across Justin's shoulder and embraced him. "Thank you for bringing us here!" He knew that mere words could not show his feelings. His heart's exhilaration was boundless. "Praise be to Allah!"

Rashad looked back to find Omar and Peter laughing and embracing in celebration. He remembered how mistrustful Omar had been of Peter and Justin. *And now look at them!* Oh how complete his joy was! He would cherish this day forever!

But then he remembered the terror he had endured within the monastery. His heart went cold. *The infidel and his blasphemous idols! Praise be to Allah for delivering me from Hell!* Yet Allah had used these infidels, this hell, to save Omar's life. *This is the Devil's deception!* However, for all of his alarm, Rashad felt his heart blanketed by a calming serenity. He began to see the experience at Saint Luke's as something different. He couldn't explain it but he wondered if what he had thought of as the depths of Hell were in truth the Gates of Heaven. He saw the others laugh and cry together. His friend was well! Omar had been healed! It was indeed a miracle! *Praise be to Allah!*

He saw his friends laughing and celebrating and he laughed with them. However, his cynical mind wasn't about to yield to his heart's airy musings. *No! This is the work of the Devil!* His joy was clouding his perception of what had truly happened in the monastery. As his heart and his mind battled each other, Rashad sensed the white-haired monk at his shoulder.

The monk said nothing but Rashad knew it was time to leave. He instructed Omar to lie back down on the litter so they could carry him back to the ship.

"That mat will not be necessary," the white-haired monk said, smiling.

Rashad was not certain that he had understood the monk but he asked Omar to stand. "Are you able?"

"I feel as if I could climb a mountain!" Omar replied. He looked at Rashad, as if to ask his permission, and stood up, effortlessly. Omar, wide-eyed and laughing, grabbed Rashad. "I am well, Rashad! I am healed!" He embraced his friend again and shouted with unbridled joy as he ran across the courtyard, through the gate and into the road. Rashad followed and Peter was soon on Rashad's heels.

Justin stayed to thank the white-haired monk. "Thank you. My friend is well now."

"Yes, I know," said the monk, beaming at Justin. "But it was your faith in Christ Jesus that saved your friend. If you hadn't believed it could happen, your friend would still be on that mat."

"Thank you," Justin said again, backing away from the monk. He smiled, turned, and sprinted to join the others. The monk's words hadn't quite registered with him yet. It would not be until later that Justin would appreciate fully what he had encountered that night at the monastery.

Eleni awoke in Rashad's cabin at dawn. Her sleep had been fitful. In reality, she had probably not slept at all. Few of those who had remained on the ship did. Eleni pulled herself out of the bed and quickly ran her fingers through her long auburn hair, hoping to undo the effects of her restless sleep. She dipped her hands into the waterbasin and splashed the cold liquid onto her face. She gasped as the icy water sent a chill through her. After she had dressed, Eleni made her way onto the deck. The sailors waited anxiously for the return of Rashad and Omar. There were murmurings among the crew as to why Omar had been taken to the monastery. Why had Amin failed to cure him? He was the best physician in Damascus. Some suspected their two friends would not return from the Christian holy place.

Soon a loud rustling arose among the men. "They're back!" Eleni said to herself with some apprehension. Then she saw them, Rashad, Omar, and then Peter with Justin, walking at first, and then running to the ship to show their companions the miracle that had befallen them.

Eleni wept as she saw the men return triumphantly. She dropped to her knees and crossed herself three times. She clutched her hands together and thanked God for the miracle. As Justin ran up to the ship, Eleni stood and went to where he was boarding. They embraced and held each other tighter that they ever had before.

"You saved Omar's life, Eleni," Justin said to her proudly.

"You also acted as God's instrument in this, Justin," she reminded him. "Your faith, too, as well as Peter's and Rashad's, healed Omar." Justin fell into her hazel eyes and kissed her.

Rashad and Omar, inundated by questions from their fascinated shipmates, tried to explain what had happened to them in the last two hours. Peter joined Justin and Eleni after he spoke briefly with Amin.

By midday, the celebration began to wind down. The sunny weather prevailed and the wind picked up by the third hour. The ship sped around the southern coast of Rinia, past Siros, and on to Serifos. At Serifos, Rashad docked to reprovision the ship. After the evening meal, Rashad and Omar went ashore with ten other men. Peter found Justin and Eleni sitting on the deck amidship and sat down next to them.

"How are we doing, Peter?" Justin asked.

"Couldn't be better, except, of course, if we were already in Venice," Peter replied.

"Ever the pessimist, aren't you, Peter?" Eleni joked.

"I merely choose to be more realistic in my outlook," Peter replied.

"Sometimes I think you'd just as soon be at the end of your life," Eleni quipped, "so you could look back and say, 'Sure glad that's over; now I can really enjoy myself!'"

Peter sneered good-naturedly at her. Justin tried to restrain himself but he soon joined Eleni in laughter.

"We all have our own strategies for negotiating this veil of tears we call life," Peter began. "Why endure our flawed life on earth if it's nothing but a mere conduit to a perfect eternity in Paradise?"

"What good is a perfect eternity in Paradise," Eleni retorted, "if it's not preceded by a flawed life on earth?"

"She's right, Peter," Justin said, smiling. "One can only appreciate perfection if one has experienced imperfection."

"Justin, when did *you* aquire such wisdom?" Peter joked. "That sounds like something your Uncle Theodore would say."

"Peter's right, Justin," Eleni said, continuing the feigned appreciation of Justin's newly found sagacity. "Perhaps you should write a letter to the patriarch, or Michael Psellos, and expound on this theory."

Justin smiled. He didn't mind being the butt of their joke. He knew that he had often victimized others in the same harmless way. Collecting his due was to be expected.

It was just over an hour before Rashad and his men returned. The ship was quickly made ready and soon they were under way. The sun was low in the sky and dusk approached. They sailed west, toward the declining orange orb. Luminescent rays of red, yellow, and orange shot forth from the glowing globe and painted the gently billowing sea.

By midnight, they passed Melos and by the next day's dawn, they were off the coast of Ananes. Justin left the cabin for the deck and found the crew at prayer in the morning overcast. The waves' crests and troughs widened their differences. The swells grew to seven feet. At the moment the wind was moderate, out of the north-northwest at fifteen knots. Justin found Peter and Rashad at the bow and asked for their assessment.

"The weather has definitely taken a turn for the worse," Rashad said.

"If the wind picks up and these swells get deeper, we could be in for a rough ride," Peter added.

"What should we do if that happens?" Justin asked.

"Find something solid and hold on," Peter answered. "You and Eleni should stay in the cabin. If anyone falls overboard in a storm he's as good as gone." Rashad nodded in agreement.

By midday, the weather worsened. The swells grew to ten feet and the wind jumped to thirty knots. Justin and Eleni were tossed about the cabin with each wave's crest and trough. The water easily penetrated the ship's deck and imperfect walls. The bedside table lay on its side on the floor. The wash basin fell off of the table two hours earlier, sending water across the floor. Nothing remained on the walls; everything was on the floor. The bed itself became mobile and was no longer a safe place. Justin and Eleni stood against opposing walls, hanging on tightly to any projection available.

On deck, Peter and Rashad hurried from mast to mast or any other structure that could hold them. Rashad had ordered the sails down to limit the wind's hold on the ship, but this didn't help much. The roar of the wind and waves impaired even the simplest communication. The crew had to yell to each other to be heard. Yet, the cold, wet crewmen stoically manned their stations. The fury of the storm soon amplified itself. Peter had no idea where the ship was headed. She was totally at the mercy of the waves, who tossed her about like a toy.

Peter saw three of the crewmen lying motionlessly on the deck on the port side. Perhaps they had collided with each other, but whatever the mechanism, the three could easily be washed overboard by the next big wave. As the ship reached the trough of the wave it was riding, Peter shot over to the impaired sailors and grabbed them. He struggled to pull them to the middle of the ship, losing his balance several times on the wet deck. He saw a large wave approach. If he didn't move he and the others would be washed overboard.

Rashad ran to Peter and grabbed him with one hand and grabbed one of the sailors with the other. "Wave!" he yelled in Peter's ear.

Peter quickly looked up at the sea and saw that the ship had climbed to the crest of the giant wave and was about to descend into a cavernous trough. He held on tightly to the three unconscious sailors as he felt Rashad tightened his grip his arm. The ship fell precipitously. The crew held on dearly to prevent being launched over the plunging bow. One unlucky sailor lost his grip and slid headlong from the stern on the slippery deck past his shipmates. He dug his fingernails into the deck and screamed for Allah to save him but he rapidly slid forward. His shipmates reached out for him. Those who were quick enough were able to grab a limb but his wet skin and the force of the rolling sea dashed their efforts. The unlucky sailor slid under the railing and over the bow, falling into the water just ahead of the ship. As he rose up from his plunge into the sea, the vessel rode over him, sending him to a cold, watery grave.

Inside the cabin, Eleni and Justin held on as well. There were one or two times that one of them would lose his or her grip and go crashing into a wall or into the door. Fortunately, Rashad had bolted the door so it could not serve as a point of unplanned exit for them.

The storm finally ended an hour and a half later. Peter and Rashad inspected the ship carefully. Only the one man had been lost. The three unconscious crewmen recovered. The storm had only lightly damaged the masts and the rigging.

Rashad raced to the cabin to check on Eleni and Justin. Peter surveyed the sea around the ship. It had calmed considerably but still remained rough.

"That was very unpleasant," said Rashad to Peter as he came up to him from the cabin. "Justin and Eleni are well."

"We're lucky we're still afloat," Peter said. "Who was the man we lost?"

"The son of one of my neighbor's," Rashad sighed. "This was his first voyage with us."

Peter's heart sank. "I'm sorry, Rashad." He couldn't help but feel reponsible for any misfortune that befell the crew. It was, after all, for Justin's, Eleni's, and his benefit that this journey had been undertaken.

"Peter, we could have just as easily lost him off the coast of Cyprus on our return to Damascus." He changed the subject as he scanned the water ahead. "Do you have any idea where we are?"

"I have no idea," Peter replied. He looked up into the sky and found it difficult to find the sun in the darkened sky. However, in he south, the black nimbo-cumuli inched apart and the sun pried its way into view.

"It's still about midday," Peter hypothesized.

"Yes," Rashad agreed.

Rashad steered the ship ninety degrees to the midday sun. Their next destination was roughly due west of their last postion.

"Eventually, by heading west we should spot land before sunset," Peter speculated.

"The only problem being," Rashad noted, "which way did the storm take us? Were we blown east or south? The wind was out of the north-northwest when the storm began, so it's unlikely we were blown north or west."

"We'll come across land soon and then we can re-orient ourselves."

The crewmen jumped into their work. They re-rigged the sails and soon the ship plowed westward through the choppy sea, a fifteen knot wind coming over the starboard bow. Justin and Eleni ran onto the deck and joined Rashad and Peter amidships.

"I take it that is one of the more treacherous elements of sailing," Justin said.

"One of them," Peter answered.

"One of many, my friends," Rashad added. "One of many."

A crewman spotted land at the twelfth hour. Celebration erupted on board the ship. But which piece of land was this? Some one would have to go ashore. As they approached the land mass from the south, Rashad ordered the ship in as far as it could go without running aground on the sandy beach ahead.

"I'm going ashore," Peter announced as he watched the anchor splash into the water.

"I thought that you and Eleni and I were going to stay on board at all times," Justin protested. "I don't think that's a good idea."

"Justin," Peter retorted, "we're lost. I need to get our bearings."

"Rashad can do that," Justin continued.

"He and I discussed it already. I know the waters better . . . It just makes more sense."

"It's too risky. You could be caught!" Justin argued.

"If I'm caught, there's still a chance Rashad can get you to Venice. If we can't find out where we're going, then we're all lost. We've got to take this chance." Peter noted the position of the sun and added, "If I'm not back by sunset, leave."

The next sixty minutes were extremely tense for everyone on board. No one doubted Peter's abilities but the uncertainty and danger of their predicament left its mark. The sun's nether portion slid below the horizon but heavy cloud cover muted an otherwise dazzling sunset. Rashad and Justin searched the shoreline anxiously. There was no sign of Peter and soon it would be dark.

"What will we do if he doesn't come back on time?" Justin asked.

"Go after him," Rashad said in a matter-of-fact way.

"That's exactly what I thought you'd say."

Peter swam ashore with only his tunic, skirt, and knee-length lace-up boots. The evening's chill grew as the daylight faded, undoubtedly making Peter's situation more complicated.

"Are we leaving?" Eleni asked as she joined Justin and Rashad.

"I'm afraid there's been a change of plan," Rashad announced.

"We're going to go find Peter," Justin added.

"Good," she said.

"Are you coming with me, Rashad?" Justin asked.

Suddenly Omar inserted himself between Rashad and Justin and said something in Arabic to Rashad.

"It appears that we have another candidate to rescue Peter," Rashad said.

Justin was surprised. "Who, Omar?"

"He insists," Rashad said, relaying Omar's firmness to Justin.

Justin hesitated. "Rashad, I'm not sure that Omar —"

Justin was cut short by one of the crew. Soon others were cheering, pointing at the shore. There they saw Peter running into the water. About thirty yards behind were fifteen light infantrymen in hot pursuit. When the water was up to his waist, Peter dove into it and swam as fast as he could toward the ship. Some of the soldiers divested themselves of their weapons and swam after him. The others threw lances, rocks, sticks, and whatever they could find at Peter. One rock grazed his left ear and cheek, stunning him temporarily, but he quickly recovered and continued on toward the ship.

The sailors cheered wildly for him as he inched closer to the vessel. Fortunately, the antagonists' remaining projectiles fell harmlessly into the water. As Peter neared the ship, the crew launched various missiles at Peter's pursuers. When Peter was within a few feet of the ship, the soldiers gave up and returned to the shore. Justin and Rashad lowered a rope ladder, and Peter nimbly scrambled up to the deck.

"Peter!" Justin cried, hugging his friend, "What the devil happened?"

"Long story!" Peter shivered. Rashad brought him a blanket and led him to his cabin. Justin and Eleni followed.

Omar ordered the crew to raise the anchor and prepare for immediate departure. The sails flew upward and grabbed the passing breeze, sending the ship slicing through the black water that shimmered irregularly in the moon's reflection.

"Kithira," Peter announced breathlessly, "this is the southwestern shore of Kithira."

"So we are not as far off course as I thought," Rashad noted.

"Six to eight hours of smooth sailing should bring us to Cape Matapan," Peter added. "And from there—"

"Tell us what happened, Peter," Eleni interrupted. The others echoed her request.

"Once I was ashore, I walked about a mile or so to a small village. There, I asked an old man where I was," Peter explained. "Once he had told me, I turned and walked back toward the beach. It couldn't have been simpler. However, as I returned to the beach, I was stopped by five soldiers."

"What did they want?" Justin wondered.

"The usual questions: Who was I? What was my business there?"

"So when did the running begin?" Justin asked.

"Everything seemed to be going well until one of them alerted the sergeant to my wet clothes. I imagine they weren't used to people in soaking wet clothing wandering through their village at sunset."

"So how did you escape?" asked Rashad.

"I grabbed one of them and pushed him into the others. Knocked them all to the ground. Then I ran. The sergeant blew his whistle, and soon, about a dozen others came from every nook and cranny of that little town. Somehow, through dodging, cutting back, and even jumping or diving over or through them, I made it out of the village. From there I just ran like hell to the beach."

"We're glad you made it, Koumbarro," Justin smiled, slapping his buddy on the shoulder.

"And thanks for waiting," Peter added, "but you should have been long gone."

"Peter," Eleni said looking him in the eye, "we couldn't forgive ourselves if we left you." Justin and Rashad agreed.

"You are exhausted, my friend," Rashad told Peter. "I'll have Omar bring you some food and then you will sleep here in the cabin." Peter raised his hand to object but the expression on Rashad's face made it clear that he was accepting no alternatives this evening.

"Okay then," Peter acquiesced.

The others said good night and left the cabin. Justin poked his head back in and said, "We need you to be well rested, so get some sleep."

"All right, all right!" Peter grumbled. "Good night." He breathed a long deep sigh and lay on the bed.

When Omar arrived with the food five minutes later, Peter was asleep.

CHAPTER 22

At midnight, Justin was sound asleep on the deck next to Eleni. He felt something touch his shoulder but he ignored it. The touch returned with more force. "Wake up," he heard someone say gently. He felt warm breath on his left ear. "Wake up!"

Justin opened his right eye, then slowly opened his left eye and looked about. When he saw Rashad's face, not a foot from his own, he shuddered. He quickly lifted his head to speak but Rashad put his finger to Justin's lips, encouraging his continued silence. He motioned to Justin to follow him to the bow, which the sleepy soldier did.

The crewmen on duty were the only other people on board who weren't asleep. The night air was cool and Justin grabbed a blanket from a stack near the bow. He wrapped himself in it as Rashad brought two stools. Justin sat, still clinging to the new blanket, gleaning whatever warmth it had to offer. Rashad remained standing.

The calm black sea bore transcient faint white punctuations. The cloud-covered moon could offer only scant light. The ship glided gracefully over the dark waves as the cool breeze brought a shiver to Justin.

"Justin," Rashad began, as Justin's eyes closed, trying to return him to the restful sleep he had been enjoying. "Do you remember what happened at the monastery?"

"Yes, of course," Justin replied, rubbing his eyes.

"Well," Rashad sputtered, "do you remember everything?"

"What do you mean?" Justin detected Rashad's uneasiness. "What's wrong, Rashad?" He was wide awake now. "Are you ill?"

"No, no," Rashad replied.

"Is Omar—"

"Omar is fine, too." Rashad sat down next to him and spoke to Justin as if he were revealing a terrible secret. He whispered so the crew couldn't hear him, which was a moot point as none of them spoke Greek. "Something happened to me that night."

"What?" Justin asked.

"Something that I can't forget."

"I'll never forget either, Rashad. It's not everyday you see someone so sick healed—"

"No!" Rashad interrupted. "No. Something else." He hesitated before he continued. "Something, Justin, something happened to me."

"What do you mean?"

Rashad looked like he couldn't find the right words to say. "I haven't been able to sleep," he continued.

Justin looked back at Rashad, eagerly awaiting his words.

"I can't sleep without being awakened by visions of that place," Rashad answered. "Justin," he continued. "That place, I hear it in my dreams."

"The monks?"

"And I see things when I close my eyes."

"What things?"

"Those things in the monastery," Rashad answered. "The icons."

Justin still wasn't following.

Rashad's voice grew grave. "The icons—"

"Yes?" Justin asked, encouraging Rashad to continue.

"I keep seeing their faces," Rashad went with difficulty. "And sometimes," he said uncertainly, "sometimes they speak to me."

"What are they saying?"

"They just say my name. They speak to me as if they know me. They call to me the way my father used to."

"What?"

"They don't let me rest . . . What happened that night?" he asked as he clutched Justin's hand. There was fear in his voice.

Justin thought for a moment before answering. "I think it was a miracle, Rashad," he answered gently. "Omar was healed by the

Lord through Therapeftikos." When Justin saw that his answer didn't satisfy Rashad, he added, "I think something happened to all of us. If you asked Peter, he'd probably tell you the same thing. It's not every day that God reveals himself to us so directly."

Rashad still wasn't satisfied by Justin's simple answers. "Justin, how did you feel in the monastery?"

"I'm not sure I know what you mean."

Rashad paused for a moment and collected his thoughts. "I felt as if I were an outsider, an alien."

"Well, you're not Greek—"

"No, I mean I felt alien to God, at least to the Christian God."

"*Christian* God?"

"I felt that all I had learned of Allah, the Koran, the Hadith, was burned to cinders by a fire that was started in my soul that night. The image of Jesus rising from his tomb, the brilliant light surrounding him . . ." Rashad shook his head. "*Esh-Hadu Ina La E-LaHa illa Allah wa Esh-Hadu Ina Muhammed Rasoul Allah!*"

Justin knew enough Arabic to recognize the first tenet of Islam: "There is not god but Allah; Muhammad is the messenger of Allah." *But what was Rashad telling him?* Did the power they experienced in the monastery that night challenge his beliefs? As a Christian, Justin should rejoice at this lost sheep being reclaimed in the name of Jesus Christ, but was the anguish this poor man experiencing God's will? Was this what the Apostle Paul endured after being blinded on the road to Damascus when he was still named Saul?

"How can I make this God leave me?" Rashad begged.

"Leave you?" Justin was surprised at such a request. "I don't know," he added sympathetically. "Are you sure you *want* Him to leave?"

Rashad looked at Justin, at first, with an indignant and suspicious look. Then he smiled. "No," he replied slowly, "I'm not sure that I do."

"Rashad, I can't imagine what you're going through right now," Justin said, putting his arm on Rashad's shoulder. "We *all* experienced a great power that night. I think you need to remember that the same power that healed Omar is with you now. It's the same power that haunts you."

Rashad recoiled. "What do you mean, Justin?"

Justin found it difficult to continue in this vein for fear of Rashad's reaction, but he emboldened himself and spoke. "The Christ you saw in the icons," he said carefully, "healed Omar's fever and—"

"Now he wants something from me," Rashad interjected.

"No," Justin continued, "he doesn't want something *from* you."

Rashad narrowed his eyes. "What?"

"He wants *you*."

Rashad grunted incredulously. "I cannot believe that, Justin. What I experienced that night frightens me! I can't sleep!" He looked away and thoughtfully added, "Yet it also amazes me. I feel someone is reaching out to me. That's what's bothering me. In many ways, that night was the worst of my life but some of it I want to experience over and over again. I feel something inside my soul that has never been there; it feels good and I cannot reconcile these new feelings with my faith."

Justin didn't know how to respond.

"This would be blasphemy to any Muslim. Please tell no one, but those icons made Allah more personal, more approachable." Rashad looked away. "What am I saying? This doesn't make sense! I don't know what to believe! I don't dare explore my feelings about this any more. I cannot! I feel as if I am following a trail off a cliff!" He threw his hands up. "This is insane! What am I doing?"

"Rashad?"

"Yet, I can no longer believe what I have believed for all of my life. I am trapped between what I have always known as the truth and what my heart is telling me is the truth. I don't know which way to go, Justin. I am like a ship without a rudder."

Rashad's candor impressed Justin. He smiled at his friend and asked, "Have you spoken to Omar?"

"No. I cannot."

"Do you think he feels as you do? He seems friendlier toward Eleni, Peter, and me."

"I believe he is being appreciative for what you did for him. I don't think he truly knows what happened at the monastery."

"You haven't told him?" Justin was surprised.

"Justin, how could I? I'm not certain what happened there myself. Besides, he would not believe me." Rashad looked away from Justin.

He saw his tormented friend's furrowed brow and leaned closer to him. "Is there anything I can do to help you, Rashad?"

"No." Rashad looked at Justin's face and saw its sincerity. He smiled back and chuckled, "Now I know why my brother Nagib liked you so much, Justin Phillipos." He grabbed Justin's hand and clenched it tightly. "You're a good man!" Rashad said as he threw an arm around Justin and embraced him.

Justin looked up at the moon. The clouds around it had cleared and the silvery orb glowed proudly, sending its light over the crenulated sea. Justin pondered his friend's dilemma. How could he hope to understand Rashad's anguish? His faith had never endured such a tremor, a violent shaking that would not stop until little remained standing.

Peter was at the bow as the sun rose. The overcast had returned and the sunrise was less than spectacular. He changed the ship's heading from north-by-northwest to northwest after she had passed Cape Matapan. The wind, still through the night, picked up. It came out of the northeast.

Eleni and Justin arose well after dawn. The cool morning offered a good reason for them to cuddle under a blanket.

"What did you get up for last night?" Eleni asked.

Justin wasn't surprised that his wife had detected his absence. "Rashad wanted to talk to me about something," he answered, not wanting to betray his friend's confidence.

"It was about the monastery, wasn't it?"

"I didn't say that."

"Rashad's not been the same since."

"I don't think he wanted me to tell anyone."

"You didn't."

"Why didn't I notice this? Peter hasn't said anything to me."

"He probably doesn't know either."

"So how do you know?"

"Women can see these things."

Justin chuckled. "Well, since you already know . . ."

"Yes . . ."

"It has definitely had an effect on him."

"Such as?"

"He feels that the Lord visited him in the monastery and now he's unable to stop thinking about it."

"What did you say?"

"What could I say?"

"You just listened?"

"I said what I could but I don't think I answered his questions. I told him that I was here to help if he needed me. What else could I say?"

"Probably nothing."

"Please don't tell him I spoke with you."

"I won't," Eleni promised.

By the tenth hour of the following day, the ship had sailed past Sapientza, Loutra Killinis, Zakinthos, and Kephalonia. It was now off the east coast of Ithaca, the home of Odysseos, ancient King of Ithaca, and the wiliest of the Greek soldiers who had besieged Troy. Eleni remembered that great hero as Peter and Justin inspected the rocky coastline. She recalled the cunning genius who feigned madness and sowed his fields with salt to avoid recruitment into the Greek forces. She thought of Odysseos, the clever general, whose brainchild, the Trojan Horse, subdued mighty Troy and led to the slaughter of her men and the slavery of her women and children. She thought of Penelope, Odysseos' wife, apart from her husband for the ten years he battled the Trojans and for the next ten years of his "Odyssey," when he wandered the Mediterranean, longing for home, at the whim of circumstance and the gods. She shared her husband's craftiness and was able to delay the troop of suitors who infested her home for the many years of Odysseos' peregrination.

"The weather continues to be a friend," Rashad said as Omar and he joined the three.

As they exchanged greetings Eleni looked closely at Rashad. She saw he was more at ease and less tormented than yesterday. Perhaps his talk with Justin had soothed his wounded soul. Maybe the revelation he had experienced had rooted itself deep within him. She saw that Omar had gone through a change of sorts, as well. He was certainly more kind and attentive to them since his healing, but it wasn't apparent he'd gone through what Rashad had.

"The wind couldn't be better," Peter added. "How are the crewmen?"

"Quite well. They are in excellent spirits." Rashad directed his attention to his map. "Peter, where would you recommend we reprovision? Kerkira?"

"That would be an excellent choice," Peter began. "That island was a favorite for me when I was in the navy. It has a tremendous variety of foods."

After conferring with Omar in Arabic, Rashad added, "I estimate that we'll be there about this time tomorrow."

"Perhaps even earlier," Peter suggested.

Peter was right. They reached Kerkira just after midday. They reprovisioned quickly and smoothly. The slight sweetness of the island's water was particularly satisfying. They added salted fish, breads, and dried fruits to their diminished stores. Soon the crew had the ship under way. The tall triangular sails billowed as the ship glided into the open sea.

An hour after setting sail, the crewmen began the first of their afternoon prayers. Justin noticed that Rashad was not among them. He went below to find Rashad in his cabin.

Justin's sudden appearance startled Rashad. "Justin!"

"Rashad," Justin began, "shouldn't you be at prayers?"

Rashad looked down and started to sob. "I can't," he cried. "I can't. They don't fill me like they used to."

"Rashad—"

Rashad looked resolutely at Justin. "I'm no longer one of them."

"One of what?"

"I am no longer Muslim."

"What are you saying, Rashad?" Justin was shocked.

"I am no longer Muslim."

Justin stared back in disbelief. "No longer Muslim?"

"He came to me again last night." Rashad didn't have to explain to Justin what he meant. "He told me that he was the way to Heaven, that he wanted me to join him in the journey there."

After a long silence, Justin asked uneasily, "What did you say?"

"Yes," Rashad answered softly. "I said yes."

Justin was frozen. He should have been ecstatic but he was shocked, why, he couldn't say.

Rashad drew closer to Justin. "I am a Christian now," he whispered. The dark secret revealed, Rashad embraced Justin with both arms and held him tightly.

Justin slowly wrapped his arms around Rashad as he heard his friend whimper. He wondered why the sadness held his friend so tightly. But he knew that Rashad's tears were tears of joy as well. He had found a new life as a follower of Christ. Yet Justin knew what hardships Rashad's new status would bring. The man's life was forever changed. Conversion from Islam was a capital crime in the Muslim world. To return there and confess his new faith would be signing his own death warrant. He would have to leave his family. Rashad was probably thinking of them and wondering why Christ had revealed Himself at this time and in this way. Justin felt Rashad gently push him away.

"Teach me a prayer, Justin."

"A prayer?"

"A Christian prayer."

Justin looked into Rashad's eyes and saw a longing for understanding. His experience had been devastating and he needed continued healing. "Well, Rashad . . ." Dozens of prayers flashed through his mind but which was the best? Which was the right prayer? Then it came to him. "Ah, here's a good one," he began. "Our Father . . . ."

Rashad smiled at his friend. "Our Father . . . ."

CHAPTER 23

Two days later, the ship put into port at Dyrrachium. Peter announced that he expected them to be in Venice in a week. It was here at Dyrrachium, at the entrance to the Adriatic Sea that Peter had received his first command, a dromon, a fast galley, a few yards smaller than Stathopoulos' ship. She was a good ship, fast as the wind, strong when she needed to be, and very forgiving of miscalculation. She would always hold a special place in Peter's heart. He thought of her as he looked over the bow of Rashad's sleek ship as it slipped into the busy port.

As they docked, Omar and Rashad noted the two Roman war galleys that were docked as well. Rashad briefly spoke with Peter and then led five of his men ashore to buy supplies and food. Again, the time in port was brief and the ship was under way just after midday prayers. She continued on a northwest course out of Dyrrachium. The golden sun radiated brightly in the clear blue sky. A moderate but steady wind blew out of the northeast. The tall white triangular sails filled with wind and led the ship forward smoothly.

The day remained pleasantly uneventful. Rashad managed to slip away from the crew and spend an hour with Justin. Of course, he wanted that day's conversation to take up where the previous day's had left off. Like many of the Muslims of his time, he knew a fair amount about Christianity. Justin did his best but Rashad had many questions that Justin found difficult to answer, which was unusual, as the average Roman took pride in discussing the most minute details of Christianity. But Justin was honest with Rashad and expressed his faith sincerely. Rashad appreciated that most of all.

"You're a good man, Justin," Rashad said, patting him on the shoulder. "Perhaps when we get to Venice, I could find a priest who could answer more of my questions."

"When we get to Venice, you should speak to my Uncle Theodore." Justin laughed. "He knows more about the Bible than any priest!"

"Very well, I'll consult your uncle, Justin." Rashad laughed along with Justin, thinking it strange that a layman would know more about the subject than a priest.

By the evening of the next day, they made port at Ragusa. They reprovisioned early because this was the last Roman port they would pass. This point also marked the ultimate extent of Peter's maritime expertise. From here on, every port was outside of the Roman Empire. This could mean that Peter, Justin, and Eleni could relax, for they were beyond the Roman authority. However, it also meant danger as they were also beyond the protection of the Roman navy. The waters beyond here were far more treacherous; pirates were plentiful and ports were not always welcoming to foreigners, especially those with dark complexions.

At Peter's urging the crew purchased extra food and equipment. The ship left Ragusa heavily laden, slowing her some, but Peter convinced Rashad that it would be safer to be at sea and moving than to put in two or three more times. Pirates often chose to lay in wait for those ships heading for port. Ambushes occurred regularly near busy ports.

By the middle of the following day, the wind lessened considerably, although it was still at their backs. Peter and Rashad frequently exchanged glances but didn't need to speak. They shared concern over the vessel's vulnerability under diminished power. By evening, their silent prayers were answered and the wind picked up but the sea remained calm. Peter was convinced they should try to stay away from the sea-lanes if possible to avoid trouble. Rashad agreed.

The following morning, dark clouds filled the sky and the waves grew as the wind increased. The wind now came out of the southeast, which was unusual for these waters. Peter shook his head and said to Rashad, "Well, we've been lucky so far but I don't like the way things are looking."

"We should stay closer to the islands," Rashad suggested. "The wind may have less effect on us that way."

"But the pirates will be harder to avoid," Peter added.

Later, the wind increased again and rain began to fall. Peter turned to Rashad and begrudgingly admitted, "You're right, Rashad, we'd better hug these islands for a while." They both knew they had been lucky in the last storm. Now they were in waters that neither of them knew and the map Simon had provided them was untested. They were completely at the mercy of any storm. Peter spotted a long thin island ahead and suggested that they proceed along the eastern coast of this cay, staying between these islands and the mainland until the storm passed.

Among these islands of the Illyrian Archipelago, the wind and the waves lessened, but the storm continued nonetheless. The crew quickly trimmed the sails and braced for the worst, although this maritime upheaval proved to be considerably less severe than its predecessor. None of the crew or cargo was lost and Rashad was able to maintain course without difficulty. Within three hours, the storm became a memory. Most of the clouds deserted the sky and the sun reclaimed its rightful place in the heavens. The sea was again calm and a moderate wind continued to blow out of the southeast. Rashad ordered the crew to reset the rigging and the sleek vessel once again sped through the sea.

"Do you think we should head back out to the open water, Peter?" Rashad asked.

"I would recommend it," Peter agreed. "Every island I see is a potential hiding place for a pirate ship."

Rashad ordered the helmsman to steer the ship west to the open sea once they had cleared the island off the port. The island itself was several miles long but they'd passed most of it.

Peter studied the small rocky green islets off the starboard. To him, these verdant peaks of oceanic mountains resembled ships themselves. If he imagined just a little, Peter could see them moving through the still water. He imagined invisible crews manning these vessels of earth, stone, and greenery. Off the starboard bow, he also imagined that two proximate islets were doomed to collide. He could hear sailors, perched in the mast-like trees, excitedly shouting their reports to their respective captains. The green decks below teemed with vigorous activity as panic seized the crew of each isle. The cool-headed captain of each vessel tried valiantly to prevail as a collision loomed. But the unavoidable did not come to these earthen ships; time itself spares them from catastrophe but keeps them from safety. One island remained still just as close as the other; the crew and captain of each stayed vigilant, never relenting, always guarding against the calamity that would never come.

Astern, Justin helped Omar reassemble the provisions. Justin struggled with his Arabic and Omar even more with his limited Greek but they completed their work. Justin looked out over the stern and saw the ship's wake slowly dissipate into the sea around them. Occasionally one of the ripples would make its way to the shore of a nearby island. Justin smiled, soothed by the regular propagations of the wake and the regular churning of the sailing ship through the water.

Justin looked to the bow, where Peter and Rashad studied the map and compared it to the local landmarks. So far, the map proved reliable. It ruffled in the breeze as the prevailing wind blew across the starboard bow. Suddenly, one of the crewmen raced forward and grabbed Rashad's arm. He pointed to a ship approaching quickly off the starboard stern, running at forty-five degrees to Rashad's course. Rashad saw the long ship's large single red rectangular sail and long oars and showed Peter.

"Norman longboat!" Peter shouted. "Get below!" he shouted as he approached the others. "Get below! Pirates!"

Justin ran to Eleni and took her below to Rashad's cabin. "Lock the door!" he ordered as he headed back on deck.

Justin joined Peter and Omar amidships. Rashad spread the word and soon the entire vessel was on alert. Her sails were fully rigged. "Can we outrun them?" Justin asked Rashad.

"The wind is at our backs," Rashad answered as he worriedly looked back at the rapidly approaching longboat. "Under these circumstances, that square sail gives him the advantage. And he is considerably lighter than we are."

Justin anxiously watched the pirate ship, praying for another foot or two between them and the danger. But it was now obvious. Soon she would cut them off.

"What if we turn around?" Peter asked.

"We'll sail right into them!" Rashad objected.

"They're almost on us! That boat's faster and more maneuverable than we are. We are heavier and can move better into the wind. Our only hope is to surprise them."

"And *collide* with them?" Rashad continued to protest.

"We'll take out the portside oars," Peter answered. "She'll be paralyzed."

"No!"

"Then be prepared to fight to the death!"

Justin detected doubt in Peter's voice. He wasn't sure Peter's argument was valid but it seemed the only option available to them. They both looked across the starboard and saw the longboat closing the gap between them. Justin looked back to Peter who cursed under his breath. "Rashad! We must act now!"

Rashad said nothing.

"It's our only chance!" Peter insisted.

Rashad begrudgingly nodded his head and told Omar the plan. At first the first mate raised his eyebrows but Rashad insisted and the first mate raced among the crewmen, issuing orders and preparing the ship.

Peter looked at the orientation of the lateen sails. They were rigged to starboard. *Perfect!* "Starboard, Rashad," Peter ordered gently. "On my signal."

The captain nodded.

Justin turned to Peter, hoping for an explanation but Peter's attention was now on the rapidly approaching Norman vessel. When she was two hundred yards away, Peter nodded to Rashad who gave the signal to the steersman who turned the rudder hard to starboard. The ship groaned as she abruptly turned about to starboard. She slowed as her bow turned from due west to northwest.

Justin saw the longboat approaching the ship. *My God! This is the end of us!* He dropped to his knees and bowed his head in supplication. He felt the ship continuing her turn to starboard. She was at ninety degrees to her former course, heading due north. The wind still filled her sails but the Normans were fast approaching. *Dear God! In the name of Christ I beg you!*

The ship let out a loud groan and Justin opened his eyes. The lighter Norman vessel continued to close the distance between the two ships. He again looked at Peter who patiently waited for the ship to complete her one-hundred-eighty-degree turn. As she did, she headed straight for the pirate longboat.

Rashad's ship was now at forty-five degrees to the wind. She had slowed but like all ships rigged with triangular sails, she could still maneuver. Peter's face showed his determination. Rashad's showed his uncertainty.

"This *will* work, Rashad!" Peter said calmly.

The longboat was now fifty-five feet away and the pirates were ready to board Rashad's ship. Peter watched the longboat carefully, then turned to Rashad and shouted, "Now!"

Rashad gave the order. The helmsman pulled the ship to port and directly at the longboat. The pirates turned their stearing board quickly to starboard but not quickly enough. The bow of the sailing ship splintered the longboat's portside oars as she sped past the pirate ship, leaving her disabled.

As the sailing ship sailed past the crippled longboat, Rashad and Justin embraced Peter and cheered at the top of their voices. "That was incredible, Peter!" Rashad added. "Where did you learn to do that?"

The attack devastated the crew of the longboat, throwing the captain, a giant of a man, into the middle of his oarsmen, where he struck his head on the end of an oar. The collision threw several of the crewmen out of position. But just as a wild beast is most dangerous when it's wounded, the pirate captain's fury pushed them to immediate action.

As the sailing ship splintered the last of the longboat's portside oars, the captain ran to the stern with his first mate. Along the way, they gathered two grappling ropes. When they arrived astern, they threw them with all of their might toward the stern of the passing sailing ship. The first mate's rope fell short but the captain's firmly grabbed the stern gunwale of the sailing ship. The captain raised his fist in triumph and a loud roar erupted on the longboat.

The abrupt tug at the stern of his ship alerted Rashad and Peter that they were not out of danger. The crew, who had been, until a second ago, enwrapped in the thrill of their daring escape, looked astern to see twelve of the pirates pulling rabidly on the grappling rope, inching their vessel closer to the sailing ship.

The captain quickly inspected his ship's portside and saw that half of the oars on that side were shattered. The damage to the hull was mostly superficial. He was in no hurry to attack his quarry. There was no way for them to get away this time. When he was satisfied with his vessel's seaworthiness, he ordered his men to attack. A dozen pirates were the first wave of the attack. They brandished swords and maces as they ran toward the bow, screaming their warcry as they came.

Rashad and Peter ran to the stern with Omar and Justin, gathering up about half of the crew to expel the interlopers. The crewmen grabbed whatever they could: swords, boat hooks, hammers . . . . One of them brought a lance, another, a bow and quiver of arrows.

The pirates continued to storm over the stern rail. They were outnumbered nearly two to one, but were better equipped than Rashad's crew and were particularly fierce. Two of them lunged into four of the crewmen with wild abandon. The rest poured toward the bow, hacking and jabbing as they went.

With their swords, Peter and Rashad quickly dispatched two pirates. Justin proved equally valiant and sent two other pirates over the side with a boat hook. Omar climbed twelve feet up the main mast and flew down upon the pirate first mate, slashing his throat with a knife.

The rest of Rashad's crew did not fare well. The marauding pirates were seasoned killers, borne out by their rapid slaying of ten of the crew in the first fifteen minutes of the battle. The pirate captain was particularly vicious. With one blow from his long sword, he sliced through two Arabs. Anybody who came within three feet of him was soon dead. The pirate crew saw this and rallied behind their captain. They knew that the ship would soon be theirs.

Eleni heard the fracas above. Most of the action had moved amidships and that things weren't going well at all. She had to act. She was their only chance. Eleni slowly opened the cabin door and crept up the stairs to the deck. She poked her head up from below and saw the action on deck move toward the bow. Unfortunately, her instincts were correct. The ship would soon be lost.

Eleni quickly ran to the stern and looked over the rail at the deserted longboat. She desperately inspected it. *There must be something here.* Then she saw it. Amidships was a small brazier, still burning low. At the bow were four short javelins. She would have to make do with what she had. She shot a glance toward the bow of Rashad's ship, then turned back to the longboat, took a breath, and shimmied, feet first, over the rope, across the small cleft between the boats. Her smaller size and agility helped in the crossing. When she reached the longboat, she threw her right leg over the gunwale and pulled herself onto the pirate ship.

Once there, Eleni ran to the brazier. She found a wool blanket nearby and used it to grab the charcoal-filled vessel by its hot ends. With ease, she spilled the glowing coals on to the longboat's wooden deck and set the corner of the blanket in the embers. She ran to the bow and retrieved the four javelins.

Rashad and Peter fought the pirates, side-by-side, on the starboard. Omar and Justin tried to hold the pirate advance on the port. The pirate casualties climbed but the Arab sailors continued to fall, too.

The pirate captain was at least two heads taller than Justin. His long golden hair was tucked under his conical iron helmet. His flowing red beard was stained by the blood of his victims. No one had layed a hand on this titan. His maniacal abilities and long sword had decimated Rashad's crew. He wielded his long blade with such skill that those unfortunate enough to cross his path were slain or maimed. His advance was ruthless; it terrified the Arabs and inspired the Normans. So far, he had not encountered Peter, Justin, Rashad, or Omar but as he and his men pushed Rashad and his crew toward the tapering bow, a collision was inevitable.

On the longboat, Eleni gathered the four javelins together. They were light and easy to carry. She threw each one individually onto the stern of the sailing ship and returned as she had come, over the ropes that held the ships together. She looked back at the longboat and saw that the embers of the brazier consuming the wool blanket she'd placed among them. By the time she got back on board the ship, the deck of the longboat was afire.

When Eleni turned to retrieve the javelins, a burly hand grabbed her arm. A pirate smiled menacingly and said something she didn't understand. He laughed and pulled her toward him. Eleni thought quickly. He was a strong man so fighting him would be useless. She offered only token resistance and looked around as quickly she could. How could she get to the javelins?

The pirate grabbed her head and pulled it toward him. He pressed her face into his and smeared his sweaty lips over hers. Eleni spat at him so he'd move his head away. He laughed at her and forced another kiss on her. This time, Eleni bit his lip as hard as she could. He screamed in agony and then backhanded her across the face, sending her to the deck. He grabbed his lip and growled when he saw his blood.

The pirate reached down for her but Eleni quickly rolled away. He lunged at her and grabbed an ankle but Eleni kicked him in the head and hopped away. The burly Norman shot up and ran after her. She dove for one of the javelins and seconds later, the pirate dove for her. As she landed on the deck, Eleni grabbed the javelin with both hands and quickly rolled over onto her back, pointing the short spear upward.

The Norman realized his misfortune only after his body landed on Eleni. He felt weak and then coughed on her. When he saw blood on her face, he knew it was his. He gasped and grunted and collapsed on top of her.

Eleni struggled frantically to liberate herself from the massive corpse on top of her. She pulled herself free and wiped the blood from her face. There was no time to lose. She grabbed the other javelins and ran toward the bow.

The pirate captain finished off another of Rashad's crewmen. He pulled his massive sword from the chest of the unfortunate man and looked for his next victim. He spotted Omar and prepared his huge weapon. As Justin battled another pirate, he saw the gigantic captain approach and shouted at Omar, just as the attacker was upon him. "Duck!" Justin yelled in the best Arabic he'd ever spoken. Omar complied, falling to the deck. The captain's blade landed in the thigh of one of his own crewman. The wounded man cried in anguish as the sword sliced through his hamstrings and lodged in his femur. The pirate captain callously freed his blade from his crewman's thigh and the wounded pirate collapsed.

The pirate captain was directly ahead of Eleni. She gasped, watching the Goliath move toward Omar as she hurried forward undetected. Omar's defense was a short sword. He called to Rashad who was busy fighting off two pirates. Justin was closest to Omar and he shouted to him that both he and Rashad couldn't come to his aid. Omar tried to call for Peter but the severity of the moment dried his mouth. Speech was impossible.

The pirate jabbed at Omar with his sword. Omar moved to the side and lunged toward the attacker. The mighty pirate backhanded him with the hilt of his sword and Omar fell away. The crashing blow momentarily stunned the Arab, making it difficult for him to find his feet. As Omar stood up, the pirate hacked at his left side. Again, Omar moved aside and avoided injury, but when he dove out of the way of the pirate's sword, he collided with another pirate and was knocked to the ground. This time, the giant pirate ran up to his fallen prey. It was time to finish him. Omar struggled to get up. The pirate captain waited for him. Omar tried to yell for Rashad again but the huge pirate had him. There was no way out.

Eleni ran to the main mast, clutching three javelins in her hands. The pirate captain was ready to finish Omar. Eleni hesitated. *Can I hit him from here?* She had thrown sticks and stones, but not a weapon of war. Should she try to run him through? *He's far too large.* She heard Omar scream for Rashad. *I've got to do it now!* Eleni dropped two of the javelins and grasped the third tightly in her right hand. She took a deep breath, stepped out from behind the mast, and ran forward. The mighty giant glared at his quarry, helpless on the deck. He raised his massive blade over his head and let out of war cry as he swung the sword forward. Omar screamed, anticipating his death any moment.

But the giant's war cry halted abruptly. His arms froze above his head. He felt a burning in his back, just under his left shoulder blade. He grew weak, dropped his sword, and collapsed in front of Omar. There was a loud *thunk* when his head hit the deck. Thirty feet behind the fallen titan, Omar saw Eleni standing where she'd launched the lethal missile.

The pirate captain's unforeseen death abruptly stopped all of the fighting. The Normans and Arabs alike froze in disbelief when the monster's lifeless body crashed to the deck. When he failed to move, the pirates panicked. They quickly disengaged from the fracas and ran sternward toward their longboat. They ran past Eleni as if she weren't there.

The Arabs, emboldened by the death of the pirate captain, gave chase, Omar in the lead and Rashad and Peter right behind. When the pirates reached the sailing ship's stern they found their ship ablaze. They turned around to find Rashad's crew nearly upon them. It didn't take long for each of them to choose the uncertainty of the sea over incineration in their longboat or certain death at the hands of the vengeful Arabs.

Justin stopped amidships and embraced his wife. He lifted her off the deck as he held her tightly. They laughed and cried and kissed and embraced. They could hear the triumphant crew yelling wildly as the defeated pirates swam away. Peter cut the rope that held the two vessels together and Omar used a boat hook to push the blazing longboat away. The crew cheered as the pirate ship floated away, smoke billowing from her deck. Omar led the ship's complement amidships to Eleni. Justin beamed as the elated crewmen cheered around them.

"Eleni," Rashad began, "we all owe you our lives! Thank you!" He took her hands and gently squeezed them.

"Justin, is there anything your wife can't do?" Peter asked, hugging Eleni.

Omar came up to her, bowed, said something in Arabic, and bowed again. The rest of the crew followed Omar. Each bowed to her and thanked her. Eleni modestly accepted their praise. However, the elation ebbed as the crew returned to their fallen comrades. Thirteen of the crew were slain and twelve were badly injured.

Amin gently washed their gashes and gouges with cool water. Omar prepared bandages for the physician. Eleni ran to Omar and silently offered assistance.

Peter and Rashad saw how difficult it would be to continue their journey to Venice. They were short on able-bodied crewmen to sail the ship. Duty shifts would be increased and the effect on the crew would be telling.

"We'll need favorable winds to get us to Venice," Peter began. "We don't have the manpower for sustained maneuvering against headwinds."

"I don't want to put in at any other ports until we are at Venice," Rashad added. "Another pirate attack will be the end of us. We're well-provisioned now but in less than a week, our supplies will be exhausted."

"Yes. And that makes the wind that much more critical."

Justin and Eleni overheard the conversation while walking toward them. "Then we will have to pray for good winds," Justin said.

"Yes," Rashad agreed, looking at Justin and Eleni, "we will."

Their prayers were soon answered. The wind blew out of the east at twenty knots. The white lanteen sails billowed in the forceful wind. The ship gracefully sliced through the calm, green-blue sea. Amin and Rashad met amidships. Most of the wounded were recovering, although slowly. Three of the more seriously wounded succumbed to their wounds. Amin led a brief funeral service and their lifeless, shrouded bodies were ceremoniously delivered to the sea.

The late summer sun shone in the cloudless sky. The extra provisions that Peter requested served them well. The ship stayed out at sea and cruised steadily as her crew recovered from the pirate attack. That evening at sunset, Peter ordered extra portions of food for the hard-working crew.

Justin and Eleni joined Omar, Rashad, and Peter. They celebrated their victory with dried fish, bread, and apples, and relived their latest adventure, thanking God, praising Eleni, and mourning their fallen comrades. The exhausted soon crew retired. Peter led a small watch that remained at their stations until midnight. Omar and a second watch relieved them at midnight and tended to the ship until dawn.

The next morning was overcast. Some of the crewmen of the second watch surprised everyone by catching fish before sunrise. The wind speed dropped to fifteen knots but maintained its favorable direction. The overcast day was uneventful; something appreciated by all. The low-hanging clouds twisted the declining sun's rays into a polychromatic panorama: blues and purples complementing the vivid reds, oranges, and yellows. Eleni and Justin held each other as they drank in the spectacle before them.

"Justin," Eleni began, "can you imagine what it will be like to see our families again? I can see your father smiling proudly."

"That's about as emotional as he gets," Justin chuckled. "I think your mother will be a sight to behold." They both laughed. "She won't be able to contain herself!"

Eleni lapsed deep into thought at the mention of her mother. She again felt the longing for her that she had experienced during her residence at the Palace Bucoleon. She smiled. They would have so much to share, she thought but as she remembered her own perilous voyage, her heart sank. Certainly her parents' journey to Venice was not without its own dangers. Eleni remembered Stathopoulos, the storm, the pirates. *Dear Lord! Were they alive? Had they been captured and sold into slavery? Did they arrive in Venice safely? Please, God, let it be so!*

"Justin," Eleni began, "what if we arrive in Venice and find that our families . . ." she hesitated, "aren't there?"

"Eleni, Giovanni Rossi has made that journey dozens of times. They're safe; I'm certain of it."

Eleni looked sharply at him. "But Justin—"

"We *must* believe that!" he interrupted. "I know that our prayers for them have not gone unattended by God. They will be there!" he added forcefully. Then he calmed down and looked tenderly at her. "Wasn't it just a few days ago that you were chiding me about my lack of faith?"

She smiled back. "Yes, it was." His faith had grown in these last days. It is indeed a gift to be able to believe easily. Few people had this gift, although many claimed to. She knew it did not always come easily to her. Children certainly had it. The Lord had confirmed this when He said that we are to come to him as children, hearts open, ready to believe. "You're right, Justin," she said. "We must believe." Her heart kept whispering to her, between her mind's firm declarations of doubt, that her husband was indeed correct. For her own peace of mind, she decided to listen to her heart, not her mind.

Peter walked over to them. "Another beautiful evening at sea!" he sighed.

"It is wonderful," Eleni and Justin agreed.

"Justin," Peter inquired, "could you take the first watch tonight?"

"Sure. I'd love to, Koumbarro."

"Thanks, Justin. Rashad will relieve you at midnight." Peter grabbed a blanket, found a quiet spot on deck, and fell asleep within minutes.

Eleni yawned and hugged her husband. "Peter's got the right idea," she said. She could see that despite his earlier declarations, Justin was still having his doubts.

Justin was slow to answer. "Yes," he grunted his agreement. "Rashad has offered the cabin for us tonight. Why don't you go to bed? I'll join you after Rashad relieves me."

Eleni gently pulled her husband's head toward her. "Our families are fine, remember?"

Justin looked into her bright hazel eyes and smiled. "I remember." He smiled and kissed her as she wrapped her arms around his neck and sweetened their embrace.

"Goodnight, Justin," Eleni whispered, releasing him.

"Goodnight, my dear. Sleep well." His eyes didn't leave her as she walked across the deck.

Rashad arrived promptly at midnight. Justin was still seated on the deck. To him, the hours had flown by.

"How was your watch, Justin?"

"No problems, Rashad. The crew changed shifts an hour ago. The wind has picked up."

"Good! Very good!"

Rashad sat next to Justin but looked out at the sea, as if to avoid Justin's eyes.

"We've made good progress," Rashad said without turning to Justin.

"Yes, we have."

"My crewmen are the best."

"I've noticed," Justin said. He knew this chit chat indicated a feeling of trepidation.

"Peter's quite a seaman," Rashad said, a slight quaver in his voice.

"Yes, you told me that yesterday."

Rashad hesitated before he spoke. "Justin . . . ."

"Yes, Rashad?" Justin replied, anticipating.

"You've been very helpful to me, Justin," he began, "I mean, about the monastery and Isa. Thank you."

Justin recognized "Isa" as the Arab name for Jesus. "You're welcome," he said, knowing that there was more to come.

"I have been saying the prayer that you taught me . . . ."

"Oh, that's good," Justin sensed Rashad's need for encouragement.

"I've taught it to Omar," Rashad added, knowing it would surprise Justin.

"Omar?" Justin was flabbergasted. "Why did —"

"Two nights ago, he asked me about the monastery . . . ."

"Oh?"

"I told him everything, even about our discussions."

"What did he say?" Justin asked uneasily.

"At first he reacted violently. He said that the idolatrous infidels had seduced me. He cursed the day we first found you in Anatolia."

"Did he threaten you?"

"Almost. As I said, he was very upset at first. Then I reminded him that we have known each other for many years. I told him how hard it was for me to face this."

"Why did you teach him the prayer?"

"I told him more about Therapeftikos and the icons. I told him that," Rashad struggled for the right words, "he owed his life to the Christians."

"What did he say?"

"He denounced it all as magic, witchcraft. He condemned me as a traitor to Islam."

"Then what happened?"

"I told him about my nightmares, the icons, and finally his healing. And then I told him about my doubts about Islam and about the feelings I now have in my heart."

"What did he say then?"

"He spat in my face."

"Rashad, I'm sorry."

"But then he remembered how long we've known each other. He apologized and said he felt confused by what I was telling him. Then he left. The next day, he acted like nothing had happened. Until last night . . . ."

"What happened then?"

"Your wife saved his life that day! Don't you remember?"

Justin smiled sheepishly. "Yes."

"That night, he came to me and asked my forgiveness. Of course, I gave it without a second thought but he said he was afraid. He appeared as I did when I first spoke to you of the monastery."

"What did he want?"

"He told me he was ready to listen to me. He realized that the miracle at the monastery had healed him and he felt that Allah used Eleni to save his life. Surely, if a man had saved his life, he'd have paid it no heed, but for a woman to do so, that could only happen through divine intervention." Justin chuckled. "So I did as he asked: I taught him the Lord's Prayer this morning."

"Does he want to speak to me?" Justin asked.

"No, Omar isn't ready for that yet but he's still curious and asks me about many things."

"Can I help you more?"

"Later. You have been very helpful. Thank you for your patience."

Justin stood and started toward the cabin below decks. "And how are you feeling, Rashad?"

Rashad chuckled. "I feel that I am at the beginning of a very long journey. A very long journey."

Justin smiled again. "I wish you the best in your journey."

"Thank you, Justin."

In the next two days, more and more of the wounded crewmen returned to their duties. Amin's dutiful attendance, as well as the continued prayers of the crew and their guests, sped the healing. Peter and Rashad reviewed the map. By the next morning they would pass Tergeste and, from there, would cruise past Aquileia by midday. They'd be in Venice by the following morning.

Rashad and Peter reminisced about the dark tunnels of Saint Barbara's convent. Peter laughed when he remembered how Justin looked in a nun's habit. They remembered the storms and their near-capture by Stathopoulos, and their heroic battle against the Norman pirates. Emotion overcame them and they embraced.

Ironically, it was the adventure that they didn't mention that weighed heavily on both of their minds. To Peter, the monastery had been an uplifting experience, confirming and reinforcing his faith. Obviously that early morning's events had some kind of effect on Rashad. He wondered what had gone through Rashad's mind at that time but he couldn't reach out to his friend and ask him. Here was someone with whom he had negotiated some extremely dangerous situations; each had placed his life in the hands of the other but the closeness they felt didn't transcend the spiritual plane. Perhaps this was Peter's doing. He was a very private man, especially when it came to God. After all, he hadn't even discussed the monastery with Justin.

Rashad had a great deal of respect for Peter. Their friendship, though still relatively young, was strong. He would feel at ease discussing anything else with Peter, except the monastery. That was most likely why he chose Justin who was much more approachable than Peter. Or was it because Justin had known his brother? He didn't know, but he felt fortunate that Justin had agreed to speak with him that night. Justin's easy manner and his willingness to listen made the experience a good one for him. His decision had been rewarding. His soul, after so much torment, was resting easily. He still had questions, dozens of them, but he knew the answers would come, given time.

The ship eased into the harbor at Tergeste and anchored there. A sudden storm had made the large harbor a more appealing place to be than at sea. Within an hour, the storm abated and the ship continued toward Venice. By midday, the sailors could see Aquileia in the distance. Excitement spread; they knew this next port would be Venice. After all of this time and the loss of so many of their comrades, they were but a day from their destination.

Rashad had never been to Venice but he knew many traders who traded with the Venetians frequently. Most of them had been to the city. He tried to remember what his friends had told him of this cluster of mud islands, located in a tranquil lagoon at the northern tip of the Adriatic Sea.

That night, everyone on board celebrated the approaching end of the long journey. They prepared extra food and played music to accompany the evening repast. When all had had their fill of fish, fresh fruits, and bread, the crewmen sang and played games with great joy. At midnight, Rashad reluctantly ordered the crew to work or to sleep. They'd have plenty of time to celebrate in Venice.

By the middle of the next day, Peter, sitting attentively at the ship's bow, caught sight of the entrance to the Venetian lagoon. He felt a particular sense of satisfaction along with his nearly uncontrollable joy. Their odyssey was nearing its end. He went to Rashad and pointed out the lagoon.

Although none of the crewmen spoke Greek, they knew what Peter was talking about when he repeatedly said "Venice" to their leader. They stirred excitedly. Rashad gently reminded them that their work was not done. He ordered the crew to prepare to dock.

Justin stood with Eleni and looked ahead at the oncoming land. "They'll be there," Justin whispered.

Eleni hugged him and kissed his lips. "I know."

The ship cruised through the channel between the two thin islands that guarded the Lagoon of Venice. Justin joined Peter at the bow. He saw the group of small islands that made up Venice. Their ship was not alone in the lagoon. Five large galleys appeared out of nowhere and three small sailing ships soon joined them. The crews exchanged greetings as the ships passed toward the same destination.

Rashad's ship approached the city from the southeast and followed the other ships to a large channel that separated the cluster of islands into two halves. The southward-facing docks swelled with activity. As the ship pulled into one of the docks, Rashad hugged Omar and shouted out in celebration. He ran to his crewmen and guests and embraced them all. As the jubilation spread, it didn't go unnoticed by those on the wharf and nearby boats.

A short, thin man on a distant wharf took particular notice of the noisy ship. He walked toward it, paying particular attention to three of those on board. Eleni and Peter spoke with Rashad and didn't notice him, but Justin happened to catch a glimpse of him out of the corner of his eye. He didn't think much of the young Venetian at first until he noticed the man staring at him. He automatically stared back. Then Justin saw the man say something as his face grew pale. Soon the man ran up and down the wharf, looking as confused as could be. *What's wrong with that fellow?* Justin slowly recognized him. "Giovanni!" he yelled to the man. "Giovanni Rossi!"

The short man suddenly came to his senses and ran toward the ship. "Justin? I can't believe it's you! Justin! Thank God you are safe!"

The crew set the gangplank and Justin rushed down to Giovanni. They embraced and laughed and cried. Justin looked at him soberly. "Our parents?"

"Are at my father's! Everyone is well! "Eleni?" Giovanni asked.

Justin turned and saw her looking down at them. "Giovanni!" she yelled. She ran to him and embraced him and kissed his cheek. "Oh thank God! It's so good to see you!" She suddenly looked uncertain. "Our parents?"

"They're fine!" Giovanni reassured her. "They're all fine!"

"Oh, thank God!" she cried. She buried her face in her husband's chest and let her tears flow.

As Justin comforted her, he could feel the tears welling up in his eyes. "Thank God!" he whispered to her, "thank God!"

Giovanni met Rashad and shook Peter's hand and he welcomed them all to Venice. He led Justin, Eleni, Peter, and Rashad through Venice to his father's house. Omar and Amin opted to stay on board with the crew. As they left the docks, they proceeded north through a forum. At the eastern edge of this square was a new church that Peter stopped to admire.

"Saint Mark's Basilica," Giovanni informed him.

"It looks exactly like the Church of the Holy Apostles in Constantinople," Peter said under his breath. He delighted in the five-domed church in the shape of a Greek cross. *Beautiful!* He reflected on the largest central dome and each of the four smaller domes at each of the four extremities of the cross. *Exactly like the Holy Apostles!*

"The first church was built in the early 800s to house the body of Saint Mark," Giovanni explained as they all made their way to his father's house. "Fire destroyed the church ninety-five years ago. This structure was completed only eight years ago. Earlier this year the mosaics were started."

They arrived at the Rossi house within a few minutes. A servant greeted Giovanni as the five of them entered the home. Giovanni's father, Ludovico, just happened to be walking down the hall when he noticed his son and his guests.

"Lord Christ above!" he gasped, running toward Justin. They embraced and the older man patted Justin on the back. "Your father will be so . . ." Ludovico burst into tears and couldn't complete his sentence.

Giovanni introduced the others to his father. The older man hugged Eleni, whom he had met but once before. He gently kissed her on the cheek. He gripped Peter's and then Rashad's hands as he welcomed them to his home.

He smiled at Justin. "So good to see you again! Come with me." Justin felt his heart pounding. At long last, he was going to be with his family again and Eleni with hers. He thought of his father. Only a soldier could appreciate what he and Peter, let alone Eleni and Rashad, had been through. The moment he had been waiting for so long was finally here.

Justin looked at Eleni and saw her wipe a tear from her eye. She tightened her grip on his hand as Ludovico led them down the hallway and to a great room at the end of the hall.

Justin almost didn't recognize his father. Basilios sat in a large chair, disengaged from everyone. He looked like he hadn't slept in a month and had lost weight. The gray in his hair had spread beyond his temples and covered most of each side of his head; his once powerful eyes seemed weak and weary.

Eleni's mother Aspasia busily chatted with Justin's mother, Martha. One could never guess that these women had just fled their homes and traveled hundreds of miles by sea to an unknown city.

Eleni's father, Demetrios, spotted them first. "Eleni! Justin!" he yelled. "Dear God! Look! They're here!" He ran to them and embraced his daughter and then Justin. Aspasia and Martha joined him at their children's sides, crying for joy. "Thank God you are here! Thank God!" Warm embraces and kisses followed. No one could get enough. "Thank God we are all together now!"

Last of all, Basilios, looking at them as if he couldn't believe his eyes, joined them. When it finally hit him that Justin was standing in front of him, the always stoic Basilios melted like hot butter. He bawled like a child. "You're alive!" he cried. "You're alive! Thank Christ you're alive!" Justin held his father tightly. "Thank Christ!" he whimpered over and over as he collapsed into his son's arms.

"Yes, Father," Justin said, trying to comfort him, "I'm alive." He, too, wept as his father continued to hold on to him. Justin turned his head and saw his mother was behind him, tears streaming from her eyes as she gazed with joy and relief at her beloved son.

"I knew God would protect you," Martha said. She crossed herself and hugged him from behind.

Aspasia Nikopoulos embraced her daughter tightly. "There was never a doubt in my mind that I would see you again."

"How did you know, Mother?" Eleni aked as she stepped back a bit.

"Every night, the Lord sent me a dream and every dream ended with you in my arms, just like now."

"Dreams, Mother?"

"They were the strangest dreams imaginable: First you were in a convent, then in a ship on a stormy sea, and once you were attacked by pirates!"

"Pirates?" Eleni asked uneasily.

"I know it's silly."

Only with difficulty did Eleni conceal her amazement at the accuracy of her mother's prescience. "No, Mother," she smiled, "Your dreams were not silly."

"What do you mean?"

"You have always told me that God talks to us through our dreams."

"The pirates were real?"

Eleni hugged her mother tightly. "We will have a great deal of time to tell our stories, Mother. For now, I just want to hold you!"

"And I you," Aspasia added with a tear.

Justin introduced Rashad to his and Eleni's parents. They welcomed Peter, too. Justin's uncles, Alexander, Leo, and Theodore had gone for a walk in the city with Justin's brothers and Eleni's sister and their spouses. Messengers were summoned to bring them back.

Ludovico brought food and wine. They celebrated by punctuating the meal with tales of both journeys to Venice. The parents' journey was fairly uneventful. The weather was most cooperative, except for a mild storm off the coast of Kephalonia. Ludovico had obtained special privileges from the Roman government. His ships were never searched and oftentimes were allowed to sail with Roman warships if they shared the same destination. They were lucky enough to encounter a Roman galley off Dyrrachium. The ship carried an emissary from the imperial court to the court of Hungary. It was on its way to Tergeste and it had guided them through the pirate-infested waters of the Adriatic.

Peter told their story to Justin's and Eleni's families. They listened quietly, the women frequently crossing themselves during the telling. Needless to say, the tale of Justin's and Peter's adventures in Anatolia and the events that followed left the parents fascinated. When Peter told of all of their experiences in Constantinople and at sea, a surprised Aspasia looked at Eleni and gasped. Her daughter smiled back at her. Aspasia crossed herself and later told Eleni, "It truly was an angel that sent me those dreams!"

When the others returned from their outing, the celebration was reinvigorated. Peter happily retold their story and the parents enjoyed hearing it again.

Uncle Theodore was most impressed that his powdery gift to Justin had played such an important part in Justin's adventure. "I knew it would serve you well, Justin!" he beamed.

As night fell, the newly arrived voyagers were exhausted. Giovanni showed them to their rooms and Justin and Eleni fell into each other's arms.

"It's over, Eleni," Justin sighed. "Thank God! It's finally over!"

Eleni embraced her husband and kissed him as if they had been apart for years. When she released him, she whispered, "Justin, my darling. I am with child!"

Part IV

EXILE

CHAPTER 24

The thick morning fog was just beginning to lift from the waters of Venice's lagoon when Justin reached for his cup. The cool water felt good going down. He had stared into this soup for over an hour and he hadn't seen a thing, not that he was trying to. He'd been lost in thought. They had arrived in Venice over two and a half years ago but Justin wasn't thinking of that. On this morning, like any other of the past two years, Justin's mind was in Constantinople.

He turned toward the bed in the corner of the dimly lit room. There, he saw that Eleni had dozed off while nursing their new daughter Aspasia. The baby continued to suckle, oblivious to her mother's light snoring. A midwife had delivered her in this bed three weeks ago. This gift from heaven had jet-black hair and lots of it.

In the other corner of the room, his older daughter, Martha, who in two months would be two years old, turned over in her small bed. Eleni and Justin had followed the ancient custom, naming their first daughter after Justin's mother and their second after Eleni's. If their daughters had been sons, the same custom would have applied, with their sons acquiring the names of first Justin's father and then Eleni's father.

Martha had taken to her father early and cried inconsolably when he was not around. It came as no surprise to anyone that when she was nine months of age, the first word from her mouth was "dadda." Upon awakening, she would immediately find her father and give him his marching orders for the day. Of course these always included finding her a small toy or something sweet to eat. Her favorite indulgence was a ride on Justin's shoulders.

She found it most convenient that her father was equipped with an ear on each side. How better to guide her steed than by purposeful tugging on one ear or the other? Justin chuckled as he thought of her. *How much like Eleni she is!*

The baby grew fussy and Justin walked over to her. Her breakfast had been interrupted when her mouth drifted from her mother's breast. Justin gently rectified the situation without awakening Eleni. He bent forward, his face within a few feet of his new daughter. Aspasia's little gray eyes suddenly open and he looked into them. *Such a beautiful child!* She looked at him and studied his face. *What are you thinking, little one?* Justin tried to interest her in his little finger but she would have none of it. She concentrated on her mother's breast but, every now and then, her curiosity would get the best of her and she would steal a glance at her father. Justin would smile back at her when she did so. He kept watch on her, treasuring every glance she shot his way. Soon Aspasia tired of both eating and playing with her father and drifted off to sleep.

Justin stood up and walked to the window and when he got there, he turned and looked back at his family. He crossed himself and thanked God for these precious gifts.

A soft rapping at the door broke Justin's concentration. He quietly slipped over to the door and opened it. On the other side, he found Uncle Theodore holding a letter in his hand.

"Justin," Theodore whispered, "I knew you'd be up. I've got a letter here . . . from Rashad!"

Justin moved quickly. He slid out the door, closing it as softly as he could. "What's this? A letter from Rashad?"

Theodore smiled. "I knew you would want to see this. Come with me." He led Justin down the corridor to a sitting area. They sat facing each other.

"It seems as if he left just yesterday," Justin began. "I still remember their baptisms."

Rashad and his men had stayed for over a month and were eager to leave. They had been away from home for a long time and the Venetians had confined them to that hostel by the docks. Rashad and Omar knew it was unfair to ask their men to endure anymore.

"Do you think they told their men of their conversion and baptism?" Justin asked. "Rashad told me he would find the appropriate time. I don't know when that would be. The Koran forbids a Muslim to leave the faith, you know."

"Of course." Theodore replied.

Justin thought of the new burden Rashad and Omar had acquired. "What did you talk about with them anyway? We've never discussed that."

"What do you mean?"

"What did you say to them that convinced them to be baptized and embrace our faith?"

Justin's uncle sighed. "Justin, nothing that I said had any impact at all. They had questions about details, tiny, insignificant, theological details. They were already convinced of what they were going to do. Talking to me only confirmed what they had decided before. Maybe there was something you told Rashad on the ship."

"I told him very little, Uncle. He had more questions than answers when I finished talking to him. I told him to speak with you to get these questions answered."

"Justin, as you know, I've learned a great deal about many things in my correspondences. I have several correspondents among the Saracens, in Cairo, Baghdad, Damascus, and other places. We would debate the merits of our faiths freely, each respecting the views of the other. I learned a great deal about the Mohammedans and also a great deal about my own faith in our Lord Jesus Christ. I believe I gave a good account of Christianity."

"Did any of your correspondents want to convert?"

Theodore laughed. "It takes more than an intellectual exchange to change a man's faith, especially men like Rashad and Omar. They have to experience Christian love, not just hear Christian rhetoric. Men often see God's wisdom as folly."

"And God sees Man's wisdom as folly," Justin added.

"I see you remember our last conversation on this subject," Theodore chuckled. "Approach the Lord as a child, Justin, always as a child," he added, his tone more serious. "No, Justin, I believe that Rashad was right. Someone spoke to him that night in the monastery on Delos."

Justin's eyes grew wide at Theodore's suggestion. "Do you think he was called?"

"He was chosen," Theodore said calmly but emphatically. "Unlike many, Rashad would have weathered any theological debate easily. I could have spoken endlessly of God's grace and His Son's atoning death on the cross, and His miraculous Resurrection but that wouldn't register more than a pillow being dropped at Rashad's feet. The monastery . . . that hit Rashad like a a bolt of lightening."

"But what about Omar?"

"He saw what was happening to Rashad. Omar knew that his friend's faith, once very strong and secure, had been shaken to its foundation by that night in the monastery."

"Why didn't either of them tell the crew at that time?"

"Would you have?"

"Yes!"

Theodore roared with laughter. "That's because, Justin, you are like no other man on Earth! God bless you!" Theodore stood and hugged his nephew. "I don't think that Rashad and Omar felt strong enough to confront their friends."

"Well, after talking to you, they were ready to be baptized."

"We talked about many small things, nothing in depth. Rashad and Omar knew what they wanted, or should I say what they needed. They had made the decision long before they spoke to me." Theodore sighed. "It's hard to believe they left over two years ago. I still wonder what their journey to Cyprus was like. I still, after all this time, can't imagine the reaction of the crewmen when Rashad and Omar told them they'd left their faith and would be staying on Cyprus."

"Rashad has never told us much about that in his other three letters," Justin added.

"I wonder what the crew were saying about Omar and Rashad as they sailed back to Tripoli. They could have turned them over to the authorities. It was a wise decision not to travel overland with the crew to Damascus. They would have been found out, I'm certain, even if the crew did not betray them."

"I imagine they were quite angry."

"Angry . . . disappointed . . . or confused?"

"He had been their leader and friend for a long time," Justin said, remembering those crewmen who had saved Eleni, Peter, and him. "They knew him before and they saw what Omar's healing did to him. Perhaps it was out of their great respect for Rashad that they didn't have him arrested."

"They loved him like a brother, or even a father. And how much like brothers was it for Rashad and Omar to give up their shares in the cargo they had brought home? That was very generous but also very expedient."

Justin sighed as he remembered those old friends. "Uncle, why doesn't God reveal himself to all people?"

"What do you mean?"

"Why don't all people believe in God? Why do some doubt that Christ is the Son of God?

"Justin, that is a very good question, one that I'm not sure I can answer. However, I can tell you this. One man sees the blossoming of flower in the spring and shouts praises to God. He sees God in all around him. Another may be shot in the heart with an arrow and, by all reckoning, should be dead. However, he survives. Or he sees the healing of a man given up for dead by the physicians. You or I may call that a miracle and jump for joy, thanking God. Yet this fellow may see it as just a chance occurrence in nature. Do you remember the old philosopher—"

"Lucretius."

"Ah, you are a great pupil, Justin."

"But why is that so? Why doesn't the second man see that hand of God in these things?"

"God gives us the right to choose to believe in Him."

"But why? Why don't we all see Him and believe in Him? Why does he allow some to be blind or distracted by that other than the truth?"

"Because He loves us and knows that we cannot be forced to love Him. What kind of love would that be?"

"So He abandons us?"

"No, quite the contrary. He says He will never do that. He knocks on the door to our heart all of the time, waiting for us to open it."

"I think I've heard that in church."

"Of course you have. He wants to come in but will not force His way in. He loves us that much."

"So how does the Faith spread?"

"Jesus told his disciples to take the Gospel to the ends of the Earth. He charges us with spreading His message and He gives us the power to do so."

"But there are so many that don't believe.'

"The Lord isn't finished yet."

"There are so many things about our faith that I do not understand."

"And so many that I don't understand."

"That doesn't bother you?"

"Not really. What I do know more than makes up for what I don't know. The Apostle John said that God is love and he that loves knows God."

"That sounds like a good place to start."

"Yes, Justin. You're right about that," Theodore added as he tossled Justin's hair.

"How about Rashad's letter?"

"Of course." Theodore held up the letter and read it silently. Without looking up from the page, he announced, "Judging from the date on this letter, it has taken over six months for it to get here."

"Over a month more than his last one," Justin noted.

"Rashad says that his wife and children have adjusted well to their new home on Cyprus," Theodore continued. "He's met other Arab Christians in Nicosia."

"It was one thing for Rashad to tell his crew that he had converted, but to tell his wife Fatima? That would be extremely difficult!"

"Well," Theodore began, "he certainly went about it the right way; he sent for them from Cyprus and told her after they had joined him."

"That must have been difficult for both of them."

"I'm surprised she converted so soon,"

"She must be a very understanding woman,"

"Rashad was rather matter-of-fact about it as he described in his second letter," Theodore said. "But what else could she do? The Koran forbids the marriage of a non-Muslim man to a Muslim woman. If she left him on Cyprus, she and her children would have been alone in Damascus."

"Rashad has many brothers. They would have taken care of her." Justin paused thoughtfully. "I think she loved him too much to let him go."

"Yes, Justin," Theodore said, as if he had not considered that before. "That's probably why."

"What else does Rashad say, Uncle?"

Theodore returned to the letter and read onward. "Oh!" he exclaimed. "What's this?"

Justin looked curiously at his uncle.

Theodore put down the letter. "Omar is to be married!"

"Really?" Justin asked, his face all smiles.

"He is marrying the daughter of an Arab shoemaker!" Theodore quickly returned to the letter. "They are to marry . . . Saturday!"

"This Saturday?"

Theodore read the sentence again and then glanced up at a calendar on the wall. "Yes!"

"Justin," Peter said as he walked through the doorway. "Eleni's mother sent me to find you. Your daughter Martha refuses to eat her breakfast until her father comes."

Uncle Theodore got up from his chair, chortling. "That Martha is just like her mother." He patted Justin on the back and left the room.

Justin and Peter joined the others in the great dining room, which was abuzz with conversation as usual. Martha's face lit up when her father entered the room.

"How's your breakfast?" Justin asked, sitting down next to her.

"Good," Martha replied. She looked at the untouched piece of bread in her little hand. "Want some?" she asked as she shoved it into her father's face.

"No thank you, sweetheart. I'm going to have something else."

"Yogurt?" she suggested, then slid her untapped bowl in front of him.

"If I have some, will you finish it?"

"Oh yes."

"Promise?"

"Oh yes." Martha grabbed a spoon. "Open your mouth!"

Just then, Eleni walked in with the baby and struggled to keep from laughing at the spectacle of Justin, his mouth wide open, patiently waiting for his precocious daughter to feed him.

"Ummm! That's so good!" Justin said after Martha carefully placed a dollop in his mouth.

"Want some more?" she asked, hoping he would comply.

"You promised you'd eat the rest, Martha," Justin reminded her.

"I did?" Martha's feigned forgetfulness brought a laugh to those around the table.

"Yes, you did," Justin said. He rose from the table and kissed her on the head. "Now you be a good girl and show Yiayia Aspasia how well you can eat your breakfast."

"Yes, Father," she answered half-heartedly.

Justin joined the other men at another table where the conversation centered on Ludovico's latest trip to Alexandria. He had been gone nearly a month. While he was there, he had procured some fine Egyptian cotton cloth, which would bring a high price, and Ethiopian gold, which he planned to sell to the local goldsmiths.

"Any news?" Justin asked.

"Nothing new from Constantinople," Ludovico replied sadly.

Basilios walked over to his son and took him aside.

"I know you are eager to return to Constantinople but I want to tell you that the day may never come," Basilios said. "After all, it's already been two years; you've got a family now. I don't mean to be blunt but I don't want you to be disappointed. I'm trying to be realistic."

"Father," Justin began, "don't you miss our home?"

"Not as much as I missed you when you were away from us."

"Don't you want to go back?"

"Perhaps, but everything I love is right here with me, thank God. Don't you feel that way?"

"Well, of course, but I still wonder what happened to everyone: the emperor and empress, Alexios Comnenos, even Zervas."

"You're not content with being safe and with your family?"

"Father," Justin said, his frustration with his father growing, "I won't sleep well until I know. These are all people who played an important part in my life not long ago. I feel a bond with them."

A look of incredulity took over Basilios' face. "The emperor played you for a fool and Zervas treated you like a dog. Why on earth would you give a damn about either of them?"

"I don't know, Father, but there is a sore in my gut that won't heal until I know."

Basilios embraced his son and tried to be as consoling as he could be. *You're too much like your mother, Justin.*

As he returned to his breakfast, Justin saw a servant appear at Ludovico's right hand. He whispered something into his master's ear. Ludovico whispered something back to the man and the servant departed.

After the meal, Ludovico found Justin sitting with his wife and children. "Pardon me, Justin," he interrupted.

Justin stood up and noticed a look on Ludovico's face that required his attention. So he kissed Eleni on the cheek and followed his host out of the room and into the man's study. "Yes, Ludovico," Justin asked. "What is it?"

"This message arrived for you this morning," the host answered, handing a small crumpled piece of parchment to him.

Justin took the tattered parchment and read it. His face clearly displayed his befuddlement.

"What's this all about?"

"I have no idea," Justin said as he raised his head from the paper. He looked at the letter again. "Thank you, Ludovico," he added and quickly walked down the hall to his bedroom.

Justin stepped into the bedroom where Eleni was nursing Aspasia and Martha was napping. He said nothing but Eleni saw the perplexed look on his face and the letter in his hand.

"What's in the letter?" Eleni asked, knowing the source of his confusion.

"It's from Zervas," Justin said as if it were a summons from the devil himself. "He wants Peter and me to meet him at the basilica . . . Saint Mark's."

"Zervas! Here, in Venice?" The baby had drifted off to sleep and Eleni quickly placed her in her cradle. "That can't be good, Justin! If he knows you're here—"

"Then so do the Dukas," Justin calmly completed her thought.

Peter had overheard Eleni in the hall. "Justin! What's this about Zervas here in Venice?" he demanded.

Justin opened the door and showed Peter the letter. He quickly scanned it and shook his head.

"It's a trap, Justin! Obviously he knows where we are. Why doesn't he come here?"

"But how does he know you're here?" Eleni wondered.

After a moment's pause, Peter and Eleni said, "Simon."

"No—" Justin tried to say.

"So he's betrayed us to the Dukas after all!" Peter fumed. "Comnenos is behind this somewhere!"

Justin lost his patience. "Just wait a minute you two! Let me read the rest of the letter to you before you come up with any more cockeyed ideas!"

Peter and Eleni were thrown off by Justin's sudden outburst.

"'I cannot fully express my deep regret,'" Justin read, "'for my involvement in the damnable treachery of the Dukas—'"

"That *treachery* almost got us killed!" Peter interrupted.

Justin looked up from the letter at Peter. That was all that was necessary to silence his choleric friend.

"'After you saved my life in Armenia, God spoke to me. His chiding seared my guilty soul.'" Justin looked up at Peter to forestall an anticipated comment. "'Now I am like the Apostle Paul, a changed man. I hope I demonstrated that the last time I saw you in Constantinople.'" Justin looked up again at Peter who was unconvinced.

"'That good deed nearly cost me my life. Fourteen months later, my act of kindness toward you was betrayed to Caesar John Dukas. I was brought before Emperor Michael and the caesar at the Sacred Palace, and was told my life was at its end. In the morning, I was to be taken to the Hippodrome and, before the usual thousands of spectators, my arms and legs were to be hacked off and the rest of me burned alive with a dozen other traitors.'"

"I would have paid to see that," muttered Peter.

"The man *did* save our lives, Peter," Justin reminded him.

Peter rolled his eyes defiantly.

"'But I was delivered from my prison cell by the grace of God and a short man who came through a tunnel in the floor.'"

"This sounds familiar," Eleni said.

"'I followed the man into the dark, cramped passageway to a room, I know not where. I was blindfolded and given instructions about how I was to leave Constantinople. I was led, like a blind man, down a long winding path to a wharf. While I was still deprived of my sight, I was put in a ship's hold where I was allowed to remove my blindfold, but only after my companion had left the hold. I was left alone for what must have been a week, my only fellowship with the rats that constantly stole my bread. My hosts also provided me with good water and wine but I was in darkness save whatever sunlight made its way through the floorboards of the ship's deck. When we reached port, I was again blindfolded by a man whose face was hidden behind a mask. He led me off the ship and placed me in the care of another who brought me to an inn. He took me to a room and I heard him drop a bag of coins on the table. He instructed me to stay in the room until the following morning. He reminded me that to disobey was to be killed.

"'After he left, I pulled off my blindfold to find myself in a comfortable room, generously supplied with food and drink. The moneybag on the table held more than fifty gold noumismata. The next morning, I ran to the innkeeper to find that I was in Trebizond. He handed me a note that informed me I was being watched. If I left the city, I would be hunted down and killed.'"

"Mother, Father!" Martha noisily announced that she was now awake.

"That wasn't a very long nap," Eleni said.

"Yes, it was," Martha countered, nodding her head.

Eleni knew there was no arguing with her daughter. "I think Yiayia Martha has something to show you," she said as she scooted Martha out of the room.

"Truly, Mother?" Martha asked excitedly as they walked out the door.

"Thank you, Eleni," Justin whispered to his wife.

"Well . . . what else does he have to say?" Peter asked.

"Oh, *now* you're interested in Zervas' letter?"

"Just read it!"

Justin smirked at Peter as he continued. "'Three weeks ago, the innkeeper handed me a letter from my liberators telling me that the Dukas had learned of my presence in Trebizond and that I was to leave immediately. The innkeeper directed me to a certain ship in the harbor. There, the captain locked me in the hold but offered me any comfort he could. When I arrived in Venice yesterday, he told me that you were staying with the Rossis and suggested I meet with you.'"

Justin looked over the page at Peter who was still unconvinced of his nemesis' metamorphosis.

"'I know that you have ample reason to distrust me. I was your worst enemy, a demon! But I swear to you by the Holy Virgin Mary and Our Lord Jesus Christ's most precious blood that I am telling you the truth!'"

"Ha!" Peter blurted out. "That devil's lies will not go unpunished!"

Justin continued, unmoved by Peter's outburst. "'If you could find it in your heart to see me, meet me in the chapel under the north dome of Saint Mark's Basilica as soon as you can. I swear to you I will be alone.'" Justin briefly looked up from the letter at Peter as if to ask his advice before he continued. "'I have a sealed letter from your friend in Constantinople—'"

"Friend?" Peter interjected. "I wasn't aware we had any friends left in Constantinople!"

"'I eagerly await you at the basilica. Again I swear to you by all that is holy that I am alone and come as a friend. Zervas. '"

Peter studied Justin's face and saw a familiar look. "No, Justin!" he warned.

"I'm going," Justin announced.

"Justin, don't be a fool!"

"I believe him, Peter."

"I'm not going to let you drag me into this, Justin!"

"I haven't asked you to come with me."

"Can't you see that it's a trap?"

"I believe him and I'm going," Justin said resolutely as he put down the letter and reached for his cloak.

"I'll get Eleni to stop you!" Peter threatened.

It was too late. Justin was in the hall and headed toward the door.

CHAPTER 25

The outside of the basilica was quite plain: red brick walls in the shape of a Greek cross with four equal-sized domes at the end of each limb of the cross surrounding a large central dome. Justin walked in through the west portal. Artisans studied the walls and ceilings. Drawings were visible in some areas and a few mosaics had been started. Those that were further along in their construction abounded in gold, just like the churches in Constantinople. The construction of the new church had begun just ten years ago and the church was yet to be consecrated. Still, many of the locals chose to pray in the small chapels, knowing that their prayers would be enhanced in a church that contained the relics of Saint Mark.

Justin had heard how the crafty Venetians had surreptitiously transferred the body of the saint from Alexandria to its new home. The Venetians knew that the Muslim Egyptians would not allow anyone to remove the saint's body from their city. All foreigners leaving Alexandria had their possessions searched. Keeping this in mind and knowing Islam's proscription against touching, let alone eating, any unclean animal such as a pig, the Venetians packed the body in a barrel of pork and sent it through customs. The Egyptians didn't dare touch the barrel once they learned it contained pig meat. Needless to say, the inspection was brief and the saint's body soon arrived in its new home in Venice.

Justin found his way to the chapel under the north dome. There he found a man praying. *Too thin to be Zervas.* Justin looked around. *Nobody else.* He walked over to the man and kneeled next to him. After a half minute, the man got up, crossed himself, and walked away. Justin cursed as he watched him leave the church. Then he noticed a note on the floor where the man was praying.

"Thank you for coming," it read. "Please meet me in the alley north of the basilica."

Justin sighed impatiently. *What next?* He slowly got up, crossed himself, and left the basilica where he had entered it. He found the small, dark alley and cautiously walked thirty paces forward. He stopped and looked around. Nobody. After a second thirty paces, he stopped again. Still nothing. Exasperated, he turned and walked back to the church. Suddenly he felt a hand over his mouth and a knife against his ribs.

"Captain Phillipos?" a familiar voice asked.

"Yes," Justin nervously answered.

"Zervas. Follow me."

The hand over Justin's mouth and the knife in his ribs disappeared. When Justin turned around, he saw the back of the thin man from the chapel. He followed the man as instructed to a small walkway off the alley. When Justin reached him, Zervas poked his head back into the alley to be certain they hadn't been followed.

"I'm sorry about the knife, Captain, but one can never be too cautious."

"Certainly, Tribune," Justin replied. He felt the front of his neck for any sign of injury.

"It's good to see you, Captain Phillipos," Zervas said as if Justin were a long lost friend. "Thank you for trusting me." He offered his hand in friendship.

Justin grasped it and studied his former enemy. Zervas was but a shadow of himself. He was at least thirty pounds lighter and his beard and hair nearly all gray. His hands, once muscular and forceful, were now thin and frail. Justin uneasily forced a smile but was determined to satisfy the curiosity that brought him there. "You mentioned a letter . . . ."

"Ah, yes," Zervas replied as he retrieved a parchment from his tunic and handed it to Justin. "I imagine you'll want to read it. Go ahead."

"No, Tribune. I'll read it later." Justin looked Zervas in the eye and asked, "What happened?"

"Captain?"

"Tell me what happened."

"I thought the letter I sent earlier was quite explicit."

"No. I read the letter. I'm talking about after the battle. Tell me what happened afterward. What happened to the emperor?"

Zervas sighed. "Yes," he began. "Let's sit." He led Justin down the walkway to a bench that was separated from the square by a lilac hedge. "Do you want to hear everything?"

"Everything."

"Very well," Zervas began. "One of Romanos Diogenes' personal guards told me this a few weeks before I was arrested. He was with Diogenes the whole time so I believe his story is reliable."

Justin looked impatiently at Zervas. "Undoubtedly."

"Yes, well, once the situation became hopeless—"

"You mean after Andronikos Dukas and you withdrew the reserve at the height of the battle," Justin added coldly.

"Yes, may God forgive me," Zervas continued, crossing himself three times. "Those who could flee did so, but Diogenes refused to leave the field. He fought like a titan, dropping any Turk that came near him. Even when his horse was killed under him, he fought on. He must have killed twenty Turks single-handedly until he was wounded in the hand by a lance, arrow, or sword; it isn't known. Then he was too weak to hold his sword and surrendered."

"Oh dear God," Justin muttered as he crossed himself.

"He refused to identify himself as the emperor. That night, he lay awake among the dead and wounded. The next morning, he was brought before the Seljuk sultan, Alp Arslan, in chains, dressed as a common soldier. Some of the Turkish officers had said he was the emperor and threw him before the sultan's feet. However, Alp Arslan refused to believe them, even after several of the sultan's envoys who had seen Diogenes before identified him as the emperor.

"Then Basilacios, you remember that he was captured early in the battle?"

"Yes."

"Basilacios was brought before Alp Arslan and asked to identify the prisoner. Once he recognized his sovereign, Basilacios dropped to his knees and the sultan was convinced. He then rose and ordered Diogenes to kiss the ground before him. As he did so, the sultan stuck his foot on Diogenes' neck."

Justin couldn't believe what he was hearing. The mighty Romanos Diogenes, Emperor of the Romans and Christ's Vicegerent, humbled by an infidel barbarian.

Zervas saw Justin's reaction and continued. "But the sultan immediately helped the emperor up and gave him the respect due a fellow ruler. Apparently the whole thing was a gesture to show that the sultan had triumphed over Diogenes, which of course he had."

"With a little help from you and the Dukas?"

"I am guilty, Captain." Zervas crossed himself again. "Afterward, Alp Arslan went out of his way to show Diogenes every courtesy. He even shared his table with him."

"What happened next?"

"The sultan gave Diogenes his terms of surrender. In truth, they were quite light. The empire would surrender Manzikert, Edessa, Hieropolis, and Antioch. Diogenes also promised an alliance with the sultan to be cemented by the marriage of one of his daughters to one of the sultan's sons."

"Not too harsh," Justin agreed, although the thought of his own daughters marrying a Turk was repulsive.

"Even the emperor's ransom was moderate: one and a half million gold pieces and an annual tribute of a quarter of that amount. The sultan originally demanded ten million gold pieces but when the emperor protested that the imperial treasury could never come up with that much, Alp Arslan reduced the ransom."

Justin was surprised. This Alp Arslan sounded like a reasonable man, not the leader of a barbarian hoard.

"The only problem was that the sultan had to get the emperor back on the throne to reap the rewards of his victory. I don't know if Diogenes knew that the Dukas had betrayed him. Nonetheless, the sultan saw there was no time to waste. Only seven days after the battle at Manzikert, the sultan sent the emperor back toward Constantinople with those from his army who had survived the battle. He even escorted Diogenes for part of the journey and provided two emirs and a hundred Mameluke warriors for the remainder of the journey. It wouldn't have done him any good, though."

"Why not?"

"His defeat had disgraced him. The Senate and the army would not have permitted his return."

"So what did he do?"

"Diogenes was able to find several units still loyal to him and added them to his army. He anticipated a quick return to Constantinople followed by full restoration of power. The rebuilt army was fairly large and I'm certain the emperor felt confident that, between his army and his political allies in the capital, he could easily restore order."

"Well, what happened?"

"The Dukas were waiting for him. Since Diogenes had left on his campaign, they had been systematically eliminating those who supported him."

"Senator Kastros?"

"Imprisoned by Metropolitan Mavrites on the eve of the battle. Probably dead now."

Justin shook his head. *Dear God!* He crossed himself again.

"Once the news of the emperor's defeat reached Constantinople, John Dukas seized control of the city and the empire. He declared Michael competent to rule and placed him on the throne."

"Did the emperor make it to Constantinople?"

"He had no idea what had happened in the capital. As he neared Dokeia with his army, he was surprised to find a Roman army confronting him."

"The Dukas?"

"Constantine, the caesar's youngest son. He defeated Diogenes."

"Was he captured then?"

"No. He escaped with most of his army and marched south. Near Adana, his troops collided with a second Roman army."

"Commanded by Andronikos Dukas?"

"Yes."

"And you were there, too. Weren't you?" Justin growled.

Zervas looked downward. "Yes. I was. Andronikos easily subdued him."

"He was better off with the Seljuk sultan."

"Indeed," Zervas admitted. "Diogenes had had enough of battle so he decided to surrender. In the negotiations, he agreed to renounce all claims to the throne and leave public life for a monastery. Andronikos relayed a guarantee from his cousin Emperor Michael that Diogenes would be spared under those conditions and no harm would come to him. Three metropolitans endorsed the promise. With the Church involved, Diogenes thought that not even the Dukas would fail to honor such an agreement."

Justin was certain he knew where this story was going. His throat grew dry as he anticipated hearing of Romanos Diogenes' ignoble end. When Zervas hesitated, Justin insisted he continue.

"I must admit that Diogenes was treated shamefully. Andronikos put him on a mule and forced him to ride in shame over five hundred miles to Cotiacum."

"While the others rode their magnificently dressed horses!" Justin railed at Zervas. "How dare they degrade the man like that! He was the emperor, for God's sake!"

Zervas continued without emotion. Justin could hear the shame in his voice, shame Zervas knew he could never escape. "They pulled him off the mule and threw him on the ground," Zervas slowed his speech, "held him down and brutally blinded him with daggers that they had smeared in horse dung."

"Good Christ!" Justin yelled. "How could you watch that happen?"

Zervas dropped to his knees. "Captain Phillipos!" he cried as he grabbed Justin's hands. "Captain, please forgive me! I'm so ashamed! Please forgive me!"

"Stand up, Tribune!"

"No, I can't!" Zervas cried.

"It is for God to forgive you! Stand up! Stand up and tell me where he is! Where is Emperor Romanos Diogenes!"

Zervas slowly resumed the story. "The three metropolitans were powerless to do anything. Some say they protested this grievous violation of Michael's guarantee, but the assailants paid them no heed. Diogenes was reduced to a pathetic blind man."

"Where is he now, Zervas?" Justin snarled.

"In a matter of days, Diogenes'eyes were alive with worms. He was in agony but no one heard him curse God or man." Zervas' eyes filled with tears. "To the contrary, he continued to thank God for all that the Lord had given to him. He continued to bear his indignities like a saint."

"Where is he now, Zervas?" Justin was nearly yelling.

Zervas dropped to his knees again and bawled. "He died a few days after the blinding!"

"Dead?" Justin couldn't believe what he had just heard. "Murdered by Andronikos Dukas! Oh Lord Christ, what manner of men are these?"

Zervas stopped wailing but remained on his knees. "The Dukas allowed Evdokia to leave the nunnery where they had confined her to give him a lavish burial on the island of Proti, where he had built a monastery some years before."

Justin could not accept what he had just heard. He knew that over the centuries, Roman emperors had been deposed, killed, mutilated. But the fact that he knew Romanos Diogenes and knew the treachery that led to this once proud man's fall and humiliating death made the entire situation horribly surreal.

"Evdokia was forced to become a nun after being confined there. So was Anna Delassena of the Comnenos clan. She was accused of plotting to restore Diogenes to the throne and was forced to endure a mockery of a trial."

Justin thought back to his meeting with Alexios Comnenos in the Basilica Cistern on the first day of this unending nightmare he was in. *With his mother on trial and later confined to the convent, he had no choice but to cooperate with Michael.* Justin looked down at Zervas. He offered him a hand and said, "Please stand, Tribune. I need to know more."

"Certainly, Captain," Zervas said as he stood.

"Do you know what became of Strategos Nikephoros Bryennios?" Justin asked, remembering how much he admired that brave soldier.

"He was pardoned by Michael and he retained his rank. Last year, he crushed a revolt among the Bulgars. I heard rumors of such revolts throughout the empire. Needless to say, Michael is ruling poorly. A gold noumisma no longer buys a measure of wheat. Prices are up everywhere and the people are unhappy."

"It would appear that Caesar John Dukas is much better at scheming than ruling."

"Indeed."

"What about Strategos Tarchaniotes?"

"Captain, he was in league with the Dukas as well."

"How?" Justin gasped.

"He led his army away from Khelat on Andronikos' orders. He's probably living comfortably off of his reward from the caesar. Emperor Michael," Zervas continued, "has refused to honor the treaty with the Turks agreed to by Diogenes. There have been reports of increasing Turkish raids in Armenia and Anatolia. Some fear these will be followed by an invasion. The Dukas have failed to respond. Michael has not sent emissaries to the sultan to discuss the situation."

"Perhaps the emperor is misinformed."

"Michael Dukas remains a foolish and incompetent young man. His Uncle John is making all of the decisions at this point and he's too busy securing his position to worry about the empire."

"And Psellos . . . and the patriarch?"

"Like jackals following lions. They've taken what they can from this kill. However, rumor has it that Psellos may be falling out with Michael, his former pupil."

"Have you heard about Tribune Michael Attaleiates?"

"The Dukas allowed him to return to Constantinople. He has started a monastery and is writing."

"But they knew he was one of the emperor's men."

"No doubt he's being watched. By himself, he's no threat to them, especially if he keeps to his monastery."

A loud crash not twenty feet from them abruptly ended their conversation. Justin and Zervas ran to inspect the commotion. When they arrived at its source, they found Peter on the ground with a sword blade at his throat. A tall man wearing a black cowl stood over him. Justin pulled his sword and the assailant pushed the blade against Peter's throat, nearly breaking the skin.

Justin froze. "What is the meaning of this?"

"A word with you, Captain Phillipos," the mysterious stranger demanded calmly.

How does he know me? "Speak then!"

"I mean you no harm."

"Then let that man go!"

"He attacked me."

"Let him go!"

"Sheath your sword and I will let him go."

Justin hesitated.

"You have my word. Sheath your sword and I will release Captain Argyropoulos."

He knows Peter as well! "Release him!"

The stranger pushed the blade tighter against Peter's neck.

"Justin!" Peter yelled. "I suddenly find this fellow very trustworthy! Put your sword away!"

Justin refused to yield.

"Captain," the stranger said as he pulled off his cowl. "Is this any way to treat a man who once saved your life?"

Who is this? Who has saved my life? He's far too tall to be Simon. I don't recognize his voice. Justin slowly stepped forward and looked into the man's eyes. He dropped his sword to the ground as his memory revealed the stranger's identity. "It's you," he said. "In the Mese."

Peter felt the blade leave his throat and sprang up. "It *is* you!"

The stranger sheathed his sword and said, "Yes. I am Constantine Papakostas."

"You were Mavrites' man!" Zervas said.

"I was also his executioner," Constantine added. "He betrayed me. Andronikos Dukas sent his men to kill me but I escaped. I knew Archbishop Mavrites was behind the action so I swore vengeance."

"And we certainly witnessed that," Justin interjected.

"Why are you in Venice?" Peter asked.

"I tried to stay in Constantinople after I sent that devil back to Hell but when the Dukas learned of his death, they turned the capital upside down to find his killer. I was a prime suspect. They knew I was still alive and had a score to settle with the metropolitan.

Staying in hiding was getting more difficult every day. I still had a few friends whom I could trust and they directed me to a Jew."

"Simon," Peter interjected.

"Yes," Constantine continued. "He said he knew you and when the time was right, he would send me to you."

"It would seem that Venice is the repository for all enemies of the Dukas," Peter smirked.

"For the last two years, I was kept in many hiding places. The Dukas were finding former friends of Diogenes every day. One evening, Simon came to me and announced that the time had come for me to leave the capital. The next thing I know, I'm in the hold of a cargo ship headed to Venice."

"Welcome, friend," Justin said. He extended his right hand.

"Yes, welcome," said Peter and he, too, shook Constantine's hand. Then Peter turned around and examined Zervas.

The tribune stood quietly as he remembered the abuse he had sent Peter's way.

"Tribune," Peter began. He was in complete control of the situation and nothing could make Peter feel better: His former nemesis, his worst enemy, now standing vulnerable before him. "So good to see you again," he taunted.

"Captain, I—" Zervas said humbly.

"That's right! It's me, Captain Nitwit," Peter jabbed sarcastically.

"Peter," Justin interrupted. "That's enough."

"No, Captain Phillipos," Zervas said. "Captain Argyropoulos is entitled to some fun at my expense."

"I believe that Captain Argyropoulos is obliged to forgive you seventy times seven," Justin retorted.

"Justin!" Peter snarled.

"He's a changed man, Peter. Be gracious enough to forgive him."

Zervas slowly extended his hand toward Peter. "Captain . . ."

Peter balked. He looked at Justin. The resolve on his face could not be broken. He looked back at Zervas and then at Constantine who nodded, encouraging him to release Zervas from his hatred. Peter looked Zervas in the eye and extended his hand. "Tribune, welcome to Venice."

CHAPTER 26

Constantine Papakostas thanked the messenger and examined the sealed parchment. "Captain Phillipos!" he shouted down the hall. "There's a letter for you! From Constantinople!"

"A letter from Constantinople?" the tall dark woman asked as she walked toward him. "From whom, Constantine?"

"I don't know, Lucretia," Constantine replied to Giovanni Rossi's twenty-year-old sister. They had fallen in love in the nearly five years Constantine had been in Venice. Many were anticipating an engagement soon.

"A letter?" Justin asked as he ran toward them. "From the capital?"

"Yes, Justin!" Constantine answered, handing the letter to Justin.

Eleni was right behind Justin; Peter and Zervas were right behind her.

Justin broke the seal and said, "It's from Alexios Comnenos!"

"We've been here for seven years," Peter snorted, "and this is the first letter he sends!"

"Michael Dukas has been forced from the throne!"

"We must tell the others!" Eleni said. "Bring them into the great room!"

"I'll help!" Zervas and Lucretia said simultaneously.

Justin led the others down the hall to the great room. Soon the entire household joined them. Six-year old Martha and five-year old Aspasia came escorted by the grandmother who gave each her name. Basilios came with his two-year-old grandson who bore his name.

When all had settled, Justin started the letter again. He read, "'Michael Dukas has been deposed!'"

The news sent loud murmurings through the gathering. Could they return to Constantinople now? Were the Dukas still in power? Had John Dukas replaced Michael with one of his sons?

"It appears," Justin continued, his voice raised to quiet the families, "that a eunuch named Nicephoritzes gained Michael's trust. His uncle the caesar and his allies were pushed aside. Even Michael Psellos was sent to a monastery."

"Stupid fool," Basilios grunted.

"'Nicephoritzes' reckless administration,'" Justin read, "'pushed costs too high. Peasants were starving and the townspeople grumbled at the rising bread prices.'"

Aspasia Nikopoulos and Justin's mother crossed themselves, shaking their heads and pitying their former neighbors.

"What about the Turks?" Peter asked.

Justin scanned the letter quickly. "'Within three years of the battle at Manzikert, the Turks spread into Anatolia by the thousands!'"

"What did the army do?" Peter asked.

"Not much. 'The caesar refused to deal with the Turks until it was too late.'" Justin looked ahead. "Peter. Do you remember Roussel de Bailleul?"

"I remember that barbarian bastard!"

"After Manzikert, John Dukas rewarded him richly for his help in eliminating Romanos Diogenes. He was sent with the Norman and Frankish cavalry into Anatolia to deal with the Turkish raiders who were ravaging the countryside. After arriving in the middle of Turkish territory, he set up a free Norman state. The Dukas were so outraged by this that they promised the Turks they could retain the lands they held if they helped capture Roussel."

"The fools," Basilios growled.

Justin read, "'Most of Roussel's men were captured but he escaped. Comnenos led an army into the Anatolia and returned him to the Dukas in chains.'"

"Good!" Peter interjected.

The others laughed at Peter's contempt for the Norman.

"Roussel's mutiny was the first of many," Justin continued. "Soon after Roussel's capture, Nikephoros Bryennios—"

"Bryennios?" Peter interrupted, excited to hear the name he'd come to respect because of his valor on the field at Manzikert.

"'Nikephoros Bryennios was made governor of Dyrrachium sometime before. He grew tired of Michael Dukas' incompetence and, in November of last year, he marched on Constantinople with his army.'"

"And he took the city?" Peter asked, hoping the answer would be yes.

"'A short time later, Strategos Botaneiates from Anatolia announced his revolt and marched on the capital as well. Michael released Roussel to my supervision and sent me with an army against the usurpers who were waiting outside the city. In March, riots over food prices broke out and the eunuch Nicephoritzes was captured by the mob and killed. Michael Dukas expeditiously surrendered his throne and withdrew to Saint John Studium monastery. The next day, Botaneiates entered Constantinople.'"

"And Bryennios?" Peter asked.

Justin scanned forward and stopped abruptly.

"Justin?"

Justin set the letter aside and wiped a tear from his eye.

Zervas, who sat near him, gently took the letter from Justin and read to himself.

"What happened to Bryennios?" Peter demanded.

Zervas drew a deep breath and answered. "He was captured by Comnenos and later blinded."

"My God!" Peter said in disgust. The others, too, expressed their incredulity.

"Comnenos denies any responsibility for this and condemns those that did it."

"I never did trust that bastard," Peter said under his breath.

"Comnenos is now the new emperor's chief of the army."

"And the Dukas?" Justin asked, speaking for the first time since he'd heard of Bryennios' blinding.

"Michael is a monk. Andronikos and Constantine have agreed to help the new emperor."

"And the caesar?" Constantine Papakostas asked.

"He's going to end his days as a monk, like his nephew."

"Is it safe to return?" Eleni asked.

Zervas read onward and then put the letter aside. "No," he replied sadly. "Comnenos says it is not."

The room was silent. Zervas' reading had taken all hope from their hearts. Would they ever return home?

Peter ran from the house and didn't look back. When he reached the Piazza San Marco, he stopped in front of the basilica and looked at the western portal. This beautiful church had become a frequent refuge for him but today's disappointing revelation drove him onward. He ran through the square and into the narrow streets of Venice.

My God, you forsake me again! Seven years being away from home is not enough? I'm tired of being a prisoner, no, a slave, to fate!

Peter stopped when he arrived at a dock on the Grand Canal. Ahead, he saw a repulsive but very familiar sight to anyone who spent time in Venice: a slave auction. These poor wretches came from the north, most of them. Pagan Lithuanians had been captured in raids on their homeland by Christian Germans. Slaves brought a good price in the notorious slave markets of Venice so they were brought here from all over Europe, the Levant, and North Africa.

Peter looked at them closely, all women or young children. The men had undoubtedly been killed. His anger and frustration dissipated as he saw them, one after another, given to a happy buyer. The gloomy sight sobered him. *Dear Lord Christ, please forgive my selfishness. I am an exile but I am still a free man.*

"What do I hear for her?" the slaver asked, raising the arm of his last prize. When no one announced a bid, he pushed her long dark brown hair out of her face, revealing her dazzling blue eyes.

Peter saw her and felt his heart skip a beat.

"Ten imperial gold noumismata!" one eager customer answered.

She's beautiful! Peter studied her sculptured cheekbones, her alabaster skin, her smooth, tapering nose, and her supple lips.

"Fifteen!" yelled another.

When Peter's eyes met hers, his heart melted.

"Twenty!" yelled the first bidder.

"I hear twenty!" said the slaver after a suitable pause. "Twenty-five, anyone?"

The first bidder smiled and rubbed his fat hands together.

Peter looked at her again. Her blue eyes called to him, "Help me!"

"Twenty-five?" the slaver asked again.

Peter tried to look away but couldn't.

"Twenty imperial gold noumismata is the current bid. Do I hear twenty-five?"

She stood like a proud queen, a prisoner of unworthy captors as the wind whipped her dark brown hair across her face. Her eyes, bluer than any sea Peter had seen, made one last desperate appeal.

"Twenty-five!" Peter shouted, surprising himself more than the others.

"Ah yes!" the slaver chuckled. "Twenty-five from this gentleman!"

Peter saw the relief on her face.

The first bidder glowered at Peter and rapidly checked his purse. He reluctantly turned to the slaver, shook his head, gathered together the other seven slaves he had purchased that morning, and departed.

"Very well!" declared the slaver. "Sold to the red-haired gentleman."

Peter stepped forward toward the slaver and the beautiful woman he held by his powerful grasp. When he reached them, his head entered a cloud.

"Here she is, sir! All yours for twenty-five imperial imperial gold noumismata!"

Peter, keeping his eyes immersed in those cool blue windows to her soul, slowly reached out his hand and touched her hand. It was warm, soft, graceful. He felt a comforting warmth ascend his arm.

"Twenty-five gold noumismata, sir," the slaver reminded Peter.

Peter responded as if he had been awakened from a deep dream, punctuated by a fantastic dream. "Twenty-five?"

"Twenty-five, sir," the slaver said cheerily.

"I, uh," Peter stammered. "I believe I'm a little short."

The slaver slowly pulled out a long knife and held it to Peter's throat. "We frown on people spending money they don't have," he sneered. "You see, she's high quality merchandise. If you can't pay for her, then I shall have to call on Count Bertino and apologize for the inconvenience, give him the girl for half the twenty he offered, and beg his forgiveness!"

"I'm sorry!" Peter replied. "What if I could get you the money? Today?"

The slaver carefully looked Peter in the eye. "Very well but there will be a surcharge."

"Surcharge?"

"Yes. The price is now forty imperial gold noumismata!" the slaver replied as he pulled her away.

"Forty?" Peter screeched.

"You want her or not?"

"Yes, of course!"

"Forty imperial gold noumismata. By sundown!"

Peter quickly turned and walked away. *Forty gold noumismata! Where on Earth could he get that much money by sundown?* Thoughts swirled through his head so rapidly, he nearly collided with a fishmonger's cart. *I must get it, somehow!*

When Peter returned to the Rossi house, he rushed inside and accosted the first servant he found. "Where is Seniore Rossi?"

"The library," the maid said.

Peter didn't wait for her to finish taking her next breath. He sped down to hall to Ludovico's library and burst in without knocking, surprising Ludovico and Basilios.

"Good Lord, Peter. What is it?" Basilios growled.

"I'm very sorry," Peter stammered, "but I must speak to Seniore Rossi! It's very important!"

Both of the older men were taken aback by Peter's unusual behavior. Basilios looked at Ludovico as if he were asking his host if he wanted him to throw Peter out. However, the levelheaded merchant knew that the situation required a more delicate touch.

"Basilios, my friend," Ludovico said smoothly, "perhaps we can continue this conversation another time."

Basilios' face showed his indignity but he complied. "Yes, this evening," he said, more as a demand than a request.

"Yes, this evening," Ludovico assured him. He hung his hand on his friend's shoulder and walked him to the library door.

"Thank you, sir," Peter said as Ludovico closed the door.

"How might I help you, Peter?"

"I suddenly find myself in need of forty imperial gold noumismata."

"Forty?" Ludovico laughed. "Did you buy a boat or something?"

Peter looked back at him silently.

"Peter, you, Justin, and the other Greeks have been working hard for me since you've been here. I hope that what I have provided you as your host has been sufficient to meet your needs."

"Oh, it has, sir! One could not ask for more!"

"As you are doing now."

"I guess I am sir."

"May I ask what it is for?"

Peter rubbed his forehead as he bent his head forward. "Well, sir . . . ."

"Peter, that is a large amount of money."

"Yes, sir." Peter found it difficult to find the words. "I saw someone . . . ."

"Yes."

"I was at the slave market today —"

"Slave market!" Ludovico fumed. "Lord Jesus Christ! I am amazed the doge still tolerates that abominable trade! What in God's name were you doing there, son?"

"I saw this woman, a slave —"

"You want money to buy a slave? You won't get it from me!"

"No! No, sir! That's not what I mean!"

"Then what do you mean, Peter!"

"I'm in love with her!" Peter blurted out.

Ludovico was flabbergasted. "In love?"

"Sir, I offered to buy her to keep her from another man who already has many slaves."

"In love, you say?"

"Yes, sir. She's the most beautiful creature I've ever seen. Her eyes spoke to me."

Ludovico chuckled to himself. He held out his arms. "Come here, Peter." When Peter came over, he embraced him. "I'll have your forty imperial gold noumismata this afternoon."

"I'll pay you back . . . with interest!"

"Peter, you work so hard for me as it is. You've taught so much to my young sea captains and you break your back at the warehouses and at the docks. It is my pleasure to give you the money, especially for such a noble cause. God bless you, Peter."

"Thank you, sir! And may God bless you, too!"

Peter rushed out of the library and collided with Justin, knocking him to the floor.

"Excuse me, Justin!" Peter begged.

"That's quite all right, Koumbarro. Where are you going in such a hurry?"

"I'll have to tell you later," Peter replied and raced out of the house.

"So what exactly are you looking for, Constantine?" Zervas asked as the two of them perused the shops near Saint Mark's.

"Jewelry, I'd say."

"For a woman?"

Constantine blushed. "Yes."

"Ohhhh," Zervas chuckled. "Anybody I know?"

"You know as much as you need to, Tribune. Now, are you going to help me or not?"

"Certainly, my friend. How about a gold bracelet? Seniore Verdi has several beautiful ones."

"That sounds like a good place to start."

As they neared Verdi's shop, Zervas spotted a vendor selling carved ivory and took an immediate interest. "Constantine, I would like to see what this fellow over here has," he said, pointing to the ivory vendor. "Will you need me in the shop?"

"No. I'll find you there when I'm finished."

"Very well, my friend, thank you," Zervas said as he detoured to the ivory seller.

The young ivory merchant had several nice pieces. Zervas examined an intricately carved casket. *The workmanship is spectacular!*

"Just in from Constantinople yesterday, sir," said the young proprietor.

"It's quite beautiful," Zervas said. "Do you mind if I look at it?"

"No, sir," the merchant replied. "I have more inside. I can bring them out if you wish."

"No, that's not necessary." Zervas studied the object carefully. *Exquisite!* "How much for this one?"

"Thirty."

"Thirty?"

"Too much, sir?"

"It's probably well worth it but I'm a bit short now."

"Perhaps another time."

"Yes, perhaps. Good day."

"Good day to you, sir."

As Zervas turned toward the goldsmith's shop, he heard a voice.

"You like ivory, sir?"

Behind him was an old man. "Do you like ivory, sir? I have a friend who has beautiful pieces. Much less expensive than this fellow. Very high quality."

Zervas hesitated.

"He's right over here, through this alley."

Zervas looked toward Verdi's shop. *Constantine must still be inside.*

"Just for a short time, perhaps," Zervas said, following the man into the alley.

"I'm certain you won't regret this, sir," the old man said as they arrived in the darkest part of the alley.

Zervas looked back toward Verdi's again. *Still inside I guess.* As he turned, the old man fell on him with a dagger. Zervas put his hand up just in time to block the deadly blow. This *old man* had the strength of a young athlete. He grabbed Zervas with his other hand, pulled him to the ground, and leapt on his belly, dagger in hand. Again Zervas was able to block the deadly blow but his assailant now had the advantage. The attacker quickly pinned Zervas' free hand to the ground with his knee.

"The Dukas send you this gift, Zervas!" a much younger voice said.

Zervas recognized the voice immediately. "Aristotle Markos!"

"Those will be the last words from your mouth, traitor!"

Markos cocked back his arm to drive his dagger home. As he threw his weight into the fatal blow, a thunderbolt of human flesh blasted him off of Zervas' body.

"Constantine!" Zervas yelled and jumped up to help his rescuer.

Markos and Constantine battled furiously in the dirt of the alleyway. Markos still held the dagger but Constantine was able to hold the weapon away from his body. Zervas ran over to them and pulled Markos' arms apart from behind. Constantine broke free and delivered two powerful blows to Markos' jaw. Markos fell to the ground, dropping his dagger as he did so. Constantine nimbly seized the weapon while Zervas pulled his stunned assailant up from the dirt.

"You bastard!" Zervas howled. "I should kill you here and now!"

The still-stunned Markos did not reply.

"Tribune!" Constantine interrupted. "Not here!" he added. He took a step toward the basilica. "We'll take him to the constable."

Zervas glared at Markos as he pushed him forward. "Very well, Constantine. It is certainly better than he deserves!"

Zervas held one of Markos' arms behind the assailant's back, his dagger against the small of Markos' back. As Constantine led the way to the constable's, Zervas drained his vitriol into Markos' ear. But when they neared another narrow alley, Markos purposely stumbled forward and rolled Zervas over his shoulder.

Constantine turned when he heard the commotion and saw Zervas fall to the ground. He rushed toward Markos, who was now free and reaching for second dagger in his cloak. Constantine stretched out his hands and grabbed for Markos' throat just as the villain found his dagger. Zervas saw the two of them fall to the ground and rushed to help Constantine. Markos broke free just as Zervas arrived but Zervas had the dagger ready and ripped open Markos' neck.

Markos tried to scream as the blood spurted from the open artery. He fell, dying before his head hit the ground.

Zervas ran to Constantine, not ten feet from him, who lay supine in a pool of blood.

"Constantine!" Zervas yelled as he ran to his friend.

With great effort, the rapidly breathing Constantine slowly opened his eyes.

"Constantine!" Zervas saw the bloody hole in his chest. "Dear God!"

In between his last, rapid respirations, Constantine managed to speak. "Lu—cre—tia!"

Zervas looked into his friend's dead eyes and then at the gold bracelet he held in his left hand. "Oh no!" He wailed. "Dear Christ, no!" He clutched Constantine's head to his breast and wept. "Oh Lord Christ! Why, my Lord? Why?"

CHAPTER 27

"There's a man here asking for you, sir," the servant said as Justin opened the library door.

"For me, Anna?"

"Yes. He says he's an old friend of Captain Phillipos."

"Old friend?" Justin asked, as he followed her into the hallway.

"Says he last saw you ten years ago."

"Ten years ago?" Hundreds of thoughts raced through Justin's mind.

"What is it?" Peter said as he saw the perplexed look on Justin's face. He and his wife of two years had just returned from a walk around Venice on this beautiful Sunday afternoon.

"Oh, hello, Peter, Ruth," Justin said when he saw them.

After Peter had purchased Ruth's freedom, she moved in with the Rossis and helped with the family business. The priest at the imperial embassy baptized her and christened her with her new name not two months after Peter had found her. They were married six months later, Justin stood as Peter's koumbarro and Eleni was the matron of honor. In the last three years, she'd learned Greek and Italian and proved to have a good head with numbers. Ruth and Peter's union had produced one child, a boy with blue eyes, just like his mother's. Peter named him, as custom dictated, Theophilos, after his father, whom he never knew.

"Hello, Justin," Ruth said as she gently rocked her sleeping two-month old in her arms.

"Anna says there is an old friend at the door for me. Hasn't seen me in ten years."

"Hmmm," Peter replied suspiciously.

"Oh," Anna remembered, "he said something about going through a tunnel with you . . . ."

Justin and Peter looked at each other. "Simon!"

They rushed toward the door, leaving Anna and Ruth in their wake. When they arrived at the front door, they were not disappointed. There he stood in all of his proud diminutiveness.

"Captain Phillipos? Captain Argyropoulos?" Simon asked. He had an enormous smile on his face.

The two larger men simultaneously embraced Simon with all of the enthusiasm that ten years of separation had pent up.

"What, no disguise this time?" Peter joked.

"How do you know that this is what I really look like?" Simon teased.

"Simon," Justin said, "it's good to see you again."

"Yes," Peter chimed in.

"It's good to see you too," Simon said.

"What news do you bring?" Justin was impatient.

"Simon?" a voice from the hall cried. Eleni rushed forward with her one-month-old son, Demetrios. "Simon, it's you!" Eleni handed the baby to his father and hugged the new arrival.

"It's good to see you too, Missus Phillipos," Simon chuckled.

"How did you arrive?" Eleni asked. "Have you been exiled from Constantinople as well?"

"Quite the contrary, Madam," Simon replied. "And this is your son?" Simon brushed his fingers over the baby's head. "He's very handsome, like his father."

"Thank you," Eleni said.

"Your first child?" Simon asked.

"Fourth," Justin answered proudly. "We've two girls and another boy."

"My! God has blessed you many times over!" Simon said as he watched the baby grab at his fingers.

"What news do you bring?" Justin repeated.

"I bring good news but I believe it's news that all in this household must hear."

"You couldn't tell us just a little bit?" Justin coaxed.

"No, my friend. That would spoil it for the others," Simon chuckled. "Gather everyone together and I'd be happy to share."

Zervas happened into the hall and saw the celebration at the front door. As he walked forward, Simon's eyes met his.

"Tribune!" Simon said. "I'm glad to see that you have settled in well."

"Little man!" Zervas replied. "My little savior!" Zervas lifted Simon off the ground and wrapped his arms around the smaller man. "I never thought I would see you again!"

"To tell you the truth," Peter interjected, "neither did I."

"I had my doubts as well, my friends," Simon said. "Now, where can we gather together? Where are your parents? They need to hear this, too."

As Justin, Eleni, and Zervas left the hall to find the others, Simon heard, "Simon, I've heard a great deal about you." The voice was Ruth's.

The master of disguises could not hide his amazement at this young woman's striking beauty. "Madam, you have the advantage over me," Simon said.

"Simon," Peter said proudly, "this is my wife, Ruth."

"Captain," Simon said, "it would appear that you and Captain Phillipos have been equally blessed in your choice of wives."

"Thank you, sir," Ruth responded.

"And a child as well!" Simon gasped, stepping forward to see the baby.

"Our first," Peter said.

"A double blessing for you, Captain Argyropoulos! A double blessing!"

"Simon Bar-Levi!" Basilios roared. "May God be praised! What news do you bring, sir?"

"News for all to hear!" Simon said as they embraced.

By now all of the others had arrived. They each greeted Simon and the Rossis made his acquaintance as well. Ludovico shepherded them all into the great room and yielded the floor to Simon.

"Thank you for your hospitality. It truly is my pleasure to see my old friends again and to meet some new ones. As I said, I have good news for all."

"Well, out with it then!" Basilios interjected, to the amusement of all.

"Alexios Comnenos has acquired the throne. He has sent me to extend his personal invitation to return with me."

The room erupted in excitement. Several crossed themselves, nearly all were in tears. Husbands hugged their wives, Leo and Alexander hugged each other, and Zervas dropped to the floor, weeping tears of joy. Justin and Eleni embraced each other tighter than they had in a long time.

"We're going home, Eleni!" Justin cried. "Thank God we're going home!"

"Justin," Eleni said, burying her head in his chest. "I thought this day would never come!"

Justin looked over Eleni's shoulder at Peter and Ruth. He held her tightly but Justin could see a look of profound uncertainty on her face.

"When may we leave?" Uncle Theodore asked.

"An imperial galley is anchored in the harbor and is at your disposal," Simon answered.

Ludovico found his way over to Basilios. "Congratulations, my friend!" he said as he embraced him.

"Ludovico! Thank you for keeping us these ten years! You are a great friend!"

"No more than you, Basilios! I owe you my wealth and my status here in Venice. I know you would have done the same for me."

"A thousand times over, my friend! A thousand times over!"

"I have some other good news as well," Simon announced at sufficient volume to regain the group's attention. "Captain Phillipos, Captain Argyropoulos, you have lost those ranks."

"What?" Justin wondered.

"You have both been promoted to *turmarch*."

Zervas quickly moved over to Justin and Peter. "It seems that you are now my superiors! Congratulations to you both," he said, offering Peter his hand.

"What a strange turn of events, Tribune," Peter laughed. "It is now my turn to abuse you!"

Zervas and Justin laughed as Zervas threw his arms around both Peter and Justin.

"I believe this celebration calls for wine," Giovanni Rossi announced as servants came forth with the beverage.

Alexander and Leo shouted their approval.

As the wine was poured, Justin, Eleni, Peter, Ruth, and Zervas pulled Simon aside.

"So what happened, Simon?" Peter asked. "Last we heard, Michael Dukas had been overthrown by Nikephoros Botaneiates."

"The usurper entered the capital in triumph following the bread riots. The empire was a shambles. The Turks were moving in from the east and Slavs were revolting in the west. The papacy was encroaching upon the dominion of the patriarch of Constantinople by crowning a papal vassal king of Croatia and spreading his influence along the eastern Adriatic. The Pechenegs and Hungarians increased their raids into the Balkans, throwing the empire into more chaos.

"Alexios Comnenos was the empire's most successful general, having never lost a battle and keeping the empire together by the strength of his own will. Botaneiates saw this and knew he needed a hero to be part of his administration. Comnenos never cared for Botaneiates, but when the old man offered him the rank of *noblissimus* and the position of commander-in-chief of all imperial forces, Alexios couldn't refuse, for to do so would have meant imprisonment or death.

"After a year in power, Botaneiates could see he had lost control. Military insurrections continued as the Turks swallowed up almost all of Anatolia by last year. Botaneiates did nothing to improve his popularity with the people when he married Michael's wife, Maria of Alania. Michael had renounced his marriage to her when he became a monk. But the fact that there was no official divorce granted by the church and that this was Botaneiates' third marriage didn't sit well with the clergy or the people.

"And if that weren't bad enough, Botaneiates violated a third convention by not acknowledging Michael's four-year-old son Constantine, the true heir to the throne, in any way at all. Even Romanos Diogenes said he was co-emperor with Michael when he came to power.

"Alexios' popularity grew as Botaneiates' fortunes dwindled. Last year, Empress Maria, correctly reading the mood of the people, adopted him as her son. Botaneiates, a weak man if the truth be known, did nothing. He surprised everyone by ordering Alexios to undertake a new campaign against the Turks. That meant Alexios had the army and the authority he needed to overthrow Botaneiates.

"Germanus and Borilus, both barbarians of the lowest level, held a great deal of power in Botaneiates' court. Alexios' rise to power came at their expense. His closeness with Empress Maria was particularly damaging. She had created an extensive spy network that was at Alexios Comnenos' disposal. He had to be eliminated, so Germanus and Borilus decided to act immediately.

"However, Comnenos was one step ahead of them. He and his brother Isaac slipped into the Palace Blacharnae on the Golden Horn and made for the imperial stables. They made off with several horses and hamstrung the rest to prevent any pursuit.

"They galloped away to the monastery of Saints Cosmas and Damian where they met Alexios' brother-in-law, George Palaeologos. George's wealth made him a very influential man. They then moved on to the army, which had assembled to the west at Tsouroulos." Simon paused and smiled. "You'll never guess what happened next?"

"Okay," Peter growled, "what?"

"They got some help from an unexpected source," Simon continued.

"Caesar John Dukas," Peter said coolly.

"How on Earth did you know that?" Simon asked. The others shared Simon's amazement.

"I knew that Comnenos would never sever his family ties. They offered him too much power, which is what he wants. And who had the most power in Constantinople outside of the imperial court? Caesar John Dukas, retired, but not eliminated." Peter sat back and crossed his arms with self-satisfaction. "Tell us what happened next, Simon."

"Alexios sent word to the former caesar asking his help. When Dukas arrived, he came with a group of Turks he had met as he rode his horse toward Tsouroulos. He also convinced a tax collector headed for the capital to join him.

"Two days later, the army marched on Constantinople and camped outside the walls. There were still units loyal to Botaneiates guarding the city but careful reconnaissance showed that certain Germanic tribesmen guarding the Adrianople Gate had an interest in helping Alexios Comnenos. George Palaeologos met with their leader and finalized an agreement. As night fell, Palaeologos' men climbed ladders over the bastion of the German position and, at daybreak, on Palaeologos' signal, the gates opened from within. Alexios' army poured into the capital, meeting little or no resistance.

"Botaneiates saw no point in resisting and offered to adopt Alexios as his own son. He made him co-emperor and gave him control of the government, while he retained his imperial title and privileges. John Dukas advised rejecting the offer, which Alexios did. When Botaneiates heard the news, he went to the Cathedral of Saint Sophia and abdicated. He was sent to a monastery where he reluctantly agreed to join the brothers there."

"And now Alexios Comnenos is emperor?" Justin asked.

"Yes, Captain—I'm sorry—Turmarch Phillipos. And he wants you to join him in restoring the empire to her former glory."

"Where have we heard this before?" Peter whispered to Justin.

"I must return to the embassy," Simon announced. "I will return in the morning to take you home!"

"I can't believe this day has finally come!" Eleni said as Justin and she prepared for bed. The children had been put to bed hours ago and were sleeping soundly.

"Eleni, I haven't seen you this happy—"

"Since our wedding day?" Eleni held Justin close to her and kissed him. Detecting reservation on his part, she looked him in the eye. "You have a strange look in your eye, Justin. What's wrong?"

Justin pulled her close and sighed. "I should be the happiest man in the world. I'm returning to my home with my wife and family."

"But . . . ."

"In many ways, Venice has become our home. Our children were born here. We've spent the last ten years of our life here. Constantine died here."

"Justin, we are Greeks, not Venetians. Their ways are strange to us, their faith different enough to chafe even the most liberal interpreter of True Orthodoxy."

"I can't help but wonder why God led us here if not to have us stay here."

"The Jews spent generations in exile in Babylon and the Lord called them back when the time was right. Now the time has come for us."

"I will leave a big part of myself here . . . ."

"As will I, but this is not our home." She kissed him again and then a second and a third time. "Come home with me."

Justin ran his hands through her long auburn hair. He kissed her, his passion growing as he drew his hands over the back of her neck. Eleni moaned softly, feeling his delicate touch spread to her shoulders and upper back. She reacted by pulling him closer to her and sliding her hands below his waist. This time, it was Justin who let his pleasure be known. He inhaled deeply and buried his head between Eleni's breasts. He kissed them gently as she kneaded his thighs and stroked his loins. Justin slid his fingers between her legs and detected her readiness for him, but Eleni acted first. She slowly pushed him to his back and deftly facilitated their course. She leaned forward, again offering her breasts to him, a gift he welcomed. With every gyration and fluctuation of her hips, Justin's pleasure soared. And the pleasure was not his alone. Eleni groaned in aphrodisial ecstasy as Justin punctuated her ossilations with powerful thrusts of his own. This union had been too long delayed; and the heights to where they brought themselves had only rarely been attained before. But as with all passion, it had its climax; this one sapped every ounce of strength available to them. Eleni collapsed on Justin, soaked in perspiration and drained of fire. His exhaustion had preceded hers by seconds but he was no less vanquished.

In the morning, Justin and Eleni awoke together.

"Are you ready to come home with me?" she asked, knowing full well his answer.

"Home and anywhere else you wish me to go."

Later that morning, after attending a matins at the imperial embassy chapel, Justin and Eleni assembled their children and their meager belongings and made their way to the wharf where Comnenos' galley was waiting for them. Justin and Eleni saw Simon and greeted him. As Eleni talked to Simon about the trip ahead, Justin surveyed everyone around him. Zervas stepped on board the galley and looked around. Justin's uncles Alexander and Leo were next, followed by Theodore and Aunt Anastasia.

"Are you ready to go, my dears?" Aspasia asked her daughter and son-in-law as she carried their youngest child in her arms. "We are finally going home!"

"Yes, Mother!" Eleni smiled. "I can't wait to see our home again!"

"Justin," Basilios said as he and Justin's mother came to him. "Excited, son?"

"Yes, Father."

"I'm going aboard as your oldest daughter's escort. She insists."

"And what about Mother?"

"I'll have to fend for myself," Martha joked as she followed Basilios toward the galley.

Justin looked around again. His brothers, their wives, Eleni's sisters, and their husbands, nearly all of them were there. Ludovico, Giovanni, and the rest of the Rossi family were there as well. But he didn't see Peter.

"Eleni," Justin asked nervously, "did you speak to Peter or Ruth this morning?"

"No. Something wrong?"

"They're not here."

"You're right. I don't see them. Maybe, wait! There they are!"

Justin saw Peter and Ruth approaching the wharf and noticed something wrong. "They're bringing nothing with them."

"What?"

"Look. Except for the baby, their arms are empty." Justin ran to Peter, hailing his friend as he ran.

"Peter!"

"Good morning, Justin," Peter said with a smile.

"Ruth, good morning. Where are your things? You know it's a long journey ahead."

Eleni arrived and greeted Peter and Ruth. "You're not ready?"

Peter sighed. He grabbed one of Eleni's hands and one of Justin's. "We're not coming," he said firmly but with a detectable hint of regret.

"Not coming?" Eleni and Justin asked in unison.

"I can't see myself going back to help Comnenos," Peter said. "I've never trusted him. You know that, Justin."

"You don't have to accept the commission, Peter," Justin said. "Come with us. We're your family."

"Yes, Justin," Peter said, "but I have a new family now."

"Peter—?".

"I've been wandering my whole life, looking for a home, a family, my own family. Now I have one . . . here in Venice."

Justin couldn't accept what he was hearing. He wanted to grab Peter and pull him on to the ship. He met his friend nearly eleven years ago. Together they had survived the horror of battle and the treachery of the Dukas. They spent a decade together, watching Justin's young family grow and had became as close as brothers. Justin shuddered at the thought of separation. Then Justin looked at Ruth and the baby sleeping in her arms and his heart warmed. How could he be so selfish? How could he deny this new life to his friend? It was now Peter's turn and his life was taking its own path, a path that led in a much different direction. Justin's anxiety about losing his friend gave way to excitement for his friend's new life. "Yes, you have a family now, Koumbarro," Justin said. "A beautiful one at that."

"The three of you will always be part of our family," Eleni said. She stepped forward and hugged and kissed Ruth and then Peter.

"Yes, don't forget that," Justin said as he embraced them.

"Have a good journey," Peter said. "You will always be in our prayers."

"And you in ours," Justin responded. "Write to us. Visit us." Justin added, doubting if contact could be maintained.

"God bless you," Eleni cried, hugging and kissing them one last time.

"God's peace to you both," Ruth and Peter said together.

"Good bye, Ruth. Good bye, Koumbarro," Justin said as he took Eleni's arm and walked aboard the galley.

The crew, eager to depart, made ready as Justin and Eleni set foot on board. The waving, tears, and good byes continued as the galley pulled out of the dock and toward the lagoon. Justin's eyes didn't leave the wharf until it was out of sight. Peter and Ruth did not move until the galley was but a speck on the horizon. As Venice grew smaller and smaller, the last ten years again flashed again through Justin's mind: his wedding, the emperor and the empress, the Dukas, the battle at Manzikert, Rashad and his men, their incredible journey to Venice, the birth of his daughters and sons, and Peter's and Ruth's wedding and the birth of their son. He dreamt of Ruth's and Peter's new life in Venice and smiled.

"Good bye, Peter," Justin said. "Go with Christ."

CPSIA information can be obtained
at www.ICGtesting.com
Printed in the USA
BVHW072028010720
581819BV00001B/4